It was never just about the cards...

The BRIDGE CLUB

10th Anniversary Edition

8 women • 5 decades • 1 unimaginable request

PATRICIA SANDS

Including 8 bridge hands from Canada's Audrey Grant

This is a work of fiction. Names, characters, organizations, places, events, and incidents are either a product of the author's imagination or are used fictitiously.

ISBN: 979-8-55-409731-7

Cover design by Sharon Clare

Praise for *The Bridge Club*

"In its tenth anniversary edition, *The Bridge Club* captures the heart of its members, spanning forty years of close, intimate friendship. Sands, through her expert storytelling, weaves the lives and loves of eight women, capturing life's greatest challenges with honesty and courage. Readers looking for a timely tale of sisterhood and the power that comes along with it will be moved by the rarest of friendships and the final act that proves their strength and worth."

—Rochelle B. Weinstein, *USA Today* and Amazon bestselling author of *What We Leave Behind, The Mourning After, Where We Fall, Somebody's Daughter*, and *This Is Not How It Ends*

"*The Bridge Club*, a captivating tale of friendship by Patricia Sands, celebrates its tenth anniversary, but the story is as relevant today as it was a decade earlier. Sands, a gifted storyteller, presents the reader with the best of Girl Code, female empowerment and unbreakable bonds ... no one can control the cards she is dealt, but *The Bridge Club* serves as a refuge and a lifeline to cushion the outcome with unconditional love, sensitivity, unity, and strength."

—Lisa Barr, award-winning author of *Fugitive Colors* and *The Unbreakables*

"The story of the eight women in *The Bridge Club* offers a rare insight into the choices we make as individuals and as members of a beloved group. Told with great compassion, it demonstrates the depth to which women will go to support one another through life's journey. I highly recommend this thought-provoking book."

—Judith Keim, author of the Fat Fridays series

"In this heartwarming tale, Sands has woven eight slice-of-life stories into one seamless narrative full of characters so real I wanted to be part of their circle. *The Bridge Club* is a testament to the enduring, transformational power of women's friendships."

—Kerry Anne King, bestselling author of *Whisper Me This* and *A Borrowed Life*

"*The Bridge Club* is women's fiction on an epic scale—an achingly beautiful story of female friendship and living life to the fullest. You'll find yourself thinking of your closest, dearest friends and appreciating them more than ever. The novel also raises thought-provoking questions about important moral choices the characters face. Be sure to keep your tissues handy. If you loved *Firefly Lane* and *The Ya-Ya Sisterhood,* you will treasure *The Bridge Club.*"

—Julianne MacLean, *USA Today* bestselling author of *A Curve in the Road*

"A deeply touching story about the bonds of friendship, about finding our way, and the ability to dig deep to navigate the most challenging turning points in life. Patricia Sands captures readers from the atmospheric outset, drawing us in to this group of strong women. A poignant tale that left me truly grateful for my friends."

—Alison Ragsdale, bestselling author of *Dignity and Grace*

"A friend in need is a friend in deed. 8 Women. 40 Years. *The Bridge Club* is one engaging book by award-winning author Patricia Sands. A literary tribute to the lifelong friendships between women right up to the mind-jolting end. Read this book, then ask yourself: How far would you go for a friend? "

—Marilyn Simon Rothstein, bestselling author of *Lift and Separate*

ALSO BY PATRICIA SANDS

The Promise of Provence

Promises to Keep

I Promise You This

Drawing Lessons

The First Noël at the Villa des Violettes

A Season of Surprises at the Villa des Violettes

Lavender, Loss and Love at the Villa des Violettes

DEDICATION

With love and thanks to the amazing women of my Bridge Club.

~ Barb, Bonnie, Candace, Cathy, Delia, Jinty, Mary, Myrna, Poopsie

This Tenth Anniversary Edition is dedicated to the memory of
Bonnie Hays, gone too soon

PROLOGUE

Silent night, holy night.
All is calm, all is bright.

It wasn't Christmas and it's not about religion, but whenever I think of that night, those words filter into my head. Kind of bizarre, I know, but that's how thoughts are sometimes.

The winter storm that consumed the weekend had finally moved on. As often happens, the unpredicted disturbance came at us out of nowhere, much like the shocking news months earlier that bound us together for these two days.

Winds had raged sporadically. Snowfall had fluctuated from light to blinding, including everything in between, but there was never nothing.

Left in the storm's wake were drift-filled roads, the work of savage gusts whipping the snow across the flat, vacant fields of Simcoe and Grey counties. The white barrage had swirled and funneled as it was sculpted into uneven peaks, trapped between the fencing that bordered the road. Trapped, as between the proverbial rock and a hard place, which was how you might have described this group of friends. But you would have been mistaken. We had chosen to be there.

Dangerous whiteout conditions brought traffic to a halt as roads had been closed around midnight on Friday. Through sheer luck we had left early enough that afternoon to miss the worst of it. Trust me, you don't want to be out there when you can't tell which way is up.

Now, on Sunday evening it was suddenly peaceful. Quiet. Still. A silent calm filled the post-storm air and cast a surreal shroud over the landscape. The pristine snow reflected the moon's soft glow, making the night appear more like dawn. Had we not been so distracted, we would have appreciated the beauty of it all.

Too numbed by what we had experienced on this weekend to even notice the cold, we stood on the crest of the hill by the farmhouse and watched.

In the distance, a fluorescent blue beam revolved on the cab of a snowplow. Piercing the dark, the probing rays brushed across the mounds being carved along the narrow side road. Blinking red and yellow lights lined the truck warning of its massive size. Following in tandem was a bulky SUV with amber hazard signals flashing. Last, and somewhat diminished by comparison, were the headlights on the unmistakable silhouette of a funeral-home hearse.

The pulsating throb of the combined lights created a slow-motion kaleidoscope silently sliding toward us.

We waited.

That's how this story ends. Let me tell you how it all began.

1

"Feast or friggin' famine."

That's how the locals referred to the random pattern of snow accumulation in the popular Georgian Bay ski area, two hours north of Toronto. Global warming had not spoiled their hopes this season for a white winter. In fact, records were being set. A feast it definitely was.

There's a certain serenity artfully forged by a fresh blanket of snow. Flaws of nature, and of man, are fleetingly hidden, and to some people a sense of peace prevails. To others, it's all about the shovel or the drive.

As snowfalls go, this one was perfect, with the big, soft flakes true fans of winter love. Intricately and delicately fashioned, some fell in clumps, becoming fluffy, floating puffs as they swirled and drifted through the dusk, adding to the already whitened landscape.

Peering through her reflection in a lightly frosted window, Pam's eyes followed random flakes as she desperately tried to focus on something other than the reality the weekend would bring. Being the daydreamer of the group, she surely could distract herself. So she thought.

With considerable effort, she willed the beauty of the winter scene to nudge aside the anxiety crowding her mind. Her imagination transported her inside one of those glass balls her dear godmother kept on a shelf in her Victorian china cabinet so long ago. "Back in the day," as the kids say now. Snow globes. The kind with the ceramic winter setting that you turned upside down and right side up again to start the tiny white particles twirling around. How many hours of her young life had she spent mesmerized by them?

"Get a grip," she pleaded silently, "my brain feels like a snow globe right now with all my thoughts swirling about."

Some of those globes could be wound up to play music, she recalled. Forcing herself to be drawn once more into the hypnotic motion of the storm, she became faintly aware of tinkling winter melodies from somewhere in the vast archives of her treasured memories. Warm recollections enveloped her of family, friends, laughter ...

It was laughter now that pulled her back into the present. Low, amused chuckles gave way to uncontrolled bellows and hoots. Rich sounds of great good humor and easy conversation that signal close friendships and not simply cocktail party small talk.

"More wine, anyone?"

The clinking of bottle meeting glass mixed with the laughter and chatter.

"We'll have more dip back here, and pass the pâté while you're at it, please!"

"Mmm—artichokes and Asiago. We've come a long way from the days of soup mix and sour cream."

"Hey, I still like those old dips!"

"Me too!"

"Well, these hors d'oeuvres are to die for, but that's nothing new!"

"I could live on Antoine's pâté. Apply it directly to my hips, though!"

A sudden warning interrupted the festivities. "Whoops! Hold on ladies, and cover your drinks! We're heading into a whiteout!"

The conversation stilled momentarily. Seatbelts were double-checked and bodies swerved as Bonnie over-steered to correct the trajectory of the huge Suburban. This was one of the perils, after all, of a mobile cocktail party in the midst of a winter storm.

Marti squeezed her eyes closed and gritted her teeth. She hated it when this happened even though she knew these nasty combinations of wind and snow were all too common.

Danielle quickly crossed herself and murmured a hasty Hail Mary, her normal reaction in such a situation. She was the only one in the group who would actually describe herself as deeply religious and considered it her responsibility to make certain any prayers or exhortations to the Almighty covered all these special friends. She knew she would need her faith more than ever this weekend.

Devout as she was, Danielle could also out-swear anyone in the group and now, having finished her Hail Mary, she let fly a few choice words. All of her profanities were in French, which sounded more impressive than the more commonplace English swear words. Besides that, in her rapidly spoken French anything she expressed was basically untranslatable, so she could say whatever she wanted. She was not a potty mouth, but rather an utterer of good solid curses when the moment called for one. If you go to confession regularly you receive some special dispensation for swearing, she claimed.

Everyone else waited calmly, at least on the surface, for the moment of uncertainty to pass, as it always did. These women had come to know that those "hold your breath and hope for the best" moments in life—no matter how long they seemed—eventually did pass.

"No problem," Bonnie reassured them. "It was a small one! Holy crapoli, I'll be more than happy to reach the farm. I can't recall driving up in such a heavy snowfall for years."

"Hooray for skid school training, Bo! Stellar driving job, as usual!" praised Jane as she saluted with her glass before taking a long sip, almost draining it. She knew the need for her calming drink had nothing to do with the driving conditions.

"Easy for you to say, sitting back enjoying your wine and relaxing," Bonnie muttered. "Being the designated driver is not a simple task, you know, ladies, particularly when you're chauffeuring a traveling party without a beverage yourself!"

"But Bo, you don't drink anyway," Cass reminded her, "so what are you going on about?"

"Uh ... I was looking for a little sympathy, that's all. Actually a soda water would go down very well right now, with a twist of lemon."

Reaching back for the cooler, happy to have any minor task that would bring relief from her worries, Lynn quickly filled the order and passed it up to Bonnie.

"Thanks, that hits the spot!" Bo suppressed the urge to admit it wasn't as effective as a vodka martini. For the past twenty-six years she had resisted every temptation to have alcohol touch her lips. Anticipating the challenge of this weekend might be the acid test.

"Twenty minutes to go and right on schedule. Got the stew ready to throw in the oven, Dee?"

Dee laughed, hoping it didn't sound forced. "I'd be crazy not to with you foodies!"

"Got that right!" The others chorused positive responses that were almost too enthusiastic.

Cass leaned over to turn up the radio as they sang along to

"Lucy in the Sky with Diamonds." Of course they knew all the words.

Nothing seemed amiss, in spite of what they all knew was going down in the next forty-eight hours.

Pam quietly considered the number of years these eight friends had repeated the scenario. This was the Bridge Club's annual cocktail party on wheels in the twelve-passenger Suburban from Bonnie's farm, driving north for their annual ski weekend.

They had it down to a fine art after forty years: one bottle of red, one bottle of white. That was the limit for the trip. The wineglasses were a necessary but not particularly desirable plastic. If they were going to break the law by having wine in their moving vehicle, they at least tried to be somewhat responsible about it.

Bonnie was a non-drinker, or as she would quickly correct you, a recovering alcoholic, even after two and a half decades. Outgoing and undeniably the loudest member of the Bridge Club, she had claimed permanent ownership of the designated driver title. She was also the most experienced at handling the lumbering Suburban, for which the others were immensely thankful. Particularly Marti, who almost needed sedation to travel the winter roads and who drank no wine en route. Nevertheless, along with all the others, she had rarely missed one of these road trips.

The Bridge Club: eight women, close to hitting their sixty-five-year speed bump. They were never anything remotely resembling Desperate Housewives or Ya-Ya candidates but simply great friends since their footloose days of finding the way through their early twenties.

During those heady days of the mid to late 1960s they had,

in various combinations, lived, worked, studied, traveled, and certainly partied together. Not only at home but also, to their great surprise, overseas. Friendships had been formed at school, parties, and work. A couple of them had known each other from childhood. Out of a very large circle, these eight women had connected during the preliminaries of getting to know each other and continued to build on that.

Coming from small towns in Ontario, trips to Montreal or across the U.S. border to Buffalo were major excursions when they were growing up. As young adults, it had been a thrill to join the masses tasting the new freedom ushered in by the peace/love, or sex/drugs, or anything else you can think of and rock 'n roll of the psychedelic 60s.

Hordes of liberated twenty-somethings, including most of these eight young women, invaded Europe that decade, backpacking and hitchhiking, renting "wrecks," riding the rails with Eurail passes, or getting around by whatever means their budgets would accommodate.

The Age of Aquarius had spawned a generation eager to explore the planet. The blossoming of affordable air travel opened the doors. *Europe on $5 a Day* was the bible, and wandering that part of the world was, for the most part, a safe, exciting adventure.

In the late '60s, they were lured back to the opportunities and energy of the emerging urban Toronto scene, their explorations completed for the time being. The young women began to settle into their lives with more structure and growing responsibilities. Most assuredly though, this by no means eliminated the good times. They did know how to party.

Quickly reconnecting through lunches, dinners, parties, and spontaneous bridge games, it was a no-brainer to get organized with a monthly commitment to meet at each other's homes and maintain their valued friendships. From early on, their ability to share the best of what women offer each other had been obvious. It was too good to let slip away.

Apart from this, that classic card game of skill and chance was the common denominator that brought them together. Each had been introduced to the challenging but enjoyable pastime of bridge by the time they were in their late teens or early twenties.

Taking turns hosting, the young friends gathered on the first Tuesday of every month with no guest, no spouse, and no "outsider" invited. Eight was the number needed for two tables of bridge. It made perfect sense, really, even though they all had friends who at one time or another suggested they would be happy to join in. The Bridge Club, as they had christened themselves with a collective guffaw, knew only too well that anyone who had not been with them from the beginning and shared in their experiences would be bored stiff listening to them reminisce ad nauseum.

Typical of the time, they were a homogeneous collection from white middle-class families. The opportunities for cultural diversity in Canada in the 1960s were not what they were even twenty years later. In fact, as crazy as it sounds today, having one Roman Catholic and another Jewish member in the group was fairly progressive for those days. Not that it mattered to them.

At first the primary object, they all agreed, was to play bridge. More dilettantes than serious competitors in those early days, they soon found it equally important to simply enjoy each other's company and get caught up on the latest. The chatter was effortless and continuous: the joys, the pains, the hopes, the secrets, the gossip, the mundane, and the adventure. Life, played out by each one in her own way. Separate but, at the same time, shared intimately with each other.

They moved easily within their individual spheres, sometimes overlapping with each other but more often not, and came together each month to compare notes, laugh, cry, vent, or simply relax.

Their dedication to the addictive card game had followed an interesting, arguably predictable progression when they looked back on it:

1968–1978

Bridge was played with relish for the first couple of years, until the cocktail hour stretched on in a haze of cigarette smoke and sometimes completely precluded dinner. Sleepovers were not uncommon. Love affairs, marital issues, and the shift from acting like kids to having them were their headlines for this decade. The background music: the Beatles, the Stones, anything Motown, Joni Mitchell, James Taylor, Crosby, Stills, Nash, and Young, the Guess Who, Queen, Gordon Lightfoot, Bob Dylan.

1978–1988

Families began to flourish in their own distinct combinations, or not. Careers were becoming established or were struggling. Important choices were presenting themselves for endless discussions, and the cards were set aside—except, that is, in times of crisis. When the talk got too intense, without fail, a few hands of bridge would be the calming factor. The background music: the Beatles, the Stones, anything Motown, ABBA, Burton Cummings, Miles Davis, Sinatra, Fleetwood Mac, the Eagles, Leonard Cohen.

1988–1998

For the most part they liked who they were. They recognized the strengths they had developed and were up front about what still needed work. Family dynamics were shifting and mid-life issues were challenging as they steered each other through the vagaries of menopause. Lingering over inexpensive but decent wine and appetizing meals perfected through the years, it was during this time that nostalgic mutterings about serious bridge often surfaced. The cards were on the table with greater regularity. The background music: the Beatles, the Stones, anything Motown, Oscar Peterson, Shania Twain, Lloyd-Weber soundtracks, Eurythmics, the Tragically Hip, Blue Rodeo, Elton John.

1998–2007

The fourth decade brought much less alcoholic consumption (but not abstinence, let me assure you), healthier food choices (but *always* dessert), one lone smoker (unless there was excessive alcohol), and earlier nights for those whose schedules now included caring for aging parents. Life's impending chapter of retirement signaled new opportunities, more eagerly anticipated by some than others. The cards were back on in a serious way. The background music: the Beatles, the Stones, anything Motown, classic jazz, U2, Diana Krall, Coldplay, Sarah McLachlan, Classical 96.3 FM, golden oldies.

The constant from one decade to the next was the endless conversation and camaraderie that carried them together through the passages of their lives. All to the beat of the background music.

Until the late 90's there were no cell phones or internet.

There was never a shortage of opinions. At times there was dissention—particularly when Canadian politics was the topic. Cass's steadfast commitment to the New Democratic Party's social tenets clashing with Bonnie's true-Tory-blue Conservative Party ideals provided good entertainment.

The lively exchanges were often passionate, but whether the issue was negative or positive, nothing changed the deep love of their country and the life it offered each person. Lucky them, they all agreed, to live in the true north strong and free. Although getting away for part of the winter wasn't a bad idea!

In the fourth decade of the Bridge Club, the events of 9/11 had introduced a sad and unfortunate new perspective to the world. These women could remember, as teenagers, the fears created by the 1962 Cuban Missile Crisis. It was their first experience feeling threatened in their country, which always seemed safe and removed from any such danger. The Cold War, with its talk of bomb shelters, brought the realization that North America was vulnerable to nuclear attack. This dark side of the 1960s, with the assassinations of the two Kennedys and Martin Luther King Jr. as well as the unpopular war in Vietnam, had awakened political awareness and a desire for activism to a greater extent than generations before.

After 2001, those early, uneasy fears resurfaced with the pervasive lingering threat left by the new type of terrorism and the atmosphere of suspicion and paranoia it spawned.

Who didn't feel that the world seemed to stop spinning on its normal axis? Combined with dire warnings of climate change and the reckless abuse of our planet—not to mention the standard violence making daily headlines—there was much to lie awake worrying about. There was a sense that life for their children and grandchildren faced the possibility of unimagined change and challenge.

These ordinary, average women, like so many others in so many cultures and so many countries, recognized the blessings in their lives and did not take them for granted. They also spoke with passion of their frustration with political decisions that often made no sense to them. Through efforts both large and small they tried to make positive contributions to the world around them and have their voices heard, even if the sound did not travel far. They were involved, concerned, and productive.

"Eighty percent of success is showing up," to quote a Woody Allen line, as Jane often did. These women always showed up.

There were differences, to be sure. Opinions were clearly expressed and a solid verbal kick in the butt was as quick to surface as a nod of approval. Conciliation, compromise, and forgiveness were guaranteed. Even though the process might be painful, never were words spoken that were not meant. They just didn't do it. Heated debate, yes. Disagreement, of course. Disrespect, never. Throughout the years, incredibly, none had ever spoken a hurtful or unkind word to another—even privately amongst themselves.

Not that there weren't ever pissy comments; they could actually be pretty good at it when called for. But without a word of a lie, they never uttered them about each other. Not even during killer PMS days—or, in later years, when the dreaded hot flashes and mood swings of menopause wreaked havoc.

From the beginning of their friendship, each of these women had been able to focus on the positive of whatever lay before her, although sometimes they needed each other's help to find it.

Approaching sixty, without a doubt, caused them to be even more aware of how time was flying by. As they constantly reminded one another, every day was a gift and never a given. *Carpe diem*. They certainly gave it their best shot. Why wouldn't you? they asked.

You shouldn't conclude this group was too good to be true, but believe this you must. It's the bottom line of what the Bridge Club is: a precious commodity in a world where gossip, deceit, and doublespeak flourish. What had to be said, including times when one did not particularly want to hear it, rose from a foundation of trust even when it was in firm opposition. There was never any doubt that this was the ultimate safe harbor.

It wasn't about remembering each other's birthday (random) or scheduling other social engagements (even more random). Their individual social lives were mostly entirely separate, apart from sharing details and experiences in conversation with the Bridge Club. Those were the least important aspects of what they shared. Truly, they were a sisterhood and simply wished each other well. This was friendship at its purest; boring it wasn't.

Since their ages were all within a year of each other, when "the big 4-0" loomed it was decided that a joint celebration over a long weekend might be a good idea. It was and they continued to repeat it every five years.

The group sixtieth birthday weekend had occurred the summer of 2005 at Lynn's in-laws' cottage. Nestled for over a hundred years amid the pines on a gentle slope overlooking the natural beauty of Lake of Bays, the classic wood-framed house offered a welcome retreat. This part of cottage country was an easy two-and-a-half-hour drive from Toronto, a weekend pilgrimage that was a long-established summer rite for thousands heading north for R&R and a break from the city. Driving up on Thursday to avoid the heavy traffic was the only way to go, experience had taught the BC.

The hottest hours of the day were spent at the weathered boathouse, where the women languished on the sun-washed dock, dipping frequently into the clear lake to cool off.

Ever-present background music interrupted conversation from time to time as they broke into song or dance, and more often both. Jimmy Buffett's music dominated the afternoon and the replay button was hit repeatedly for "Changes in Latitudes, Changes in Attitudes". The last line, declared their mantra decades before, was belted out with great gusto, *"If we couldn't laugh we would all go insane!"*

A Sunfish sailboat and cedar-strip canoe, along with enough kayaks for all, provided a diversion when the urge struck, replacing the motorboat, water skis, and windsurfing rigs of younger years.

"You know," Bonnie commented, with a lazy grin, "I'm really enjoying just looking at all that stuff from the dock." Years before that kind of talk would have been enough for Bo to instantly end up in the lake. Now there were a few murmurs of agreement.

As the afternoon sun began to dip, bug spray was generously applied before the *de rigueur* hike through the woods. After that each went to do her thing whether it was to take a shower, a nap, or to tuck into a quiet spot with a book.

Evening cocktails were served in the screened-in porch, which provided a panoramic Technicolor view of each magnificent sunset. Reminiscing went on with seemingly greater intensity than usual. The women were unanimous in their shock that sixty years had flown by, but weren't neurotic about it. Although the mirror argued against it, they all agreed for the most part that they felt as good as they ever had.

With classic good humor, the aches and pains they experienced now were described as simply tradeoffs for the hangovers of the early days. In general they had been fortunate health-wise, not to minimize a few major incidents. Diabetes, hip replacement, cholesterol and blood pressure issues, and even breast cancer had become part of their history. Diets, exercise, and the latest trends in health and wellbeing were a regular part of their chatter, as they exchanged their latest strategies. Their post-menopausal bodies sometimes had their own agenda, they had all come to learn.

"HRT is the only way to go," Lynn had told them years before, sweat dripping off her forehead from yet another hot flash. "Humor Replacement Therapy ... not hormone!" They knew the value of laughter and of taking time to smell the roses no matter how crazy life was.

True members of the sandwich generation, there were now aging parents to factor into some schedules. A few were discovering the joys of being a grandparent. It was helpful and reassuring to collaborate on ways to adjust to the changes the years delivered and the realities demanding to be faced.

The saying was that sixty was the new fifty, but they agreed that still didn't cover it; make it forty at most. They felt great in spite of that damn mirror. Rampant optimism reigned most of the time. They were lucky and they knew it.

Part of the usual reflection of that "60th" weekend included a suggestion by Jane over the Friday night cocktails.

"Pick one issue from the last forty years."

"Are you serious?"

"*Merde*!"

Jane nodded as she elaborated, "I'm referring to one instance when each of us turned solely to the Bridge Club for help. We've all had our share of ups and downs. Some of it difficult, some of it sad—"

"Some of it scary."

"Some of it devastating."

"Yup, the bad stuff was bloody awful at the time, that's for sure."

"And the lesson learned: all of it was ultimately survivable, even when it first appeared it might not be," offered Dee as she raised her fist high in a power salute, repeated by the rest.

"The stuff life is made of," agreed Pam.

"That about covers it," continued Jane. "Most of these situations—like the marriages, divorces, separations, kid issues—that we always shared with each other were often dealt with in our own family circles and support groups. I'm talking about other stuff."

"Even when we had other support, we always could count

on the BC as a sounding board and a source of relief. No doubt about that," offered Marti.

"Hah! Saved my bacon more than once, that's for sure," Cass exclaimed with a vigorous nod.

"We needed it as the perfect place to vent, swear, and whine when we couldn't do it anywhere else," reminded Danielle.

"On the other hand, there's no better group to have the best laugh in the world with—even if it's totally inappropriate," chuckled Bonnie, who had the loudest, most contagious laugh and could get them all completely out of control in no time flat.

"Exactly," replied Jane, refilling wine glasses as she spoke, "so I'm talking about something when we needed just us. I'm referring to a time when we felt we could rely only on the Bridge Club for support. I know we've all had more than one issue where we couldn't or didn't want to involve anyone else. Think about it."

The challenge was received with the requisite groans and mutterings. Each would disclose her response on Sunday over breakfast. Some knew immediately what the answer would be, while others wanted time to think about it.

"Oh, this will bring back memories, that's for certain," said Jane, beaming her usual self-confident smile, "although my answer is a no-brainer."

"Ya think?" laughed Lynn.

It was a given that they could each identify experiences, some lasting longer than others, when family or other support was not the answer and the BC had come to the rescue.

"Like a life raft," said Cass with conviction. Then her voice caught slightly. "That's how you've always been for me."

"You've nailed it, Cass. The Bridge Club has been a life raft, keeping us afloat when we needed it. Maybe we should call this issue our SOS," suggested Lynn.

"But it wasn't that our souls needed saving, was it?" Marti questioned as she reached for wine.

"Right, that doesn't quite catch it," agreed Lynn.

"How about 'sink or swim'?" offered Bonnie as the corners of her eyes crinkled with laughter.

Chuckling, the others had to admit there was some merit to that. They'd had their moments, no argument there.

"But really, it was all of us supporting each other at a time when turning elsewhere was not an option. In my case, not even to my faith," Danielle added emphatically.

"How about 'support of sisters'?" Pam suggested. "That could define SOS for us."

They liked it.

The cards were dealt and a bridge game filled the rest of the evening.

2

CASS'S SOS – 1972 AND ON

When Cass declared her SOS had lasted thirty years, the rest of the group fell about laughing. She wasn't kidding, and the more she explained her reasoning, the more the Bridge Club could see her point.

"The analogy of the Bridge Club as a life raft really fits for me, if you stop to think about it. As opposed to you landlubbers, I've spent a good chunk of the last forty years—yikes—on boats. And with more than a few relationships drifting in and out, I've needed to know that rescue was out there."

After joining in the laughter briefly, Cass took on a look of serious reflection. "I'm not just referring to my bank account either! Honestly, I don't think you realize how much you've given me, in so many ways."

Christened Cassandra to honor her great-grandmother, she was called Sandra by friends and teachers throughout her public school days. The day she left the small town of Guelph for Toronto's big city lights, an easy hour away, she became Cass. It just felt right.

From an early age, she had sensed an artistic, nonconformist inner self ready to burst through the conservative veneer wrapped around her like a well-loved tartan by her family. The solid values and traditions of Guelph's early Scottish settlers were deeply rooted in that quiet community, known primarily for the agricultural college established in 1873.

At the age of eighteen, Cass eagerly embraced university life in Toronto. A bachelor degree in nursing science became her goal balanced, in her view, by a busy party schedule.

Once out of the nest, Cass blossomed into the stereotypical flower child of the '60s. Tall, slim, and blond, with a classic beauty that attracted no shortage of dates, she relished her new independence.

With an infectious sense of humor that was more than a little off the wall, she could be counted on to end frequent late-night bashes wafting about, lost in her own private bubble. Jazz, ballet—whatever kind of interpretive dance movement you want to call it—she would flit gracefully around partygoers who were in various states of sobriety on the floor, leaning against walls, or draped over furniture. Eyes closed, with a dreamy smile that created an aura around her, and in no need of an audience, Cass just did it.

Her first encounter with Pam occurred as they bumped into each other racing to the front door of their university residence with seconds to go until curfew. Flopping into the well-worn leather armchairs in the hall entrance to catch their breath and trying to make certain their giggling did not wake others, they whispered their introductions. The next thing they knew, an hour had passed.

Living in other residences and pursuing completely different degree programs for the previous two years, they hadn't met. However, when comparing notes now, they laughed as they realized they'd been at more than a few of the same parties. Taking a closer look, Pam recognized Cass as the "Dancing Queen".

The more they talked, the more they felt they had known each other forever. Their small town childhoods, dreams for life in the big city, and cautiously disclosed fantasies of seeing the world were much alike.

In no time, tall, blonde Cass and short, brunette Pam became fast friends. Graduation two years later presented opportunities to follow their dreams.

Many of their peers were off backpacking, hitchhiking, or picking up odd jobs in western Europe. Cass and Pam agreed it was a no-brainer when they decided to work and save money in order to join the traveling hordes. It was an exciting possibility and it appeared to be so easy. The times were definitely a-changing, Bob Dylan promised.

Exactly one strictly-budgeted year later, the young women were on their way.

They hit the starting gate of their adventure at Expo '67 in Montreal, as a warm spring replaced the typically bitter cold of Quebec winters and visitors from around the world flocked to the site. This World Fair was surely a defining Canadian experience in 1967, representing the pinnacle of the nation's hundredth anniversary (in spite of Charles De Gaulle's infamous "*Vive le Quebec libre!*" outburst).

The week flew by as Cass and Pam experienced the cultural offerings found in the ninety pavilions representing sixty-two nations from around the world. From culinary to sports, science to the arts, industry to history, life was explored within the Man and His World theme. Exhibits, films, art, demonstrations, as much as dining areas, served generous portions to taste and savor.

Wining and dining with groups of young people they met from all over the world, some evenings they would sample the pubs of the fair. On others they would taxi downtown to experience the decades-old effervescent nightlife found along Rue Crescent for the Anglophone flavor and the Quartier Latin for the Francophone. With late closing hours, raucous bars and nightclubs, and superb jazz, Montreal never disappointed, Expo or no Expo.

Those seven hectic days in May whetted their appetites for the experiences awaiting them across the sea. "*Formidable*!" they kept telling each other in exaggerated French accents, laughing as they did.

They couldn't believe they were actually doing it, actually about to live the dream.

The journey exploded into full throttle excitement as the exhilarated pair boarded the Cunard steamship line's *Empress of Canada* to sail down the majestic St. Lawrence River into the Gulf of St. Lawrence and across the Atlantic.

What followed was an unforgettable year of working, traveling, and generally having a blast in Europe in spite of a shoestring budget. Shoestrings went a lot farther in those days.

Easily finding employment through a temp agency within a week of their arrival, they rented a cavernous South Kensington bed-sitting room from Lady Sonia Lloyd-Thurston, a five-time-divorced former aristocrat. Now somewhat diminished financially, she made ends meet by renting her two bedrooms and sleeping in her parlor. With a personality to match her flaming red hair and the vocabulary of an army sergeant, she was well past her best-before date and like no one the girls had ever met. Never hesitating to share her dubious wisdom and experience with her boarders, to their amusement she insisted they pretend to be her nieces from Canada whenever she had visitors. Every day wrote a new page in the adventure.

Their flexible jobs, Pam as an office temp and Cass doing temp medical locums, offered opportunities to explore near and far as soon as they had the money. Quickly becoming intrepid travel junkies, they kept records in their diaries, promising they would return to that side of the Atlantic even after this party was over.

From their first taste of the British experience, they were hooked. London in 1967 was the place to be: Carnaby Street, the Beatles, the Stones, mini-skirts, bell-bottoms, the Summer of Love—it was all happening. Nothing made a greater impact on the London scene more than the June release of *Sgt. Pepper's Lonely Hearts Club Band*, the album that changed music forever. The Beatles, already recognized as musical revolutionaries, became oracles of a new age: a new kind of "cool." It was quite a ride.

In August, three months after their arrival in London, an overnight ferry transported Cass and Pam through rough seas to Holland. Marti, Jane, and Lynn had flown from Toronto to Amsterdam, and after a noisy reunion they piled into their rented rusty pea-green VW van with curtained windows.

"Pam's still a bit wobbly from the boat, so I'll take the first shift at the wheel," Cass told them as they piled into their ultimate hippie-mobile. "Fasten your seatbelts and prepare for takeoff." Along with cheers of excitement, an exhaust-stinking backfire heralded their departure. They would experience that noise and smell often. Breakdowns threatened, but ultimately the van did not disappoint.

The five friends shrieked through steep switch-backed mountain roads, pulled off narrow coastal highways in the baking midday sun to dash into the Mediterranean, and argued over maps as they navigated their way through country after country. They held their breath at sights more beautiful than they had ever imagined. It was a never-to-be-forgotten whirlwind of an adventure—a three-week "if it's Tuesday, it must be Belgium" laugh-filled, awe-inspiring, excursion.

"Okay," Lynn said as they had one last feast of beer and Vlaamse frites back in Amsterdam on their last night,

"Everyone pick a favorite memory. Hiking in the Alps? Swimming in the Med? Getting lost? The history? The scenery? The food? The guys? It's not going to be easy."

"You know," said Cass, "we've got to keep making dreams come true. The five of us having all these new experiences together has been unbelievable. I'm going to smile for the rest of my life when I think about it."

"And when Pam gets her ten thousand photographs developed, we're going to have a blast looking at them," Jane said with a laugh.

It was simply the coolest time ever, they all agreed.

Later that autumn, Bonnie spent a week on Cass and Pam's bed-sitting room sofa, regaling them with the details of her voyage on the luxury liner the *Queen Elizabeth II* and her scotch-infused encounter with the actor Peter O'Toole. It could only happen to Bo! She was on a reunion trip organized by her former high school classmates from Bishop Strachan School for Young Ladies, where Bonnie never fit the mold yet was always popular.

Cass and Pam were in complete agreement that the visits of old friends and the making of so many new ones from around the globe were a big part of the amazing experience they wished would not end. The novelty never faded of being surrounded by centuries of history combined with the excitement of the music, fashion, and social interaction their generation was discovering during Britain's Swinging Sixties. Along with that, the opportunity to travel to such diverse cultures and countries in just a few hours and not at great expense was something they were reluctant to leave behind.

Inevitably though, a year later, it was time to return to reality, become gainfully employed, and get on with life.

Cass was welcomed back to Toronto General Hospital, where she had worked the year before going abroad, and settled into her comparatively boring routine reinforced by a wealth of memories. By the end of the next year, a new adventure had begun for her.

"First comes love. Then comes marriage. Then comes Cassie with a baby carriage," teased Bo, whooping with laughter as Cass rolled her eyes.

It looked like that childhood rope-skipping rhyme was to be Cass's prophecy. As much to her surprise as many of her friends, she became engaged to Art, a serious medical student with a magnetic personality and the sexiest dark eyes she had ever seen. He was completing his residency at the hospital where she was an emergency room nurse, fulfilling her parents' dream. It wasn't long before they discovered each other at the monthly staff parties, which had a reputation of their own in the history of Toronto hospitals.

Art was a change from the pot-smoking, poetic, and philosophical all-night party guys she had dated for years, and possibly that novelty attracted her initially. He did have a wicked sense of humor and a way of convincing her that he was right even when she had her doubts. Wasn't it time to leave her flower child days behind and settle down? he whispered in her ear.

Walking down the aisle on her wedding day with her parents on each side and Art's smile beaming at her from under the *chuppah*, Cass felt a momentary pause within herself. She had completed her conversion to Judaism with commitment, pleasing Art's family and eliminating what might have been a barrier to their marriage. Settling down with Art seemed what fate had planned, and she was a big believer in fate.

Without noticeably missing a step, she caught the eye of Pam, her predictably tearful maid of honor. The look signaled her hope that she was doing the right thing. God knows she wanted it to be so.

Her bliss as a newlywed offered such promise. Art joined a well-established clinic and an upwardly mobile lifestyle soon followed. They moved into a big house on a secluded lot in the middle of the city, bought a C&C 28 (boat number one), and joined an exclusive yacht club all in quick succession. Her first taste of sailing came as they christened the *Artful Dodger* on a breezy summer afternoon before taking an inaugural run around the Toronto Islands. Cass couldn't believe the exhilaration and freedom she felt as they flew across the waves of Lake Ontario. The more time she spent on the boat that summer the more aware she became of the strong connections she was feeling deep inside. She couldn't explain the sense of longing when she wasn't out on the water, but she felt it without question.

Although not without some hesitation, Art encouraged Cass when she expressed a desire to leave nursing and pursue a film degree at York University. To their surprise and pleasure, she became pregnant halfway through her second year. Life was a blur of activity, and they had little time to consider whether any of it meant anything. Art's psychiatric practice was flourishing (his specialty in family and marriage counseling), so there was certainly no problem with income, although his hours were long.

No one would have been able to predict the problem when it arose. It seemed Art was extremely successful in giving thoughtful counsel in every marriage but his own.

After two years that saw their relationship spiral downwards at an alarming speed, Cass was out the door with their young son under her arm along with a couple of paintings, her weaving loom, and some clothes, which did not include any of the designer pieces her husband had regularly encouraged her to buy.

"Oh goddamit, Cass! Don't tell me!" exclaimed Pam with surprise and concern, as she opened the front door to find her friend balancing baby and belongings.

"When you told us last week you couldn't live with the situation anymore, I thought Peter and I had persuaded you to take things one step at a time, go to counseling, or at least get the proper legal advice," Pam said with a questioning look. She was still standing at the open door, too shocked to move.

"I was convinced to do that until today, and then I snapped," Cass said, her resolve appearing to slip. "I was folding laundry and trying to figure out why I felt so awful, when I realized..." She paused, biting her lip and lowering her head before she looked back up with renewed determination. "I realized I simply didn't care about the relationship anymore. I was empty."

Pam stepped closer and wrapped her arms around Cass and Jake before she drew them inside.

As Pam took the suitcase from Cass and put it on the floor, Cass shifted Jake in her arms and held him even closer to her, her words flowing non-stop. "I know you told me what the legal consequences would be, but I'm done, finished, totally through with being a part of that marriage. I know what I'm leaving behind and I know I'm not doing it the right way, but it's the way I have to do it."

Taking Jake and giving him a warm, squeezy hug, Pam led the way into the living room. They settled into the couch with synchronized exasperated sighs. With a questioning look, she asked Cass about the next step.

"Well, I was hoping we could bunk in with you for a few days while I look for an apartment. I'm sorry I didn't even call first. That was crazy..."

"Hey, you know where the key is. Of course you should have come here!"

"Will Peter mind?"

"Silly. He won't mind you being here, but he's going to be upset with what you've done! You may have walked away from what is owed to you. No question about that! Oh yikes! He should be home soon. Does anyone else know?"

Frowning, Cass replied, "Nope. Not even Art. I've left him a note, which he won't find until he arrives home after his tennis match this evening. I can't tell my family. They love Art, and when I tried to talk to them about our difficulties, they all gave me the feeling that I just wasn't trying hard enough to make things right. Everybody is going to be really ticked with me."

Pam closed her eyes and let her breath out slowly. "Jeez, Cass, how on earth is this all going to play out? I bet Art calls here before the end of the evening."

"If he does, you can't tell him I'm here. You can't! Say you know where we are and that we're fine, that we're not alone and he shouldn't be worried. I told him this in the note, but just tell him I've promised you I will phone him tomorrow." Cass's voice broke slightly.

Pam threw her head back and rubbed her hands up and down her face in frustration. "Cass, Cass, Cass, slamming the door like this means you are walking away from a lot of financial support that you deserve but probably won't get now. Peter explained to you exactly what the law says about walking out on a marriage. And what about Jake? How fair is this for him?"

The color drained from her face as Cass nodded. Jake had climbed back into his mom's lap. She hugged him tightly and kissed the top of his head. "Don't assume for a second I haven't agonized over this—not for me, but for Jake. It's been torture, but I have to do this. I refuse to stay in this unhappy and hurtful state any longer. The tension in our house isn't good for him either."

Pam reached over and unpacked the bag of toys Cass had brought along as Jake eagerly slipped to the carpet. Oblivious to the drama around him, he was quickly distracted as Cass continued, "I know what the problems will be, and I'm prepared to deal with them. I can get a job. You know me. I don't need a lot of money to be happy. I can provide the basics for Jake and myself, and as angry as Art will be with me, I know he will give Jake all the financial support the laws demand and all the emotional support he can. He's a good dad."

In one motion the two friends put their arms around each other and had a quiet cry while Jake happily sat on the floor playing with his toys.

The unexpected houseguests remained for a short time, until Cass located an affordable apartment. Finding a good daycare program for Jake, no small feat in itself, and a position in healthcare (temporary, she promised herself), she placed her university program on hold and put all her efforts into making their life calm. She was disappointed, but determined that she had made the right choice and wouldn't look back.

After some urging from the BC and her family, she agreed counseling might be helpful and she felt she owed it to Jake as much as anyone to be certain their problems were chronic and not simply temporary.

For well over a year, she had confided in the girls a litany of instances where Art had been inappropriately critical of her in front of others. What he said to her in public didn't begin to compare to what he saved for her in private. Sometimes what he wasn't saying hurt more.

He wasn't physically hurtful, but he was verbally and emotionally abusive, even though most of his comments were softly spoken. It was as if he was purging some anger or frustration that was eating away at him. Cass sensed she wasn't living up to his expectations, which in turn caused her to be tense and things often would escalate. She would look for quiet times and calmly try to talk about it to him, as was her style. There were times they would seem to make some headway but more often Art would explode and stomp off or Cass would become mute with frustration. Days of icy silence followed. Art saved his kind, humorous demeanor for the outside viewer, and what lay beneath was an immense surprise to anyone who glimpsed it.

Pam admitted she and Peter had been shocked a few times overhearing Art muttering hurtful criticisms to Cass during friendly doubles tennis matches and casual bridge evenings. Cass, in the meantime, retreated more and more within herself even as she recognized, somewhere deep inside, that this was only adding to the problems.

In the aftermath, she and Art attended some counseling sessions together and individually. He had been blindsided by Cass walking out. Shell-shocked actually. After all, marriage counseling was his specialty. He knew, in theory, what it took to build a solid relationship and keep it going. Obviously he hadn't practiced what he preached. Cass wasn't prepared to live in a marriage without the respect she deserved.

Counseling only appeared to reinforce in Art that he was right and she was wrong, and that was the end of it for him. He simply did not understand why Cass would not learn from his comments. He perceived them helpful rather than harmful and accused Cass of being overly sensitive. Cass looked at him with astonishment when he said he was simply attempting to be a Henry Higgins and help Cass to reach her full potential. At this point Cass could only see him as Svengali.

The therapist was successful in guiding Cass to look inside herself and recognize that she was equally responsible for some of the frustrations that caused conflict in the marriage. Cass seemed to bring out the worst in Art and could only conclude that she was a disappointment to him. The differences in their upbringing and personalities, which had seemed so complementary at first, were now tearing them apart.

"The most important thing I've learned from counseling is that you don't go into it to save a marriage. You go into it to find out who you are," she told the Bridge Club. With a look of remorse she described how her starry-eyed reaction to that first blush of romance and the excitement that ensued had obscured the fact that theirs was a less-than-perfect match.

More than one of them noticed Cass subconsciously rubbing her finger where her wedding band was now missing. They knew, no matter how it appeared, the breakdown of her marriage was a source of great sadness to her.

"So what I understand now, without question," she continued, "is that trying to live up to certain expectations of the lifestyle we were chasing created anxieties I had difficulty recognizing. I tried to turn into someone I wasn't. I just want to be me again."

The divorce was on.

Now she was over thirty, a single mom on a rather limited income. In those days when a woman left a marriage she wasn't entitled to much of a settlement. Divorce law was in need of an overhaul, and it would happen too late for Cass. There were moments of despair and great guilt over the change she had brought into Jake's life.

"Kids are the innocent victims of divorce, no matter how you slice it," Bonnie commented to her one evening, "and in my area of social work, we are usually dealing with the after-effects."

Nodding slowly, Cass agreed, "No matter how right I know this is for me, I know the effect this will have on Jake. I need to make things good for him."

"Right on! We know that's exactly what you will do," Pam asserted.

"Yup, you know me. B positive is my blood type and my philosophy!"

These monthly Bridge Club evenings, she always said,

gave her an outlet to vent, which left her feeling energized and positive most of the time. Phone calls during the weeks were always appreciated as well. Although she had made friends at work and had family to chat with, it was only in the Bridge Club that she could be totally up front about her feelings.

Someone in the group always had a night or the odd weekend to babysit Jake and give Cass some time on her own. Often the visit was accompanied by a bag or two of groceries and treats that didn't fit into her well-managed budget.

Most importantly, Jake did not want for anything. Art, as Cass had predicted, did not shirk his parental responsibilities, no matter how furious he was with her.

She never did complete that film degree but returned to a nursing position in a clinic with people she quite liked, and her artistic juices flowed through her weaving. The pleasing textures and colors of the natural fibers along with the soothing motion of the shuttle provided a calm oasis and she wove dreams as she worked.

Cass, even as she struggled to adjust as a single mom, and Art, who soon married again, made certain they were both the best parents possible. An amicable, although distant, relationship developed between them.

Cass had joined a public sailing group (boat number two), a clever way to continue her passion on her now limited budget. On her weekends off, with Jake at his dad's, she'd fly across the waves on Lake Ontario, refining her sailing skills and becoming a sought-after team member for the weekly races. Her post-race social skills did not go unnoticed either. The girl could still party and easily adjusted to whatever situation she encountered, collecting new friends as she went.

During those years of transition, the BC was with her through the ups and downs, which included more than a few new men in her life. Although rarely without one, she wasn't a woman to be with just anyone, so finding the right fit proved more of a challenge than she had imagined.

"So far," she reported, "they've been all show and no go."

Lounging at Danielle's dining table late on a Bridge Club Tuesday, she passed around a joint to those who cared to indulge and reflected on her current status. "I have to admit, these last few years haven't been as easy as I thought they would be. The best thing is that Jake is doing fine. He's happy with me and at his daycare and at his dad's."

"And that last part is very cool," Pam said. "If Jake is happy, you will be too."

"Pass the J, please," said Marti.

When she got her breath back after a deep pull, Marti clapped her hands and pushed her chair back to stand up. "Bravo Cass. We're proud of the way you've taken control of things, and heaven knows it hasn't been easy. You've accomplished a lot on a limited budget, and the only complaining we've had to put up with was the shortage of quality men around."

Cass nodded in agreement. "You can't say I haven't given the search my best effort. You know this, but I have to say it again: all the time you girls have spent with Jake has been a huge help to me. All the times you've picked me up when I've been feeling down. Thank you. I love you. Oh man, I think I'm becoming maudlin—must be the grass."

"Get a grip, Cass," laughed Pam. "I know I'm not just speaking for myself when I say spending time with Jake is an absolute delight. It's not as if you need us to help very often anyway. You're a great mom."

"Thanks! It's always good to hear words like that. The most important man in my life is Jake. Nothing compares to him."

Pausing, she rolled her eyes, tapped her chin with her finger, and grinned broadly as she went on, "But a close second has to be Burton Cummings. He's been the only guy in my bedroom for many months. My God that guy can sing! Unwinding late at night, I just lie on the bed and listen to his latest album over and over and over again. 'Undun' is my bad day theme song."

"What would we do without music in our life?" Jane asked no one in particular as she popped a Guess Who cassette of Dani's in the stereo. They all belted out "American Woman" with Burton as they cleared the table and boogied around the kitchen, taking turns washing and drying the dishes.

"One of these days I'm going to buy an automatic dishwasher. Everyone seems to be getting them," muttered Danielle as they settled themselves at the card tables.

Months later, as Bonnie was bringing in platters of her famous spareribs from her BBQ, Cass mentioned she'd had a few dates with a guy named Dirk since the last BC evening. Everyone immediately gave her their full attention.

"He's fifty though, with an adult daughter. Kinda scary. I was sort of hoping I'd meet a young stud muffin, not a geezer," Cass laughed, making a wry face.

"Fifteen years is quite a difference," Dee cautioned.

"Oh well," sighed Cass, "it probably won't amount to anything anyway, but I have to admit, he's popular at the marina and great fun at our parties."

As the months went by, Dirk's name popped up with increasing frequency. A sailor and carpenter, he remained fit, so the age issue didn't seem to be a factor. After two years of hanging out together they finally bought a townhouse, where they settled with Jake, and began to work on a dream they discovered they shared.

Two more years passed until there was no doubt in her mind about the plans they were making. Cass decided it was time to spring the news.

"*Mon ostie de saint-sacrament de calice de crisse*," whispered Danielle.

"You're going to sail where, and for how long?" shrieked Bo.

With everyone's face frozen in a state of shock, Cass excitedly repeated herself.

"Dirk and I are working on a three-year program to prepare ourselves to sail around the world. We're going to take courses, save the money we need to buy a good seaworthy boat (number three), and when Jake is thirteen, we're going to live our dream! I am sooooo excited!"

With that, she began to dance around Jane's living room, which was not particularly large, grinning like the Cheshire cat on some serious grass.

"And for how long, Ms. 'Round the World Sailor? A few months? A year?" Jane called from the kitchen, where she and Lynn were putting together the salad and bruschetta to go with the vegetable lasagna. They exchanged looks of amazement before joining the others to hear the rest of the announcement. Dinner could wait.

Still hopping up and down, Cass threw her arms over her head, squeezed her eyes tightly shut, and shouted, "Forever! We really intend to make that boat our home and sail the world until we're too old and tired to do it anymore. We'll anchor in different places for extended times when we need to or want to, and we'll work if we need money. Who knows where we will end up?"

"That's totally radical," said Jane. "What a plan!"

"I'm psyched!" Cass said as she tried to control her enthusiasm.

As expected, Danielle had already crossed herself and sent the first of many prayers that would follow off to St. Christopher, the patron saint of travelers. She'd have to get a medal to hang in their boat, she thought to herself. It couldn't hurt.

Cass continued, "We're been researching and reading about others who've done the same thing. We have a lot of work to do and a lot of learning, but honestly, we believe it's ... well ... our destiny. Crazy as it sounds! Dirk is an excellent cabinetmaker, as you know. I've bought an industrial sewing machine to repair sails and make cushions, biminis, stuff like that. So we should be able to make a bit of money as we move around."

Pam pulled her down to the couch and put her hands on Cass's shoulders, facing her squarely. "You're not kidding, are you? It sounds like you've already made up your mind and the course is set!"

"But what about Jake? He's the light of your life. You're going to leave him?" Danielle asked, her expression horrified.

"How does he feel about his mother sailing off into the sunset without him?" asked Dee solemnly. She was the prime worrier of the Bridge Club. Travel to exotic places really did not excite her, even though she enjoyed listening to the adventures of others. A golf course in British Columbia or the Carolinas in the winter was as far afield as she desired to go.

Cass became serious now.

"No question that's the most difficult issue, and I wouldn't even consider going if he said he didn't want me to. He's been sailing with us so often, I think he loves it almost as much as I do."

"So what is the plan for Jake?" Danielle repeated, unwilling to let go of the issue.

"It's actually a good one, and he's been very much a part of it," Cass replied, her eyes sparkling.

"We'd expect nothing less of you, Cass," Pam said.

"Okay ladies," interrupted Jane, "let's move this to the table. Dinner's ready. Looks like bridge will be delayed tonight. We've got to hear more details, Cass!"

As they sat around the dinner table, Cass continued, "Art had suggested to me several years ago that he would be happy to have Jake go to a private school when he's a bit older, if he so desired. Well, he does. The plan wasn't necessarily for him to board or live out of the city, but he is dead keen to attend Lakefield Preparatory College. You know it. It's on the Trent Canal, just north of Peterborough. We've gone up to have a look, and it's a fantastic place—"

"It's where Prince Andrew went," interrupted Bo. "Remember? They have great academics combined with all sorts of athletics, including a first-class sailing program."

"Exactly! Jake has a couple of friends there, and he's unbelievably excited about it. He'll spend short holidays with Art and come to the boat for the longer vacations wherever we are. Art has even offered to help with airfare if it's a problem. I'm still in a daze, just shaking my head constantly at how this all is working out."

"Hey, that's nice of Art," Pam noted.

"Yup, we're working things out," said Cass.

"Lakefield is a first-class school! Our nephew goes there, and we've driven up a few times to visit," said Dee. "What an opportunity for Jake."

Cass agreed heartily. "I'm thrilled for him, although I know it'll be a major adjustment for all of us."

"Cass, we know you and Dirk are serious sailors, but wow, are you up for all the challenges in this kind of life?" asked Lynn.

Bonnie, sitting next to Cass, turned to her with a frown. "It's not going to be easy to convince me. Think about it. Foremost will be the challenge of spending your life with Dirk the Jerk in a confined space. You often say the townhouse doesn't have enough room for the two of you!"

In the beginning of their days as a couple, Dirk quickly became known by the nickname he had given himself as a self-deprecating nod to his grumpy disposition. It was all in good humor—for the most part. He wasn't exactly Mr. Personality, but they could see he was good to Cass in his own way.

He had even cooked dinner for the Bridge Club on a couple of occasions (the only spouse or partner to ever dare stick around for that). Besides being an excellent cook, carpenter, and sailor, he was great in the sack, Cass reported, and that was very important to her.

Cass was sure it was a good relationship at this time in her life, and marriage was not important to either of them. Been there, done that, they both said. She knew she had her friends' support as long as she was happy and the problems were not serious. She had to admit, Dirk wasn't always the easiest person to get along with, but he didn't take it out on her like Art had. At worst, he was cantankerous at times. Could they survive in that small cabin together? All they could do was give it their best shot, and they were both committed to that.

For just over three years, as advertised, Cass and Dirk planned and organized. They took courses in boat maintenance, including repairing ripped sails and doing overboard underwater emergency problem solving. Cass canned provisions. Dirk built in all the required safety features for transoceanic navigation. They were as prepared and informed as possible.

After Jake's bar mitzvah, he began preparing to live with his father and stepmother until the next school year, knowing that he would spend some longer holidays and summers with his mom no matter where she was. To everyone's credit, Jake was cool with this. He was a bright, confident teenager who was emotionally connected to all the people in his life in just the right way, but he was also looking forward to the independence of going away to school.

Cass had to admit that Jake's dad was as responsible as she was for making certain Jake had a stable, happy life in spite of the divorce. Art was a good man, she readily acknowledged now, and she regretted the tension and anger that had accompanied their breakup. Obviously they were not meant to be together, but she was happy they had reached a level of mutual respect.

Cass was able to leave knowing her son didn't feel she was abandoning him. Jake was about to begin his own new adventure at private school, and he was excited about that. Plans were already in place for him to fly to the Caribbean to meet them for the December holidays, and in summer he would join them in Europe. Cass would think of him every day—that was a given.

Another dream was about to begin.

On a bright, crisp September Saturday in 1988, the Bridge Club gathered on the dock at Humber Bay Yacht Club amid excited friends and family to wave the sailors off. As everyone held a glass of champagne, Pam moved to the front of the group. Jake, understandably overcome with emotion, had earlier asked Pam to "make a speech" for him to send the adventurers on their way. He was standing in the cockpit of the boat with his mom as they prepared to cast off.

Pam gave Jake the signal to ring the boat's brass dinner bell, a gift from Bonnie. Getting everyone's attention before she began to speak, she fought back tears. Jane had already slipped her a Tissue.

"I've known a few folks who had a so-called midlife crisis at forty and made a change in their lives, Cass, but none have matched this one! Actually, I'm kidding you about the 'crisis' part, because as we've all seen, you and Dirk planned carefully for this voyage. Not only have you educated yourselves and prepared for all the challenges that may arise, you've also educated us. You made certain that those you love and who love you feel happy and comfortable with your decision. I know I don't have to tell you how excited Jake is. As much as he will miss you, he's eagerly anticipating the new adventures in his life as well. He asked me to remind you of this. As we wave farewell to you and the trusty *Xanth*, we want to *command* you to keep in touch with us, as we will live this adventure vicariously through your letters and tapes. We wish you both safe waters, strong winds at your back, and smooth sailing always. You'll be in the hearts and on the minds of each of us landlubbers as you follow your dreams. Yo ho ho and a bottle of rum! Godspeed!"

Three rousing cheers followed, as the crowd saluted the adventurers. Jake gave Dirk a hug, followed by a long, love-filled embrace with his mom, and then hopped onto the dock and untied the last mooring line. Cass and Dirk toasted in return and then, eyes bright with emotion and excitement, they cast off with everyone waving and cheering. The sound system was on full blast, and the strains of Styx's "Come Sail Away" lingered on the waves until they were well on their way toward the horizon.

They began their quest by navigating through the intercoastal waterway of the eastern seaboard in the States, until it spilled them out into the Atlantic. From that point it was serious sailing down to the Caribbean, where they spent the winter island hopping as they prepared the boat and themselves for the spring trans-Atlantic crossing. Danielle's St. Christopher medal hung from a peg right above the shortwave radio.

Not only had Cass needed to deal with her absence from her son, but there was the Bridge Club as well. She was not prepared to lose that connection—her anchor, as she called it —and thus the plan was hatched. Since serious bridge was not yet back in vogue on their monthly Tuesdays, the girls decided if they wanted to play, they would simply have a roving "dummy" that would move to the second table once the bidding at the first was completed. The idea of introducing a new member to the group was not considered.

A week or so before each BC Tuesday, Pam would receive a

cassette tape in the mail filled with Cass's inimitable musings and details of that month's adventures. It was an ideal way to share the journey, and they felt so very clever for coming up with the idea. In return, they would record a tape of the evening with their individual comments and stories of the happenings in their own lives to keep Cass up to date, which frequently ended with laughter-filled, incoherent chatter as they talked over each other in their usual way. It would be sent off to whatever postal station Cass had indicated as the next stop.

Amazingly, the system worked most of the time. The tapes Cass sent were saved by Pam in a special box, along with any postcards and letters received from her so she would have them on her return.

Cass and Jake used the same system, although she also wrote a letter or postcard to him without fail once a week. Her commitment to him never wavered, and he knew it.

They sailed the world having the adventures they had fantasized about—and some they never could have imagined. Her tapes told tales of people, places, and situations more likely to be found in fiction. Their experiences covered the entire spectrum from terrific to terrifying.

Terrific included flying across wild seas with perfect wind and wave conditions; meandering along slightly elevated canals as if floating on a cloud above the flat, windmill-dotted landscape of Holland; enjoying fresh fish from the BBQ and local white wine from Cassis, as a light Mediterranean zephyr lazily caressed them along the Cote D'Azur.

Terrifying was waking to find themselves in a maelstrom with forty-foot waves, lasting twenty-four hours but feeling like forever; the loud crack of the forestay breaking in heavy seas, far from a port; navigating the north coast of Scotland, offshore oil rigs, tankers, and fish nets included, in a full-on Scotch mist.

"Someday I'm going to write a book about this—or get

someone else to," Cass frequently told Dirk. "I still have moments where I can hardly believe we're really doing it!"

Dirk would sometimes remind her of the plan. When he was slipping over the side of the boat in his wetsuit to do a repair in frigid, stormy waters, he had growled, "Make sure this goes in that damn book of yours!" At other times as his fingers lightly stroked the smoothly rubbed tiller and they drifted lazily by spectacular scenery on a perfect day, he would murmur with a smile, "This might need its own chapter."

A tight budget was the underlying reality of their existence. In winter months particularly, they might be permanently docked for extended periods, with work to do on the boat or with poor weather holding them at bay. Dirk would pick up extra jobs doing repairs on other boats and building cabinetry. The industrial sewing machine was a godsend. Cass had learned to repair sails and with orders for cushion covers and other boat accessories she soon turned her talents into a small cottage industry.

They didn't earn much, but it was always enough to keep going. Along with a small savings account they budgeted their carefully itemized spending. The upside of these extended stays was the chance to explore the culture at leisure. An added bonus was the friendship formed on and off the boat.

A winter surrounded by the history and stark beauty of Malta; an autumn in the Netherlands, celebrating Thanksgiving with other Canadian sailors; six weeks in a Turkish fishing village discovering acceptance at its warmest level and telling time by the Muezzin's call to prayer—all part of another side to the sailing adventure that offered its own rewards.

The Bridge Club even managed to see Cass on her foreign turfs on a few occasions.

Moored off the Amalfi coast their second winter out, Cass and Dirk befriended an Italian couple anchored in a neighboring slip. Bartering is a vital part of the sailing culture. It was agreed that in return for sail repairs and cabinetry from Cass and Dirk, they could have the use of a farmhouse in Tuscany for several weeks during the summer.

Cass brilliantly thought it would be just the place for the BC's forty-fifth birthday celebrations, and so that August, it was. Dirk gallantly offered to visit his daughter in England, appreciating how Cass would treasure a Bridge Club reunion.

What a time the eight of them had discovering that magnificent part of Italy for two weeks. Using local bus service for the most part, they explored Florence, Sienna, San Gimignano, and many small villages in between. Their local daily market supplied the produce, prosciutto, cheese, figs, and chianti classico that became their standard evening meal after their lunchtime eat-a-thons of the freshest pastas, the richest sauces, the most tender veal, or simply the endless varieties of delicious panini. It would be impossible to top this birthday celebration, the BC agreed.

Two years later, the fifth year of the big sailing adventure, Lynn and her husband were in Denmark, where she was to participate with her rowing crew from Bracebridge in the World Masters Olympics. Cass had told her they might be in that area around that time, but nothing was certain, given the unknown factors of weather and boat repairs.

Sight-seeing in Copenhagen, Lynn and Jim were taken on a water taxi tour of the city and its harbors. As the ride was ending, Lynn asked the guide where a visiting Canadian sailboat might dock in this area. He offered a few options, then asked the name of the boat.

"*Xanth*," replied Lynn.

"How do you spell that?"

No sooner were the letters off her lips than, with great surprise, the guide pointed to the boat they were passing. There it was.

In a flash, they were past the boat with no opportunity to

stop and their shouts lost. The tour ended shortly afterwards. They drove directly to the mooring, and a loud, joyful reunion ensued. Cass was astounded. Reveling in the coincidence, they shared some good times together during the week, enjoying every minute of this twist of fate. Cass was ecstatic to have Lynn and Jim relax with them on the *Xanth* and showed them how they lived. Lynn's competition became all the more special to have one of the BC standing with Jim hollering their lungs out as the Canadians rowed to a thrilling second-place victory in their class.

With refreshing cold beers the post-race drink of choice, Cass and Lynn entertained the others at their table, relating the incredible quirk of fate as the water taxi was passing the *Xanth* at the precise moment Lynn asked about it.

"It's all about timing," said one of Lynn's teammates.

"Exactly, or as our Bridge Club puts it," explained Cass, addressing the long table of celebrants, "this is a perfect example of the ancient Chinese art of Ti-Ming. Get it?"

There were some confused looks, so Lynn explained, "The Bridge Club latched on to this play on words so long ago, none of us can remember who first introduced it. We all thought it was very funny and it stuck with us. Whenever we talk about the coincidental timing of something, we always refer to it this way: Ti-Ming, like a Chinese expression. Does that help?"

There were smiles and nods of understanding, but Cass and Lynn later commented to each other that not everyone would find it as amusing as they did. It was a Bridge Club thing.

Most years Cass was able to return to Canada for a visit with Jake and her mom around Christmas. The odd time she was tight for money, the BC managed to find a way to get her a flight, usually thanks to Marti's Air Canada pass. Every year, Jake spent part of his summer vacation on the boat. Having these reunions from time to time made the experience of leaving everything behind easier to deal with, and the years flowed into each other as swiftly as the waters *Xanth* sailed.

Even when there was smooth sailing, the ride in the cramped quarters became bumpier and stormier as time went by, and after almost eight years the voyage was over. Cass boarded the plane home with some disappointment that it was ending, but not an ounce of regret. There had been great days and terrible days. There had been times of exquisite beauty and peace, unparalleled excitement and challenge, and unforgettable terror. She would, in all honesty, treasure the entire journey: the good, the bad, and the ugly.

Pam got the call, first from Jake and a day later from Cass, confirming she would be flying in later that week. She had lived her dream far longer than many people ever do. In the end, though, the cabin had ultimately, as predicted, become too small for the two of them, and someone had to go. Dirk was turning into a grumpy old man, and although he did not want Cass out of his life, he had agreed that perhaps some time apart would be a good thing. She was pretty sure that "some time apart" was going to last forever.

So now what? Going back to nursing was a last resort, as these years away had shown Cass that her happiness lay outside the mold. She'd always felt it deep in her heart, but it had taken this journey to reach a place where she was willing to give herself permission to live the way she wished. The fact she was almost flat broke gave this new reality a particular sense of urgency.

Back in Toronto, the networking began. Spring was in the air, and boat owners might still be hiring for summer contracts. Contacting old friends from her sailing days, Cass was hopeful something might turn up. She wished she knew, or for that matter even had a hint of, what she was looking for. The truth was she really didn't know. She figured the more people she spoke with and the more she scoured the ads, the more options would present themselves. Now there was also the amazing Internet, albeit in its infancy, a wealth of information.

She bunked in at Pam's place in Halton and Pam was delighted to have her old friend around after all those years at sea. Cass felt a bit like a freeloader but knew the support was genuinely offered. With her parents in a seniors' residence now, Cass really didn't have a convenient family place to stay. Besides, Pam had let her know she would be seriously ticked if Cass did not stay with her. It was simply a no-brainer, Pam insisted.

After a few weeks, lingering over a late Sunday breakfast, Pam said, "You know, Cass, I'm really glad you're staying with me so I can share firsthand in the next adventure. We never know what's going to happen next with you. I'm glad Jake's apartment at university is as big a dump as the rest of our kids', so you weren't tempted to crash with him."

Cass ran her fingers through her multi-hued hair, now sun-bleached and naturally streaked with those platinum shades of gray that blend so naturally for blondes. "Dump or not, he wouldn't have appreciated his menopausal mom moving in, no matter how temporary it was! Now I just have to figure out what I do next, and I have to tell you, my B positive attitude is feeling rather anemic these days! Nothing seems to be clicking work-wise."

Pam took a deep breath. It was a concern that had been growing for weeks since Cass had returned. "I know this isn't like you, but I'm worried you may be slipping into depression. You're sleeping a lot and don't seem very peppy. You haven't been yourself for a while."

Cass frowned. "Uh huh," she murmured with an uncustomary air of dejection, "I've been kind of worried about that myself. I've never felt so down, I must admit. I'm questioning myself at every turn, beating myself up about selfish decisions in my life that have brought me to a brick wall. I just don't have a vision of what I am going to do now."

Pam nodded, relieved to hear Cass acknowledging how she was feeling.

"Instead of jet lag, I've got serious boat lag! Accepting the fact that I'm not going back to *Xanth* in a few weeks is a lot tougher than I imagined." Cass stood and gazed out the window for a while before she continued, "I really hoped I could find some kind of work at one of the yacht clubs, then I thought maybe I could just be a gofer at one of the new film studios in the city and work into something there. Not so easy, I've learned."

"No thoughts about going back to nursing?" Pam asked, knowing it wouldn't be a popular choice but a practical one.

"Aw, Pam, I know you're probably right," Cass replied, wrinkling her nose and nodding slowly with a look of resignation. "I just may have to go that route after all. It's just that I've gotten so far away from living with a schedule, it's going to be a real challenge to go back to one."

"Understood. But what about doing temp nursing placements, like you did when we were in England five thousand years ago, until the right thing comes along?"

Cass spoke slowly, mulling over her words. "That's not a bad idea. I've got to start earning some money."

"I know it's not what you want but it might be worth a shot for now."

"I'll pull myself together and make some appointments with agencies starting tomorrow to see what's available. Thanks."

"And listen," Pam added, "if you want to see my family doctor about how you're feeling, I know he would see you, even though he's not taking new patients. Just let me know and I'll make the call."

Cass gave her a crooked, wry smile. "I appreciate you giving me a nudge. It'll make me more conscious about my mental health as well as my job-hunting. Really ... I'm fine. I didn't realize I was moping that much. Obviously I have been, though, because the other day when Bo dropped by, she told me to pull up my big-girl panties and get on with life. Remember?"

They laughed, recalling the conversation. "Oh, that's her kindly social worker persona coming through again."

Having taken the morning Go train into Toronto a few days later, Cass sat in a downtown Tim Horton's. She had just completed an interview with a medical employment agency, which added her name to their lengthy list of temp applicants. It hadn't been a particularly encouraging meeting.

Kick-starting the rest of her day with her standard double-double and highlighting employment ads, she glimpsed a familiar face pass by the window. But from where? It took a few seconds of flipping through memory files before the light went on. Tortola, BVI! She and Dirk had spent several weeks anchored there in the early days of their adventure. Richard was the name Cass put to the face she thought she had seen—a grizzled, fun-loving soul of the sea who freelanced as a captain-cum-mechanic/jack-of-all-trades nautical with a well-established reputation, making him much sought after in that part of the world. What on earth was he doing in Toronto when he had seemed settled in the Caribbean for life?

Quickly draining her cup, she dashed out.

Some things are just meant to happen. Ti-Ming.

Cass looked to her right and saw no one familiar. Lingering for several minutes, she was about to leave when Richard stepped out of the bookstore onto the sidewalk not more than a few meters away. Spotting her at almost the same moment, his burly frame shook as he burst into laughter.

"Good God, Cass! Is that really you? I thought you were sailing the world, and here you are standing on a sidewalk in a boring shopping strip in bloody Toronto! How did that happen?"

Returning the laugh and smothered in the grip of his huge bearhug, she gasped, "I only arrived back a few weeks ago. The voyage came to an end, but it was quite the ride while it lasted! Now I'll turn your question around: what on earth are you doing here?"

"Came up for an interview, bizarre as that sounds. There's a couple from here that are chartering a beauty ninety-two-foot ketch for March and April out of Tortola, and they've asked me to take charge. How's that for exciting? They've had a few unpleasant experiences in the past, so they wanted to meet me in person and be certain of their choice. I've got a return flight south later this afternoon."

"You wowed them, I have no doubt."

"You betcha! What's better though, they wowed me, which is a nice change after some of the schmucks I've gotten stuck working for. They're more than a little comfortable financially without a touch of snootiness and very experienced sailors. They're just the kind of folks you'd want to work for, because you know they appreciate a job well done. So there you go, that's my scoop. What are you up to? Surely you're not turning into a landlubber."

"Funny you should ask. I really don't know how to answer that question, because I've no idea what I'm going to do. I've been networking former contacts, checking the ads, but really not getting anywhere. I'm putting all my energy into not collapsing in a slump right now, so you are a definite bright spot in my day!"

Taking Cass by the arm and checking her watch, Richard said, "Look at that, will ya? The sun's almost over the yardarm! Let's grab some lunch and a beer or two, if you have time. You need to tell me just where in the world you and Dirk managed to go on your amazing quest. At least give me the quick and dirty version! I thought of the two of you so many times over the years—especially whenever I happened to see a C&C 38!"

That night was BC Tuesday at Dee's, so Cass stayed in the city for the rest of the day. The cocktail hour was energized as she reported her coincidental run-in with Richard. Cass's excitement and optimism filled the room, her change of attitude noted by Bonnie and Pam.

"Too bad he's not staying around for a while. He sounds like fun," laughed Danielle.

"Wait, wait, wait!" Cass waved her hands, barely containing her enthusiasm. "I haven't told you the best part! We had lunch, with me doing most of the talking as he plied me with questions about our travels. And then the most surprising thing happened..."

Now Cass was on her feet, grabbing a startled Pam to demonstrate how Richard had suddenly reached across the table and held her at arm's length. She described his look of complete incredulity as he exclaimed it dawned on him that he had just the job for her. "He said he was in charge of hiring the rest of the crew and needed a cook; he said I would be perfect! He recalled more than a few great meals on our boat, even if many were remembered through an alcoholic haze."

In the middle of the living room, Cass was still gripping Pam by the arms, and now the two of them were bouncing up and down together, shrieking with delight.

"Go for it!" shouted Jane with her customary exuberance.

"You did say yes, right?" questioned Pam in between bounces and shrieks.

Cass nodded vigorously, her green eyes sparkling. "Without a moment's hesitation! The money is decent and it's a start. Richard will book my flight and I'll leave at the end of the month. I'll stay with him for two days before we begin the charter."

"It's sounding better all the time—if you get my drift," said Bo, with an exaggerated eye roll.

"Any chemistry there, Cass? After all, we do know the quickest way to get you out of a downer is some good sack time," Marti said knowingly.

"Sorry to dash your hopes, but he's in a very committed relationship with a super scuba instructor named Margie, and he mentioned over lunch they were still going strong. Marriage isn't an issue for them, but fidelity is. Nice to hear, huh? Anyway, I had more than enough excellent sack time with Dirk the Jerk to last me a lifetime, so I'm ready to dedicate myself to celibacy for a while."

There was collective moaning.

"I've retired my title as the *Shagadelic Queen*," Cass threw in for a laugh.

"Ha! Consider your audience, woman," Dee warned her with a smile.

"We know you better! Some of us more than others," Pam reminded her with a sly wink. Cass grinned at the memory of when they were young and traveling the world.

"Trust me on this, my dear friends. The horizontal lambada is no longer my favorite dance. Well, for the time being anyway. I really need to get my life together and figure out what I'm going to do with it before I get bogged down in yet another messy relationship. I'll just take along my trusty battery-operated Casanova that you girls so thoughtfully gave me as a welcome-home gift."

Marti snorted with laughter. "Gawd, we do know each other well, don't we?"

Cass went on, "Okay, okay, back to the important topic! So! Isn't this amazing and exciting? I can't believe how it happened, but then, as we know—"

"Ti-Ming at work again!" interrupted Bo, leaning over to pass around the veggies and dip.

Cass chuckled in agreement, munching on a carrot stick, then became serious. "I also need to say thank you yet again for the group support, encouragement, and energy. You have no idea how much you've helped me these past weeks. Once again, the Bridge Club keeps me afloat. Lucky me to have all of you!"

"Works both ways, Cass. As we all know," Jane said, smiling.

"As a matter of fact, Jane, I'm going to tell the gang what you did, because I'm so blown away by it," said Cass with a look of gratitude.

"Really not necessary, Cass ... really—" Jane started, modestly looking away.

"Jane insisted on giving me a check for five thousand dollars to bank and use until I get on my feet. How is that for amazing? Paying you back will be my top priority when I finally get a real job."

Jane shook her head and assured Cass there was no rush. "I really did it for selfish reasons," she said with a smile, "so I would stop worrying about you for a while. As Woody likes to say, *Money is better than poverty, if only for financial reasons.*"

Everyone laughed and at the same time praised Jane's thoughtfulness.

Changing the subject, Jane exclaimed, "Back we go to Canada Post for the next two months entrusting our tapes to the mailman."

"Wait a sec. Now we can graduate to CDs! We'll give you a CD player/recorder as a bon voyage gift! I've got an extra one and I'll bring it over tomorrow," promised Bo.

Beaming with pleasure at this turn of events, they headed to the dinner table. After dessert they took advantage of the fact that all eight were present to have a serious game of bridge. The evening ended with good-bye hugs for Cass—once again. For how long, they wondered, but then with Cass you just never knew.

That was the beginning of Cass's next chapter (boat number four). She spent two months island-hopping in the tropical paradise she recalled so well from her early cruising days with Dirk, relishing the soothing contrasts of turquoise water, white sand, and lush greens. There were sunsets that brought her to tears.

Preparing meals on the yacht was effortless with the well-stocked galley. At times she pitched in with the crewing to feed her love of true sailing and to give somebody a break. There had been a few days of rough weather where her obvious experience became highly valued as others of the crew were seasick and pre-occupied in the "head." The opportunity just to be on such a fine craft, let alone help sail it, was a dream come true.

The owners, Dave and Steph Kelly, were an impressive couple, as Richard had promised, and when they didn't have guests they ate with the crew. It was a great atmosphere—a diverse, interesting, small group.

Cass wished it would never end.

However, the end was just the beginning for her, as it turned out. By the time the boat docked back in Tortola, a new opportunity had presented itself.

That ancient Chinese art of Ti-Ming was at work again.

Having recently terminated an employee who had spent more time looking after his own private interests than doing his job, the Kellys had been searching for someone capable and personable to fill the slot. As Cass listened to their proposal one evening during the second last week of the cruise, she had instantly known this was the job for her. As soon as they were in an area with good phone service, she wanted to run it by the BC, and Jake, to get their feedback.

This month the BC evening was at Jane and Sam's new condo in Yorkville, and they had just finished a tour. As the cork was removed from the second bottle of wine, Jane announced she had a voicemail for all of them and put the phone on speaker mode.

With increasing joy they listened as Cass spoke in measured tones, trying to contain the excitement in her voice.

"Girls, this is too good to be true. I mean, tell me I'm not dreaming. They've offered me a permanent job back in Muskoka! The Kelly family has owned an enormous cottage property and a small resort on the adjacent property on Lake St. Joseph for five generations. They've been searching for someone to hire as a general overseer of both properties and work with the resort manager to co-ordinate their business and social commitments, which are many. As a bonus, in the winter, I can come south with them to cook when they cruise."

Her enthusiasm began to tumble out with her words as she described the job offer in detail. The BC already knew she liked the couple and seemed to have established a good working relationship with them.

"I wanted to run it by you to see if any downsides jumped out. They've given me one of these new cellular phones to use so I can get my affairs in order—as if I had any. I'm so blown away by the offer I'm nervous about jumping at it before I realize something important is missing. They've suggested I think about the proposal and let them know by the end of the week, so I have lots of time. I left a message for Jake with all the details before I called you. Sorry I couldn't call when you were all together. Have a slurp for me. Can't wait to see you in just two more weeks! Okay girls, discuss and then get back to me!"

After Jane wrote down the cell phone number and disconnected, the room was full of excitement.

"Wow! This does sound tailor made!" Lynn could barely contain her enthusiasm. "Could anyone have come up with something better for her? The environment she loves, challenging, interesting, good compensation. It's a kind of outside-the-box job for our outside-the-box Cass."

"Maybe the resort manager is a hottie," Bo threw in.

"Seriously, I have the feeling that Cass has finally come home with this job. She lived her dream of sailing the seas until she had enough of it, and now she has fallen into the type of work that has the potential to keep her happy," Pam said hopefully. "She deserves that."

"And she may possibly even save some money," added Dee. "She deserves that too!"

"And close enough to make it to Bridge Club Tuesdays —bonus!"

Before Cass flew back to Toronto, the deal was done and a contract signed. The Kelly's led busy lives filled with business and social commitments. A priority was to focus on ideas to revive the resort property and attract a new clientele while maintaining commitment to their loyal customers.

They respected Cass's input, recognizing that her years of traveling had exposed her to a multitude of unique experiences from which they could all benefit. Cass was able to use skills she always knew she had, like doing repairs and other physical kinds of work that gave her tremendous pleasure. Enrolling in computer courses, she readily embraced the challenges this emerging technology offered, and her employers were impressed.

Cass dared to believe she was at a place in life that gave her great fulfillment for the first time since she left Dirk on the boat in Turkey. Her promise of celibacy was wearing a bit thin, but to her surprise she was still committed. The fact that she felt she was "waiting for something good" and not simply over the hill made the difference to her. She still had hope. For a change, she hadn't let having a man in her life become a priority.

Living on the cottage property in a slightly dilapidated boathouse that oozed atmosphere and history was right up her alley. The lapping of the waves lulled her to sleep, transporting her to dreams of faraway places that had been part of her life.

There was ample room for the weaving loom she had retrieved with glee from one of the barns on Bo's farm. It had been stored with the few pieces of furniture and treasured odds and ends she was unable to part with when she and Dirk had set off so many years before. What a pleasure it was to welcome these pieces of her past back into her life.

By juggling her work hours, Cass was also able to volunteer one afternoon every second week at the local hospital.

Most evenings she immersed herself in working on the loom. In a short time she had discovered a local co-operative where the members spun and sold wools culled from the llamas, sheep, and angora goats raised on surrounding farms. Many of them were skilled weavers who were only too happy to share their techniques, and workshops were frequently organized. She soon rediscovered the talent that she had shown when she wove at home while Jake was a baby. At the encouragement of a local artisan, she began turning out work that gradually became sought after in the various local shops. This in turn gave her the opportunity to save some money and, after repaying Jane's generous loan, to bargain for reasonable monthly payments on a sleek, swift second-hand laser (boat number five).

The competition amongst the various sailing clubs in the Muskoka Lakes was fierce but friendly, and there was a fine sense of camaraderie. Life in cottage country suited Cass more than she had imagined. She loved her work, put her heart into it each day, and her efforts did not go unnoticed.

To make life even better, Cass had arranged to have the first

Tuesday and Wednesday of each month off. She could do the three-hour drive to the city for the Bridge Club night and combine it with lunch or dinner with Jake before heading back north. Since Lynn and her family were practically neighbors, the two of them would often drive down together.

Jake was following in his father's footsteps and studying medicine at the University of Toronto. Relaxed and respectful to each other, Cass and Art were both proud of their son and the fine young man he had become. Cass loved having Jake back in her life on a regular basis and was grateful her long absences had not broken their bond.

Two years after she had settled into this very satisfying time of her life, things got even better. The manager of the nearby marina was also a sailing enthusiast. Cass had become friends with him as they competed in the weekly races. Nick Robertson was a widower with two grown children and two grandchildren and very involved with his family and the community.

It turned out—as she revealed to the BC only after she was convinced of it herself—he thought Cass was the best thing since sliced bread (his words). He treated her with respect, melting her anxieties about her graying hair and extra pounds with his loving smile, and they never ran out of conversation. He had a wicked sense of humor, was ready for anything whether fun or laborious, played a cut-throat game of Scrabble and even a decent game of bridge! What sealed the deal, Cass reported with a grin, was that along with all these good things, he was a hardcore Guess Who fan from the 70s. She felt it was kismet.

"And, on top of everything else," she added with a laugh as she fanned her face with her cards, "he sends me the sweetest cards and notes! I'm not kidding! Can you believe at the age of fifty-something, I'm falling head over heels in love?"

"Bravo," hollered Bo, giving Cass a standing ovation.

"Go for it, girl!" shrieked Jane, leaping to her feet with the rest of the women.

"You deserve someone like him, Cass," Pam said softly as she wiped her eyes and went around the table to give Cass a hug.

They all gave Danielle a look, knowing what to expect. In true form, she raised her eyes upward and quietly whispered, "Thank you, God!"

Not too long after that Bridge Club evening, following a particularly exciting race and several cold beers in the clubhouse, Cass had broken her vow of whatever and fallen into bed with her new love. Cass had thought her former partner Dirk a good lover, but this time around she got to go places she'd never been.

Before breakfast the next morning he put on her Etta James CD, fast-forwarded to "At Last," and while the coffee brewed they slow-danced around the kitchen.

For the first time, she sensed she was finally grounded. She had her son and family regularly back in her world, a challenging job that she loved, enough money to save some for a change, her steadfast friends of the BC along with a slew of new ones, and now ...

"Ooh la la, ladies," Cass sighed, her eyes sparkling, at the next BC evening. "I do believe for the first time I'm in love with someone who loves me just as much in return. I've never felt anything like it. There's a mutual respect, a sense of equality that I realize was missing in my other relationships. And as an added bonus, I think he's hot! Those Freedom Fifty-five ads never mentioned this! It really never is too late to begin again, is it?"

"*Mazel tov*, dear friend," Jane said, as she passed the tissue box to Pam and the others grinned.

It had been a long time coming, they agreed, as the cards were shuffled.

DEAL #1

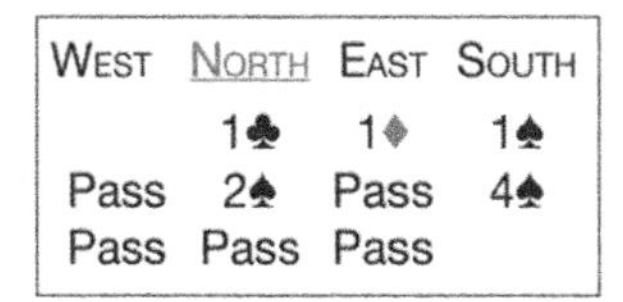

West	North	East	South
	1♣	1♦	1♠
Pass	2♠	Pass	4♠
Pass	Pass	Pass	

North
♠Q 10 6 4
♥K 6
♦6 5 4
♣A K J 10

Dealer:	North
Vul:	E-W
Contract:	4♠
Declarer:	South

West
♠9 2
♥9 8 5 3 2
♦Q 3
♣9 7 6 4

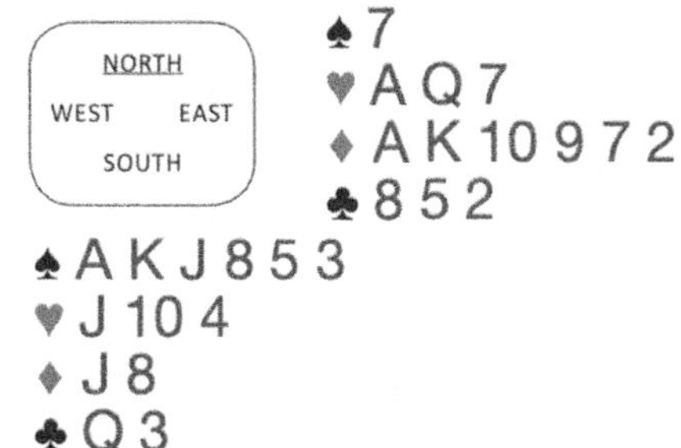

East
♠7
♥A Q 7
♦A K 10 9 7 2
♣8 5 2

South
♠A K J 8 5 3
♥J 10 4
♦J 8
♣Q 3

Suggested Bidding

North opens 1♣ with 13 high-card points and no five-card major. East overcalls 1♦, and South responds 1♠. West passes, and North raises to 2♠.

East passes. South, with 12 high-card points plus 2 length points for the six-card suit, has enough to go right to 4♠ once the spade fit has been found.

Opening Lead

West leads the ♦Q against 4♠, top of the doubleton in partner's suit.

Bridge Quiz:

How does East plan to defeat the contract?

How can East communicate the plan to West?

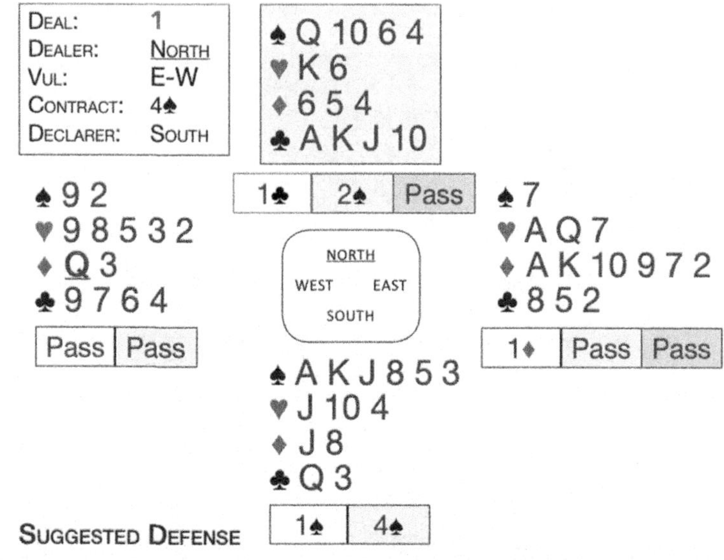

Suggested Defense

East likes diamonds but needs West to lead a heart at trick two to trap dummy's ♥K before declarer can discard heart losers on dummy's clubs. So, on the first trick, East should give a discouraging attitude signal by playing the ♦2.

When the ♦Q wins, it's tempting for West to continue with another diamond. West, however, must pay attention to East's discouraging ♦2 signal. East is unlikely to want West to lead a club, so East presumably wants West to lead a heart. West shifts to the ♥9, top of nothing. The defense gets two hearts and two diamonds to defeat 4♠.

Suggested Play

If the defense starts with three rounds of diamonds, declarer can ruff the third diamond high, draw trumps and discard two hearts on dummy's extra club winners. Declarer gets ten tricks: six spades and four clubs.

Conclusion

The defenders need to use signals to take a defensive heart finesse. To defeat the contract, East must give a discouraging diamond signal and West must be watching.

3

JANE'S SOS – 1977

At the age of thirty-two, Jane discovered a part of herself she never knew had been missing. High up in the southern Pacific ranges of the Coast Mountains of beautiful British Columbia, she realized just how much she was going to need the Bridge Club support to let the rest of her world in on the news.

Commenting to anyone who was listening, she drank in the view as the chairlift approached the summit and then grabbed the bar, preparing to exit.

"When I'm up here, it's as close to flying as I'll ever get. Harmony Bowl! There's no better name for this piece of the planet."

With that she adjusted her bindings, pointed her skis down the fall line, and just let go, effortlessly carving her own trail over the untouched mountainside. Popping through mogul fields from time to time for a change of pace and then slipping onto the adjoining runs still covered in freshly fallen snow as light as feathers, she praised herself one more time for rising early with the other powder hounds. Now the skies had cleared, the sun was out, and the conditions, combined with the always mind-blowing view, were almost too much to handle. She floated. She flew.

"Heaven, I'm in heaven..." she sang, and then laughed out loud as she anticipated what was coming next. Her whoop of pleasure filled the valley.

Jane had been coming to Whistler from Toronto with her mother since she was a toddler. At that time, it was simply known as Garibaldi and took five or six hours to reach from Vancouver, including a train ride from Squamish. It was a summer pilgrimage thanks to her grandfather's Canadian Pacific Railway pass, and they would stay with her grandparents for a month.

The first ski lifts were built in 1965. Soon the road access improved, and winter visits became possible too. She knew these mountains intimately in summer and winter. Magic they were, simply magic! The season didn't make any difference, as each one had its particular beauty and rewards. If push came to shove, though, she would have to say a perfect winter's day on the Whistler slopes was her very favorite. As she developed into an accomplished athlete, she knew her experiences there had strongly influenced her determined personality and strong connection to nature and sports.

Jane's energy and zest for living was boundless, and the Bridge Club affectionately referred to her as being "fully caffeinated." As a teenager she had determined her motto was "Ask me the impossible," and she applied that to her life in every way. As she matured, she radiated good health, both physical and mental.

On the other hand, she was able to relax when she knew she needed to. Frequently these downtimes were accompanied by the peaceful clicking of knitting needles, a favorite quiet time activity. Ski socks were her specialty.

Skiing in conditions like this always made her feel as if life couldn't get any better. However, on this particular day she knew there was an additional factor involved. Something she had always hoped for but had nearly given up on. She was in love! Pure and simple.

After all these years, she had fallen deeply in love, and the best part was that her feelings were returned in full. She had been in a few fine relationships through the years, but for a variety of reasons, mainly an inability on her part to make a commitment, they hadn't lasted. Without exception, she remained good friends with all her ex-boyfriends.

Now here she was, in the place she most loved in the world with someone whom she might also soon describe in the same way.

After three months of intense dating, they had planned this two-week trip to be in their own world and determine their next bold steps. If all went as the couple believed it would, they had decided to move in together upon their return home and gradually let friends and family in on their news. The first part of that plan was the easy part. The latter presented the challenge.

Making a sweeping turn, Jane looked uphill to see if Sam was keeping up. No problem. Stopping together at the top of the ridge on the next part of the run, Sam slid her skis on either side of Jane's. Jane turned her head to casually share a kiss. With the cold tips of their noses touching, they looked into each other's eyes, threw their heads back, and laughed until the crisp air caught in their throats.

"You told me how perfect this would be," gasped Sam, "but every day has been better than I imagined ... this view, these conditions ... totally tubular!"

"Let's go! It's not finished yet!" Jane hollered over her shoulder as she took off again. Her ponytail bobbed wildly as she worked her knees rhythmically through some enormous bumps.

At the end of several high-speed runs and a few mellow

cruises, they collapsed with a combination of exhaustion and exhilaration on the deck of the pub at the foot of the chairlift. Sucking back the local Kokanee beer as the Eagles' "Hotel California" blared from the outdoor speakers, they sat with grins that wouldn't quit.

"What a way to end a vacation and start the rest of our lives," they toasted with their frosted glasses..

It was Sam's first visit to Canada's most western province, but Whistler was like a second home to Jane.

They were staying at the rustic log cabin her grandfather had built on the shores of Alta Lake just down from the historic original Rainbow Lodge. Sent to British Columbia in 1915 as a land assayer with the Great Pacific Eastern Railway, this son of Russian Jewish immigrants had become hopelessly enamored with the wilderness and brought his young wife to join him. The cabin belonged to Jane's parents now, but they seldom used it and one day it would be hers. She was at peace here.

Jane felt proud to be the one to introduce Sam to the beauty and pleasure of these mountains, the village such as it was, and the surrounding community. What's more, the weather, which could at times be unpredictable, had been perfect the entire time. The conditions on the ski slopes had been outstanding, day after day. Jane decided it was an omen.

As they took a last look all the way up to a point above the tree line, the vision of the luminescent-blue glaciers on the highest peaks locked in their memories. Remnants of the most recent ice age, they were a powerful reminder of the lasting effects of nature and the overwhelming spirituality of the beauty enveloping them.

"Even the scenery is extreme! I can't get enough of it," Sam exclaimed as they loaded the car to head for Vancouver the next morning.

Just as they knew it would, the departure day had arrived way too soon, and now they would wind their way back down the Sea to Sky Highway to the Vancouver airport. Highway 99, its original name, followed along historic pathways used for generations by the original Coast Salish people. Then came the stampeding hordes of treasure seekers heading to the Caribou Gold Fields in the 1850s gold rush. The route was narrow and dangerous, but the development since the mid-60s had changed that out of necessity. Now it was wider at its most threatening points and actually had railings at some of the most spine-tingling turns.

"From the first time I drove this road, I loved it," laughed Jane. "It was such a thrill! They've taken some of the fun out of it with the new railings."

"An opinion not shared by most, I'm guessing," Sam laughed back.

All the sports in this area were challenging, and driving this road was no exception, even with the railings and in spite of Jane's opinion. The route would take them from the paradise of Whistler with its glaciers and back-bowl skiing through the dense woods and imposing rock faces of Garibaldi Provincial Park. Slowly the scenery would transition to the coastal rain forest at Horseshoe Bay, before they arrived at the inevitable gridlock on Lion's Gate Bridge. The landmark suspension bridge would bring them to beautiful Stanley Park and on into the city of Vancouver.

They would leave behind the majestic peaks of these Coast Mountains, reflected so clearly in the mirrored surfaces of the cluster of small lakes scattered through the upper valley.

"God damn!" Sam exclaimed, taking one last look at their view. "It's so vivid! This scenery is just *so* in your face—the peaks, the lakes, the sky!"

Jane simply smiled.

Even the new development of the area, for the most part, complemented the alpine setting. With natural materials of log and stone blending with the surroundings, there was a sense that the environment was being respected. Runs were being cut, lift lines dug, and lodges built on the adjoining Blackcomb Mountain, with a completion date just a few years away. The change had been monumental over the past ten years, but not everyone was happy about it.

"Change," pondered Jane as she guided the car down the narrow lane that served as their driveway, "it requires understanding, trust, and acceptance. I hope my family has that in abundance."

At this point in her thoughts, she was not referring to development at Whistler but rather to the challenges that lay before her upon her return to the "real world," beginning the next day. For now she would continue to focus on the beauty of this familiar drive and allow it to calm and strengthen her spiritually, as it always did.

After a quick forty-five minutes, they were suddenly staring at the imposing Stawamus Chief as they rounded the bend into the town of Squamish. No matter how often she did the drive, the Chief was always overpowering, looming over the small town nestled at its base.

The second largest granite monolith in the world, next to the rock of Gibraltar, it was becoming a Mecca to climbers with its immense vertical walls and deep chasms formed by glacial erosion millions of years ago. It offered challenges and thrills for climbers of every skill level. That, along with the unique windsurfing conditions found in the choppy waters of the Squamish Spit, added to the draw of this part of the world.

In the early days, the putrid smell of the local pulp and paper mills would announce your imminent arrival, but even that was fading with progress. There had been a certain tradition in holding your nose and complaining loudly about the stink!

"I almost miss that part," Jane chuckled as she described it to Sam.

From this point down, the highway was carved from the side of steep cliffs that fell straight into the Pacific. Stretching towards the horizon, a distinct blue-hued light blanketed the cluster of islands that dot Howe Sound.

"What an awesome effect," Sam exclaimed.

Jane nodded. "This combination of light and color truly can only be captured by the naked eye. Artists, in all different media, have managed to create some magnificent reproductions, but nothing matches this visual ... actually being here."

With her practiced eye, even as she drove, Jane showed Sam how to spot majestic bald eagles perched high in the pines. From November to March this was a traditional wintering location, with the shallows of the Squamish River offering feasts of chum salmon.

Not anxious to end the drive, they made a quick exit for coffee at the Roadside Diner in Klahanie, with its perfect view of the 1100-foot Shannon Falls cascading down to announce the start of spring thaw. In the depths of winter, adventuresome ice climbers attacked it with picks and crampons.

The highway carved through the impenetrable forests so famously captured by Emily Carr's strong brushstrokes. Finally what seemed like an odd transitional moment shifted them. They began to pass the vertigo-challenging homes hanging precariously over the Pacific, as the growing urban sprawl replaced the treasure trove of nature's bounties they had just left behind.

"That drive alone is worth the trip out here," declared Sam as they sat in the anticipated traffic jam waiting to cross the bridge into Vancouver.

It wasn't often you could drive through the city without a traffic delay somewhere, but the reality was there were few options. You simply had to adopt the easy, laid back West Coast mentality and not be bothered by traffic—or anything else.

Today this was a welcome challenge. They knew they were going to need that same attitude at home.

Banks of daffodils, from the palest shades of cream to the brightest of yellows, had burst into bloom along the road winding through Stanley Park. Deep blue wild hyacinths carpeted the forest floor. The rhododendron and azalea bushes blazed with colors of every shade and provided a show that only the West Coast climate could guarantee in this gardeners paradise. Throughout the city, planters overflowed with multi-hued mounds of pansies, tulips, and hydrangea, reminders of the spring yet to arrive in Toronto.

Within the hour they were lined up at the airport to check in for their flight home, and before they knew it they were touching down at Pearson International Airport.

“Back to reality,” Jane muttered as they deplaned. Sam held her for a long minute and whispered good luck.

“Just keep reminding yourself of the belief we have in each other and the strength we’ve discovered in this amazing love we share,” said Sam with a look of determination.

“I know,” replied Jane, her dark eyes flashing. “It will carry us through whatever we have to face in this next little while. Onward!”

Picking up their bags, they climbed into separate cabs and headed off to change their lives. They both had important talks ahead of them before Jane moved into Sam’s apartment at the end of the month.

Jane knew without question that the BC would be her first responders. Her parents would be the next challenge. The fact that Sam was not Jewish would not go over well with her family, but that was just the beginning.

Sam was leaving the next morning on a three-day business trip and they would see each other after that. In spite of careers in very different professions, they had met when the Ontario government put together a taskforce from all areas of education and business. Sam, as an accountant, was one of the number crunchers. Jane had been teaching Phys Ed for ten years in elementary school and had been seconded from the classroom for a year to work on a committee researching changes to programming to help instill fitness and sports as an integral part of children's lives. A major emphasis on this was developing in the 70s, and she was committed to the project. She also loved the fact that scheduling was entirely up to her as long as she put in her hours.

On a blustery Tuesday, two nights after her return, Jane walked through the door at Lynn's place, her usual bright smile tempered by an unexpected anxiety. Sporting a ruddy glow thanks to the combination of wind and sun on the mountain slopes, she hugged her way around the room as everyone commented on her healthy appearance.

"Oops, I'm just going to visit the loo before I sit down. Traffic was crazy," she said to Lynn and dashed down the hall to the powder room. Quickly closing the door, she backed against it and shut her eyes, breathing deeply. She had anticipated feeling nervous, but this was completely out of character for her. Slowing her breath, she leaned on the sink and looked at herself in the mirror. In her reflected face she saw her happiness. It was obvious. This sudden anxiety was natural, she told herself, but she refused to let it overtake her happiness. She could go out there and do what she planned. "Ask me the impossible," she repeated silently as she opened the door.

"Okay, turn down Sinatra and fill your glasses," she directed the group once everyone was settled. "If I ever needed your support, my friends, now is the moment. I have what you might call news."

With drinks poured and munchies on the table, Jane began to talk and, in so doing, she began the rest of her life. Exhaling slowly, she set her glass on a coaster on the coffee table. "As you know, I've just come back from two weeks in wonderful Whistler."

"Rocky mountain hiiiiigh," sang Cass, "We know it's your *most* favorite place in the world."

"Got that right! I had the best time ever and—"

"You're in love! You met somebody there!" shouted Marti, sending drops of wine flying as she banged her glass down and threw her arms in the air.

"Oh my God, we can see it all over your face! Marti's right, isn't she?" Cass asked gleefully.

"I've never seen you look so smitten!" Lynn pointed out. "This must be serious."

By this time, Jane had her hands over her face, but her grin kept slipping out the sides.

"Yes! You're right," she said through her palms. "I can't quite believe it myself, but it's true. I'm in love—deeply in love. Oh-h-h, it feels so fine to hear myself say it this easily."

"And? So, who is it? Where did you meet him? Details, we need the details, all of them!" Danielle demanded, beaming with anticipation.

Dropping her hands from her face, Jane took a deep breath as her ebony eyes met those of each woman.

"Okay, well ... oh ... here's where it gets tricky, so I'll just say it. But first I need to ask you to think before you react. Think of how well you know me and all the history we share..."

"Jane, for heaven's sake, what's the problem?" asked Pam sympathetically.

"It's not that there's a problem, but this is a turning point in my life and really it involves all of us. It's a major issue—that I know. I'm trusting that our friendship is strong enough for all of you to accept this—"

Reaching over to take Jane's hand, Dee interrupted reminding her that the racial barrier had been broken years before when she married her Kenneth from Barbados and had to endure the wrath of her family, as well as the prevailing 1970s attitude toward mixed marriages. It hadn't been easy, she reminded Jane.

"Are you walking in my shoes?" Dee asked tentatively.

"N-not exactly. I am in love—and that's the easy part. This is the part that's not so easy, but here goes..." She paused for a few seconds.

She could feel her pulse hammering in her throat as she pushed the words through her lips, "I'm in love with a woman. Her name is Samantha Harper." Inhaling deeply, the rest of her words tumbled out. "There. It's out. The first time I've said it out loud. I know this will be a surprise, and I'm sorry if you're shocked—"

Quickly crossing herself, Danielle closed her eyes and silently speed-prayed, not wanting to believe her ears and feeling badly that Jane would see the look of distress on her face. They never hid their feelings, though, and this was not the time to start. As if they ever would. Dani knew this was going to be an issue for her. Anything remotely connected to this subject had never touched her life, and she was all too aware the church considered homosexuality a great sin. She simply could not fathom it.

To say the room was silent would be an understatement.

Jane used the pause to regain her usual confidence before continuing, "I'm sure you're flipping through your memories now and thinking 'But, she dates guys, and she's had boyfriends and—'"

"My God, Jane," Marti interrupted with a quizzical expression, "haven't most of us fixed you up with some guy over the years? What's this all about?"

"You're right, I've met some fabulous men thanks to you. If you really examine those relationships, you might recall that they didn't actually last all that long, and I always had an excuse why not. "

"But..." was heard from more than one corner of the room. Bonnie had walked across the room to refill her wine glass and returned with the bottle to top up everyone else's. Plunking it down in front of her, she muttered, "Oh crap, just get me a straw for this bottle, will you? It's going to take more than a few glasses of vino collapso to get my head around this conversation."

Rolling her eyes, Lynn removed the bottle as soon as Bonnie sat down. "Cool it, Bo. Enough is enough."

"No more interrupting," Jane pleaded, throwing her head back and closing her eyes tightly before she continued. "I met Sam at a conference a couple of months ago. We were seated at the same table in the morning workshop, and all of us in that group decided to go for lunch together. She and I got chatting and discovered we knew some people in common through our jobs. It was a good group—lots of conversation and laughter. It was a two-day conference, and when we bumped into each other the next morning we decided to sit together for the session. A few others—both genders I might add—hooked up with us and we did lunch again. Several of us exchanged phone numbers to perhaps get together another time."

Legs were crossed and uncrossed. Drinks were drained and refilled. Everyone was listening attentively to process the reality of Jane's words.

"A couple of weeks later, one of the guys called some of us and suggested we meet at Stop 33 at Sutton Place after work. I was free and planned to go. It's such a lively place to be—always such a buzz in the crowd. Always such a great view."

"Always such a big bill," muttered Lynn, at which they laughed, relieved to have an opportunity.

"I have to admit that I did find myself hoping that Samantha might be there too. Didn't think anything of it though. That wasn't unusual, right? I mean, we all meet terrific new people from time to time and our circle of friends is richer for it."

There were low, affirmative responses.

"She seemed glad to see me too, and although we mingled, we did spend most of the time talking to each other or in the same group. It was a great evening and later as everyone was beginning to wobble off in different directions—they do make a wicked martini there—Sam asked me if I wanted to grab dinner downstairs in the bistro."

Bo interrupted, "You're so right about their martinis, Janey, but enough details. Cut to the chase. Tell us how the falling in love thing happened."

"Trust Bo to get right to the point!" Dee said.

Jane nodded with a wry smile, "You're right Bo. That's the part I need to tell you."

"During dinner, just like before, the conversation and laughter flowed so easily. We were comfortable together and commented how it seemed like we'd known each other for years. Partway through our decaf coffee, Sam just looked at me and—right out of the blue—said she felt compelled to tell me that she was a lesbian and was tremendously attracted to me. She hoped I wouldn't be shocked or insulted or repelled by the admission, and do you know, I felt none of any of those reactions."

"What? You weren't even a little surprised, Jane? I can't believe that," said Lynn.

"You're right, Lynn. It's hard to believe," agreed Jane. "I suppose..." She paused for a moment, looking up in thought. "Yes, I suppose I was surprised. It was all so out of context. But it passed quickly, and I tell you this very honestly. I let her words sink in for a moment and then I realized that I felt pleased. Quite pleased."

A long sigh could be felt around the room as everyone tried to breathe normally again. They were looking at each other with incredulity, as if searching for an expression somewhere in the group that would say they should just relax, an expression that would encourage them to be over the moon for her because she was in love. So far, it wasn't happening.

She continued, with a noticeably anxious tone creeping into her voice, "Sam said she was a bit shocked herself at being so open with me, because this was not her style and she usually kept her personal life private from new people. She said she had not been able to stop thinking about me and was on the verge of calling me herself when Greg called with his invitation to Stop 33. She said that if I was offended by what she had just said, she would understand. She hoped that at the very least we could remain friends and she would silence the other emotions she was feeling."

Jane paused and looked around the group, scanning each face for some reaction. All eyes were wide with astonishment, glued to her as her friends were inwardly running through their own emotional checklist.

Sipping her wine, Jane went on, shaking her head. "I was stunned at first as I realized I was actually feeling good about this. I told Sam that I had been thinking about her as well, but it didn't occur to me it might have been in the same way. Her words had allowed me to open something inside that I had never acknowledged."

"I can't begin to imagine how you could think rationally about anything at that point. Wasn't your mind racing?" blurted Danielle with a look of complete horror on her ashen face. "*Merde*! How did you manage to compose yourself? Holy Mary, mother of God, I'm having trouble thinking just listening to you." She was also struggling to control the tears that were building in her eyes. In all honesty, she did not want to hear what her friend was saying. She didn't want this to be true, even though she wasn't sure exactly why.

"Dani, I know it sounds crazy. After the first few minutes,

my mind wasn't racing, but I simply wasn't sure what I wanted to say. Like I said, I really kind of felt, well, flattered I guess. Weird, I know. I asked her if we could just talk about this slowly, and about ourselves, so I could sort through the emotions I was experiencing."

"And?" asked Lynn calmly, hoping to divert Jane's attention from Danielle.

"And that's just what we did. We talked and talked and then got into our own cars and went to our own places. Sam said she wouldn't call me and that she realized I was probably having some pretty bizarre thoughts about what she had said. She felt it best that I call her when and if I wanted to. I called her two days later."

"Jane," Marti questioned with a slight hesitation, "did you know ... uh ... or think or suspect ... well, that you were..."

"A lesbian?" Jane finished the question for her.

Marti looked her straight in the eye, nodding with a perplexed expression. Nobody else said a word.

"You know, I don't think I ever truly knew what I '*was*'. I don't think I was hiding anything from myself or anyone else. What shocked me about that night was that I *wasn't* shocked by the revelations. Slowly a lot of things started to make sense. I could clearly recall the avoidance issues I had in so many relationships, my inability to truly bond with any of my boyfriends, no matter how great they were."

"And there were a couple of more than great ones," offered Cass. "I could probably use some of their phone numbers."

"For sure," Jane said, smiling at the memories. "I had some great experiences with several of those guys. I like men—immensely! I can't even say that I didn't enjoy sex with some of them, but now that I've experienced this relationship with Sam I can feel what was missing. This really is the first complete relationship I have ever known—physically and emotionally. I have to tell you it's better than anything I ever imagined. I think

I have always been drawn to women, but being socialized the way we are, I would never allow myself to pursue thoughts about anything other than friendship."

"Well, it's not like there are a lot of fine lesbian role models to be found," said Cass. "I mean, people are somewhat more open since the '60s, but there's still a long way to go."

"True," Marti said, nodding, "there seems to be a backlash now and that concerns me."

Dee interrupted with a typically anxious worry. "Jane, I feel awful saying this but I'm kind of afraid for you. I'm afraid people will be unkind and hurtful. We'll all have to keep this a secret. It doesn't seem right but I really feel ... well, scared..."

Jane quickly jumped in on Dee's pause. "Society needs to learn so much more about respecting differences. Acceptance, understanding ... I guess it will be a long road but I've made my choice."

There was an oppressive silence before Pam's wavering voice got their attention. "Jane, we're all stunned, but of course we want to support you. I can imagine how difficult this is for you to share—no matter how good you feel inside."

"Exactly," said Jane, a frown settling in, "I feel so sure about my feelings. It's a sense of finally understanding myself, but I'm worried about the reaction my family will have and also the other important people in my life—like you. It was important to me to tell you all together—just like we always do."

She paused, dropping her eyes for the moment, not wanting to see if there was disapproval on any of these faces that she loved like family. Quickly, in a way that occurred quite naturally when this group was facing a challenging issue, each woman, with one notable exception, responded in her own turn. They admitted there were mixed feelings at what she was telling them. They had to be honest. They always were. But tonight Danielle was struggling.

"I'd be lying if I said I wasn't surprised," said Bonnie,

pouring a straight vodka, which did not go unnoticed. "I would never have suspected for a moment that you were, uh..." Siphoning half of her glass, she cleared her throat, "It just never crossed my mind."

"Mine either," agreed Marti. "I just thought you were picky and the right guy had not turned up."

Then Lynn, who had known Jane since they were together in nursery school, spoke up. "You know, I did occasionally entertain the thought that you might be a lesbian. No particular reason. There was just something. And to be honest, what would I know? I think I've only read one article about . ..uh..." Her face reddened as she searched for words. "But I guess, like the rest of us, when it came to your love life, I simply didn't dwell on it and—"

"Yeah," Cass interrupted, looking confused. "It's not like you were acting any differently towards guys than the rest of us. You know, giving us hints or anything."

"That's because," Jane answered, "as I said earlier, I didn't realize it myself. Sam reaches me in a way no one has before. Corny as it sounds, our hearts and souls connect, and the intimacy and honesty we share just blows me away. I think this is how true love is supposed to feel, and I've never been there before ... as much as I tried to be with some of my boyfriends. I feel like I finally fit into my own skin, and for the first time I feel happy and at peace with myself. Can't you tell?"

"It's so obvious, Jane. It really is," murmured Pam, her eyes glistening with emotion.

"Ti-Ming. Good thing you went to that conference," Cass said, laughing in her supportive way.

"As the saying goes, the truth will set you free," Marti offered, at the same time glancing at Danielle, who had almost vanished into her corner of the sofa and had not said a word since her earlier outburst. Looking flushed and uncomfortable, Danielle was not making eye contact with anyone at this point.

"I can't say that I'm thrilled for you," said Bonnie, gripping a chunk of hair on top of her head and twirling it furiously, "because I know your life won't be as easy in this relationship as it would be if you were in the magic kingdom of 'coupledom' with a guy. The way society expects you to be. That's just a fact and we all know it. Issues around kids, possessions, family, even your job—all sorts of things—will be more complicated. Some people aren't going to be able to accept this as your choice. You know we're here for you in whatever way we can to help, to listen, or to do anything you ask, but not everyone in your life is going to react this way. Not at first anyway. Are you prepared for that?"

"But this is the 70s, and the times they are a-changing," said Cass, channeling Bob Dylan as she was known to do.

"Not a-changing fast in every way though," Marti interjected. "I'm embarrassed to say that I have a lot of friends who are very anti-homosexual. Um ... there's a new word now – homophobic. I know it's from a base of ignorance but it's out there, big time. I'm a little more used to gay guys since I've worked with so many in the airline business, and I hear a lot of snickering and mean comments."

"Janey, Bo is right," agreed Pam. "There are many people who will think you are sick or just plain weird. You're going to have to be very careful how and to whom you disclose this. That's part of the reality we're talking about here."

Jane nodded as she said haltingly, "I'm ready to deal with outsiders, and I'm not about to announce my choice to the world. I know what you are saying is true. I'm really worried about my family though. They're very old-fashioned. I know they'll feel hurt and confused and won't be able to grasp this at all. It's going to be a horror show. Nothing like this has happened with anyone we know. At least as far as I'm aware."

"It might not be as bad as you are expecting," suggested Cass softly as she reached for Jane's hand.

Clasping Cass's hand in return, Jane's voice broke as she said, "Thanks Cass. You're such a flower child, always looking on the bright side and not worrying about taking risks. I hope you're right. I really feel I've found strength and courage from my relationship with Sam, and I hope I have enough of what it takes to get me through this process. I just don't want to hurt anyone I love."

"And they won't want to hurt you either but they'll be shocked at first, and that's exactly what might happen. You'll have to be prepared for that—and be ready to forgive," suggested Lynn, who knew the family much better than the rest.

"Yes," Jane said with a sigh, "I want to move on so badly that I do feel ready to deal with whatever lies ahead. Telling all of you was the first hurdle." Her eyes welled with emotion and she smiled faintly. "Thank you for ... being you..."

Her voice trailed off as she looked at Danielle, who was still jammed into a corner of the couch, her mascara smeared and eyes red. She and Pam had been sharing the Tissue box although their tears were for very different reasons.

"If you believe it, you can achieve it," encouraged Marti in an effort to lift the mood and shift the attention away from Danielle. "How did you get through the last three months without breathing a word to us?"

"That was the most difficult task so far," replied Jane, brushing her long, sun-streaked brown hair back from her face with her fingers and twisting it into a French knot. "Keeping secrets isn't the way we operate, is it? I simply had to know with total certainty that I was making the right decision before I let you in on it. The two weeks at Whistler left us both with no doubts."

The room was quiet. Everyone seemed to be considering what a major issue it was for Jane to feel she needed to tread lightly when she always approached life with gusto.

Feeling it was time to inject a little humor into the conversation, Jane asked, "And to top it off, Sam's a movie fanatic, like me! Guess who's her favorite filmmaker?"

Without a pause they all yelled, "Woody Allen!"

"Of course." Jane grinned broadly, a steadfast Woody Allen fan since she saw the film *Play It Again, Sam* years before. She quoted him often, usually to the BC's amusement but sometimes with great poignancy.

"He's got a new movie, *Annie Hall*, coming out next month and the previews are awesome. Can't wait!"

Pam had been pacing the living room. Pausing mid-step, she asked, "Jane, have you thought about just moving in with Sam and introducing her simply as your roommate for a while?"

"Thash a good idea," Bonnie interrupted with a noticeable slur that caused a few alarmed glances.

"That way," Pam continued, shooting a frown at Bo, "everyone could get to know her as a person and become friends with her before you let the world know the full extent of the relationship."

"That might not be a bad way to go, Jane," agreed Marti.

Jane shook her head vehemently. "Nope! Definitely not! Sam and I feel strongly that would be deceptive and the reactions might be even more negative because we covered up the truth. We don't want speculation. We want to be open and honest right from the get go."

"Got to give you points for that," said Dee, and after a few seconds of reflection they agreed they wouldn't expect anything less of Jane. She always faced life head on, just like she approached sports. She was a leader, heading things up whether they were committees or teams or the cast of her local little theatre. She would meet this squarely as well. Dee had concerns but agreed that deception never looked good on anyone.

The talk continued through dinner. There were thoughts and feelings still to be shared and sorted through. Danielle's input was noticeably absent.

Finally the conversation slowed as they cleared the table for dessert, although the karma in the room felt out of kilter as far as Danielle was concerned.

Jane knew she was still the same Jane she had always been, but she also understood it might take some of these friends a bit of time to realize that. There had to be some space, some time to let this all sink in.

"Okay ladies, here's a diversion," Pam announced, smiling as she pulled a packet out of her purse. "I've finally brought the photos from our ski weekend, and as usual they are quite hilarious. Sorry it took me a while to get them developed."

The laughter and comments that accompanied the pictures provided exactly what they needed to feel more relaxed. Everyone was relieved to move the conversation in a different direction.

"Enough chat, already," declared Cass once the photos had made the rounds more than once. "It's time for some bridge."

The cards were brought out, shuffled, and dealt. It was time to think about something else before they called it a night. This was a truth they had discovered long ago: no matter what issue held center court during one of their Tuesdays, if things got really serious, they made sure they played a few hands of bridge. It just felt right.

As they were bidding the first hand, Jane stretched her arms to the ceiling in a gesture of thanks and said, "Once again, the Bridge Club comes through. I have to tell you, I was so anxious about tonight. I honestly didn't know how all of you would feel."

Bo put her cards down and walked around to Jane's chair. Grabbing her softly by the throat, she gave her an affectionate throttle and shake before her arms slid around Jane's shoulders. “Oh, for heaven’s sake, Jane! Surely you have more faith in us after all these years!”

Jane’s eyes moistened. “Well, we haven’t faced anything like this together, and, goodness knows we’ve all cracked our share of queer jokes over the years—myself included. I mean, who would’ve guessed?”

“Hurry up and bid please, Cass. We’re moving on at this table,” said Lynn, trying for a little levity. More than a few of them swallowed hard as they began to play.

As the evening was breaking up, Jane asked Lynn if she would consider going with her when she planned to break the news at home. Fortunately her parents were leaving in a few days for their annual two-week vacation in Florida, and she had decided to wait until their return to begin a process she suspected could be painful.

“You’re like a member of our family, Lynn. After all the years our parents have been friends. Coming to dinner with me is nothing you haven’t done on a regular basis through the years, so it won’t appear odd. They love and respect you, and it might help if they see you are okay with this.”

Zipping her jacket, Lynn nodded a quick yes and put her arm around Jane. She could sense her anxieties. “Of course I will.”

A reverse receiving line fell into place at the door as everyone gave Jane a warm hug on their way out.

There was a moment of hesitation as Jane and Danielle faced each other. Looking down, Danielle struggled for composure and then burst into tears. There was an awkward moment, and then Jane simply grabbed her, like always. “Dani, I knew you would have the most trouble with this. I’m sorry it’s hard for you. Keep talking to me and we’ll work it through, I know we will. Nothing’s changed between us, no matter what you think right now.”

Danielle snuffled and nodded as she stiffly pulled back and made a quick exit.

"You'll have to be strong, as you normally are," said Pam as she turned to step into the frigid night air and watched Danielle hurrying to her car. "The most important thing is that you know in your heart what you feel is right. The people in your life who love you will come around. It might take some longer than others, but it will happen. For those who don't come around, just know that the problem is theirs, not yours."

"I know," Jane replied. "That doesn't make it any easier, but I know. *Que sera, sera.*" For the first time in a few hours, her typically bright smile made an appearance, radiating hope and a relief that this first big step had been taken.

There would be phone calls and lunch dates over the next few weeks as they continued to offer Jane support and a safe harbor in which to lay bare her feelings. They all reassured her, even a still somewhat reluctant Danielle, she had only to ask and they would do whatever they could to help.

An established routine since being on her high school track team, running was a favorite part of Jane's day. She had always done it for the exhilaration of the exercise, but now she recognized it as a way to relieve her anxieties, a problem she had seldom experienced. The more she worried, the more she ran.

Three weeks later, Lynn met Jane at the Grenview exit from the west end Royal York subway stop. Soft lights were shining warmly through the leaded glass windows of this attractive enclave of Tudor-style homes as they walked the ten minutes to the welcoming front door of the classic two-storey house where Jane had grown up.

"A little bit of England far from England" was the motto of the visionary Robert Home Smith when he developed the neighborhood after the Bloor Street bridge was built over the Humber River in 1924.

Winter-bare branches of oaks and maples, many centuries old, created graceful archways over the quiet streets of this quiet, established neighborhood. Jane's had been one of the first Jewish families to move into the area in the late 1950s, and it had taken some years before they truly felt settled. Even now, more than twenty years later, they still had to drive a half-hour along Eglinton Avenue to reach the closest synagogue.

"I'm beside myself. I haven't been able to sleep thinking about how I'm going to tell my parents about Sam. In fact, Dee came over last night for a few hours. I worked myself into a terrible state, something I never do, but I didn't want to make any more demands of you."

"I know. She called and talked to me this morning to bring me up to snuff. She said that Sam had suggested last night that you have one of us with you tonight. We were both impressed with Sam's sensitivity and intelligent approach, Jane. It's been a pleasure getting to know her these past few weeks. I'm certain that given time, your parents will grow to love her."

Jane spoke softly. "I honestly haven't given this much thought. I was just caught up in what was happening to me. I was so happy and excited about my relationship with Sam that until now I haven't considered my mom and dad. I've been completely besotted and self-centered. I can't believe it. They're *not* going to get this. I just know it."

Lynn nodded her head slowly. "I've been thinking about it too, and I've made a few trips to the library for books about homosexuality and how families cope. I have to tell you, there isn't a lot of literature that's worth reading. So much is just medical reviews, but I figured I'd better try and be more informed before you drop the bomb."

When there was no response, Lynn looked over to see tears streaming down her dear friend's cheeks. Taking her by the arm and stopping in the middle of the sidewalk, Lynn wrapped her arms protectively around Jane and spoke with compassion.

"This is so unlike you. I can only try to imagine what you are feeling. This situation involves love on a whole bunch of different levels and an acceptance of a way of life many of us just can't understand. It's not going to be easy at first. There's no way around that."

Jane sniffled through her tears. "I know, I know. It's just that my parents are so wonderful. They've been the best in every way, and now I'm going to cause them a lot of pain."

"Not necessarily," said Lynn. "You're going to tell them something that's going to be a shock at first. But you may be surprised once it sinks in. Your parents love you and want you to be happy. We know that."

"Yes, but I know they want me to be happy with some wonderful man and give them grandchildren and build a life like the children of all their friends. Like all my cousins. The way they always dreamt it would be."

"Jane, your parents may be more perceptive than you give them credit. Our folks aren't always quite as old fashioned as we believe. They read a lot. They're thinkers who spend a lot of time out in society. They've lived life, for heaven's sake. They may be more prepared for something like this than we know. If this is truly what you want in your life—and it looks to me like you have no doubt about it—then you simply must forge ahead. The bottom line for them will be that this is good news. You are happy and in love. It just may take some patience to get the message through."

"That's what Dee said last night."

"Well, there you go. Let's get in the house and start that ball rolling."

Over a drink before dinner, Lynn kept the conversation going with updates about her family and her parents' recent train trip to Lake Louise. Jane managed to bombard her with questions about it every time the talk slowed, although she knew this was only going to work for a short time. As they sat down to a delicious beef brisket dinner, the talk turned to Jane's trip to Whistler. Naturally her parents were curious about the state of the cabin and property and the extent of the new development on the mountains. Lynn realized they were not aware that Jane had gone with anyone. Somehow they managed to keep the chatter flowing throughout the meal.

After clearing the table, they were returning to the living room for after-dinner coffee when Jane caught Lynn's eye with a look that said she was ready.

Watching her parents settle into their respective chairs, Jane was struck by how they had aged. They seemed a bit smaller and frailer tonight. She was their only child and had arrived later in their lives, when they had almost given up hope. Her dad was getting close to retirement, and her mom was becoming more and more like her grandmother. Why was she doing this to them? She felt a strong desire to simply strike up a conversation about nothing in particular and call it a night.

But she had a mission this evening, she reminded herself. It was time to be truthful. It was time to live her life openly, and she desperately wanted her parents' eventual understanding and acceptance. Having Lynn there had been a wise decision. She would be able to give credence to Jane's words simply by her presence and her comfort with the situation.

Pulling up a footstool in front of her parents' matching recliners, Jane sat facing them and clasped her hands around her knees. Before she could speak, her mother asked, with a look of concern, "Is everything okay, dear? You seem so serious. You're worrying me."

"Oh Mom, you've always had a sixth sense about things, haven't you?"

"It's how mothers are. Isn't your mom the same, Lynn?"

Lynn chuckled, smiling as she nodded in agreement.

Jane took a deep breath. "Mom and Dad, I do have something to tell you. It's something really important to me, and I hope you will understand."

Looking at her with a mixture of curiosity and concern, his head cocked and brow furrowed, her dad gently pressed, "For heaven's sake, Jane, what is it? Are you all right?"

"Yes, Dad. I'm fine. In fact, I'm probably better than I have ever been, but—"

"That's wonderful sweetheart," he encouraged. "So why is this difficult?"

"Well," she hesitated, "I've met someone ... and..."

"Oh," her mother interrupted, sensing she knew what was wrong, "And he's not Jewish, right?"

"Well—"

"Don't worry, Janey," her father interrupted. "If it's serious, maybe he'll consider converting. A lot of young men do, you know."

"Oh, Irving," her mom broke in, reaching over to pat his arm, "it's probably way too early to even think about such things. Besides, we have to be more modern about this. We're a far cry from orthodox, and—what do they call it—oh yes, mixed marriages are becoming far more common. We have to think of Jane's happiness first. Tell us more, Janey. I'm so thrilled you've met a special fellow."

Desperate to get the conversation back on track, Jane reached out and grasped a hand of each parent as her words tumbled out. "Please, please ... listen to me. It's not about being Jewish. It's not about meeting a special fellow. I'm in love with a woman and I'm moving in with her and I know it's the right thing for me. I realize I've been missing something in my life no matter how hard I searched. Now I've found it, and I'm still the same me, only better. I know this is a shock ... and I'm sorry ..." she took in a deep breath before her words kept coming. "I just want you to know that it's a good thing. It's the right thing. I simply never knew it. I hope in time you can understand."

Amid this flood of words, Lynn had quietly moved over to the arm of Jane's mother's chair and placed a comforting hand on her shoulder.

Lynn rubbed that shoulder lightly now as Estelle Spivak looked up at her with a mix of confusion and shock. Lynn met her gaze, patting her shoulder gently, and nodded. Then Estelle returned her attention back to her daughter, her jaw clenched and eyes wide. Irving Spivak was motionless, blinking as though he needed to clear something from his eyes. As Jane had anticipated, they were stunned, perplexed, and speechless. She hadn't intended to blurt everything out. The torrent of words had been unstoppable once it began. But it was out, all of it.

"Oh my goodness, Jane," her mother said, her voice hoarse, "what on earth does all this mean? Are you certain about this? Perhaps you just need some help, you know, like counseling. Talk to Doctor Black or something or I ... I..."

She fumbled with her hands and looked to Lynn with wide, desperate eyes. Lynn squeezed her shoulder tightly and spoke quietly.

"It's taken a lot of courage for Jane to be open and honest about this with you," she said, looking from one to the other, "and with me. I was surprised—like you. I've had time to adjust and come to understand that she is clear about this. I know the last thing she wants is to have you unhappy."

"Well, I can't see any way she's making us happy with this announcement," her mother replied as a small tear escaped from the corner of each eye. "I simply don't believe it. How did this happen? What's wrong with her? How can we understand? How can anyone understand?"

Mr. Spivak continued to sit silently upright in his chair, staring at this young woman he would always see as a little girl, who was sitting at his feet beseeching him with her gaze to understand. Beseeching him to love her for whom she was and always had been. Their beloved only daughter, the young woman of whom they had always been so proud, their bright and shining star, as they always referred to her.

Realizing this was as far as the matter could go at this point, Lynn proposed that perhaps everyone needed to sleep on it before discussing it further.

Reluctant to leave her parents in distress, Jane suggested, with some hesitation, that she might sleep over tonight in her old room, as she did from time to time, so they'd be together in the morning.

Mr. Spivak finally spoke, keeping his voice as flat as possible to conceal his pain. "Jane, I think that's a good idea. Please do stay."

Jane's parents embraced Lynn and thanked her for being with them tonight and for being such a good friend to Jane. Lynn tried to lighten the mood by saying she had never been known to miss an invitation to one of the Spivaks' famous dining experiences over the years they had known each other.

The evening ended abruptly, with Jane's mother excusing herself with a bad headache and Jane's father helping her mom up to the bedroom, both looking ashen.

Sitting at the kitchen table, the two friends stared mutely at each other. After a minute or two, Lynn reached over to stop the nervous tapping of Jane's always well-manicured nails.

"You're going to drill a hole right through the table."

"I knew it would be bad," Jane whispered, letting out a long sigh, "but I didn't visualize it like this. I thought we would talk and I would tell them about Sam. I didn't expect the door to slam shut like this."

"I don't think the door has slammed shut at all. It's just gotten stuck and needs some work." Lynn replied. "I think your parents need to absorb this shock before they can begin to talk about how they feel. Give them some time. See what tomorrow brings. Your idea of staying over is brilliant, and I think it will help—a lot. No matter how your parents act in the morning, promise me you'll remain calm. You might need to do a great deal more listening before you start talking again."

They parted after another hour or so. Lynn had to teach in the morning. Jane was going to take the day off.

As Jane climbed into her old four-poster, still with pink linens like the ones she loved as a teenager, she prayed to get past the horrible sinking feelings she was experiencing. She longed for sleep to offer her a brief escape from this reality. Tomorrow had to be a better day.

After quietly crying into her pillow, she lay staring at that familiar ceiling and gave a start as she felt a soft hand lightly stroke her hair. At first it seemed like a memory from her childhood, until she heard her mother gently whisper her name.

"Janey?"

"I'm awake, Mom," she groggily responded and moved over to make more room. "Lie down with me like you used to."

Her mother settled on the bed beside her daughter, who had been a woman for many years now, and they instinctively joined hands as they had on so many nights over so many years, when comfort was sought and love was shared. The moon's glow softly lit the profile she had gazed upon with such pleasure from the moment of her daughter's birth.

For several minutes they lay with not a word between them, yet they expressed so much. Slowly her mother began, "I love you."

"I love you too, Mom."

"I'm sorry if I hurt you earlier. I didn't mean to."

"Me too," said Jane as her tears once again broke loose. "I just didn't know how to tell you and dad ... everything kind of came spilling out."

Her mother's voice was throaty but still clear. "I'm not sure there is any way to know how to talk about things like this without words and emotions getting out of control. I still don't really know what to say, but dad and I want you to know that above all, our love is always there for you. We're going to need a lot of help to understand what you've told us tonight, but we want to do that. Am I making any sense?"

Jane could barely make her mouth move as she wrestled with her tears and sobs. "Oh, Mom ... thank you..."

"No matter what, my darling daughter, you will always be our bright and shining star."

She turned to put her arms around her daughter. Cradled in the safety of each other's arms, the two women wept softly for things they couldn't change before they fell asleep.

When she awoke in the morning, her mother was gone, but love and hope still filled the space on the comforter next to Jane. What an apt name for this bedspread, Jane thought, looking at it in a way she never had before. She knew she would be able to face the day and felt encouraged that the path of this journey would be smoother.

It took several more visits by Lynn as well as her own parents after she explained the situation to them. They had all been long-time friends, and this support was helpful to Jane's parents.

"After all," Lynn's mom had said, hoping to remind Estelle and Irving of a much earlier memory, "we learned a lot when Cousin Betty from Montreal turned out to be one of 'those people,' as we ignorantly said then, and we were all shocked to death when it first came to light. No one would believe it! Thirty years ago, homosexuals were shunned and treated like lepers. Many in our family were very upset with me when I finally stopped acting like an idiot and talked to Betty again. We had always been close, and I just couldn't believe that she had changed. And lo and behold I discovered she hadn't. She was the same lovable cousin, and we enjoyed many happy times with her and her friend. My goodness, we humans often create such unnecessary conflict in our lives."

It took many evenings with Jane and her parents, talking, questioning, searching, and more than once shedding tears. Jane's father, surprisingly, was able to accept the reality of Jane's feelings and choices sooner than her mother, who kept blaming herself for missing some important aspect of parenting throughout Jane's life. Jane told them about a support group for families of homosexual children. There weren't many resources like this at the time, and indeed secrecy was still very much a part of this lifestyle.

Lynn and her parents accompanied them to a series of those meetings. Marti, Cass, and Dani attended some sessions with Jane as well, as much to be informed as to support Jane and her parents.

Initially the Spivaks found it less embarrassing to ask their questions of Lynn, who shared some books she had borrowed from the library. She encouraged them to read about lesbian issues and parents who faced the same unexpected shift in family dynamics that they were experiencing. It was easier for them to express their shock and surprise to Lynn and her parents. The security of that long friendship offered the opportunity to contemplate their thoughts and words and begin a journey towards acceptance. They felt there were not many people with whom they could share their struggle.

The last thing the Spivaks wanted was to cause their daughter more stress than she was already feeling. It took them several weeks before they felt ready to meet Sam, although Jane had shown them photos and answered all questions about her as well as she could. Determined not to make it a sales promotion, Jane absolutely needed to sense her parents genuinely were open to accept the relationship without prejudice. It was the only way.

They would have to make a paradigm shift from a very old-fashioned attitude to see the relationship for what it was in spite of gender and to accept the love the women shared. Easier said than done. Time and patience were the critical factors here.

In the midst of a casual telephone conversation with her mom more than a month later, Jane had a feeling the timing was right.

"Mom, would you and dad like to come over for coffee on Saturday afternoon? You can meet Sam and we can spend as much time together as you like but you won't have to feel locked into sitting through a meal. If you only want to stay a short while that won't be a problem."

Her mother accepted the invitation and asked what she could bring. Jane sensed a note of nervous relief in her mother's voice. "Yes, we won't stay long. I'm going to be busy preparing for the holidays. Passover is coming up and..." Estelle paused now and Jane did not break the silence. Then her mother said softly, "And maybe we will all feel comfortable about being together for the *seder*..."

Progress, thought Jane. She would see how the coffee date went before committing to anything else. The last thing she wanted was to rush things.

At the next BC night, Jane and Dee confessed to the group they had been going to a duplicate bridge club once a week. Jane said she found the serious competition just the thing to bring a little balance to her life at the moment.

"Sam goes to the squash club while I play duplicate. The night out is a good break for both of us."

"Oh trust Jane. Now she's playing extreme bridge! Just don't start getting carried away with any of those fancy duplicate conventions with this group," warned Bo, giving her an exaggerated evil eye as she shuffled the cards at her table.

Jane joined in the laughter, before adding, "No worries! And by the way, I'm happy to report the bumps in my life are becoming easier to deal with, although it's still slow going with my parents. But guess what ... we're celebrating Passover together this weekend."

DEAL #2

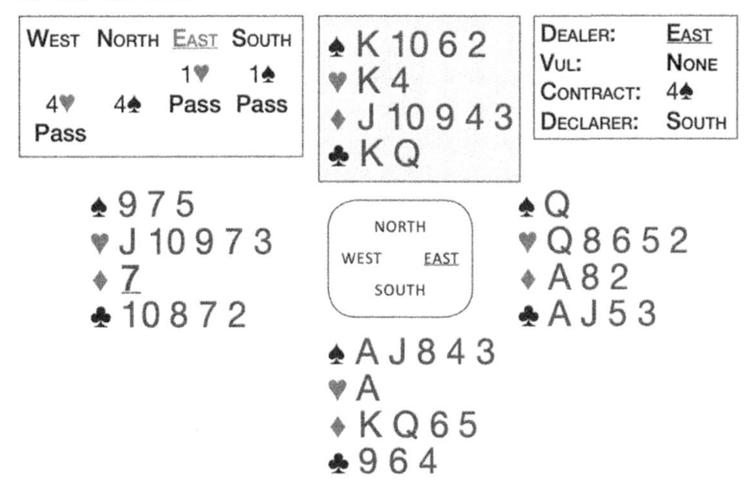

SUGGESTED BIDDING

East opens 1♥ with 13 high-card points plus 1 length point for the five-card heart suit. South overcalls 1♠.

West has the weakest hand at the table but can make a preemptive jump to 4♥. The partnership has at least a ten-card heart fit and West has a potentially useful singleton diamond.

North has too much to pass and, with four-card spade support, chooses to bid 4♠ in case 4♥ is making. The 4♠ bid ends the auction.

OPENING LEAD

West knows the partnership has at least ten combined hearts, so the defense won't be able to take more than one heart trick. West applies the Defenders' Plan and leads the ♦7 against 4♠, hoping to get one or more ruffs.

BRIDGE QUIZ:

What contribution can East make at trick two so the defenders can maximize their trick-taking potential?

What does West play to trick three and why?

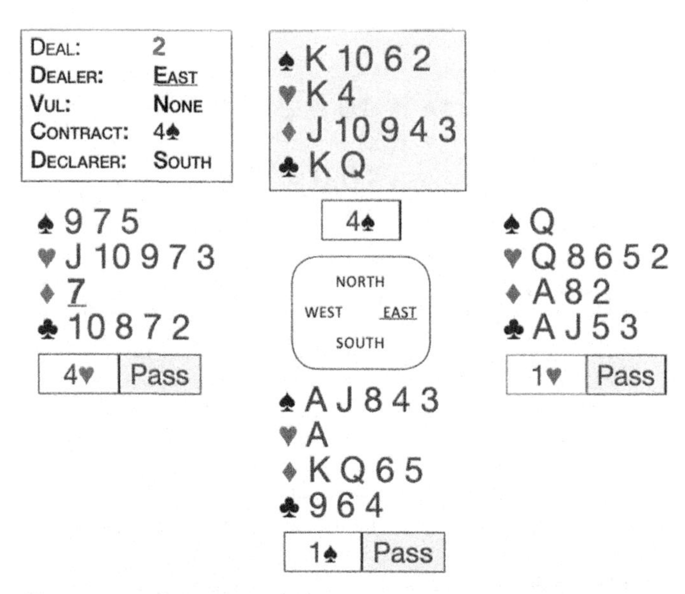

Suggested Defense

It is expected that West would lead hearts, the suit bid and raised by the partnership. East suspects the ♦7 lead is because West has a singleton. East wins the ♦A and leads back a diamond for West to ruff.

Since East opened 1♥, West would usually try to get back to East's hand by leading a heart. East knows that won't work on this deal. To tell West to lead a club rather than a heart, East returns the ♦2 for partner to ruff. This is a suit preference signal for the lower-ranking suit, clubs. At trick three, West leads a club to East's ♣A and gets a second diamond ruff.

Suggested Play

If West leads a heart after getting the first diamond ruff, declarer wins, draws trumps, and loses only three tricks.

Conclusion

Both defenders apply Defenders' Plan to imagine their trick-taking potential. They use a suit preference signal to figure out how to get two diamond ruffs.

4

BONNIE'S SOS – 1984

Bonnie's SOS was all about taking responsibility for one's choices and sticking to those decisions. She insisted she could not have succeeded without their help, but the Bridge Club knew the bottom line was that Bo had done the larger part on her own.

Sharing the classic brick century farmhouse, thirty minutes west of Toronto in Halton County, at first with her parents and later her widowed mother, Bonnie was to the country born. At age thirty-eight, after her father's death, she took over running the family's long-established dairy farm, with the help of their farm manager.

The rich, rolling farmlands of this historic county were settled for the most part by United Empire Loyalists and British immigrants beginning in the 1780s. Agriculture remained the core of the area's economy, but change was coming after two hundred years. Industry and urban development began moving west toward Halton's small towns and rural villages. Bonnie's father had sensed the shift and wisely invested in property through the years, growing hay and grazing herds until the time was right.

In spite of her cosmopolitan education at a long-established private boarding school in Toronto, Bonnie's heart lay in her family's deep legacy of farming. Her assortment of paintings, pottery, and various collectibles spoke to a lifelong love affair with Holsteins. There was something about those velvet-coated black and white bovines, with their silky, long lashes framing deep, limpid eyes. As a child, she would be found snuggled for a nap in the hay-strewn stall with her 4H calf.

You never had to wonder about the thought process in the uncomplicated life of a Holstein, she always said. Bo appreciated life best when it was straightforward.

Along with the farm management, her primary commitments were to the family property development business and a popular catering company she ran with a partner. Not only could she hold the floor in any discussion, ranging from agricultural to social and political issues, but the woman could cook up a storm, and serving four or four hundred was no problem for her.

"Embrace the chaos," she reminded herself, and the BC, on a regular basis.

Bonnie had left social work some years before, when the pressure finally caught up with her. She had been deeply committed to the challenges facing childcare workers; however, the bureaucratic interference and paperwork had killed it for her.

"You can take Bonnie out of social work but you will never take the social worker out of Bonnie," the Bridge Club teased her forever. They were so right. Her natural inclination was to help people, and so she did.

In the wings, her family had been waiting for her to bring her talents into their business, which was rapidly expanding as suburbia spread its tentacles.

If one member of the Bridge Club were going to successfully

run for politics, it would have been Bo. Short and stocky, with dark hair that became blonder as she became older (as women's hair so often does), she had just the right presence—someone who could make an entrance without attracting much attention but leave having made an impression you wouldn't forget. Her unassuming manner and generosity of spirit ensured she was liked by all.

Quick-thinking, informed, smart as well as intelligent, she was a paragon of irrepressible good humor. Politics was in her blood, with an uncle having served in the Canadian Senate and a cousin in Parliament as the respected member from an important Saskatchewan riding. She would have been a natural.

Thanks to all this good standing, she managed to convince everyone for years that she didn't have a serious drinking problem. People were imagining things, overreacting, she told the BC. Yes, she knew that from time to time she drank more than was acceptable, but she had everything under control, she assured them. She could spin things as well as the most experienced politician.

The truth was, like her father, she was an alcoholic. She had been for far too long. She knew it. The Bridge Club knew it. Admitting it was another matter.

"We're going to have to plan an intervention soon. That's all there is to it," Dee said matter-of-factly.

The Bridge Club was sitting in Dee's spacious Rosedale house, with the exception of Bonnie and Pam, who were driving in together. The others had arrived at 6:30, a half-hour earlier than normal at Dee's request, so they could discuss Bo's situation, which now had reached a crisis level. Dee had asked Pam to deliberately stall when she collected Bo so they would arrive later than usual. With Pam's reputation for tardiness, it wouldn't be a problem.

The anxiety in the room was palpable as they silently watched Danielle cross herself and close her eyes in a quick prayer. *Do your thing Dani. We need all the help we can get*, each one was thinking.

"An intervention isn't exactly an act of friendship," Jane said sadly, breaking the silence.

"You're wrong," responded Cass with a shake of her head. "It might be one of the ultimate acts of friendship. We might be saving her life."

"God knows we have to do something drastic," said Danielle. "My prayers don't seem to be doing any good. I've been so worried, saying extra novenas and lighting candles like crazy for the past year."

"And your efforts are always appreciated, Dani," said Marti, picking up her glass of Merlot and tipping it in Danielle's direction. "We depend on you for that, but Dee's right. We have to take some drastic action, and we have to do it soon before something awful happens."

Lynn's foot jiggling had reached maximum velocity, as it did during tense moments. Now she uncrossed her legs, putting both feet flat on the floor before she turned to Dee. "I agree with you," she said. "It won't be pleasant, but that's what we have to do. You've known Bonnie since childhood and you're familiar with her family situation, so you're really in a position to guide us on this."

Dee acknowledged this with a grave look. "It's not as if her family is in a position to do it anyway. It's just over a year since her father died, and the rest of the family is dealing with their own issues around that. I'm not certain they would even want to recognize she *has* a problem."

"I'm embarrassed to admit I was totally ignorant about interventions until Dee explained the whole thing to me," said

Cass, pulling a bunch of brochures from her purse and passing them around. "After we talked, I called Alcoholics Anonymous to see if they had any helpful literature and dropped by their office in my neighborhood. I was sure someone I knew would see me—that's usually what happens, eh? Then the rumors would fly!"

"Thanks, Cass. That was a good idea," agreed Dee.

Dee knew about the process from a friend who had been involved in a family intervention. She asked Cass to share with them what AA had to say about it.

"Well, first of all, apparently it's an extremely difficult thing to do. The woman on the phone warned it could backfire. Bo might become angry with us for overstepping our boundaries and shut the door on all of us, causing even more problems. It's a big risk. However, she also said it's a necessary risk when the situation is out of control."

"There's absolutely no question with any of us about that," confirmed Lynn, as the others murmured their agreement.

"Right," continued Cass, "and she did say that often friends are more effective than family at carrying out an intervention, but that it will take some time to plan. She offered us the name of an experienced counselor. We have to make a list of key people—family, friends, business associates—who might be effective in the intervention. Then we all have to meet with the counselor to plan it."

Listening to herself, Cass had to wonder if she needed to take a look at her own drinking habits. She thought about how heavy handed she could be when pouring her drinks. She did love her rum and Cokes. Too often, when Jake was at his dad's and she was alone, she would drink until she passed out on the couch. Time for a reality check, she decided.

Placing another log on the fire, Dee stopped to look through the window at the gray, wintry landscape illuminated by the streetlights. "Yes, organizing an intervention is like rehearsing a play. Everyone has to memorize and practice what will be said, in what order, no deviation from the plan. It needs to be done in a loving manner but honest and firm. It's intense."

Jane exhaled loudly, her voice full of concern. "We have to let her know that her drinking is affecting more than just herself. I mean, it's not as if we haven't spoken to her repeatedly about it, but she always says she has it under control and we want to believe her, so we do. We can't give in this time."

"God knows, we've each taken our turns over the years sitting on the phone for hours with her when she was in a drink-and-dial mood," said Danielle.

"Yes, we've all taken turns lecturing her, but the fact is that she has always been an extremely high-functioning alcoholic. It's not had a negative effect on her professional life, as far as we know," Dee said emphatically, almost as if hoping to find a way of avoiding the confrontation. "The two of us have spent a hell of a lot of time together, and I can't tell you how often she has convinced me that she does not have a problem!"

"Everybody loves her. She's always so full of life and gets you laughing in no time—with or without a drink," laughed Cass, almost apologetically.

"She even plays bridge well when she's bombed," agreed Marti.

"But we know she's an alcoholic. We know that for certain. We've got to stop ditzing about and do something concrete instead of just talking about it. Eventually the drinking is going to take over, and then it will be even more difficult to try and help," Dee said, trying to get them all back on track.

"You're right. We've procrastinated far too long. We should do it before all the Christmas parties start and the temptations are even stronger," Lynn suggested as she reached for a much-needed top up of her wine. This wasn't going to be easy, she told herself.

Flipping through one of the brochures, Danielle read aloud,

"God grant us the serenity to accept the things we cannot change, the courage to change the things we can, and the wisdom to know the difference."

"That's the AA prayer."

"We better take it to heart as well," said Dee.

They debated the chances that Bonnie would even agree to join AA and participate in their twelve-step program. It seemed to them the only effective program available and yet the statistics showed that only 15 percent of those who got through it remained sober for more than a year.

"My gosh. That seems like a pretty low rate of success."

Still looking at the brochure, Danielle read on, "It says right here that alcoholism is an incurable illness. They stress the best thing family and friends can do is offer love and support as they encourage the alcoholic to stay with the program."

They agreed their plan would begin that evening. Cass would call the recommended counselor the next day to begin working on the intervention. Dee knew Pam was already on board. She had been the designated driver for Bo on Bridge Club nights for over a year now and had alternated cajoling, lecturing, and arguing with her regularly about her drinking until she was close to her wits' end on the topic.

"Okay," said Dee, "so beginning tonight, we're going to tell Bonnie that none of us are drinking with her, nor can she drink with us. I've already had Kenneth put all the liquor in the basement for tonight, and Marti, you can put those bottles of wine in the back of the pantry, thanks. Bottoms up everybody. Let's get serious about this."

They continued to plan and began compiling a list of those they thought should be involved in the intervention, until Cass, sitting by the large bay window, alerted them that Pam was edging her car into the last tight spot on the typically crammed street.

After a noisy entrance, complaining about the frigid night

air, Bonnie and Pam made the rounds, greeting everyone as usual. The new arrivals were in good "spirits": Pam due to her ever-present optimism, but Bonnie because she'd been drinking. The unmistakable air of breath mints was always a dead giveaway.

Over the past year or so, Bonnie was more often than not on her way to being sloshed when she arrived at the Bridge Club evening. It depended on the day of her drinking cycle, which consisted of getting blitzed one day and not drinking any booze the next to allow her to recover from her brutal hangovers, using her proven remedy of soup, bananas, and Coca-Cola. As a matter of coincidence, Bridge Club evenings usually fell on her drinking day. She normally kept things somewhat under control then (a matter of opinion when you're an alcoholic) so she would not be subjected to the BC's concerned admonitions.

Alcohol had been the drug of choice for the majority of their generation, which had seen the legal drinking age in Ontario change to nineteen from twenty-one long after the ladies of the Bridge Club had reached the age of consent. In their days of underage drinking, most had fake identification, and going to bars and booze-ups was the major social activity during their university days. No one would deny that they overdid it more often than not, but only Bo had become addicted by the time she was in her thirties.

The fact that she was a high-functioning alcoholic and able to appear completely in control most of the time—even when they knew she was blasted—made it more difficult to deal with. With her outgoing nature, raucous laugh, and *joie de vivre*, she could cover her tracks well, until she crossed over the final line and her normally loud voice pitched even higher, raising alarms.

"So, where's the wine?" asked Bonnie as she looked around for the usual collection of bottles.

"We're not drinking wine tonight, Bo, or anything else alcoholic, for that matter, and we're not going to at Bridge Club any more if that's what it takes to begin helping with your problem," answered Marti.

Bonnie nodded as she surveyed the scene, noticing there were no wine glasses or any beverages other than water on the coffee table.

"I've got soft drinks, tea, coffee, water—" offered Dee.

"What sort of bullshit is this?" Bonnie asked, making a sound that somewhat resembled a laugh as she lit her cigarette and flopped down on the couch. "Are we turning into the Women's Christian Temperance Union?"

"Nope," said Cass, "but we are turning into some seriously concerned friends."

"Uh oh, here we go again," Bo said, blowing smoke rings into the air.

"Bo, we're very, very, worried about you, and..."

Bonnie's face twisted into a frown, a look of displeasure unfamiliar to any of them. It seemed the conversation might not last much longer.

Pam sensed a different approach might help. Giving a timeout signal to the group, she said, "Bonnie, relax. Let's tell the gang what we were talking about on the drive in."

Bonnie crossed her legs and began twirling a chunk of hair furiously. No one told her to stop this time.

Pam recounted how, in the car, she and Bonnie had been comparing their drinking habits of the late sixties and early seventies. They reminisced—if that's the right term—about how the majority of their peers were regularly getting smashed and no one thought anything of it. There were not as many music and dance clubs in those days, so most of the time the sole purpose of being out was to drink. They were students, single, and beer was cheap in those days.

The others in the room caught on to Pam's strategy and joined in.

"Omigawd, remember the Pretzel Bell downtown, with that bizarre singer who wore ladies' glasses, or the Jolly Miller up at York Mills and Yonge? That was always such a party," Lynn recalled, causing them all to hoot with laughter at the memory of those wild times.

"Rocking to Ronnie Hawkins and the Hawks at Le Coq d'Or," Dee said, grinning.

Pam made a face, recalling her usual pattern of ending up on the bathroom floor, draped over the "porcelain pony" while the others took turns holding her hand. "And the endless trays of draft beer at La Place Pigalle downstairs on Avenue Road, when Cass and I had that apartment just a few blocks away before we went to Europe?"

"Ah yes, Hangover Haven, as it was affectionately known," Cass said to nods all around. There had been many nights some had slept on the floor or couch in that flat.

"How many times were some of us on stage for amateur night at the Brunswick House?" grimaced Marti. "Beer convinced us we were talented and amusing."

"Do you know," added Danielle, "the Brunny is still going strong, with kids today as young as we were then! My nephew was talking about it not that long ago. *Tabarnac de calisse*! Good thing all our kids are too young for that—I for one am not ready to deal with it."

"Dani," said Bo, seeming a little less tense, "you probably have the clearest memories of any of us, since you were usually the best behaved!"

"Wait just a darn minute," said Lynn. "I know we all can recall a few evenings when Sainte Danielle was one of the stars."

There was much laughter as those stories spilled out and Danielle blushed uncontrollably.

"That was then and this is now," Dee said with an unapologetic air, returning the topic to its more serious side, "and there's no reason why we can't laugh about the old days, but we can't ignore what is happening now with you, Bo."

"Well, we sure had fun in those early days," Bonnie continued, defensively, "and I didn't really think I drank any more than anyone else. At least it wasn't noticeable."

"No, we all had our moments," Lynn agreed. There was an awkward pause in the room, as they each anxiously hoped for someone to say the right thing.

Cass stood up and walked over to Bonnie. Her voice was tense as she began, "Bonnie, we're not exactly sure how to do this, and we're probably making some mistakes right now, but we've decided that we have to do something—and soon. I'd like to say I'm sorry, but honestly, I'm not because this is important, and—"

Bonnie held up her hands to halt her in mid-sentence, sensing where this all was going. "Okay, okay. Hold on a minute!"

She stopped twirling, stood up, and moved past Cass as she began pacing the room.

Everyone waited for her to speak.

It would be a very long minute, and behind Bonnie's back, Pam gave a discreet hand signal for them to be patient.

Bonnie's expression changed from anger to determination as she began, "I have something to tell you. I know you're worried. I know you've been worried for a long time."

A wave of silent head bobbing moved around the room, and Bonnie took it in before she closed her eyes briefly, inhaled and exhaled deeply, and continued, "Believe it or not, now I'm worried too—even though I'm three sheets to the wind right now ... well maybe just two ..."

Sitting beside her, Pam rolled her eyes in confirmation without bothering to mask her frustration.

Bonnie, looking unusually chastened, continued, "Driving in, after we had been revisiting the good old days, I told Pam what happened last week—five days ago to be exact. I had a luncheon to attend along with many of the top people we deal with in our business. To keep the story brief, I got totally hammered on some killer martinis and ended up out of control. I mean, *big time*, with a capital B. I ranted and made rude and stupid comments to people in a way I've never done before ... staggered around ... completely made an ass of myself ... Crap! It was brutal!"

No one interjected as she shook her head in disgust. "I was mortified the next day when I finally surfaced from my hangover."

She paused here, as a look of shame clouded her face and her voice lost its customary steam. "It's the epiphany you've been waiting for. Over the past few days, I've finally accepted that alcohol is controlling my life. I have to stop fooling myself that it isn't. I don't ever want to be that out of control again. I don't even remember driving home, and that really scared me."

"Goddamit Bo, we've all been concerned this was going to happen—or worse," Marti said, glaring at Bonnie.

"Well it finally did. I'm so pissed off with myself!" Bo looked around the room, meeting everyone's eyes with total remorse.

"Let's face it. You're not in control of your life, and you have a decision to make," challenged Dee.

Bonnie's eyes grew dark with emotion. "That's the bottom line all right. It's time for me to step up to the plate. My brother, who unfortunately saw the whole debacle, had a long talk with me the next day when I was coherent. Needless to say he was furious with me. In spite of that, he said he wanted me to play a more active part in the family business. He stressed he needed and wanted me there—*sober*."

"Hallelujah, that's great news," said Danielle, doing what she always did.

Bonnie reminded them of the strong effect her father's death had on her the previous year, a death caused primarily by his alcoholism. "I keep thinking about what a waste it was. He had a wonderful life and never appreciated it in later years because of his drinking. He still had a lot of living to do. I am today acutely aware that I don't want the same thing to happen to me."

Leaning forward to stub her cigarette in the ashtray, she looked down at the floor and didn't lift her head as she said in a soft but strong voice, "I'm an alcoholic. I know it. You know it."

Silence filled the room as they all hoped she meant what she was saying. Bonnie stood up and poured herself a large glass of water. Taking a long drink she stood with the glass in her hand. Nodding slowly, obviously giving a lot of thought to the moment, she repeated, "I *am* an alcoholic."

No one moved a muscle. All eyes remained locked on Bonnie.

"I'm finally admitting out loud what I've been in denial about for way too long. I know I need your help. You may think all your harping over the years hasn't had an effect, but I assure you it has. I've chosen to ignore it, but I can't forget it. Slowly it's been seeping into my alleged brain."

Bonnie talking about herself as an alcoholic was a break-through. Considering they had been planning an intervention before she walked in, they were struck by the coincidence. Ti-Ming.

Sitting next to Bo, who had returned to the couch and put down her water, Marti turned to face her and took hold of her hands. "If you're serious about making a change, let's do it.

"Keep talking Bo," Pam encouraged. "Let's go back to the start of when things began going bad."

Bonnie nodded in agreement and reached for her glass again as if holding it would give her some familiar support. "It'll be the abbreviated version, though, short but not terribly sweet. You know how I don't like to blather on, and besides, you've all lived it with me—"

"Got that right!" Cass interrupted. "The important thing now is to keep the ball rolling. Don't just say you're going to do something, that you want help, and leave it at that. Besides, you're not exactly sober right now, so my guess is you may need a bit more convincing."

"Okay, you're probably right," Bonnie replied, looking sheepish. She confirmed that after she made her decision to confess to the Bridge Club, she did have two stiff drinks to bolster her courage before Pam picked her up.

"First of all, the most obvious part of this equation is that alcoholism runs in my family, on both sides and back several generations, so I've had it around me all my life. I know it's a treatable disease, but there's no medical cure. Between living with the issue and dealing with alcoholic clients in my social work days, I'm educated on the subject. I know what I'm up against. I watched Dad battle it day in and day out."

"And I know," interrupted Cass, "that the first step to treatment is a sincere desire to get help. I feel like we're seeing that from you tonight, Bo. I've not felt that before."

"Yes," said Bonnie, as her hair twirling began again in earnest, "you are. I think I've hit bottom, and I'm ready to do something about it. Besides, I owe it to my mom as much as myself. I'm going to be responsible for her for many years to come, and she deserves better than this."

Lighting another cigarette, Bo continued, "Okay, here I go. After working as a social worker for a year, Jackson and I had the Woodstock experience and left to bum around Europe. Remember that, Dee?"

Dee blanched at the mention of Jackson. He had been a friend of hers at university and she had never forgiven herself for introducing Bonnie to him. It was a name that was seldom heard these days. In fact, it had seldom been heard for almost a dozen years.

Jackson Parker and Bonnie had been dating steadily for a

year when, in 1969, a spur-of-the-moment decision found them driving south to cross the U.S. border with five friends, Dee included. Word had spread there was going to be quite a party, with the most amazing music, and suddenly, loaded with food, beer, and a tent, they were on their way to the Woodstock Festival in an old Volkswagen van. What a life-changing experience that was.

Once the craziness was over, it took longer to get out of the parking lot than it did to drive all the way down there in the first place! Finally arriving home and scrubbing off the last stubborn bits of mud, with no need for further encouragement, Bonnie and Jackson packed in their jobs, sublet their apartments, and left for their own European hippie adventure.

"To be on our own, complete unknowns. Like a rolling stone... " Bonnie paraphrased Bob Dylan with a nostalgic look in her eyes.

There were some melancholic smiles in return.

"It began so brilliantly," Dee recalled, hesitating as her expression and tone changed, "and ended so terribly."

With a look of despair but a clear voice, Bonnie continued, "Understatement ... after a couple of months of traveling I realized Jackson was manic depressive. The trip came to an abrupt end as he became unbearable, out of control. I didn't know that before I met him he'd been seeing doctors and trying different medications. When we were dating I really didn't notice anything wrong. I mean, we were all suffering from some kind of angst in our early twenties."

"So true," broke in Danielle who felt the need to give Bo a chance to pause in her story, which she knew was only going to get worse. "In my case that was the only time I seriously questioned my faith. I was really tormented about it for a couple of years. Then that charismatic old priest at Our Lady of Sorrows spent months arguing with me. He was the one that helped me work through my doubt. "

"Oh I remember that well," said Jane, with a wry laugh. "Final year of uni. You were driving us crazy and then we had the miracle of Lourdes."

Danielle blushed. "*Bien* ... then I met Bryce. He was such a devoted Catholic that I happily embraced the church once again. I don't need to tell you how that situation worked out."

"That's not all you embraced," snorted Cass as they all appreciated the lighter moment.

"Sainte Danielle," as they liked to tease her, was comfortable in her role of true believer and as the Bridge Club member in charge of prayers and other matters religious. They also knew how "hot" she and Bryce had been for each other since day one.

Now Danielle looked with concern at Bonnie. "Are you sure you want to talk about this part? We all know how painful it is."

"If I'm going to put all of this history on the table, this has to be part of it. You're right, though—it's painful. There's never been anyone in my life like Jackson. I've often drowned my sorrows over what might have been. So, to continue, a couple of weeks after we got back from Europe, Jackson simply vanished, as you know. I thought I was going to go crazy. We'd been drinking a lot in Europe ... way too much. I chose to ignore it. With his psychological issues tormenting him, I wondered if he was experimenting with medication or drugs. I thought he might have gotten hurt and was hospitalized somewhere, so we checked everywhere, remember? Our families, our co-workers, you guys and other friends..."

"We blitzed the city," Pam said sadly.

Bonnie's eyes filled with tears. "I'll never forget the day I went with his parents to file the missing person report. That was brutal."

"And then the priest that Danielle and Bryce knew found him wandering downtown and refusing help. That was the beginning of a whole new learning experience for all of us."

"Right," Lynn said, "it was a complete shock to realize that no one could intervene on his behalf. The rights of the homeless to make their own choices are stronger than the rights of their families to help them. To be honest, I still don't get it."

"I remember," said Cass, "that the hostel situation in Toronto was very limited in those days, and the amount of support available for homeless people almost non-existent."

"That's when—and why—we started volunteering serving breakfast at the hostel," Marti reminded them.

"Dani, if it hadn't been for your church connections and the hardnosed efforts of that priest, we might never have found Jackson."

Bo acknowledged Cass's comment with a nod to Danielle as she agreed, "Yes, I did have Dani to thank for that, as I've often said. It was a relief to know Jackson was as safe as he could be. The difficult part was accepting that he wanted no part of me or anyone else. He just disappeared back into the murky, frightening world of living on the streets. That was my first exposure to loss and grief, and I spent most nights at home for a year or so, with my father pouring me drinks to drown my sorrow. Needless to say, that kicked up my drinking a notch or two."

"You didn't let us in much emotionally during those days, Bo," Marti said.

"We were all so young," said Bo, "and our Bridge Club nights were really my only social outings for a long time. Couldn't miss those!"

"Or you'd get the dreaded letter of reprimand from the rest of us. Remember?" Jane dragged a laugh of sorts out of all of them with the reminder of the non-existent letter they often joked about sending to any of them who missed one of their BC evenings.

Bo pulled out memories from the next ten-year period, explaining how she, like many alcoholics, became adept at hiding the truth of her problem from most people around her.

Her naturally strong personality and capable way of handling her affairs presented a distorted version of the truth. She could pull herself together and appear convincingly sober when in fact she was not.

Grasping a hunk of hair once again and twirling it absent-mindedly, Bonnie went on, "Then, as I continued in social work, I had a mentor who shared so much of her experience with me. You remember Dolores."

"Oh yes, we do remember Dolores. Not that we ever met her, but you certainly talked about her a lot. She was a mixed blessing in your life—a talented and experienced social worker but also a talented and experienced drinker," Dee volunteered.

With a nostalgic expression, Bonnie agreed, "I liked to listen to her case stories. You know, more than once we came up with some very progressive strategies for our clients. But ... you are right, there was a problem, which I effectively ignored for years. She was an alcoholic too. We would drink together as we had these conversations. I really got into it in those years. After that, I needed no encouragement from anyone and enjoyed getting tanked by myself as much as with others."

"That's when you know things are really getting bad," said Jane.

"We should have stepped in right then and there, but you always convinced us there was no need," Pam muttered.

Reaching for another cigarette, Bonnie argued, "Well, I'm not so sure you could have done anything then, because no way was I ready to admit I had a problem. Now I think I might be, although I'm not making any promises. Hey, I talk a pretty good story for a drunk, don't I?"

"You always do, Bo. You always do," agreed Lynn.

The next question was whether she would be willing to go to AA and commit to their program.

"I'm one step ahead of you," Bonnie responded. "For some years, through my work, I've known of an addiction treatment center called Havenwood. It was established in the 1960s in midtown Toronto and has a very good reputation. The program is different from AA's, and it appeals to me more. I'd like to give it a try, but I'm not making any promises. Today I can say I want to get help, but who knows what I'll say tomorrow?"

When Pam offered to call and make the first appointment, and accompany Bonnie, there was no resistance. Actually, something in Bo's demeanor kind of looked like relief.

Sensing it was time, Dee stood and motioned everyone to the table.

"Good idea. Let's eat and get the cards out," said Lynn. "I know I speak for all of us, Bo, when I say how encouraging it is to see you're ready to tackle your devils. I feel like we've all turned an important page tonight."

Pam and Bonnie left first that evening and there was a lot of head shaking in the room when the others were on their own again.

"Holy Mary, Mother of God," uttered Danielle in a solemn voice, eyes focused upwards, "thank you for answering my prayers."

"Well, I'm not sure who to thank, but man, am I grateful that it doesn't look like we need to plan an intervention. I wasn't looking forward to that! Talk about Ti-Ming," said Jane, sitting back in the couch and relaxing for the first time all evening.

"Yes," agreed Lynn, "it's unbelievable that Bo walked through the door tonight with that story to tell us."

"But she was still pretty tanked tonight," Cass reminded them, scrunching up her face and looking a bit doubtful. "Even though she's saying she wants to stop, it ain't happening yet!"

"Exactly," Dee replied, getting the wine bottles back out and filling some of the glasses offered to her, "and that's why I'm firmly convinced we still should plan the intervention and have everything ready to go in case Bo loses her resolve. I mean, we shouldn't expect miracles—even though what happened here tonight was close to one! I've never heard Bo admit to being an alcoholic before."

"That's a first for sure," Danielle said emphatically, raising her glass.

"And the critical starting point," Jane pointed out. "At least let's hope so!"

"I'll keep this list of names we put together. Tomorrow I'll call the intervention counselor to learn what we need to do next, while we wait to see what happens with that first appointment at Havenwood," offered Cass.

Exactly one week after that BC evening, Pam pulled into Bonnie's driveway to pick her up. Bonnie greeted her in her usual effusive manner as she slid into the passenger seat and they headed to Toronto for her first appointment at Havenwood. In fact, when Pam had phoned the facility she had been told that Bonnie had to make the call herself to show she was serious. Pam begged the director on the phone to understand and accept her word that Bonnie truly was an alcoholic and not be swayed if Bonnie tried to convince her otherwise. Pam didn't want this attempt to be over before it began, and she knew how persuasive Bonnie could be.

"Okay, Pam. Let's do it!" Bonnie said, a bit too loudly, as she buckled her seatbelt.

"Damn it!" Pam pounded the steering wheel with her fist. "You've been drinking! I can smell it."

"Oh, nice haircut! Wow you really had a lot taken off!"

"Bo! Quit trying to change the subject! You've been drinking!"

Bonnie looked guilty as she confessed to a short vodka and soda while she was waiting for Pam. "You know, one of the fallacies of a lot of alcoholics is that if they drink vodka people won't smell it. Not true—although slopping vodka on my shirt didn't help! Got to get me one of those designer bibs!"

"Bo, it's not funny."

"Ah, I just had a quickie to relax and get me through this first meeting. Don't worry."

"Well, I am worried. What if they don't take you because you had a drink today?"

As it turned out, Bonnie made it into the initial phase of the program. No one judged her on this obvious slip.

Surprising to Pam, Bonnie was not expected to stop drinking cold turkey. The policy was that over the next few weeks she would taper off, as they referred to it, with the acceptance that when she began her one-month live-in rehabilitation, she would be committed to never drinking alcohol again.

"That's really the biggest stumbling block for an alcoholic," the counselor said. "*Never* is a tough concept to accept. That's the reality, though, and only another alcoholic can truly understand how formidable it is to imagine the rest of your life without booze of any sort. You will grieve for the banished bottle at first and feel like you're losing your best friend. What we hope you will come to understand is that you are really slaying a dire enemy and reclaiming your life."

By the end of that appointment, Bonnie committed to coming one day a week, accompanied by Pam as her support person, until a space opened up for the month-long stint. They anticipated this would happen in three to four weeks, which would take them into early January.

The program administrator spoke clearly and slowly, maintaining strong eye contact with Bo. "This means, obviously, you're going to have to survive the Christmas party scene before you come to us. We know we risk losing people when they have to wait, but that's part of how our program operates. If an addict isn't ready to meet us halfway by cutting back and committing to prepare for the rehab, then it would be a waste of everyone's time anyway. We find the waiting period quite an effective part of our therapy."

After two more appointments, Bonnie knew it was time to walk the walk.

"One more of these meetings and then the tapering stops and a lifetime without alcohol begins. Are you still feeling ready to commit?" asked the counselor.

"As ready as I ever will be," Bonnie firmly responded, hitting the desk with her fist. "It's time."

It turned out that even if Bo thought it was time, she still needed some assistance. Pam was beside herself as she listened to Bonnie's loud, slurring voice on the phone three days later.

"Pamela, my friend! Do ya want some fish for your freesher? For your New Yearsh Eve party! I got some fresh feesh for the frisher ... I mean for the fresher ... no the freesher. Ha ha ha ha!"

"Bonnie! What's going on! You sound smashed. What are you doing? Where are you?"

"Oh ya, I'm shmashed all right. Totally shitfaced! Hmmm, where am I ... oh yeah, I'm at home ... with my new besht friend, the cookie monster ... no, no, no ... just kidding..." There was an interruption as she hiccupped uncontrollably for a few seconds and burped loudly. "I mean, the fishie monger, yup, the fishie monster ... oh hell, the guy that shellsh the fish..."

"The fish monger? You don't even like fish! Bo, I'm coming right down. Do not go anywhere! Do you hear me?"

"Oh yeah, great. C'mon down and buy some fish, cuz I'm

not buying any ... *hic* ... I hate feesh. Ha ha ha ... yup, we'll be here ... okay ... yeah, bye."

After calling her husband to ensure he could collect their sons from basketball practice, Pam set a speed record as she beat it down the snow-packed back roads to Bo's farm, a twenty-minute drive.

She burst into the kitchen to find Bonnie sitting at a glass and beer bottle–littered table with a pleasant looking young man, both of them completely inebriated.

The stereo was on full blast as Bonnie harmonized with Elvis, her all-time favorite, at the top of her lungs.

The young man was conducting and humming along, and they seemed to be enjoying themselves immensely. Bo always did know how to have a good time, hammered or not.

Turning the stereo off—the only way to get Bonnie to stop singing—Pam stared at the two of them. At least everything seemed to be more or less in order, she noted with some relief.

As Bonnie politely made semi-coherent introductions, swaying on her chair, Pam quickly assessed the situation and went outside to remove the keys from the truck ignition, which she had checked on the way in. Then she asked Luis, the so-called fishmonger, if he could phone someone to pick him up. Indignant at first, he soon succumbed to his good nature and gave Pam a number. Within minutes, she had arranged for him and his Finest Frozen Seafood truck to be collected.

Pam made a pot of strong coffee and plunked mugs down in front of the two sots. Quickly realizing any sort of rational conversation was hopeless she listened, desperately trying not to laugh as the two launched into one of the most ludicrous political discussions she had ever heard.

Once Luis was gone, Pam took Bonnie's arm to help her out of her chair. Bo's legs wandered in two different directions, until Pam managed to steer her down the hall. They made it to the bedroom, and within minutes Bonnie was out cold on top of her bed in her clothes, snoring like a steam engine.

Bo's mother arrived home from her canasta club shortly thereafter and Pam explained that Bonnie had slipped off the wagon with a loud thud.

Her mom looked sad and worried. She'd been there too many times before with her husband, and it broke her heart to see her daughter falling into the same trap. Pam hugged her, offering hopeful reassurance, and asked her to make sure Bonnie called her when she was up and about.

Around noon the next day, Bonnie was on the phone to Pam apologizing and feeling terrible, mentally as well as physically.

"I don't think I can sink any lower. I mean inviting a complete stranger into the house and proceeding to get totally pissed with him is just plain crazy. Thank goodness he was a decent guy and not some psycho. That's it. I've had it. I'm never going to drink again. I swear it."

"I'd like to trust you Bo. Prove it."

Since the next two weeks took them through the Christmas and New Year's party season, one or two of the Bridge Club kept in touch with Bonnie or her mom every day to make sure she had not slipped again. Bonnie stayed close to home, declining all invitations. She knew her problem was that once she got started she couldn't stop. If this was the only way she could maintain control for now, so be it.

By mid-January a space in the program was available and Pam delivered Bonnie to Havenwood, where she settled into the room that would be hers for the month. She swore she had not touched a drop of alcohol since the fateful fishmonger event and Pam believed her.

The program was intense, with no outside contact allowed for the first two weeks.

As Bonnie described it later, there was nothing she hadn't

heard before, but this time she needed to believe it and commit to it. This included accepting that alcohol addiction is a chronic and progressive disease for which there is no cure. Research has indicated it is genetic, and when activated, it takes control. The only hope of the addict regaining control is when the desire to stop is greater than the desire to drink.

"It's a constant battle," she acknowledged to her counselor. "I've finally taken the blinders off and I have to confess my new range of vision is frightening."

"It's a momentous journey," the counselor agreed, "and we're here to guide you as long as you feel you need us."

After two weeks, Bonnie was able to invite three luncheon guests. Pam, Dee, and Bonnie's mother arrived together. To their relief, they found her composed and confident. She wanted to succeed. She was determined.

"I'm not saying it's easy. I would give anything for a drink right now, if I'm being honest. What's different for me is that I know I simply cannot have that drink ever again. It would be like deciding to jump off a cliff. That's what it comes down to for me. Whether it's genetic or not, I am the only one making choices about this behavior, and I acknowledge that."

She paused for a moment and inhaled deeply as if to gather the air to support her declaration. "I accept that I have this incurable disease, and I'm a patient who needs to take the proper steps to control it. I am not a victim. I am in charge of me."

A few long seconds passed. Each of her visitors expressed their admiration for the strength Bonnie was showing.

After lunch, they bundled up and strolled along the snow-cleared walks in the forested property. The cold air turned their breath into puffs of steam but the sun shone in a cloudless winter-blue sky and soon felt warm on their faces.

Bonnie continued to relate her experience so far. Her desire to talk about it was obvious and filled them with hope.

"The exercise program is a good one and it's inspired me to get back into shape. Jeez Louise, I've got a hell of a job ahead of me. I figure I'm going to have to put a treadmill in front of the tube so I can still keep up with my daily shows. Having those endorphins racing through my system really helps emotionally, which surprised me. My main problem now is that whenever I think about having a drink I have something to eat instead. Oh well, I'll deal with that later. When I look at some of the other people struggling in the program I realize how fortunate I am that I'm taking the steps to get better now."

"We all know what a strong constitution you have, Bo. Your sense of humor must be a bonus in here," said Dee.

"Goodness knows it carried us through a lot of dark days," Bonnie's mother added. "You've always been able to laugh at yourself and help others find a reason to smile. I've been proud of you all your life for that."

Bonnie flashed her usual grin, acknowledging that seeing the humor when things look bleak had always been a strength of hers. "I have to tell you, my daily goal to laugh long and hard until I'm gasping for breath hasn't exactly been easy to achieve here, but I keep working on it!"

Words of encouragement hung in the air as they praised her efforts and contemplated the challenges she was facing.

Gratefully accepting the support, Bonnie continued, "Something else I've always had going is that I could last a day without a drink when I was nursing my hangovers. That knowledge helped me believe I could do it for more than a day and just keep stretching it. I just had to want it."

"Purpose and direction, Bo. I hereby give you permission to use my mantra," Dee said as they all smiled at the familiar words straight-shooting Dee had used forever to keep herself, and the BC at times, organized.

"This whole process is such a head game, for me anyway," Bonnie said. "I've always felt that my addiction to alcohol was a physical illness because I don't struggle as much as others do with cravings. But I run into trouble when I actually take a drink, because then I can't stop. Once I recognized that and decided to not take another drink, my battle was set on the right path."

Three pairs of eyes stared intently at Bonnie, attempting to digest and believe her words.

"Don't get me wrong!" she added. "Not that I haven't struggled with that decision. Not that I haven't had moments of wanting nothing more than the taste of a good martini. I'm not saying it's easy, but with the guidance I'm receiving here, I see how I can control my addiction."

"What about withdrawal, Bo? Has that been difficult?"

Shaking her head emphatically, her former social worker persona came to the surface as she said, "It's important to understand this impression is something else that's been embellished in books and movies. Not every alcoholic has the shakes and wild delirium. In fact, most of us haven't had major problems—although one guy had to be hospitalized. Most of us have had mild to moderate withdrawal symptoms that they can deal with here. Not that we haven't needed support, and we definitely have had tremendous help, physically as well as psychologically."

"We are all getting an education from Havenwood," said Dee.

They were almost back to where they began their walk and Bonnie slowed the pace for a few minutes, "I would say the most important lesson I've learned here is that I'm not responsible for my disease but I **am** responsible for my recovery. That's what is happening here."

The three visitors nodded as they appreciated the obvious impact the program was having. The moment called for hugs with Bo, long and heartfelt, before they headed back to the building.

"The resources here—gym, pool, yoga studio, library, learning centers, craft rooms and workshops, you name it—all look amazing," Pam noted.

"They are," Bonnie agreed. "We're kept busy with a strict schedule. Oh! Before I forget, tell Danielle that I'm taking the meditation classes! I couldn't convince myself to try stretching into the yoga positions, but I'm really finding meditation helpful."

"That's fantastic, Bo. We'll tell her for sure," said Dee. Pam nodded, knowing how pleased Dani would be to hear that.

"On the downside, I'm smoking up a storm, but that's an acceptable substitute for alcohol at this point. Oh well, one vice at a time." She punctuated that with a snort before they parted company with more hugs and words of encouragement.

At the end of the month's stay, those who were judged ready to move on did. There was no elaborate graduation celebration but rather solemn handshakes and embraces and an oath composed by the recovering alcoholic reaffirming the commitment to never again consume alcohol.

This was not the end of the program, and for many it took much longer before they left Havenwood. However Bonnie's assessment stated that she was ready for the next step, in which the participant returned to her normal environment with controls. It was all up to her. She was determined not to be one of the statistics who turned back to the bottle.

There was no question temptations were all around. Against the advice of the program, she still kept alcohol in the house, feeling it would be unrealistic to live without it on hand. Being a social creature that could put on the best dinner party, she wanted to offer her guests a drink if they wished. She was determined to be strong enough to handle the taboo right from the start. Taking Antabuse for the first few months gave her the control. It was an effective deterrent knowing that she would experience a most unpleasant reaction if she touched a drop of alcohol.

At first there were weekly follow-up meetings, with zero tolerance when it came to missing one. As the months slipped by, Bonnie became strong in the knowledge that she was beating her demons, and she signed on to take a counseling course with Havenwood. She hoped she would be able to give back to future people in the program. Throughout all this time, the support of family and friends reminded Bonnie over and over of her good fortune in life.

As the first signs of summer appeared, Bonnie told the BC that she was feeling positive about how things were going. She had insisted that they serve alcoholic drinks as usual at their monthly, but they all committed not to consume any liquor in her presence until she had passed the one-year mark, no matter how much she argued with them.

"The only problem is that I'm still eating way too much," said Bo, patting her stomach. "I need a new interest in my life. I'm playing so much bridge I'm dreaming about it, and I'm snacking like crazy when I'm playing, so it sure doesn't reduce my calorie intake."

"Well," Danielle sniffed, pretending to be spurned, "I've tried everything I could to entice you to come to yoga with me. That'd be a start to getting in shape."

"No, no, no, my yogini friend," Bonnie responded, pressing her palms together at her heart center with a bow, making Danielle laugh, "for whatever reason it's not for me, and you know it. You get an A+ for continuing to try to persuade me."

Danielle rolled her eyes and waved her hand. "*Pas de problème, Bo. Chacun à son goût.*"

"But if you hadn't encouraged me to check out the yoga

studio when I was at Havenwood, I never would have become involved in the meditation program there, which definitely helped my recovery."

Again Danielle waved her hand, this time to dismiss the praise. "You did that yourself, Bo. I'm so happy it worked for you."

"Present tense, my friend: *is* working. I meditate every day and consider it a critical part of my ongoing therapy. I may have a very fit mind these days, but it sure doesn't do anything for my expanding waistline."

"I've got just the answer," Dee suggested, standing up to simulate a golf swing. "I think it's time you gave golf a try, Bo. I'm going down to Pine Needles in North Carolina next month to a women's golf school. Usually four of us go, but Barbara had to cancel this year so her spot may still be available. I think you should come too."

"Golf! Me?"

"Why not?" asked Pam. "You've got a driving range just down the road from your place and new golf courses are being developed like crazy all around us in Halton County. You should give it a go."

"At the very least, it's a great time of year to go to North Carolina. The magnolia trees will be in blossom and the weather should be perfect. Come, Bo," Dee begged, "give the game a try. We'll play bridge in the evenings. It'll be great fun."

Jane was also a golfer but restricted to school holidays, so she offered to go to the indoor driving range with Bo over the next few weekends and practice together after Bonnie took a lesson or two.

"It's all about practice once you learn the basics. I can see you really getting into it, Bo. If you beat booze, you can be a good golfer. Okay, that was weak attempt at humor but it takes a somewhat similar determined mentality," Dee said convincingly, being the expert golfer she was, a former college champion.

"What have I got to lose?" said Bo with a shrug of her shoulders. "I'll give it a try. I couldn't have a better mentor than you."

Give it a try she did and was immediately hooked.

Almost a year to the day of the group confrontation that resulted in Bonnie stepping through the door of Havenwood, the Bridge Club was sitting around her dining table enjoying a fine prime rib roast accompanied by exotic vegetable concoctions.

As seconds were being passed and plates refilled, Bonnie quietly looked at each of these friends. She felt her heart swell with gratitude. Then she pulled herself together, stood, and tapped her fork against a glass to stop the chatter. "Okay, put a sock in it. I've got an announcement."

Cutlery was set down as she eyeballed the faces around the table.

Clearing her throat, she continued, "Here's what I know. Addiction is an uncontrollable compulsion to repeat a behavior regardless of its consequences. That's a fact. Here's another fact. I'm immensely proud to say I have my addiction to alcohol under control. I'm a recovering alcoholic and intend to be one for the rest of my days."

Cheers and applause filled the room. Danielle quietly did her thing.

"That's the good news. But now I have to confess I've replaced one addiction with another—and it's all Dee's fault! I'm now a golf addict, and if that hasn't driven me to drink, I can't imagine what will!"

"Got that right, Bo," said Jane, a huge smile lighting her face. "If golf hasn't, nothing will."

"There'll be no better test though, Bo!" Dee laughed.

"Seriously gang, I'm so excited. I've just put in my application to join the golf club down the road next spring. I can't get enough of the game!"

Looking sternly around the table again she continued, "I am now declaring the end to the one-year moratorium on the Bridge Club drinking alcohol in my presence. I checked the calendar, and we're close enough to the date. There will be no argument about this."

Bonnie seldom lost an argument, so the issue was settled.

She had purchased a bottle of champagne for this BC evening, and as the women toasted her with their bubbly, she raised her glass of Canada Dry ginger ale. "The champagne of ginger ales, as the ad says," she laughed loudly. "I must admit it tastes good—and even better, no hangover!

"To you for pushing me and always being there for me," she said as she raised her glass to the group.

"To you, Bo. You did it!" they toasted back, each giving a word of encouragement in turn. When the accolades were completed, Pam gave the command for them to stand around Bo at the end of the table.

"Right on, Pam," cheered Cass, "this definitely calls for a photo!"

Setting the camera on the china cabinet, she lined up the shot and pressed the self-timer before she dashed to join them.

"All right, let's get it over with," Bonnie grumbled. Then she beamed with pleasure and well-deserved pride. "Now we can play some bridge."

DEAL #3

West	North	East	South
			1NT
Pass	3NT	Pass	Pass
Pass			

North
♠ K 6 4
♥ Q J 6
♦ K 6 5 4
♣ Q 9 4

Dealer:	South
Vul:	Both
Contract:	3NT
Declarer:	South

West
♠ Q 7 2
♥ 10 7 3
♦ Q J 9 8 2
♣ A 6

NORTH
WEST EAST
SOUTH

East
♠ 10 9 8 3
♥ 9 8 4 2
♦ A 3
♣ 7 3 2

South
♠ A J 5
♥ A K 5
♦ 10 7
♣ K J 10 8 5

Suggested Bidding

South opens 1NT with a balanced hand and 16 high-card points plus 1 length point for the five-card club suit. West doesn't have the strength or distribution to come into the auction. North raises to 3NT with 11 high-card points.

Opening Lead

West leads the ♦Q against 3NT, top of a broken sequence.

Bridge Quiz:

What technique can the defenders use to defeat 3NT?

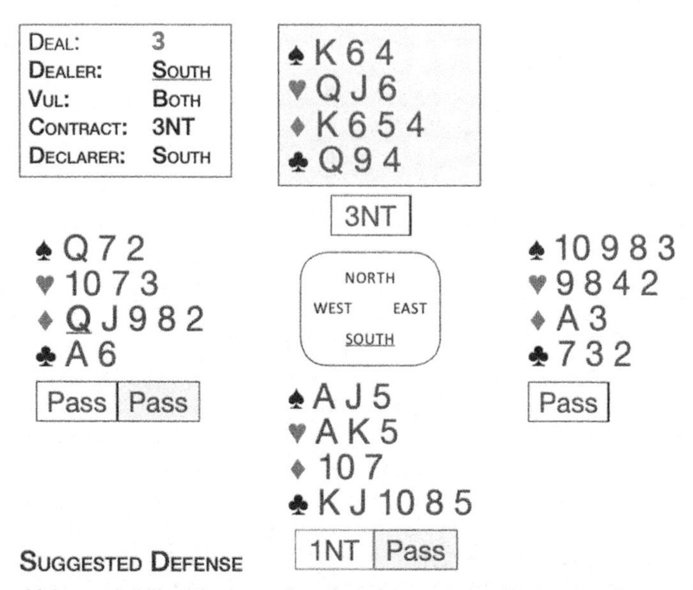

Suggested Defense

Although West's opening lead temporarily traps dummy's ♦K, if declarer plays low from dummy, East must be careful not to block the suit. From the ♦Q lead, East can visualize West is leading from a suit headed by the ♦Q-J-10 or ♦Q-J-9, so the defense can promote winners by simply driving out dummy's ♦K. East should overtake West's ♦Q with the ♦A and return the ♦3. This allows West to drive out dummy's ♦K and promote enough winners to defeat the contract while still holding the ♣A.

Suggested Play

Declarer has two sure spades and three hearts. Four more tricks are needed and can be promoted in clubs. The only danger is the diamond suit. Declarer should play low from dummy when the ♦Q is led and also if the ♦J is continued. If East wins the second trick with the ♦A, the contract is safe.

Conclusion

East's only high card is the ♦A but East shouldn't let it get in the way of establishing West's suit. If West had led a low diamond, East would have no difficulty winning the ♦A and returning the ♦3.

5

LYNN'S SOS – 1987

Lynn was the Earth Mother—a tree-hugger, composter, and committed environmentalist before many people really knew what that meant. It was simply part of who she was.

The fact she was adopted was just another natural part of her. Until it happened, Lynn would have scoffed at the suggestion that she would ever have an SOS related to her adoption. It goes to show how something as simple as listening to a radio program in the car can start a chain of events. Ti-Ming.

She arrived home with her parents (she never thought of them as "adoptive") at six weeks of age. Her birth certificate indicated she was born in Toronto. Through whatever quirks of fate, her life as a family member began in the lap of a large extended clan of grandparents, aunts, uncles, and cousins, settled in a small northern Ontario mining community. Her paternal grandfather, along with other young immigrants chasing a dream, had arrived as a prospector in the early 1900s. His five sons had followed his footsteps into the local gold mines. That's how it was in those days.

Throughout her life, Lynn had a strong sense of family.

When she thought about it as an adult, the core of those feelings was firmly set growing up in that secure small town environment of the forties and fifties, where everybody walked everywhere and knew everyone, or acted as if they did. Family history was important and passed on so much more in those days before technology filled people's lives with too much information.

Their simple but spacious frame house was filled with furniture that had arrived on the steamer from England when her grandmother and great-grandparents left behind their splendid family home in London in 1907. That handsome oak-beamed Tudor had been captured in an oil painting that hung in Gram's living room, and hauntingly in gently-faded, sepia-toned images of cherished old photographs. Their rustic home in the wilds of northern Ontario was furnished with an eclectic collection of old and new. Along with the intricately-carved, centuries-old oak tables and armoires brought with them across the sea were uncomplicated early Canadian pieces of warm pine and bird's-eye maple, crafted and acquired locally as the family grew.

The stories of her family's past came alive to Lynn through these pieces of furniture, their histories vividly recounted by her beloved Gram with her soft British accent.

When she inherited some of these treasured furnishings, Lynn took pleasure in keeping their history alive. Rubbing her hands over the smooth, well-oiled wood, she could feel the connection to those memories in her fingertips, memories she in turn would pass on to her children. Centuries of personal histories were absorbed deeply into the grains of this furniture. DNA did not matter here.

In later years, her thoughts often returned to that history and to the northern Ontario environment of her youth. The images, romanticized by time no doubt, stayed with her as she matured. Closing her eyes, she would play the montage in her mind:

Summer weekends filled with family visits and hikes through thick forests, carting bathing suits, picnic baskets, and fishing gear to the cold, crystal-clear lakes. Picking wild blueberries. Lemonade served on the front porch. Collecting wildflowers along the wooden sidewalks. The smells from her grandpa's bakeshop. Breakfast cooking on the woodstove at her uncle's cottage.

Winters long and dark. Building forts in towering snow banks. Tobogganing. Raucous hockey games, curling or skating on frozen ponds and backyard rinks. Steaming hot cocoa at the kitchen table, a respite from the biting cold. Frosted faces. Tongues stuck on metal railings. Silver birches. Saturday evenings gathered by the radio for Hockey Night in Canada.

The soundtrack included her dad's cheerful whistling, the noon-hour mine sirens and the secular chorus of pealing church bells. The clanking of metal lunch boxes of men of all ages walking to work. The rhythmic whirring of push lawnmovers. The clip-cloppings of the dairy horse hooves and clinking of milk bottles being carried to doorsteps. The high-pitched screeching of blue jays and clotheslines. Melodic summer songbirds. The shuffling of cards for family games. Hockey Night in Canada's *theme music.*

Her belief in a world that was safe and welcoming surely sprung from growing up in the comfortable familiarity of faces and places that nurtured a sense of belonging. Everyone knew who you were or where you lived and there was somehow an accounting for behavior because of that. It was the quintessential Northern Ontario childhood, at least in her memory, and she cherished it.

Native Canadian influence was prominent throughout the region and combined with the story of the rush of immigration to mine the great gold discoveries after 1911. Lynn's grandmother had captured her young imagination as she vividly shared tales from those early days. Gram had arrived with her young husband to be the first white woman in the settlement, giving birth to her earliest babies in a tent. She described how the tender care of gentle native women was her only source of support in those early years. These were stories that fascinated and intrigued Lynn from childhood.

"Can you imagine?" Lynn asked, when she first shared some of these stories. "From life in London, England, to the wilds of northern Ontario—talk about culture shock! I'll always regret that I didn't ask more questions while Gram was still with us."

The people living in towns such as this in the post-WW2 years were, for the most part, the direct descendants of these early adventurers, and the sense of ownership and responsibility to their surroundings was in their blood. People cared about their community, and about each other. Life was simple, safe, and family oriented, and it was natural to grow up feeling loved and valued.

Lynn had no hang-ups about being adopted. Her mom had made it into a beautiful story before she was even old enough to understand. In later years, the only incident she and her mom could recall happened once during an almost assuredly PMS-induced temper tantrum, when she uttered the words that probably most adopted teenagers throw out at one time or another. Her mom had given her that classic parental line that begins, "As long as I'm your mother, you will—" to which Lynn retorted, "You're not really my mother!" followed by instant regret.

To her credit, Lynn's mom just let it slide, knowing it was anger speaking. Once she cooled down, Lynn apologized and they sorted it out with a long embrace. The love of this family was deep and strong with the normal tensions and conflicts that accompany the joys of raising any teenager.

Lynn had a cousin who was also adopted and from time to time Lynn met others who were. She became aware of the mixed feelings many of them experienced, ranging from feeling perfectly comfortable to mild curiosity to torment, as they wondered about their birth parents.

Some obsessed over whom they resembled and Lynn wondered why. She knew lots of kids that weren't adopted who didn't look like either of their parents or their siblings.

As Lynn matured, she recognized she was unfazed about adoption because everyone in her family felt the same. It seldom crossed her mind. Throughout her teen years, on the rare occasion the subject arose, her parents had offered to help her search for information about her biological parents in any way they could. She only had to ask, but she never had the urge. Her dad would sometimes joke that he had two children and one was adopted, but he could never remember which one.

Her brother, five years older and her parents' firstborn, was simply her brother with normal sibling rivalries and bonds. She could not recall a single occasion when he made her feel she wasn't his sister, and she loved him all the more for that.

Most people who met her with her mother would comment on how much they looked alike, and her mom would give her a proud nudge or discreetly squeeze her hand. She loved her family and knew it was her own and they loved her equally.

Her parents enjoyed sports and encouraged Lynn and her brother to be involved and to compete for the fun of it and not necessarily the victory. "Ya gotta be in it to win it, kiddo!" her father used to shout cheerily from the sidelines. For some reason that always made her laugh and try a bit harder. Those words remained with her in every task to which she set her mind.

This was the foundation upon which she and her husband, Jim, were creating their own family history—with an ironic twist of its own.

The twist actually began with Lynn's brother and his wife, who after six years of marriage and no luck getting pregnant adopted a six-week-old son. One month later they discovered they were expecting and soon became a joyful family with the two children eleven months apart.

The second twist came when Lynn and Jim themselves went the adoption route after several years of trying to conceive. With great emotion and happiness, they brought home their eight-week-old son only to discover the following week Lynn was pregnant. They always felt this was absolute proof that this first son was destined to be theirs. Had she become pregnant a few weeks earlier, the adoption would have been off due to agency rules. Ti-Ming. Within the space of nine months, they were an ecstatically happy family of four!

Lynn would joke that adoption ran in their family. "It's a tradition," she would say with a smile.

Setting aside her teaching career, she embraced her role as a mother.

Driving in her car one day just a few days before her thirty-ninth birthday, Lynn was listening to the Betty Kennedy show on a local radio station. The discussion was about an adoption registry system that had been set up by the provincial government as new legislation had passed about disclosure of adoption information. The once highly confidential details were going to be released to interested adoptees and biological parents after they proceeded through a typical bureaucratic maze of paperwork.

Her curiosity was piqued, or maybe she just was feeling old; moving into that fourth decade had been preying on her mind more than she had ever imagined. She thought if for no other reason, it would be helpful to know her medical history. Breast cancer and heart disease in women her age were becoming more openly talked about. Maybe there were some blanks to be filled in after all.

If she hadn't been listening to that show, this whole issue might not have surfaced. *Timing is everything*, she mused, *the ancient Chinese art of Ti-Ming*. That Bridge Club interpretation always caused her to laugh out loud.

Following up with a phone call to the government offices, she obtained all the information required to proceed. To Lynn, it was a simple and unemotional process. The registry would determine if an enquiry from either side had a match in the system. If so, the Ministry of Social Services would make the initial contacts and if both parties were in agreement, a meeting would be arranged.

Legislative reforms continued to change dramatically. Soon there was a letter sent saying a search could be made even if there was no registry match. Lynn returned a form giving permission to proceed and put the issue aside. There was a backup of several years. This was a government agency, after all.

The following year, Lynn and Jim contemplated their approaching fortieth birthdays. A small-town environment surrounded by nature at its best was a lure they could not resist, and so they packed up and moved north of Toronto to the cottage town of Bracebridge with their sons, aged ten and eleven.

With no regrets but plenty of anxieties, Jim left his executive position and the security it offered. After researching the scant business opportunities in the area, he took a chance on establishing a business offering computer services. With a lot of effort and commitment, they were slowly reaping the rewards.

The move was all about lifestyle. They felt this slower pace of life was more suited to the way they wished to raise their children.

"Always make certain your home is your refuge," had been

Lynn's constant credo, "and the people in it the ones you most want to be with. It's simple."

She knew how to keep it real.

Jim's family cottage was a few miles away on Lake of Bays, where he had spent summers all his life. That, combined with Lynn's northern Ontario history, was the catalyst for the dramatic move.

On the other hand, Toronto was an easy two-and-a-half-hour drive. Bridge Club Tuesdays were not in jeopardy, and what better reason for an overnight visit. It should also be noted that Lynn baked the world's best chocolate-chip cookies, and a full tin accompanied her each month. She liked to think all those childhood days spent covered in flour in her grandfather's bakery shop had something to do with her baking skills.

With the excitement of settling into their new surroundings, the subject of the adoption registry had vanished completely from Lynn's mind. There was much to be done getting their new home in order and establishing their business and local connections, challenges they gladly embraced.

However, the hip surgery Lynn discovered she needed six months after the move, and the year-long recuperation that would follow, had not been on their agenda. She handled it with her typical good spirits and in due course was back to rowing, the hobby she had begun years before in the city. She joined the local rowing club and was soon back to good physical condition and again involved in competitions, much to her relief.

The only disappointment was when her doctor advised her to discontinue downhill skiing.

"Too much twisting and turning apparently doesn't work with my problems," she told the BC when they were planning their annual ski weekend, "but I can still do cross country skiing, so I can keep Bo company."

"Hooray," cheered Bonnie, the only one of the group who

had never taken to downhill. "At least you don't have to worry about dragging me out of the bar anymore when the rest of the gang is on the slopes!"

"Amen to that," said Danielle as the others murmured agreement. Everyone was thankful those days were over.

As the years passed, Lynn's surgery and recovery faded into the background. Jim's business grew, with equal credit to Lynn, he was the first to say, who took over much of the administration so he could focus on sales and development. The whole family soon felt they had never lived anywhere else.

Three years after her last contact with the ministry, an unexpected telephone call pulled the adoption issue back into focus.

The Bridge Club listened in surprise as Lynn updated them at their next meeting, which was at Marti's.

"So the social worker called right out of the blue. They had used Canada 411 to track me down! They believe they've located my biological mother living in Toronto with her husband, who is not my biological father."

"Okay, let's get this straight," replied Cass. "Several years ago you told us about listening to the talk show, and then I recall you told us when they sent you the form to give them permission to begin a search—"

"Oh right," Dee interrupted, "I remember, because not one of us was aware of the Adoption Registry and we had a conversation about the whole issue. Should you search or shouldn't you? Whose rights and privacy deserve protection? You know how I worry about every little detail. It's such an emotional dilemma in so many ways, but you've always been so calm about it."

"We had a real go about the whole topic again when they

sent you a form saying they were ready to proceed with searches in your birth year," Danielle reminded them. "Come to think about it, we stopped asking after a few months because you said you would tell us if there was anything to report. Wow, you had no further communication until this call?"

"Exactly! You can imagine how shocked I was to hear her words. My reaction really surprised me. As you know, it's never been something I cared about one way or the other. I guess that's why I had put it out of my mind. She asked my permission to make the contact, which I gave. A week later she called back and said that it had been a bit complicated, but she was finally successful in speaking with my biological mother. Apparently the first time she telephoned the house, the husband answered, and when his wife picked up what was obviously another line, the husband hadn't hung up."

A groan filled the room. "Ooooops."

"Good thing the social worker was paying attention," said Pam.

Jane nodded, "No kidding—eavesdropping on a call like that could cause some tension in the relationship!"

Lynn rolled her eyes. "So the social worker had to be discreet and say there was a personal matter she wished to discuss and could the woman call her back at another time? She had to do a bit of foot-dancing, because she wasn't making a lot of sense speaking vaguely to prevent the husband from understanding."

"Of course," Bo said, twirling a strand of hair on top of her head until it was standing straight up like Alfalfa in the Little Rascals. "How many times, especially in those earlier years before WW2 and even decades after, had a young woman kept her secret when she did move on with her life?"

"I can remember that even from our high school days," Cass recalled, "particularly in conservative small town Guelph. You would hear rumors about why someone had disappeared for a year. The truth was never spoken—those girls were sent out of town to get away from the stigma."

Bonnie continued to twirl and talk, "That's right. Before the sixties, there was so much shame and secrecy attached to being an 'unwed mother' that the family would do all they could to hide it. Family, friends, and neighbors, who were the source of most news in those days, were told that the young woman had suddenly gone off to help an ailing aunt, take a secretarial course, or some other academic pursuit. But in truth they would send her to a home for unwed mothers or to an out-of-town relative or family friend until the pregnancy was over."

"Straight out of a Dickens novel, isn't it? And it wasn't so long ago," Pam said with a shudder.

"No it wasn't," Bonnie agreed. "Unwed mothers were a big part of my social work caseload in the 60s."

"I'm sure some of those places were well run and kindly staffed," Danielle offered. "If I remember correctly, one called Mothercraft was also a residence where they would offer some type of basic job training. You know, opportunities for personal growth so there was not just a sense of failure and loss at the end of the day."

"I think that was a rarity," said Jane. "Thank goodness attitudes have changed."

"What happened next, Lynn? Obviously the social worker received a call back," Dee said, wanting to get back to the story.

"Actually, at first she didn't. After a few days, she tried again, and this time my biological mother answered. She was alone and could talk. When the social worker asked her if she had given birth to a daughter on my birth date, the response was a fumbling, stuttered negative reply. The conversation was short."

Dee shook her head sympathetically. "Good grief! Imagine the shock—right out of the blue after forty-three years!"

"The social worker could tell from the response that she was on the right track, but from experience she suggested that perhaps the woman needed time to think about it. She left her number again and the next day the call came in."

"And ... ?" Jane asked.

"And the social worker called me immediately to say that my biological mother wanted to meet me, and would I like to spend a day with her?"

"So?" they all asked in unison.

"I'm almost embarrassed to tell you my first response. The thought of spending a day with a virtual stranger didn't appeal to me, and I said I would simply like to meet her at the social services office." Pausing, Lynn scrunched up her face and asked, "Doesn't that make me sound like a cold fish?"

Bo hooted. "You? Never! Pardon me for laughing in the midst of a serious conversation."

"It's not as if it's the first time you've done that Bo!" Dee retorted.

"Well," Bo continued, "it's just that Lynn suggesting she's a cold fish at any time deserves a hoot. Not even close."

Lynn smiled. "Thanks for the vote of confidence. I've struggled to see if there was some deep-seated reason for my controlled response, but I think it was simply logical thinking about a situation that never consumed me emotionally."

Sitting next to her, Marti leaned in, putting her arm around Lynn's shoulder.

"I also said I wanted my last name to remain anonymous", Lynn continued. "I wanted to be in control of how much contact there would be in the future. I mean, honestly, when you stop to think about it rationally, you've no idea what sort of person you're going to meet. Other than the genetic link you share, this person is a stranger with whom you share no history."

Slowly nodding, all but one acknowledged not having given much thought to the possibility that this stranger could be someone you don't want in your life given the option.

All of them except Marti, who could speak directly to the subject. She had gone into foster care at age three and was placed with an emotionally ill-equipped family. Ultimately she had been rescued by grandparents and subsequently raised by a family friend, who had given her the love and guidance every child deserves. She was only too aware of how it was to have a biological mother that she didn't want to know and to love unconditionally the woman who, without question, had truly mothered her. They'd often discussed her story over the years. From the beginning of their friendship, Lynn and Marti had shared this connection.

Both women had been happy to educate the group on the subject, explaining that when you permanently become part of a family, through adoption or otherwise, you are just that: part of a family. It's not temporary.

Lynn had always spoken passionately on the subject, with Marti on the same page. "You evolve with the family and assimilate. It's not a part-time situation. You grow up knowing you are a son or daughter and who your parents are. You live it every day. I may be biased, but I feel it's a minority of adoptees who feel the need to search out birth parents. However they are the ones who write articles or books and get the attention. Seldom do you read an article by a happy, contented adoptee, although perhaps more of us should write about it so people see the positive side. Needless to say, it may be a more complicated issue for some older children who already have a history with biological parents."

Lynn continued describing how she felt compelled to have this meeting with her biological mother happen on her terms.

Jane was the next to comment. "I understand your reasoning. This is how you feel and that's what matters. I know someone who, as an adult, decided to do a search a couple of years ago. After his first child was born he felt motivated to find his roots, as he put it, even though he too had grown up in a loving family. He was an only child whose parents doted on him and, like you, he had always known he was adopted. The only difference is that he was two and a half years old when the adoption took place, so he sometimes was aware of a nagging curiosity about what happened in those early years. To make a long story short, there were some adoption documents with a last name on them that his mom had always told him were in a folder in her desk, and he knew he was born in Nova Scotia."

"He mounted a determined search, made contact after some initial roadblocks, and discovered his biological mother was not of terribly strong character and his biological father was an abusive alcoholic. He actually met a sibling at one point only to discover she was a bit of a deadbeat, and the brief relationship ended in a very disappointing fashion. This after having experienced a very happy life as an adored son with two fine parents."

"How upsetting," said Pam with a sympathetic shake of her head, "particularly when you take the risk and you're hopeful of a positive outcome."

"Is he further ahead by experiencing all of this?" asked Jane. She certainly knew all about taking risks. "Personally, I don't think so. But interestingly enough, he says that although it wasn't information he was happy to know, it actually did bring him some closure. It filled in some blanks."

"*Merde*! I don't know if I understand that," said Danielle. "That's painful stuff to process."

"I agree with you Dani," said Dee, "and I dislike the word 'closure'; I don't think every issue has to be considered *finished*. I think it's more important to know you've worked through something and figured out where it fits into your story. Anyway, I feel badly that your friend had to hear such unpleasant information, Jane."

"I get the way he felt," said Marti. "I get it."

"Me too," agreed Cass, "I'd just as soon have the blanks filled in."

"Not me," argued Pam, "That would be very difficult for me to live with. I'd rather not know."

"It's a tough call," said Marti, as she got up to answer the door. Explaining earlier that her day had been crazy and Chinese delivery was for dinner, she invited them to the table where they unpacked enough food to feed a small army and the discussion continued.

"Sometimes," said Dani, passing the spring rolls, "it may be better not to know. I think you would have to pray long and hard to have help with that decision. There's a classic example of a person having to live with some disturbing information and a disappointing experience that really did not need to happen. I've always said Lynn has the most healthy attitude about adoption."

Lynn smiled as she filled her plate. "I feel so fortunate, but I agree if someone has a need to know then it's important to deal with that at some point. I couldn't care less, except now that I'm forty and I've gotten this far into it, I wouldn't mind learning medical history."

"And some people who aren't adopted wish they were!" said Bo, making everyone laugh.

"Here's a perfect example: Kim Woods ... " Cass suggested, checking to see if everyone knew who she meant.

"Oh God, yes! She's gorgeous with the most upbeat outlook on life, and could headline at Yuk Yuk's with her wacky sense of humor," Bonnie agreed.

"Well, her mother treated her terribly and put her down constantly throughout her childhood," continued Cass. "As an adult Kim tried everything to improve the relationship, but the reality is that her mom has a serious personality disorder that she is unable to acknowledge. Finally Kim had to cut off communication with her so she could move on and rid herself of the terrible negativity in her life. She keeps tabs on her mom through a neighbor, but otherwise her life is much better without her. It happens. I can't tell you how many times she told me, exasperated, that she wishes she had been adopted!"

"Families come together in so many different ways. Common DNA doesn't guarantee a positive emotional connection," said Lynn. "A shared history and the emotional links formed during those experiences are what shape a family."

"Or shatter it in some cases," Marti added.

"For sure," Lynn continued. "A simple genetic bond guarantees nothing. Your friend's situation, Jane, also reminded me that part of the reason I wasn't balking at making a connection was because I gathered from the social worker there was nothing nasty like that in my history. Just the luck of the draw."

"You know," Cass threw in, "let's not forget a whole other side of this genetic connection. It would be interesting to know just how many children have been fathered by someone other than the man they believe is their dad. Many mothers know this fact only too well. I'm not saying it's happening often—just making the point that it doesn't really matter whose genes you carry."

Bonnie had been quietly listening, twirling her hair nonstop once she had finished eating. She leaned forward now to offer another perspective.

"I've a friend who was pregnant as a teenager; she went the adoption route believing it was best for the child, as she was still a child herself, and later married and had a family. She told her husband about her past experience, but they decided it wasn't something their children needed to know. She's hopeful she'll never be contacted and she wouldn't consider searching herself. Not because she doesn't care, but precisely because she does. She believes her decision was in the best interests of the child and that their lives have taken their own paths since that time. She'd feel terrible to learn that the child had experienced an unhappy life. She's hopeful it was a happy, loving life—one that she has no right to have a role in. She feels comfortable in her feelings. How can you argue with that?"

"It seems the dispute arises when the adopted child wants to search. It's a conundrum, because we all know the other side of the coin, where some women who place their child for adoption are haunted by it forever. Those women never stop hoping to reclaim the relationship and feel they do have the right to search! It's hard to argue with that too, I guess," said Dee, typically analytical.

Lynn's response to both of them was calm and unbiased. "You can't and shouldn't argue with either of those scenarios, even when you think you have a valid objection. It's such a personal issue. We've all read about adoption reunions that seem like wonderful experiences, where everyone involved has gone on to share meaningful relationships. There's no doubt that *can* happen. In fact, I know someone who went that route, and it was very positive. To each his own."

Typical of their evenings, the women expressed dissenting opinions in various degrees. They debated through the whole spectrum of adoption, but in the end they all agreed to one aspect: giving birth to a child did not automatically qualify a woman to claim the title of mother. There was much more to it. Anyone can be a biological mother, but the true 'mothering' of a child is more about life after birth than before.

"Take surrogate mothers these days," said Jane, adding a new dimension to the conversation. "There's a noble example of a woman giving birth to a child to help another woman achieve her dream of becoming a mother. It puts another spin on the definition of 'mother,' doesn't it?"

"So, back to you, Lynn. Wow, we did get off on a tangent there. What happened next?" asked Pam.

Lynn laughed, acknowledging that they were experts in digressing and talking ad infinitum on practically every subject imaginable. "Right. Okay, back to the social worker. She would make the arrangements, she said, then call me back to confirm the date and time. The next thing I knew she was on the phone again, saying that since I had moved up north, the whole matter would have to be sent on to the ministry office in our county."

"Ah yes, I do detect the nasty odor of bureaucracy," Bo muttered.

"Right. Well, the social worker was ticked about it too. There had been many recent changes within their agency and this was the red tape we had to wade through. Three weeks later I received a letter from our local office of the Ministry of Social Services saying it would take them six months to process my file."

"Government at its finest! How did you feel about that?" Bonnie pressed. Her feelings on the subject were well known.

"You know, much to my amazement, I'm kind of upset," Lynn said, looking crestfallen.

This was not Lynn's typical emotional response to anything, and definitely not the subject they would have imagined her reacting to with any distress. It was obvious that this delay was troubling her in a way they had not seen before.

She continued to explain. "I realize that now a contact has actually been made, I do have a strong need to say something to my biological mother. I don't feel I need to see her, but I most definitely have words I want to express to her, and I know that writing a letter would be good enough for me. I'm shocked at how intense those feelings are. When I think about it, what really bothers me is that now I know I have the chance to tell her what I'm feeling, and in six months' time she might have croaked. You know how things happen. "

"Nice talk," Jane exclaimed. They smiled empathetically, knowing Lynn was not being disrespectful.

"It's kind of bizarre," Lynn said. "She might have passed

away years ago and then this whole scenario never would have happened. Since she didn't, and now that the opportunity is actually before me, I don't want to lose it. Does that make any sense?"

Pam said, "Lynn, I've expressed to you before that I think I would have always been curious if I had been adopted. It surprised me that you never were bothered one way or the other about it. After you adopted Thomas and I watched how naturally you became a family and how truly you and Jim are his parents, I began to understand. I'll never forget the shower we had for you the week after you brought Thomas home. Seeing you walk through the door with your sweet son in your arms was such a moment."

"The connection was electric," Cass interjected, wrapping her arms around herself. "Mm-hmm, I still get goose bumps remembering that night."

"We all learned so much sharing that experience with you," said Jane, "I think people who were not adopted aren't able to consider the feelings rationally, although I'm not sure I can explain this. I think we have an idealized, movie-script sense about it rather than a realistic understanding. Watching you become a family really put this issue of adoption more into perspective for all of us."

"I totally agree." added Marti, "It's like anything else really. People who have shared an experience can have far more meaningful conversations about it than with those who have not been there. With my two beautiful stepdaughters in my life now I finally feel like I get it too."

"You know, Marti," Jane continued, "what we're voicing here just as easily applies to my relationship with Samantha. In the beginning, talking to other gay people was the only way for us to exchange opinions considered normal. It took time for most others to have a realistic understanding of our desire to be accepted as a couple, as a family in our own right."

"And I was among the most guilty," Danielle said, casting her eyes to the floor, her cheeks turning pink. "I'll always regret that."

Jane shook her finger affectionately at Danielle, reminding her that they had all long ago come to terms with those difficult days. "You had your own reasons and lifelong religious prejudices to overcome. You saw us as different and once you got past that everything slowly became fine."

Danielle nodded hesitantly with a tender smile for Jane, but deep inside knew she had still not forgiven herself for some of the thoughts she had harbored so many years ago when Jane first told them she was gay.

"My cousin Joyce was adopted, and for as long as I can remember it was always an issue for her," Pam related, wanting the conversation to move on from memories she knew were painful for Danielle—and Jane too, for that matter. "Because she felt she was different, I always thought that about her too. Somehow my aunt and uncle never really relaxed about adoption, which I think they felt showed a failure on their part for being unable to conceive. They weren't what you would call emotionally warm people, unfortunately. I'm convinced their insecurities caused my cousin to have uncertainties within her and that's really sad. But then one of my closest friends, from kindergarten until now, was adopted and like you, Lynn, she never really gave it a second thought, and I didn't either. In fact, I never gave it any consideration whatsoever."

"Precisely," Marti agreed, "so much of it depends on the family. If everyone is comfortable, understanding, and intelligent right from day one, it simply does not create any feelings of being different within the family or in life in general. If you have the misfortune of being adopted into a family with 'issues,' then chances are you will have adoption issues—and if you have the misfortune of being born into a family with other 'issues,' the same can be said."

"There *is* one aspect of adoption that really rankles me, I must admit," continued Lynn with an unabashed expression of annoyance, "and that's when I read in the paper or a magazine where someone is described as an adopted daughter or adopted son. When you're adopted you become a daughter or a son—period! You don't hear a parent introducing a child as their adopted child or their surrogate-born child or their in-vitro fertilized or their natural-born child. You get what I mean. I really feel this shows tremendous ignorance when I see it in print. Perhaps it's just my bias but that *really* bugs me!"

"Uh, Lynn, your foot's going to propel you into orbit if you don't stop that right now," Jane warned her with a smile.

Lynn quickly put her foot on the floor. "Well, that just shows you how much that issue drives me crazy!"

Wrinkling her brow, Cass paused a moment to absorb Lynn's words then said, "I can't say I ever really noticed when someone was described as an adopted daughter or son. I probably wouldn't notice the description one way or the other, but you are absolutely right. Someone's kids are their kids. Nothing more, nothing less."

There was unanimous agreement as Dani continued, "That's such a good example of how our circumstances in life establish our point of view. The writers of those words, none of them adopted, I will bet, do so in all innocence, and it never occurs to them how it sounds. I imagine if it were pointed out, they would agree with what we're saying here."

The conversation continued throughout the evening, with Lynn explaining exactly what it was she wanted to express to her birthmother. Things got emotional, as one can imagine. There were tears, but not Lynn's. Clearly she was untroubled with what she wanted to say. What was troubling her was that she might not have the opportunity until it was too late.

Marti was mulling something over as she listened to Lynn.

"It's so interesting for me right now," Lynn explained with

some surprise, "because I have apparently carried these feelings within me at some level recently, although I haven't obsessed over them. Being a mother myself heightened my awareness of the kind of traumatic, soul-searching experience it has to be for a woman to part with her child at birth. Who would have guessed that I would gain an even deeper understanding of the dynamics of love and adoption when our two sons came into our lives in their own special way. I realize now what I want to let her know. At this point I can even say, what I *need* to let her know."

"That's not to take anything away from the biological father too, but of course back in the day men weren't involved in childbirth," Cass pointed out.

"You're so right, Cass," Bonnie said, clearly drawing on her own social work days. "Until well into the 1980s it was quite an isolating experience for the woman, with little or no responsibility on the part of the man involved. Often the men were never even told of the pregnancy, and in some cultures sadly that has not changed."

"Well, lucky me," Lynn smiled warmly as she went on, "my mom has always said that being adopted has an extra special 'love component' to it. As she would say, my biological mother no doubt made her decision based on a loving hope for the child she carried to have a life she could not provide. The other side of the equation was the love offered by my parents in their desire to have a family. Mom never failed to paint a picture of a win/win situation, and those are the same natural explanations of love that I have passed on to Thomas."

"God bless your dear mom! Eighty and still going strong!" cheered Jane.

"Hear, hear! A toast to Louise!" as they all raised their glasses.

"Yes, she is something else," said Lynn, "but I decided not to tell her about this for now. I want to follow it through first and see what happens before I tell her the story."

Dee asked, "Do you think she'll have a problem with it?"

"I really don't. I think she'll find it interesting and quite incredible after all these years. Especially since she and Dad always said they would help me search. Too bad dad isn't alive to find out about this too. At some point I'll tell the boys, but I want to see where this all goes first. Of course Jim is on this ride right along with me."

"What do you think Thomas will have to say about it?" said Cass. "You've always told us that he's not interested in searching for his birthparents at this point."

"That's what he says. He's comfortable with the knowledge we'll help him in any way just as my parents told me. Of course he is only fifteen and might change his mind at some point. Remember, the times have changed, and he has three full pages of information on his ancestry going back several generations, except for last names of course. I think that makes a difference in terms of filling in blanks, and at this point it appears to be a non-issue for him as it was for me."

"Do you think that writing a letter is all you want to do or do you want to meet your biological mother in person?'

"You know, it's fascinating. I feel right now that saying these words to her is truly what's important to me. Once I've accomplished that, I'm not certain I'll need or want to do any more. It's not as though I've ever felt compelled in any way. I know who my parents are. They kissed me goodnight every night of my childhood. They've made me feel loved every day of my life. They've nurtured my attitude and my personality and put up with some nonsense. They've given me my values, disciplined me when I needed it, taught me about responsibility and accountability, and encouraged my hopes and dreams. They've helped me grow into the person I am today. I am their daughter."

"You'll get no arguments from us there. But now that you've gone down this road, let's think about your biological mother's feelings for a moment here," suggested Pam. "I imagine that now she has recovered from the shock of you finding her it would be difficult for her to hear that you didn't want to meet her. Don't you agree?'

There was a general affirmative reaction around the room.

"A valid point," agreed Lynn, "and I've thought about it. I think I'll follow through with meeting her but now I want to make sure that I write the letter and she reads it. The roadblock is discovering I have to wait six months. I don't have a good feeling about that."

"I guess you'll just have to be patient and hope for the best," Jane encouraged. "We're with you all the way."

"I talked it over with Jim, and he agreed I needed to do whatever I felt was necessary. As usual, mulling through it tonight has just confirmed what I'm going to do next. I will write the letter; waiting for the opportunity to deliver it will be the hard part."

Marti had not made any comment about Lynn's concern over the delay, but a plan was formulating in her head. She would make some calls tomorrow and see if there really was any chance she could help before she said anything.

"Good grief," exclaimed Lynn, happy to change the subject. "I didn't intend to take up the entire night with this! Let's clear the table and get at the cards!"

"Fortune cookies first," insisted Cass. "You know how I hate to miss a chance for a bit of good luck!"

A little luck was what Marti hoped for the next morning as she looked up the telephone number of someone she had gotten to know while working on a couple of Habitat for Humanity projects.

The next month's BC night at Bonnie's began with everyone on the edge of their chairs waiting for the update from Lynn. Unfortunately, she and Cass had run into a backup on the highway and arrived at the same time Bo's dinner was about to be served. Bo had been stalling as long as she could with this special meal.

While waiting for the latecomers, Bonnie poured everyone a glass of her current beverage of choice. "It's the best tasting mineral water I've found and I've tried them all. My nephew imports it for his food services company and it's all I drink now."

Pam pointed out it was also close to Bonnie's second anniversary of being alcohol-free and they raised their glasses high.

Bonnie beamed.

"Sorry we're so late," Lynn apologized with Cass nodding beside her when they finally walked into the house, "The traffic was the pits."

"Well, give us the headlines now," Bo urged. "We need to know what happened."

"Okay! Headlines now and details after we eat. We're as hungry as the rest of you. First, I need to do this," she said. She went straight to Marti and gave her an enormous hug, followed by a burst of kisses on each cheek.

The two women grinned at each other. "Marti," Lynn said, "you fill them in on the first part. You are awesome!"

Looking pleased with herself, Marti told them that through some charity projects she had become friends with a fellow who had a senior position in the Toronto office of the Ministry of Social Services. She took a chance and called him to see if there was any possibility of pulling some strings on Lynn's file. He was quick to explain that it was against ministry policy to take a shortcut in matters like this but he would see what he could do.

"He told me, in a nice way, not to hold my breath."

"And was he willing to bend the rules?" asked Bo. "I bet not, based on my experience in social services."

"After waiting a week that seemed to go on forever," Marti described, "he got back to me saying Lynn could call her original social worker who had been advised to proceed without delay and not forward the file. I phoned Lynn right away."

Lynn picked up the story. "So of course I called immediately and, after she expressed her shock at being told to go against policy, the social worker said she was thrilled to help. She stressed I had to be absolutely certain not to include any identifying information at this point, and I had no problem with that. I suggested I send the letter in an open envelope so that she could read it first to make certain I didn't break any rules. She agreed to do this and make certain it was put in the hands of my biological mother."

Bonnie blinked her eyes in amazement. "Wow, you got lucky there, Lynn."

"Marti got lucky for me," Lynn beamed. "I can't thank her enough!"

Marti smiled. "You know how we always say it never hurts to ask. Most of the time people come through and it just goes to prove the power of networking."

"So true," agreed Dee. "I see it time and again in our business too. The worst that can happen is that someone will say no. So how did it go, Lynn?"

"I have to say that writing the letter was easier and more satisfying than I had imagined. Of course I want to share it with you, but after dinner. Cass and I were fantasizing about your prime rib as we drove down and I'm starving!"

"Right on!" Cass said quickly, sensing Lynn could use a bit of a break. "What can I do to help, Bo?"

"Ooops, you'd better break the news, Bo. It's not going to be easy," said Pam as she handed the latecomers a glass of wine.

Bo laughed, nodding in agreement, "Sorry to disappoint you two—the others have had some time to get over the shock —no beef tonight!"

Cass and Lynn stared in amazement. "But you always do your prime rib for us. We bank on it!"

"Not tonight, my friends. Pam is going to Weight Watchers with me and I'm sticking to their plan. If I can give up booze, I can drop a few pounds too, and that's my next challenge. No beef tonight and that's that!"

The moaning and groaning carried on as they took their seats at the table, but in fact they knew whatever Bonnie served was certain to be delicious.

Within minutes, a dill and lemon–scented poached filet of sole (cooked foil-wrapped in the dishwasher) was being served, accompanied by steamed broccoli and a fragrant jasmine rice, as well as a tomato, cucumber, and feta salad. The recipes were indeed from the Weight Watchers cookbook. No one could believe the fish had actually been poached in the dishwasher.

"I've heard about that before," Jane said, "but always thought it was just another of those kitchen myths! I can't believe how well it works!"

Bonnie passed around a gravy boat. "Here's a piquant sauce for the ones I know want more of a bite. A little jalapeno goes a long way!"

For several moments silenced reigned, interrupted only by declarations of satisfaction from the diners.

After sharing each other's latest news in between bites, they cleared the table and declared that the meal was satisfying as well as being light on calories.

"Satisfying, yes," agreed Bonnie, "and I'm definitely going to add more fish to my diet, but I still say nothing beats a steak and baked potato. Beef is always going to be number one in my books, light cuisine or not."

"But in the meantime, that's great news about Weight Watchers. Go for it!" encouraged Danielle.

"Right on!" echoed the group.

When the food talk had subsided, they made themselves comfortable in the living room and told Lynn they were ready if she was. Everyone wanted to know how things were playing out.

She had hand written the letter, feeling the typewriter was not personal enough. Plus, writing by hand seemed the natural way to let her feelings flow. When she was finished, she wrote a copy for herself to share with her family later—and of course the BC.

"Just a sec, Lynn. Pass the tissues please," Pam requested, to no one's surprise. Then Lynn was given the go-ahead.

Hello May,

I can imagine how much of a shock it must have been to receive the phone call from the social worker after all these years. I was surprised when I was first contacted, as it was some time after I initiated the search. I hope my sudden appearance in your life has not been too upsetting for you or your husband and that this will turn out to be a positive experience for all of us.

I'm sending you this letter because I've heard from the ministry that it will take another six months before we can actually have contact with each other. After forty-two years it has unexpectedly become important to me to write these words, and I'm not prepared to wait. Fortunately I've been given the assurance this will be delivered to you personally.

I want you to know that as far as I'm concerned, your decision to have me adopted at birth was the best one to make. I have had a wonderful life as part of a loving family that includes my brother as well as my parents, grandparents, and a large extended clan of aunts, uncles, and cousins. I've always known I was adopted and have never really thought about it to any great extent. My parents have spoken about it in such positive terms and presented it to me as an example of strong and true love. Firstly from you, my biological mother, for having the loving concern for your unborn child to wish a better life than you could provide under the circumstances. Secondly, from my parents, for loving me from the moment they were told I was theirs and having such a strong desire to build a family.

As I've matured, I've come to recognize what a positive situation this was for all involved, although I'm also aware not everyone views it this way. I can understand that, at the time of my birth, you were the one person who must have suffered the most over your decision. I hope you had a source of love and support somewhere to help you see the good in your choice and to comfort you through difficult times. Whatever feelings of regret you may have experienced, I want you to know from my perspective there is no need for any.

Becoming a mother myself added a whole new dimension of understanding to some of the emotions you must have faced at a time when the world was a very different place. Coincidentally, one of my sons is also adopted, so my exposure to many of the emotional sides of adoption has been a full one. My husband and I have loved both our sons unconditionally since the first moment we held them in our arms. I know my parents felt the same about my brother and me. My mother is still healthy and very much in our lives, but sadly my father passed away two years ago.

I want you to know that I wouldn't wish to change anything about my life. I want to thank you for being brave enough to face the challenges that were presented to you. You had to make decisions as a young woman in a society not as forgiving as ours is today. You may have questioned at the time if you were doing the right thing. I want to assure you that the answer is yes.

I hope you've had a happy life and perhaps we'll meet one day. In the meantime I trust you will be pleased to receive this and know that those decisions you made forty-three years ago, from my perspective, were good ones. You are the woman who gave life to me.

Then you gave me the opportunity to become who I am today. For that I thank you.

Sincerely , Lynn

As tears were wiped, including Lynn's, she was filled with the same sense of satisfaction as when she had finished writing the letter. Although she had never felt outwardly emotional about it before, expressing these feelings out loud caused her to become aware of how good it felt to do so. She described how she had first read it aloud to Jim, and they had cried together as they appreciated their good fortune to be the family they are. It had simply been one of those moments when they were filled with an awareness of how things happen in life and the randomness of the play of each of our stories. Ti-Ming.

Dabbing her eyes, Pam praised Lynn for the clarity of her thoughts. Everyone murmured agreement. Lynn smiled, more clear eyed than the rest now. "It was more satisfying than I anticipated. I'm glad I've done this."

"Pass Lynn's cookies please," requested Bonnie after blowing her nose loudly. "It's time for some comfort food—but please note I'm only having one!"

"Sorry Bo!" Lynn said. "If I'd known about you and Weight Watchers I'd have used a different recipe."

Bonnie told Lynn not to give it a second thought but insisted that someone else take the leftover cookies at the end of the evening. She knew the temptation would be too hard to resist if they were left with her. A noisy argument ensued as the others decided who the lucky recipient was to be.

"All right, all right," hollered Bonnie, "pick a number between one and ten and I'll decide the winner."

Sometimes that was the only way with this group.

A month later, glasses filled, the BC was comfortably lounging amid the packing boxes in Cass's townhouse. It would be their final evening at her place before she and Dirk took off on their sailing adventure in a matter of weeks.

After listening to an update of the departure plans and trying to ignore how much they would miss Cass, the talk turned to Lynn, with everyone waiting to hear if the letter had been delivered.

"Yup," said Lynn, "the letter was delivered by the social worker herself. Then, to my surprise, she called me a week later to say she had convinced the powers that be to allow her to complete my file rather than forwarding it on to the other office. So she will now call me back to set up an appointment for the meeting. I guess when she read the letter she felt compelled to see if she could complete the reunion herself. Somehow she managed to sidestep the red tape. Cool, huh?"

"We've always said you're the most persuasive here, and this goes a long way to support that!" Cass high-fived her.

"So have your feelings changed at all?" asked Danielle.

"I have to say that they haven't. I'm grateful and happy that I had a chance to write the letter. I think I expressed myself better than I would have in person—there's just more of an opportunity to think about your words. So no, I don't really feel anything in terms of excitement and happiness to meet her. Not at all. Perhaps some mild curiosity. Actually, if nothing happens it won't bother me. Having said that, I'll probably have the meeting by our next BC Tuesday—should be interesting."

"To say the least," they agreed with somewhat more enthusiasm than Lynn. The evening carried on without a deep discussion about anything, leaving a lot more time to play bridge.

During the week, the social worker telephoned to say she

would be on vacation for two weeks. She was happy to have another colleague attend the reunion meeting at the office, but Lynn opted to wait. She liked this woman and wanted her to see the whole thing through.

In the weeks that followed, several of the BC made a point to check in with Lynn either through a phone call or a drive up to meet halfway for lunch and some outlet shopping. Quite frankly, Lynn would tease, they were doing this as much for their own anxieties as anything. Her calm attitude remained unchanged.

The Friday before the next BC Tuesday, she joined the early southbound commuters on Highway 400, destination Toronto. Jim had offered to go with her, but Lynn knew she didn't need his presence although his strong support meant the world to her.

Parked at Jane's condo at 9:30 a.m. for a quick cup of tea, Lynn had thrown in an overnight bag on the off-chance she decided to stay in town. Bonnie unexpectedly appeared to say she was chauffeuring Lynn to the meeting. Jane insisted that a glass or two of wine might be appropriate after the eleven o'clock appointment, so they would wait in the ministry parking lot. Not planning to have anyone with her, Lynn realized she appreciated the company.

Aware of the silence that surrounded her in the elevator of the Ministry of Social Services building, Lynn had a moment of disbelief, recognizing she was about to step into a room where she would meet the woman who had given birth to her.

Not unexpectedly (although it still surprised her, she had to admit), she felt absolutely calm. She had taken pains to make certain she looked her best, so somewhere deep inside she obviously wanted to make a positive impression. She wore a beige linen dress that complemented her healthy complexion and petite figure. Her curly hair, a highlighted light brown, grazed her shoulders. As always, she hoped her freckles weren't too obvious.

The social worker greeted her warmly, asked if she was ready and feeling okay, to which she nodded yes, and they went through the door to the next room.

A diminutive white-haired woman in her late sixties rose to meet her with open arms for an embrace. Lynn awkwardly returned the embrace quickly, with no desire to linger. Introductions, first names only, were made. The older woman, her biological mother Lynn had to keep reminding herself, spoke first asking, "How are you, dear?"

How bizarre, Lynn thought. But then, again, what on earth do you say after forty-three years?

The social worker suggested she would leave the room after making the introduction but both women asked her to stay.

They all sat down in comfortable lounge chairs as May, on the edge of hers, spoke again quickly, her speech soft and hesitant. Shifting nervously, her eyes glistening and voice breaking, she stared into her lap as her words tumbled out, "Your letter was very nice ... thank you. Life was so different when I was young and I ... I ... really ... had no choice. I had to try to put what happened out of my mind and go on with my life."

Pausing, she put a tissue to her mouth momentarily but indicated with her free hand she would continue. "There was a lot of torment, I can tell you. It was ... such ... a shameful situation ... a secret I couldn't share. My mother and aunt were the only ones who knew, and they hurried me out of town on the pretext of a job."

She took a deep breath and swallowed before going on. "My father never knew, never, or he would have disowned me ... probably beaten me too. Imagine that!" For the first time she looked at Lynn directly. "It became something I buried deep inside me ... I don't really know what to say to you now."

Watching May's face the entire time, Lynn felt her heart

soften over the vulnerability of this woman to whom she owed her life and yet for whom she felt no strong emotion.

May continued in a flow of words now as she turned to the social worker. "The first time you called, my husband answered the phone and was still on the line after I picked up. I'm glad you noticed that. I had no idea why your office would be calling me. When you called the second time asking your question ... I was stunned ... I had hidden the truth for forty-three years, so it was not easy to face it again. No it wasn't..." she gulped. " ... that's for sure. So then I had to tell my husband, because he never knew. He was away at war and I thought he was dead."

With that she settled back in her chair with a deep sigh, dabbing her eyes gently.

The social worker reached out, taking May's hand. "I understand. Your reaction was not unusual. It sometimes is much longer than it took you for the biological parent to come to terms with what is happening when we call."

Turning back to Lynn, May repeated how touched she had been by her letter and how healing it had been after all these years. Lynn was filled with satisfaction that she had done the right thing—for both of them.

Lynn and May were left alone. They sat down and looked at each other.

"So, what was your first impression?"

It was the first question the following night at Pam's place. Lynn began to recount the details of the meeting. Bonnie and Jane had heard it all over lunch the day before and prompted Lynn as she gave the others the blow-by-blow.

"It was so interesting," said Lynn slowly. "I just looked at this woman and thought I could be in a seniors' residence talking to any little white-haired old lady. Somebody could say this one is your biological mother or that one is and who would know the difference? I saw and felt no connection at all. All the time we talked, I kept looking into her eyes for something—I'm not even sure what—and I saw nothing but this pleasant, slightly nervous older woman looking back at me."

"She seemed kind of nervous as she was constantly fiddling with a tissue. She showed me photos of the two children she had when she married after the war, and I could definitely see similarities between her daughter and myself—even down to the style of haircut. I thought that was a funny coincidence—a little Twilight Zone-ish. She said her children did not know about me but that she would tell them and we could all meet. I really felt uncomfortable about that. I thought it might put her in a very awkward position, and for what? I have no need to bring these people into my or my family's life. I told her it wasn't necessary to do this and I sensed she felt very relieved."

"Good grief," said Cass, "why should she have to lay bare the past if it's painful and embarrassing and not an issue for you. Who knows how her family would react and how complicated it could get if they wanted to meet you as well?"

"Wait a sec," said Dee. "I think I would want to meet my siblings."

"Siblings shmiblings," Marti retorted. "All they share is a bit of DNA—no memories, no history, nothing else that connects them. Lynn's brother is her true sibling."

Pam stood up and refilled the wine glasses around the room as Lynn explained.

"For sure. Bringing anyone else into this situation is just not necessary as far as I'm concerned. I told May the most important information to me was medical history details and so she told me about her family history, which was all good—no cancer, no heart disease, diabetes, nothing really. Good, healthy stock all living well into their eighties. Then I asked her about my biological father, and that's when she told me her story that almost had me laughing out loud."

"Lynn, for heaven's sake!" Danielle said impatiently.

"Okay, okay, just listen," Lynn chuckled as she went on "and you are all going to be laughing too. It's just so ... oh ... six degrees of separation!"

"Picture this little old lady twisting her tissue in her lap and taking me back forty-three years, when young ladies did not behave quite as brazenly as we were known to do at the same age. I felt rather sorry for her, but of course I didn't know what she was going to come out with."

There was not a sound to be heard as everyone hung on Lynn's words. The wine glasses sat where they were as each woman was caught up in this experience of Lynn's.

"She explained to me how she and William, her husband, were dating at the beginning of WW2, and then he had been shipped overseas in the army. After a while his letters stopped arriving and she assumed the worst."

"My gosh," sniffled Pam, "imagine how many women shared that same experience during the war. We forget how fortunate we've been."

"Too true. Who knows how any one of us would have handled such a time," Lynn went on. "She was living with her parents near Hamilton. A friend of hers had gone up to work in northern Ontario and wrote May to say she could get her a job there too."

Lynn paused for an overly dramatic effect before continuing. "You're not going to believe where—the same small mining town where I grew up! Is that a coincidence or what?"

Exclamations of surprise and murmurs about strange twists of fate filled the room before they urged Lynn to continue.

"So there she was, telling me she moved to the town where my father's family had long been established. Of course she had no idea of this! She had a death grip on the Tissue at that point and she bit her lip, describing how the week before she was to leave to return to Toronto her girlfriend had arranged for her to go on a double date. She said, to put it in a nutshell, she had too much beer to drink and woke up the next morning with a young man in her bed."

Cass held her hand up to briefly interrupt. "Honestly, there but for the grace of God go I twenty-some years ago—or, for that matter, all of us, except for Saint Danielle of the Vestal Virgins, of course. Right girls? There was a lot of luck involved in the bed-hopping of the sixties, that's for sure," Cass admitted with a sly grin, "and birth control was pretty sketchy too."

"You practically needed a note from your parents and a medical excuse to get the pill prescribed," added Pam.

"We didn't really give it any thought in those early days, and AIDS and STDs weren't issues like today," said Marti, shaking her head at the thought.

"My gawd, we sound like we were a bunch of ignorant dimwits, but life was so incredibly different then," Bonnie said, summing it up.

Amid the chorus of agreement, Dani grinned smugly. She still liked to rub in the fact that she had been the only virgin bride of the group. The debate raged on whether or not she should really be proud of it.

"I sit before you, the result of a one-night stand," said Lynn with a lop-sided grin.

"Lynn, you do have a way of putting things right out there on the table!" Jane said. After all they had been friends since childhood, and this was a truism about her friend if ever there was one.

"Hey," replied Lynn, "it's a tiny detail in the story of my life. No more, no less."

"We've learned more than a few lessons from you, girl," Marti's voice cracked as she spoke. Since they first met in their twenties, Lynn had helped Marti work through some of her childhood issues.

"Back to the story—what happened?" asked Dee.

Lynn continued, "She said she was mortified as this wasn't her normal behavior. The young man left in the morning and she returned to Toronto only to discover many weeks later that she was pregnant. She really had no idea who this guy was, although she knew her girlfriend would be able to find him for her. But May was too distraught and ashamed to speak to anyone about it. She had to keep it a secret from the world around her. Her girlfriend never knew, nor did my birthfather. Her mother was horrified and demanded that she keep it a secret. I mean, not even her father was told. May told me he would have disowned and beaten her—imagine!"

Danielle's muttered oath didn't go unnoticed as Lynn continued the story, "Under the pretext of employment, she was whisked to live with an aunt in Toronto, who helped her arrange for her baby's adoption through the proper channels. She said she really was totally traumatized and in those days she did what she thought was right."

"Perfectly understandable," Bonnie murmured.

"Now we really enter into The Twilight Zone—*doo doo do do, doo doo do do*. This is simply unbelievable and really quite hilarious. I was in shock, I tell you! I asked her if she could tell me anything at all about my biological father. She said she knew he was a bit younger than she was. She remembered that he had lived all his life in that town and his name, she thought, was Larry ... or Barry ... or Gary ... and he had curly hair and freckles. She went on to say that she wasn't usually a big drinker, but they were all celebrating. She wasn't very clear, but she recalled he had been injured overseas in the war and had just returned home after being in the hospital somewhere."

"We're not seeing the hilarious side of this so far," interrupted Cass.

"All right, hold onto your hats ladies! Here it is. My father had a younger brother named Harry, who had lied about his age and joined the air force at the beginning of the war. He was a gunner and his plane had been seriously damaged in a dogfight, but the crew had managed to fly it back across the channel to England. He was injured when it landed badly, resulting in his being hospitalized in the UK before being shipped back to Canada. His injuries were such that he could no longer fly, and he was sent home for further recuperation before reporting to a Canadian base in a training position. The timing fits perfectly, as I had a casual conversation with my mom about it last week. He was killed in a car accident a year after the war ended. I can show you all sorts of photos of him—and his curly hair and freckles that he passed on to me. I mean if you look at pictures of the two of us as youngsters, ya gotta wonder..."

A collective gasp went around the room, followed by a very loud silence.

Danielle crossed herself quickly and stared wide eyed at Lynn.

"Holy shit!" muttered Pam before Danielle got her oath out.

"Did you tell May this?" Dee asked, fascinated.

Lynn shook her head and said she made an on-the-spot decision to say nothing of the coincidence.

"Let's face it," she exclaimed, "I couldn't believe my ears and really wasn't sure I was hearing what I thought I was. I needed some time to process it all. May continued on, relating that a couple of weeks after D-Day, she received a letter from William saying he was alive and coming home to marry her. She said to me that had she known this was going to happen she would have kept me."

"Wow. There is that old Ti-Ming thing again," Dani said in a whisper, her eyes locked on Lynn.

"No kidding," Lynn responded. "You know, from my

perspective, I'm so glad she didn't know he was returning. I really think she would have been ashamed to tell him and he might not have been too happy to hear about it. He might have changed his mind about marrying her. Who knows? So it might have not all worked out quite as well as she imagined. After all, she never did tell him until now."

"Besides that," said Dee, "you would have had a totally different upbringing and you wouldn't be sitting here with us. But then when you start to analyze things, none of us would be here or be who we are if it weren't for those small twists of fate."

"It's all a crapshoot when you get right down to it," said Bo with a cynical chuckle.

"You're right," Lynn agreed. "I think this really spotlights the nature-versus-nurture arguments, of which we've had many. Just meeting May and her husband and comparing them to my parents, I know I got the better end of the deal. I hope that doesn't sound awful, but you know what I mean, right?"

They did.

"So how did your meeting with May end?" asked Cass.

"After about an hour of chatting I didn't have anything else to ask her or say to her, and I felt we were struggling a bit conversationally. She started to ask questions about my life and I thought there was no point to start into all that. It simply did not involve her."

"Do you think you resented her intrusion into the rest of your life?" asked Cass. "I think I might."

"I didn't feel resentment," said Lynn. "It just felt pointless. What was I going to do? Tell her my whole wonderful life story, even though I have no desire to bring her into it? I mean, it was nothing personal—she simply was not part of it."

Lynn poured herself a glass of water. Looking around the room she appreciated the understanding she was feeling.

"Yeah ... I get it," said Cass, digesting Lynn's words. Other expressions acknowledged the same although emotions were high.

Lynn continued, "She suggested we exchange telephone numbers, but I said that we should simply call the social worker if we wanted to have any more contact. I honestly did not feel any desire to do anything more. The social worker had told me that May collected salt and pepper sets, so I had gift-wrapped a pretty china set and taken it with me. I gave her the package and said it was lovely to meet her. We hugged and said good-bye."

Noses were blown and sinuses cleared once again.

Lynn, the only dry-eyed one in the room, continued, "The social worker was waiting in the parking lot for me in case I needed her, and of course, so were Bo and Jane."

"Omigawd," said Bonnie, "we were out there checking our watches. I was smoking up a storm and Jane was pacing, wondering how things were going."

"That's for sure," agreed Jane. "Even though Lynn was calm and unruffled about the meeting, Bo and I were nervous wrecks!"

With a warm smile, Lynn recalled their looks of anxious anticipation.

"I could feel your concern as I walked up to you, but I was fine, right?"

They nodded in unison.

"I said then—and I've not wavered since—that my strongest emotion was one of gratitude. I felt so thankful that I had been adopted and lived the life I had with my family. I knew very clearly that I would not be the person I am today had I been raised in that other family. Of course, I was also stunned by the revelation about the possibilities around the identity of my biological father, but I said nothing to the social worker. I saved that tidbit to announce over a stiff drink at lunch!"

Jane wrinkled her brow as she recalled how she was more

of a basket case than Lynn that day. She had been so concerned the experience might unexpectedly cause Lynn some pain or confusion or be troubling in some way. She described Lynn's calm demeanor that gave credence to the unfailingly strong sense of self and of family, *her* family, which was such a familiar part of her nature and which she embodied that day as much as ever.

"She dropped her bomb about her biological father after we'd toasted the occasion with a smooth merlot and a non-alcoholic beer for Bo!" recalled Jane. "We had a rousing debate over the possibilities of the whole situation. In the end, Lynn summed it up better than anyone else could, and I quote—"

With that, Bonnie and Lynn jumped in to join her in a strong, unwavering exclamation: "That's life!"

"*C'est la vie* indeed," agreed Danielle.

Lynn settled back on the couch and looked around this circle of women, who were in their own way family to each other. "And that's the truth. It was an interesting experience and that's all it was. As my dear Gram would remind us from time to time in her soft British accent, 'We are who we are and it behooves us to always be proud of who we are.' She loved the word behooves," Lynn said, her eyes glistening for the first time that evening.

Nothing needed to be said at this moment. The quiet reflection was powerful enough.

"So here endeth the lesson," Lynn said, regaining her smile, "and after lunch at a little hole in the wall in Yorkville—"

"With the most delicious frites you've ever tasted," added Bo, rubbing her stomach.

"Bo left and Lynn and I walked back to my condo," Jane went on, "We window-shopped along Bloor and gabbed about the usual stuff."

"Then I hopped into my car and drove to my mom's for a quick visit before heading north to beat the rush hour," Lynn said. " I didn't say a word about anything to mom but just wanted to give her the biggest hug ever. I'll tell her all about it another day. After that I couldn't wait to get back to my husband and kids and the life that I love."

It was as simple as that she explained now, as she and Pam stood up and began organizing the others.

"Case closed! Let's eat and get out the cards!"

DEAL #4

WEST	NORTH	EAST	SOUTH
	1♣	Pass	1♠
Dbl	2♠	Pass	4♠
Pass	Pass	Pass	

DEALER:	NORTH
VUL:	NONE
CONTRACT:	4♠
DECLARER:	SOUTH

North
♠A 10 6 3
♥8 5 3
♦10 8
♣A K Q 10

West
♠4 2
♥A K 7 2
♦A Q 9 4
♣8 7 3

East
♠9
♥Q J 9 6
♦7 5 3 2
♣9 5 4 2

South
♠K Q J 8 7 5
♥10 4
♦K J 6
♣J 6

SUGGESTED BIDDING

North opens 1♣ with 13 high-card points and no five-card major. East passes, and South responds 1♠. West makes a takeout double with an opening bid and support for both unbid suits.

North, with four-card support for responder's spades, raises to 2♠. East doesn't have enough to compete at the three level. South, with 11 high-card points and 2 length points for the six-card spade suit, jumps to 4♠.

OPENING LEAD

West leads the ♥A against 4♠, the top of touching honors against a suit contract.

BRIDGE QUIZ:

How can the defenders get two potential diamond tricks?

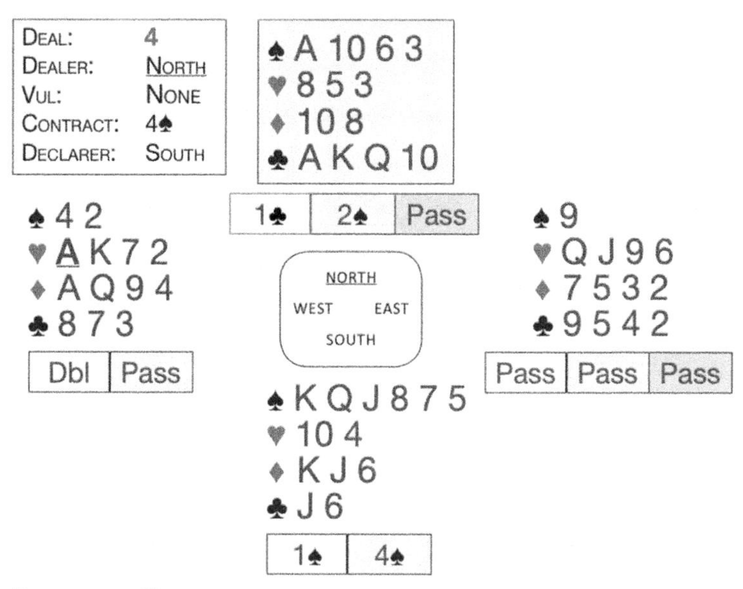

Suggested Defense

East wants to encourage West to continue hearts and plays the ♥Q. The play of an honor when partner is winning the trick shows the next lower-ranking honor and denies the next higher-ranking honor.

West wants to put East on lead to play a diamond and, knowing East holds the ♥J, plays the ♥2 at trick two. East gains the lead with the ♥J and, looking at the dummy, plays the ♦7 rather than a club. This traps declarer's ♦K and the defense gets both the ♦A and ♦Q.

Suggested Play

If the defenders don't take their diamond winners quickly, declarer can draw trumps and then discard two diamonds on dummy's extra club winners.

Conclusion

The play of the ♥Q on the ♥A shows the ♥J. East, the weakest hand at the table, plays an active role in defeating the contract by showing West where East's entry lies so the partnership can take a defensive diamond finesse.

6

PAM'S SOS – 1988/89

Pam and Peter seemed to have it all, not necessarily in the material sense, but in terms of how most people would like their life to be. Everyone knows a couple like this. A solid marriage, great kids, a close extended family, tons of friends, a husband and wife both happy and satisfied with the choices thus far and their plans for the future.

Not that everything was perfect, but they made the most of what they had and found a harmony in life.

In the early years of their marriage, before their two sons were born, Peter was fortunate to have business trips overseas that they combined with vacations to extend their travel time. They had been captivated by the pleasures and surprises of travel in Europe. The siren call of the history, culture, and beauty had begun for Pam when she and Cass had spent an unforgettable year together working, partying, and traveling through the UK and the continent when they were twenty-one. What a buzz it was to continue to explore and travel with her husband.

Nothing, they agreed, could compare to the surprise and splendor of the vistas that appeared as they drove steeply winding roads, navigating the gut-wrenching switchback turns. France, Italy, Austria, Switzerland, it really didn't matter. Even the flatter landscapes of Great Britain and Holland called to them. They couldn't get enough of the ancient history or the romance of the cobblestone streets leading down narrow laneways lined by jumbled dwellings that had sheltered life for centuries. Never tiring of the seduction of perched hilltop villages, they fantasized of one day buying the perfect ruin in the south of France with a spectacular view and gradually restoring it for their retirement. Everyone needs a dream, they would say.

Peter had a quick rise through the ranks of the high-profile company he had been with since university. He was now their youngest vice-president and responsible for the exciting new development of computer technology. He loved his work.

His family meant everything to him. His father had been killed in Hungary at the beginning of WWII and he had grown up keenly feeling that absence in his life. Becoming a father himself helped to fill that hole in Peter's heart. His commitment to his two sons and involvement in all of their interests was his primary focus. He loved his life.

Pam had chosen to be a stay-at-home mom when their older son was born, with his brother arriving a year later. It meant financial sacrifices in those early days, but to them it was worth it. She loved her life too.

Five foot two, eyes of blue, Peter would tease. With long, curly brown hair when her boys were young (her styles changed with great regularity) and an ever-present smile that made her optimistic nature contagious, Pam's response to any dilemma was, "It'll all work out." She would then commit herself to seeing that it did.

Of course they had ups and downs, but most of all they loved each other and that feeling had grown with every one of their eighteen years together.

When their sons were in kindergarten and grade one, they moved to a rustic log house in the middle of a five-acre hardwood forest with a ravine and meandering brook. It was within an easy commute of Peter's west Toronto office. The "magic forest," the boys called it.

An avid photographer since she received a Kodak Brownie camera for her sixth birthday, Pam found endless subject matter on the property to satisfy her addiction to the sound of the shutter. No matter what the season or occasion, her camera was always close at hand.

The setting was idyllic. As they turned off the unpaved country road, the gravel driveway gently twisted through the dense woods before it circled in a bright clearing where the house sat, its antique pine door beckoning a visitor to enter.

The combined effect of the simple cedar log home in the midst of the forest always elicited a "wow" whenever anyone first arrived. The boys were right. It was magic.

The Bridge Club rolled in early whenever it was Pam's turn to have them over. In the summer months an afternoon of berry picking was often on the agenda. They were only too happy to leave Pam's kitchen laden with overflowing flats of whatever was in season so she could indulge her enjoyment of providing them with her jams and jellies.

Country living offered a rewarding environment for Pam and her family, they quickly discovered. They made maple syrup each spring and roasted marshmallows over their fire pit in the autumn after spending the day raking leaves and collecting deadfall logs and branches. The boys would try to catch crayfish and frogs in their backyard stream in the summer and eagerly waited for the winter freeze so they could skate around its bends. Every season offered its own surprises as they hiked through the forest that went on forever beyond their property. They lived with nature all around them and knew they were better for it.

Biking or driving a few minutes in different directions would bring them to pick-your-own farms offering vegetables and berries, apples, and cherries in season. The country roads cutting through the patchwork of century farms, still alive and productive, filled them with a sense of well-being and a reminder of the roots of this part of the country.

To complete the equation, the nearby small towns of Milton and Georgetown offered all the necessary amenities to fulfill material needs and give social and athletic interaction. Toronto and all it had to offer was an easy half-hour drive when the traffic was moving. These were the days before gridlock.

Always open to new experiences, they continued to be avid travelers even when the boys were young. If they had an extravagance, this was it. They saved with discipline every year to make their vacation dreams happen.

The annual ski trip to Whistler became a family affair, and as soon as the boys were old enough to be interested, they had great fun researching new adventures. The most memorable trip had been six weeks to Australia and Fiji when the boys were eight and nine. The excitement of planning and preparing became a yearly ritual.

No matter where they traveled, they welcomed returning home. Pam and Peter had come to realize that the fantasy hilltop village in France had been found in their own backyard. They appreciated their good fortune in discovering a house and property they loved so completely.

The natural cedar logs of their home along with the century pine floors and the scenic views through every window gave a sense of being outside even when you were not. Skylights kept their home flooded with sunlight during the day and bathed in moonlight at night.

The master bedroom resembled a tree house as it jutted into the forest with two walls of floor to ceiling windows. The bedroom overlooked the ravine, with its gently winding stream, and on winter days you could look a long distance through the leafless trees catching sight of deer nibbling on tree bark or the odd fox or coyote skulking through. Raccoons were a daily occurrence. A porcupine bumbling slowly along or the distinctive black and white coat of a skunk appearing on milder days would bring a shout of surprise.

There was no better place to be in a snowstorm than this room. The effect was magical whether it was a light snowfall gently blanketing the frozen landscape or a wild, howling, blizzard. They would all snuggle in the big bed and watch the show.

Each spring, the trees bursting into leaf was a cause for celebration. As their younger son Jason had announced with delight one morning at the age of five, "The whole world has turned green!" Patches of white, pink, and burgundy trilliums would spread through the forest floor like an out of control underground spring flooding the woodland and heralding that season's arrival.

Summers found the room wrapped in cool shades of green that would turn into an explosion of yellow, orange, and red when autumn took control as if by the wave of a wizard's wand.

Throughout every season nature's bounty wrapped itself around them. Grand visual displays thrilled them. Simple pleasures such as the abundant birdlife of Halton County, from the tiny, round winter wrens to the majestic great blue herons, provided constant entertainment.

Sometimes what you think you are searching for is right in front of you, and that became their unexpected awareness as they had settled into their country home. There was no need to search any further. They knew they would be happy there forever.

They had such plans and hopes and dreams, for their children, for their life.

Then Peter died. He was forty-nine.

The pancreatic cancer hit suddenly and without warning. There was quick surgery with the top specialists in Toronto, a period of defiant optimism, a sudden relapse, and he was gone.

It was, in a word, unbelievable.

During the short duration of Peter's illness, he and Pam had been united in strength and the trust they would beat it. After all, hadn't everything always worked out for them?

They told their sons, then eleven and twelve, about the cancer but always spoke positively about their faith in recovery. They kept hope alive, even down to the slimmest thread, as they pursued treatment.

It didn't look good, but no matter how horrible he felt Peter pushed on. He knew he could beat it. He knew together they could do it. His belief was unshakeable. The reality was too terrifying to consider.

After they had rushed to the hospital one day in early October for a procedure to relieve some pain-causing pressure, they were offered comforting assurances. A quick overnight stay, the doctor promised them.

When Pam left the hospital that night, their parting words had been strong and positive as they kissed goodnight and embraced. Neither suspected this would be the last time. They simply would not give up hope.

But this time hope failed them.

As with a single powerful lightning strike, hope was obliterated without warning. Overnight in the hospital, his heart had stopped. The autopsy would explain how the cancer had been silently, aggressively strangling every organ in its steady advance. The doctors were amazed Peter had fought it so strongly.

There had been no time for a last—as in final, as in never

again—good-bye. The shock made it all the more difficult to accept the reality.

There would never, ever, be a moment in their lives that was more painful, more unbearable, more unthinkable than when Pam had to hold her sons as they wakened in the morning and tell them.

This was not supposed to happen.

Suddenly the whole world became empty around them, no matter what was going on or the number of people with them. Pam felt they were being sucked into a black hole.

Family and friends were there for Pam and the boys in every way, as they had been from the beginning of Peter's illness, even as they dealt with their own distress and disbelief. Pam's brother, Terry, and his family stayed with her for a few days after the funeral before returning to their lives in Kingston. He and his wife, Kit, quietly assisted in guiding her through those first days and having their much-loved cousins around had been helpful for the boys.

"The boys, our boys, my boys..." Pam kept repeating to herself, sometimes silently, sometimes aloud. The pain of her loss was immense, but the agony she felt for her sons losing their father was beyond measure. It consumed her. She was not certain she could bear it.

As would any devoted mom, all she could focus on was how to help them and in so doing try to absorb as much of their hurt as possible.

"Ask me anything, my precious boys. I know you must have all kinds of questions swirling through your heads. Ask me anything and everything."

"Why couldn't the doctors save Dad?"

"Why did he have to die?'

"Did he know he was going to die?"

"Did you know he was going to die?"

"Why didn't anyone know?"

"How did he get the cancer?"

"We thought he was getting better."

"Why didn't anything help make him better?"

"What's going to happen to us?"

"Will you have to go to work, Mom?"

"Do we have to move?"

"Why did he have to die?"

She answered their questions clearly and honestly. She needed to assure them that Peter had made certain they were looked after and would remain in their home. In later years she would remind them they were the poster family for life insurance. Although he was gone, they would be forever grateful to him. But now that did not heal any pain.

They held each other and they cried. Deeply. Sometimes loudly. Sometimes softly. It was all they could do at this point.

Every time she held them, kissed their faces, hands, the tops of the heads—with each gentle touch she tried to feel some of the pain being released from their innocent, confused, broken hearts and being pulled into hers. Her heart that at this point in time defied description, seemingly shattered into a million pieces, impossible to gather together.

Cass had been so right when she had wrapped her arms around Pam through the long distance telephone lines from some remote marina in Turkey, her voice breaking through the static. "I think you must feel like someone ripped your heart out, stomped up and down on it, and then tried to stuff it back in. That's what I think. That's how I feel you feel. I hurt so much for you."

That about covered it. Cass was bereft, deeply saddened by Peter's death and the fact that she was halfway around the world when she wanted to be right beside Pam and the boys. Pam had given strict instructions she was not to come back.

Within days, David and Jason asked to go back to school and so they did. There seemed to be a necessity in life having the appearance of normalcy that pushed them through the waves of pain that would frequently crash into them.

To add to their trauma, ten days later, Peter's devoted mother died of a cardiac arrest. The classic case of death from a broken heart, after all she and her only son had been through together. Through her wits and strength, she had saved him from the Gestapo as a young widow in Hungary during WWII. Five years later she had escaped with him, this time from a communist regime, and made their way to a new life in Canada. A smart, capable woman, she had been certain she would save him from his cancer too. They had all been certain.

It was as if the train that had first run over Pam's family had been thrown into reverse and hit them again. In the aftermath, everyone affected attempted to deal with the onslaught of this merciless loss.

The Bridge Club, their hearts crushed by these tragedies, simply did what they knew best. They quietly organized and then took turns offering support. Pam's family and closest friends were there to help in every way, but were grateful for the extra assistance. Everyone was battling their own demons and struggling to avoid being caught in the strong undertow of the waves of grief washing over them.

None of the BC had been through this kind of crippling loss before. One or two of them had lost a parent in the preceding years and had experienced that sorrow. But this was different. This death of a spouse at so early a stage in life was a lesson in grief they wished they had not been forced to learn. It was too fast, too unexpected, too painful, too unfair.

Marti stayed at the house for the week after Pam's brother, Terry, left with his family to return to Kingston. She busied herself with walks down country roads with Pam, as well as laundry, tidying, and grocery shopping even though she knew appetites were stifled. Soup or pizza was all she could convince them to sit down to. It was a start.

Bonnie alternated with Marti after that. Danielle, Jane, Dee, and Lynn picked up odd days, mostly on weekends, to give them a break. Cass kept up a steady stream of letters and postcards with the occasional phone call when her travels allowed. Pam urged her to call collect.

As long as Pam wanted them there, they would arrange it. Other friends of Pam's pitched in as well, but it was the Bridge Club who kept things organized.

Pam's mother, a widow herself of just two years, lived in the city and due to her macular degeneration she no longer drove. Friends would bring her along for visits and she offered comfort as best she could. She had adored Peter and found his loss and her daughter's pain difficult to bear. They spoke on the phone each morning, often briefly, but a necessary connection.

The boys slept with Pam those first few weeks, seeking the reassurance they still had each other. It was the beginning of attempting to accept they were now three together on this earth. There was no question they would always be a family of four in their hearts. The struggle was to find a way to turn the hurt into strength and learn to live with the ache that would be with them forever.

They were joined in the king-size bed by their beloved Wheaton Terrier pup, Maggie, and the two cats, Frisky and Fluffy, who somehow brought a sense of comfort to the huddled heap of sorrow.

The view over the ravine that always absorbed them through the floor to ceiling windows was still there. The dense forest of tall trees seeming like sentries keeping them safe, the winding brook with great blue herons and kingfishers on the lookout, the glimpses of deer, fox, coyote, porcupine, and the rest of the magic of nature, was still all around them. Right now none of it mattered.

Pam tried to remind herself their house had always been filled with such good karma, as Danielle described it. She hoped that karma would be a healing balm if they were ever able to feel it again.

Falling asleep had never been a problem for Pam, except when Peter was ill, and then her sleep was a thinly veiled cover as she sensed every change in his breathing. She had read how much good positive thinking could do and they would focus with absolute certainty for hours about his recovery, about their life continuing as it should. Fat lot of good that had done, she often thought in the aftermath. Now, incredibly, her ability to fall asleep had returned and carried her briefly away from her sorrow. She welcomed it as an escape and was thankful for it. The waking up was the hard part.

In those first seconds of awaking, Pam sometimes would feel Peter in bed beside her. At times she turned to slip her arm around him and pull herself close, before she opened her eyes to the emptiness there.

Those first weeks had been torture. Grief was wrestling her to the ground no matter how hard she struggled to stay upright. She was amazed at the force of this powerful experience. Two steps forward and one step back was as good a dance as could be done.

There were important meetings with bank managers and financial planners that would guide her in this new, unwanted role of being completely financially responsible for their lives. Thank goodness Peter in all his wisdom had long ago asked Tim, a close family friend, to go to all such meetings with her if anything happened to him. Words were simply going in one ear and out the other at those meetings. Tim would absorb the details and take the time to explain them later, helping her do what was necessary.

Some days, once the boys were at school, she simply climbed back into bed fully clothed, pulled the covers over her head, and cried until she could no more for that round. Steaming showers or long soaks in a hot bath were soothing as she attempted to pick herself up. No matter what though, she would be ready with a smile on her face to collect the boys, chauffeured those first weeks by her thoughtful friends.

Scarlet, orange and golden autumn leaves soon carpeted the property. A sight that had always filled them with such pleasure, to Pam the barren trees now only represented sadness and loss.

An early winter had been predicted.

As much as she tried to make progress, deep down she felt her battle was being lost. Six weeks had passed, and for a few days in a row she tried to ignore warnings that her ability to cope was fading in spite of her efforts.

It was terrifying, that moment when she acknowledged she was losing her grip. Thankfully she was with Bonnie when her meltdown happened. It was one evening as they returned from dropping the boys off at friends for a sleepover weekend.

In the middle of a seemingly innocuous conversation, while they drove home along the familiar back roads, Pam began to weep uncontrollably.

Bonnie braked harder than she meant to and, with a jolt, stopped at the side of the road barely missing the ditch.

"Pam, what happened just now? What's wrong? Did I miss something?"

Struggling to breathe as she sobbed, Pam's words shot out in staccato bursts. "I can't take it anymore ... I feel ... so empty ... so broken ... I'm trying ... to be strong but ... I need Peter back ... the boys need him..." Her voice trailed off as she cried harder than ever.

Bonnie took Pam's hand in hers, her own eyes filling with tears, and quietly she urged Pam to take her time.

Taking big gulps, her shoulders heaving, Pam sniffled through her words. "I can't live without Peter ... I just can't..."

"Yes you can," Bonnie countered gently. "Yes you can. I

understand it feels impossible sometimes, but you can and you will."

"N-n-no matter how hard I try," Pam wept, her voice strangled, "I feel like I'm falling down a well ... and I'm about to hit bottom ... I can't control it..." Words came tumbling out nonstop now, pleading. "I know I need to go on and build a life for us, but I can't stop this slide ... I'm trying my best and I can't stop it ... I need to be here for David and Jason but I ... I ... can't ... stop ... it..."

Rocking back and forth and sobbing into her palms, she seemed truly lost.

From her social work experience, Bonnie recognized that time was necessary here to release these bottled up feelings. She rubbed Pam's back, as she was now leaning forward with her head resting on arms folded across her knees. Pam's plaintive cries became muffled as she buried her face in her arms.

Bonnie quietly encouraged her to talk, cry, whatever she felt she needed.

Sitting back, Pam was almost whispering now, sobs wracking her body between words, "I just miss Peter so much ... I can't describe it ... I don't want to live without him ... This pain ... is unbearable..." Her fists beat on her knees with uncontrollable rage.

Bonnie reached across the seat and pulled Pam into a hug, patting her back, almost giving her a shake. Pam seemed to eventually respond as her body slowly quieted.

They stayed still together for several minutes before Pam spoke more clearly but still gulping for breath, "I miss him so much in so many ways ... I miss who I was with him ... I feel so frightened ... so totally responsible ... it's scary ... so alone ... in spite of everyone's help. I can't get on top of it..."

A long sigh escaped Bonnie's lips as she realized she had been holding her breath. Floundering for the right words—as if there were any at a time like this—she repeated, "I know, I know," and held her friend tightly.

Again they sat, only breathing, as moonlight filled the car. Bonnie offered simple words of encouragement and solace and did not try to dissuade Pam from what she was saying. Listening was the greatest gift she could offer at this moment.

As her sorrowful outburst began to subside, Pam rolled the window down for some fresh air. "Let's just go home," she said, faintly, through her tears.

Bo reached to touch her friend's arm as she put the car in gear and continued to maneuver the narrow country road. Her comforting hand rested where it was.

When she sensed Pam was calmer, Bo gently said, "I can only try to imagine the depth of your pain. No one but you can feel it, no one..."

Swallowing hard, Bo found herself wrestling with what she wanted to say. "But I understand how incredibly difficult life is for you right now. In a way," she paused, "in a way, I can sense a bit of what you are going through."

Pam sniffed loudly, wiping her face with her sleeves as she stared straight ahead.

Bonnie's voice grew softer. "Remember when Jackson disappeared from my life?"

Pam let her head drop and looked at the floor of the car, nodding despondently.

Bonnie inhaled deeply before continuing, "It was different from this, for sure, but at the same time a loss of immense proportions. I mourned his absence, and I won't ever forget how hard that was. I was grieving for what I had lost, what he had lost. You must remember those days too."

"Yes," Pam whispered sympathetically, "we knew how much you were hurting and how unable to help we felt."

Silence surrounded them again before Bonnie went on, more strongly now, "Later I battled a different type of grief when I entered rehab and gave up the bottle, thanks to all of you. Crazy as it sounds, that was a huge loss for me, and I had to dig deep to get through that. So I have somewhat of a sense of where you are. Probably only a glimmer..."

Pam nodded at the memories as Bonnie continued, "What I'm telling you now is the lesson I learned through those experiences. I appreciate why you feel the way you do—you have every right to that—but you've reached a point where you have to make a decision. Now. You have to find the strength to pull yourself out of that well on your own or get professional help."

Pam nodded again, exhaling noisily, wiping her eyes and rubbing her hands over her face, trying to pull herself together.

They stopped in front of the house and exited the car. Walking to the front door with her arm around Pam's shoulders, Bonnie continued with her train of thought, "There's a lot of excellent support out there apart from your friends and family. If you need it, let's get you there. Tonight is the starting line and you have to step over it. Try to get some sleep and in the morning we'll move on in whatever direction you say. You need to do this for your boys first and foremost, for yourself, for your family, for your future. David and Jason have lost their father. They can't lose their mother too."

It was Pam's first night with both boys away, and they had decided that Bo would stay over. It became a long evening with hours of quiet outpouring interrupted by lingering silences and many more tears. Bonnie effectively used her own experience in rehab to finally give Pam an anchor.

"When you feel you're really losing control, it becomes as basic as this—and I have Dani to thank for convincing me. Take one breath at a time. Repeat this to yourself. I am breathing in. I am breathing out. I am breathing in. I am breathing out. I feel like shit, but I'm still here. I am breathing in. I am breathing out. Focus on nothing but your breathing and eventually relief will come. Trust me on this. It carried me through many a bad patch when I thought I might die if I didn't have another drink. Trust me, my friend, and believe."

Still sleep did not come easily. Pam muffled her crying into her pillow until this night's reservoir ran dry. Then she sat on her bed, breathing in and breathing out.

She stared for hours at the night sky through the walls of glass. The vast deep was filled with stars that combined with the moonlight to spill a soft glow through the forest. Lighting a path for her, she wondered.

Straining to find some sense of her vanished strength, she was reminded of the trust and confidence Peter had expressed in a rare moment during his illness when she had lost it. Sobbing she did not want to live without him, he had wrapped her in his arms, saying with gentle firmness, "But you will live —for yourself, for David and Jason, for me. You will have a happy life again." The painful intensity of such a moment is indescribable. She could not let him down.

Bonnie slept lightly, no symphonic snoring for her tonight. She wanted to be sure Pam was safe and calm with no relapse during the dark hours.

When Pam found her friend sitting downstairs in the morning, bleary-eyed and coffee in hand as she read the newspaper, she hugged her firmly, looked her clearly in the eyes, and thanked her.

"That was a crossroads last night, Bo. I feel drained."

"That makes two of us," Bo yawned. "You had me very worried. That was quite a meltdown."

"You were right," Pam went on. "I was so far down I had to get a grip or accept that I needed help to do it. This morning feels different. You said to make a choice, and I choose to live. I choose to grow stronger."

"I wasn't sure which way things were going to go, but I knew whichever decision you made would be the right one," replied

Bonnie, an uncustomary serious expression on her face. "You just had to buy into it."

"I know the pain will be with us for a long time and the struggle isn't over," Pam admitted, "but you convinced me that I can get that elusive grip. I'm so lucky to have the support that I do. The bottom line is finding the strength within myself. I know I have it ... I just have to believe in it. Thank you for the push."

"You're most welcome." Bonnie returned the hug as she moved toward the stove. "Look at me, Pam. You know I enjoy my own company. I believe in myself. You also know I had to go through a process to be this way. Learn to appreciate yourself and not fear being on your own. It's the most important step toward taking control of your life."

Opening the cupboard she pulled out a frying pan. "Now it's time for me to cook us up a big country breakfast. You also need to start eating properly."

"Amen to that," agreed Pam.

After doing justice to the bacon and eggs, they set off through the woods with Maggie leading the way. Bonnie continued to encourage Pam to just talk, talk, talk.

"The worst time is when my eyes first open in the morning. I'm fine for a split second and then reality seeps back in and I know Peter is gone. He will never wake up beside me again. At first I feel like I can just roll over and he'll be there, that this will turn out to have been a very bad dream. It's the most difficult moment of all."

"It has to be," Bonnie agreed.

"Then I know I have to wake up the boys and we have to face the truth for another day. It's so hard to try and make sense of a world that seems to have lost all meaning."

"It's horrible," Bonnie replied. "Things like this shouldn't happen, but we know only too well they do. You mustn't lose sight of how much you have to live for and your promise to live a life that would make Peter proud, that will make you proud and the boys—and you will do just that."

"Bo, I know you're right," sighed Pam, her face lined with frustration and despair, "but at this moment life just looks like a big black hole to me. When I try to picture the future, all I see is shattered glass and dark emptiness beyond. It sounds melodramatic, but that's exactly how it seems. It's as if our tomorrows have simply vanished."

They walked through the chill air in silence for a few minutes, absorbing their thoughts, before Pam went on, "We had such plans and dreams and now I just see nothing. I can't envision anything beyond the present."

"Not yet," Bonnie said.

"Right ... but..." with this Pam straightened her back, squared her shoulders, and shook her head as if to clear it. "I will get there ... we will..."

"One breath at a time, Pam. One breath at a time."

One or more of the BC was at the house day and night. Keeping her company in the van as she drove the boys to and from school, walking and talking with her during the day, taking care of small details, cooking, shopping, listening, tidying, answering the phone, paying bills. All the stuff that needed to be done just got done.

Since Bonnie lived in the country a few kilometers outside Oakville she could be at Pam's in twenty minutes, driving straight up Fifth Line. She could take care of the daily demands at her family-run land development business as well as the dairy farm, her true love, and shuttle back and forth.

Once she felt Pam was settling into a daily routine, Bo would show up in time to pick up the boys from school with her, and then stay for dinner and overnight from time to time to fill the empty evening hours. She often drove home in the early morning in her nightgown rather than bother bringing changes of clothes with her. This always made Pam laugh. Bo knew how to work it. With her great gift of humor, she could push Pam bit by bit as everyone helped her begin to find the balance in her life again.

Other friends dropped off meals, baking, and called to see how they could help—all of it so appreciated. Actions were much easier than words at this point.

The phone rang constantly offering sympathy, friends searching for words that were so difficult to find. The mailbox was filled every day with touching memories, sorrowful thoughts, paper tears. There were days when Pam could barely bring herself to open the mail. It was impossible to read it without weeping.

"If only Peter had known while he was alive," she told Danielle one day when she dropped by. "People write such thoughtful observations after one's death. Sometimes those words are from someone on the periphery of a life who was touched in a special way by the person who is gone, someone we might not have even realized we had influenced in any way..."

Danielle looked at the stack of cards to which Pam was slowly responding. She commented on what a tribute it was to Peter for so many people to be mourning his passing.

Pam asked the question, not really looking for an answer: "Why do we wait until a person is gone before we write so eloquently about what they meant to us?"

"True," agreed Danielle, "we get so caught up in our own busy lives we don't stop as often as we should to tell people how we feel about them."

"Until a person is gone," Pam mused, lost momentarily in her thoughts. Never had the word *gone* held the deeply intense meaning it now represented to her. It was almost unbearable to hear. "*I'm sorry, Pam, he's gone,*" the doctor had gently said. Those words could never be said gently enough. They echoed for a very long time. The profound agony carried with them was unimaginable until they are said to you.

"The *deceased.*" How she cringed at that word as letters arrived from banks or other business concerns where accounts, cards, or whatever had to be changed. It made her want to scream, "He's not deceased or dead or gone. He can't be. He can't be." But he was and she knew it. Her head knew it. Her heart couldn't believe it.

She would often go into their closet and bury her face in his handsome suits and other clothes still hanging as they had always been. Inhaling deeply, she would try to catch a familiar scent of him. Searching his pockets for a tissue or piece of paper or coin to hold in her hand, she imagined him holding it in his. She would slip into a shirt of his and stand in his shoes. She slept in his tee shirts. She wasn't sure why, but somehow it helped, if only briefly.

In the early evening, around suppertime when Peter normally arrived home, she would look out the window and for a fraction of a second think she saw his headlights drawing near through the winter dark. From another part of the house she would hear the front door open and his hearty hello call out, to which the boys had always responded with a dash to greet him. But she knew he was gone. Accepting it was something else again.

It was as if Pam had used up all of her strength, body and soul, to maintain a semblance of normalcy in the midst of their pain. She had been strong when she organized the funeral with the help of her family. It had been worthy of him. She knew this even as it all swirled around her and the boys in a surreal blur. Now she felt there was nothing left. She knew she had to find that strength again, as she had promised Bonnie. Peter would expect it of her. She owed it to their sons.

As a couple they had been such a team. Pam always felt she was more than able to stand on her own two feet, never really imagining she would ever have to. It was incredible, how vacant she now felt. He was gone. And so, it seemed to her, was she.

Winter arrived early. The normally wildly celebrated first snowstorms moved through barely noticed by Pam, until the youthful exuberance of her boys pushed her to react.

On a morning walk with Marti in a nearby conservation area, to give Maggie a good run, Pam expressed her feelings. "Of course I know I'm still here, still breathing, still functioning, but I feel as if my body is a shell. On the outside I look perfectly normal, but when I look inside I see total destruction. It's as if a bomb went off inside and everything is shattered. It's such a weird sensation but so clear to me. I see pieces of my insides hanging from shards of bone. In my head I understand I will heal, but in my heart I can't imagine it."

Marti gently replied, "We all cared for Peter so much. But I know the loss we feel doesn't begin to compare to yours. It's so difficult to find words that might help. I feel like all I can do is listen and just be here with you."

Both women stopped walking and held each other in the middle of the snow-packed trail. Their muted sobs filled the crisp air and hung like frozen crystals.

"It hurts *so* much," Pam gulped, "it's *so* unbelievably intense." The words caught in her throat. Seconds passed before she continued. "I could not have imagined feeling anything like this; I never knew grief was as physical as it is emotional."

Marti hugged her tightly. "I see the agony in your eyes, your face, even in your body. And I can hear it so clearly in your voice. I've read that grief is impossible to understand unless you're the one directly impacted by the loss. For the first time, I really get that."

They moved on in silence for a while.

"That's how it is," Pam spoke again as she stumbled over a snow-covered rock and regained her balance, barely noticing. "The pain and the calm come in waves. There's no pattern so I never know when I'll get knocked down. Some of my thoughts are so illogical. I wonder how the sun can shine. How can other people laugh and joke? How can there be beauty when such tragedy has happened? I just feel numb."

Marti nodded as Pam was quiet again. The moment passed.

"You know, Marti, crazy as it sounds, I find myself hoping I'll wake up and discover it's all been a terrible nightmare. I know these thoughts aren't rational, but I can't help them."

Marti handed Pam a tissue from the ever-present bundle in her pocket these days and they dried their tears as they walked on. Maggie bounced joyfully around them as Wheaten terriers do so well.

Pam reached down to give the pup a scratch on the head, managing a half-smile. "Marti, you're doing everything you can do, and more, and I appreciate what a difference it makes." She shook her head as if to untangle her thoughts. "I'm so lucky to have all of you. I keep reminding myself how many women go through this kind of catastrophe without all of the support I have."

Marti nodded. "For sure. Many people, adults and children, must struggle on their own and deal not just with the pain of loss but also with the reality of all of the other dramatic changes in their life."

Pam fought to keep control as she admitted, "I'll always be grateful to Peter for being so responsible and planning for our future ever since the boys were born. If it weren't for his life insurance, I don't know how I'd be able to continue to raise the boys here and give them the kind of life we planned—for all of us." Tearfully, she finished, "I'll thank him, I swear, for the rest of my life ... for taking care of us."

"You're right, you are fortunate in that way, stupid as that sounds. Many families aren't left so well cared for and have to deal with serious issues like having to move, to get a job if they hadn't been working, or to bring in enough money to support their families and simply provide basic necessities."

"All that," added Pam, "while dealing with their grief. I can't imagine how they do it. I know I have many blessings to count. I mean, let's face it, I've had such a great life. I don't need to tell you all this, you've been there with me..." Her voice trailed off.

Marti picked where Pam left off, "You've been a stay-at-home mom for thirteen years and never regretted a minute. I've envied you in many ways. Besides running a busy household on a country property and being the supportive corporate wife, you do volunteer work, drive on field trips, help in the boys' classrooms, teach skiing two mornings a week, go into the city to help your parents ... I could go on. We all know how much you loved your life."

"Yup, but no income there on my part. Peter was the bread-winner. No wonder the boys worried about what was going to happen to us. In this horrible, devastating situation, we've been given a gift. I know that. I've got to force myself to focus on it, on the positive—as much for the boys as for myself."

Marti slipped her arm through Pam's without breaking stride.

Moments passed before Pam found her voice. "Peter talked to me about this when he first was diagnosed. Even though he believed he'd get better, it gave him peace to talk through everything about finances. He insisted. I resisted. It was such a difficult conversation but a necessary one. That's when he said to me, 'I don't want to die, and I'm going to fight this with all my might, but if I do die, I will die with no regrets about my life. It's been amazing. I need you to know this.' I can't tell you how those words are burned into my psyche."

She brushed aside fresh tears, which had become almost second nature now.

"Of course those words will give you strength," Marti said, her voice thick. "You and the boys will carry on as Peter would have wanted you to. It's getting through these first painful months that are part of the process. I think you're all doing the right things—talking and crying and letting the hurt out bit by bit. It's all going to help."

Pam sighed and they walked quietly for a few minutes before she continued seemingly with more strength, "I hear you. I'll be so glad when the crying eases up though ... I just can't control it. Some days it makes me crazy—and it's getting on two months now."

"Remember what Bonnie told you. One breath at a time," Marti reminded her.

"I'm trying. You'd think I would be cried out by now!"

Attempting to inject a little humor, Marti teased, "You run out of tears? You've been the champion weeper of the Bridge Club forever! Cry for happy, cry for sad, that's you Pam. Why would you ever run out of tears? But the pain will ease—this we know."

Pam's smile was weak as she agreed that Marti had a point before she continued, "Not to change the subject, but ... do you remember my good friend Maria?"

"Of course, I do. The two of you've been such close friends for ages. I remember when her husband John died suddenly from a brain tumor," recalled Marti. "Gosh, that must have been ten years ago now."

"Exactly. Peter and I were with her through that terrible experience and we couldn't believe that the same thing was happening to us. It's so bizarre how things happen sometimes, isn't it?"

Marti reached down for a frozen milkweed pod and picked away at it as they walked on.

"Well, when John died we realized how important it was to have your life in order. Never thinking it would ever happen to us, of course, we updated our wills and all of our affairs with regard to our lives and the boys. When I think of it," she swallowed hard and continued, "that was the best thing we could have done. Coping with Peter's death would've been even more complicated and confusing if we hadn't."

Nodding, Marti reminded Pam , "You probably don't remember now, but when it happened you shared Maria's experience with all of us and we got our affairs in order."

"Now that you mention it—all of us except Dani, right? Bryce absolutely refused to discuss anything about the possibility of one of them dying. We were all blown away by the mental block he had. Especially for such a smart guy."

Marti hesitated for a moment, searching back through her own memories. "Oh yeah! We couldn't believe he was so stubborn about it. Danielle had to give up trying to convince him. She organized her own stuff as much as she could. That was a valuable lesson for all of us—that everyone should be aware of the importance of wills, powers of attorney, and final wishes, no matter how old we are. It's so much easier to do when everyone is healthy and you can answer all the questions that might be difficult at other times. Some people simply don't want to even think about it, and that's a big mistake."

Pam explained how knowing that Peter wanted his body donated to science rather than buried was incredibly important. No one had to worry about making the right decision. It felt satisfying to know his wishes were being respected. She said if it hadn't been for their friend's misfortune, they might not have been so prepared.

"Because he had active cancer, he couldn't donate his organs. He changed that detail after he was diagnosed."

"You know, out of your experience, someday you may be able to help another person cope with loss," Marti said, "just like Maria helped you."

Pam's gratitude to her friend Maria was obvious. "She's been a huge support because she knows without question what I'm going through. As sad as it is for her to revisit her tragic loss, sharing her emotional experiences with me has been invaluable. She can describe precisely some of the feelings I have. She reminds me I'm normal.

Marti acknowledged how re-affirming and encouraging that must have been.

Pam nodded. "She has taught me that all sorts of weird thoughts are part of the process of working through grief, and you know what? She's so right."

Feeling no further comment was necessary, Marti changed the subject and talked about dinner ideas until they reached the parking lot and headed home. She was thankful for the option of a flexible schedule so she could give this time to her friend.

There were many walks as the weeks passed with everyone's primary focus to encourage Pam to express herself but also to find the right balance between that and therapeutic silence. Just as important was the benefit of the physical exercise. With a multitude of scenic trails close to Pam's, it was easy to spend hours of brisk walking in pleasing surroundings. The women were racking up so many kilometers of conversation on the Bruce Trail that Jane suggested they call the paths "talking trails" rather than walking trails. More and more the BC worked at mixing in news, movies, recipes, and friends' gossip, and Pam grew more interested and receptive to moving back into the real world of everyday conversation.

One particular day, Pam had other issues on her mind.

"Marti, how can I ever repay you and Bo, in particular, for your help, your time. It's an unbelievable experience, this thing called grief. So all-consuming. I try not to let the boys see how much I'm struggling with it. I hope I'm helping them to feel calm, to heal. They've their own pain to deal with, and their pain's the greatest one that I carry with me. The hardest thing for me to accept is that they've lost their father. They adored him and he adored them."

Marti, better than anyone, could appreciate the pain of absent parents. "A part of their childhood has been stolen. It's unfair."

"Exactly. I need to help them as much as I can. I have to be a mom and dad to them now. I've promised myself I'll do everything in my power to give them the life Peter wished for them. I will do that! He accomplished so much in his shortened life, and we have to take inspiration from that."

"Yes you will do it. I know you will," Marti assured her. Pam mentioned the boys had expressed some interest in going away to a camp with friends for a few weeks in the summer.

A very good sign, Marti thought to herself with more than a little relief.

On one of her visits, Lynn arrived with a few books about grief and moving on with life.

Pam was grateful and promised to get to them in due course, explaining, "I've been trying to read books on those topics, but it's almost impossible for me to concentrate. It's such an unnatural feeling for a reader like me. All I can manage is flipping through magazines."

"Do you think you carry a lot of anger inside you?" Lynn asked as they left the house to take a walk around the property. "That's so common. It makes sense."

Pam's response was calm but quick as they took the path down into the ravine. "I've read how it's normal to feel angry with the person who died for leaving you, but I really don't get that at all. I mean, why would I ever feel angry with Peter?"

"He certainly did not choose this," Lynn replied.

"Exactly!" Pam said. "I'm angry at life for robbing him of everything he still had ahead of him. I'm angry at life for taking him from me. I'm absolutely furious at life for my sons losing their father."

Picking up a frozen stick, she hurled it with all her might. Maggie excitedly tore after it.

"So to answer your question, yes, I do have lots of anger inside me but never for one second has it ever been directed at Peter. It's when I'm by myself that the anger overflows and I just lose it. I'll cry and scream and bang the walls of our empty house until I exhaust myself."

"Having said all that," Lynn suggested, "hopefully you can begin to channel that anger positively. Use it to fuel that inner strength you're trying to build."

"That's my goal," Pam's voice grew stronger as she continued, "Speaking of anger, here's what really gets me going! People who say to me that everything is in God's hands or this is all part of God's plan and we have to trust in Him."

She let out a mangled scream at that and punched her fist straight out from her arm. "I just want to plough people when they say things like that. In fact I often picture myself punching them right in the face. Sorry ... that was a bit of a rant!"

"That's not like you, Pam, but I understand the reaction."

"I knew you would. We share the same feelings when it comes to religion. It's just not our thing—and before you ask, it wasn't Danielle who made remarks like that to me."

"Oh, I never thought for a minute that it was. She knows you too well."

"And besides," Pam went on, "as we both know, Danielle is too smart and sensitive to ever impose her religious beliefs in such a way. I admire how she lives her faith on a daily basis. She's been a rock to us as well through all this."

"I agree," Lynn nodded, "between her religion and her deep

spiritual connection to yoga, she's definitely the best of the BC for spreading good karma."

"She left me a beginner yoga video, but I haven't been able to concentrate on it yet. I must admit Dani has really helped me to become aware of the positive power of yoga. How it blends the physical, mental, and emotional energy centers. I really do want to give it a try at some point."

"Danielle has a great quote that describes the connection she feels between her religious beliefs and yoga. She told me that yoga is bodily gospel," laughed Lynn. "I thought it was brilliant."

Pam agreed it was a perfect quote from Danielle. "She's so centered. Even her outbursts of profanity make sense."

"Ya gotta love it," chuckled Lynn, happy to have some levity in the conversation.

Pam smiled briefly and then shrugged her shoulders in frustration. "I just can't handle any sort of religious philosophy right now. It makes me crazy. Sorry for losing it a minute ago."

"But Pam, you know those people believe in their faith and find strength in it. They're hoping to offer you strength and comfort from it too."

"I know. I know. I mean, for example, I understand how much Danielle's faith means to her. I know what a believer she is and I respect that. I know she prayed with all her might for us and she continues to now."

"That's a given."

"I might ask," Pam added ruefully, "where did it get anyone? But I won't. There's no point. And you know I'm usually tolerant and respectful of other people's faith. I mean, it's a great crutch; it's just not mine. I would rather find my strength from deep inside myself, from believing in myself. That's what I'm working on."

"And you are doing well, even if it doesn't seem like it sometimes. It's a lot of work, but you will come out the other end."

Slowing to watch a pair of cardinals feasting on the dried berries of a thicket of high bush cranberry, they took the turn that would lead them along the frozen creek and back the way they had come.

Pam grimaced. "They say time heals everything but to me that seems like a worn-out cliché now. This wound does not heal. What I'm learning is that time allows you to figure out how to manage the pain, how to live with it. Somehow it has to make you stronger. But it will always be there, just under the surface. I mean, why should you *stop* feeling the pain of such a loss?"

"This is a learning process for all of us," Lynn sighed sadly, "and it's so much bigger than anything I've experienced. You're making progress, Pam, and your world will look bright again one day. All those happy memories you and the boys have of your life with Peter will stay with you forever in a very positive way. I believe that."

"I wish. You know, I wake David and Jason up with a smile every morning to get their day off to a positive start. They define my existence right now and there is nothing more important to me than making them feel loved and happy to greet a new day. The pain of their loss cuts through me like a knife."

"It will soften, as you explained. More time has to pass," Lynn reassured her as they walked up to the house arm in arm, the soothing sunshine warming their faces.

Christmas, always such a special family time full of traditions and fun, had come and gone before they knew it. Pam was aware vaguely that they had even been able to feel festive and happy at times thanks to the extraordinary quiet support and effortless organizing of family and friends.

Time had lost its meaning and passed in a blur. This too was not uncommon, she read. She was spending more time on her own and finding her days full with a combination of responsibilities and mundane chores. Life does go on even when you don't believe it will.

Not that it was all bad, she had to keep reminding herself. She took the boys to Whistler for the March school break just as they would have done when life was normal. This was the new normal, minus one.

They had skied and laughed even as thoughts and memories of Peter had swirled around them, reminding them how quickly life can change. At times the memories would fill them with such warmth and at others cause tears of sorrow. How he had loved that place! The boys even spoke of bringing Peter's ashes to sprinkle on his beloved runs on Seventh Heaven, and Pam was proud of them for the maturity they were showing.

Jane, of course, also had the school break off. Unbeknownst to Pam, she and Samantha had cancelled a trip to Jamaica so they could be in Whistler and ski with Pam while the boys were in racing camp. Although Pam had insisted she would be fine out there on her own, and she would have the company of Peter's sister and her husband who lived there, she had to admit it was great to have those friends out there too.

Being around Peter's sister, Ofra, and her husband, Lawrence, two of her most favorite people on the planet, had been bittersweet. They reminisced about the trip just the year before, when Peter was there and healthy and life was wonderful. It still seemed impossible that it could change so drastically, so quickly. At the same time, they felt it was healing to be together and to keep living life in the way that they always had. Change would come, but keeping past traditions alive was important and they vowed to keep this date every winter.

Another sign of healing, Pam felt, was the fact that she had taken out her camera and brought it on the trip. She had not touched it since the day she lost Peter.

As the winter months dissolved into longer, brighter days offering a hint of spring, Pam could feel the progress they were all making. She was spending most days on her own and feeling okay about it. There were plenty of daily phone calls but she was actually getting used to being by herself.

Friends, BC and others, continued to pop by and Pam was in the city weekly now to take her mom shopping. Bonnie picked her up for their "monthlies." Even in her worst depths, Pam had always managed to play bridge.

On a crisp Saturday afternoon, with patches of snow still spread through the woods, David and Jason called her outside. With great enthusiasm they showed how they had tapped spigots in the maple trees and hung the sap buckets as they had helped Peter do every year. "It is maple syrup time, Mom. We've got to get busy or we'll miss it."

Learn a lesson from these great kids, Pam told herself, as they helped her set up the propane burner in the open door of the drive shed. Next they hauled down the big washtub that would await the daily offerings once the sap got running. The clear sweet liquid would boil down here until there was very little remaining. A final boil delivering the rich, delicious syrup would happen in a big soup pot on the stove in the house. They would bottle it and share the bounty with friends.

It had always been a satisfying and sweetly delicious experience. It must be that again the three of them agreed.

On a visit one afternoon after the snow had melted and the sunshine of the longer days was warming the earth, Lynn noticed a large unplanted strip of soil by the garage that captured Maggie's attention whenever they let her out.

"There must be some good stuff in that dirt," she remarked to Pam, as they strolled across the yard to get closer to it.

Pam looked at the empty black plot with exasperation.

Sadness crept into her voice as she explained Peter had dug that new bed in the fall when he was feeling well. They had planned to fill it with hundreds of bulbs to celebrate his success in beating his cancer. It hadn't happened.

"I guess I'll just throw grass seed in there and forget about it," Pam said bitterly, blinking back tears. "We were going to call it our victory garden. Some victory."

Turning Pam to face her and grasping her shoulders, Lynn gave her a very firm squeeze. "And what would Peter think, after all his hard labor digging this out? Come on, Pam. You can do better than that. Make it something special. Speaking of special, what's in there? Maggie can't keep her little black nose out of it!"

Pam couldn't keep herself from smiling faintly as she told Lynn there were many loads of sheep poop mixed in that soil. "The stinkier the better, they always say at the nursery, and we worked it all in. Actually plants should do really well there. It's a perfect location." She kicked gently at the soil with the toe of her boot, loosening clumps as they talked.

"Gardening was something you two enjoyed doing together," Lynn reminded her, her eyes sweeping the property. "Look at all the fabulous flowerbeds you've created around here over the years. Why on earth would you give it up?"

"It's always been a passion for us ... for me ... that's for sure," said Pam. "There's something so soothing about working with the soil, watching the plants take root and flourish. I loved discovering the young shoots poking through the soil in the spring. It made me feel like I was greeting old friends." Frowning, she turned her back on the beckoning plot and looked down at her feet. "But it's just like everything else right now—nothing gives me pleasure."

Silence followed. Pam raised her eyes to see Lynn giving her a very strong squint of displeasure, her eyebrows arched, lips pursed. They held each other's gaze for several seconds before

Lynn said, softly but firmly, "You need to allow pleasure back into your life. It is still out there just like it always was but your door has been closed—with good reason—and it's time to begin opening it. Peter would want that."

Their eyes remained locked. After a long pause, Pam nodded slowly and said, "You're right. I need to finish making this garden."

Lynn encouraged each idea as Pam thought out loud, "I'll fill it full of perennials—lilies, peonies, delphiniums, phlox, and roses, lots of roses, Peter's favorites—"

"That's more like it," said Lynn, with a grin.

Pam's voice built with something close to enthusiasm as plans kept coming, "And in the fall I'll get the boys to help me plant the bulbs. A ton of them! We *will* make it our victory garden and honor his memory."

"That you will," Lynn agreed.

Poring over her gardening books and planning the new flowerbed began to give Pam a sense of purpose. For the first time in months, apart from the normal demands of the boys' sports timetables, dental appointments, and so on, she was consulting her calendar in advance with some pleasure (*thank you, Lynn*) as she worked on a planting schedule. Planning a garden meant thinking about the future. There was so much hope and optimism involved in planting seeds and seedlings and a trust that they would grow and thrive.

As Pam recognized all these positive feelings, she was reminded how applicable it was to life in general. Growth and renewal were essential elements of gardens. It was good to feel that this was what was happening in her life now. She was planting seeds for the future, nurturing hopes, and learning to let go as so much in life, just like in the garden, is beyond our control.

She would still sometimes cry and viciously kick bits of deadfall as she walked with Maggie through their woods. Other times they would quietly go deeper into the dense back forest after crossing the stepping-stones in the stream, which Peter and the boys had spent a weekend putting in place. They had all cut a hiking trail back there together, and every footstep burned with memories. She knew she could go deep enough and wail the pain out of her heart without anyone hearing her. Maggie would jam herself right up against Pam's leg, as if she sensed support was needed. Whenever Pam did this she felt a physical release, as if somehow she was attempting to empty the bottomless pit of sorrow she carried inside her. She began to realize it was not filling up quite as far now.

The comfort these natural surroundings offered was immense. The deep silence of the forest at times offered the best place for contemplation. At other times, an awareness of the birdsong, the bubbling brook, the rustling of leaves and all the sounds that penetrated the silence would remind Pam she was a guest of nature. "Yes," she thought, "Mother Nature is holding us in her arms here. I feel it. I think the boys feel it. We're so lucky to live where we do."

The small pleasures of the ever-changing canvas of the forest floor gave big returns. The display of trillium this spring filled her with hope, the reassurance that life continues on. She found herself searching out signs of familiar woodland treasures that she had greeted every year. Yellow trout lilies, sweet-scented purple violets, snowdrops, Jack-in-the-Pulpit, May apples, and wild columbine were some of the plethora of native wildflowers that appeared in abundance with the sunny, bright yellow marsh marigolds leading the way along the edge of the creek. Each species shared its particular beauty for an allotted time and then gracefully disappeared to allow another to bloom. The fact they were not letting her down, that they were returning as nature promises, was healing in its own way.

Inevitably she would find herself back at the wide ribbon of soil, which was slowly beginning to take on the shape and form of an old-fashioned Victorian perennial garden. It was clear now how it would flower in stages as the growing season progressed. Pam would talk to Maggie about it and Maggie would gaze deeply into her eyes, wag her tail at warp speed, and give her big slobbery licks all over her face. Maggie had been Peter's birthday gift for her the previous summer and, to Pam, she carried his spirit in her soft, shaggy presence. Pam had to admit this silly pup with her endless exuberance had played an important role for her and the boys in getting through sad moments.

To her surprise, her sons even took an interest in the gardening books she left sitting around. They looked at pictures of plants they thought might make good additions to their project. Shooting baskets into the net they had helped their dad install had been the only reason this spring for them to go outside, when normally they would never be indoors. Now she had them busy turning soil, edging, and hauling wheelbarrow loads of peat moss. It was becoming a family project.

Dee had a large nursery near her farm with healthy specimens of a vast selection of perennials. She would pick up Pam to spend a day poking around in the countryside before loading up her van with purchases to be added to the new garden.

"Work the soil. Attend to the soul," Dee said to her one day as they tilled the garden together. "There's so much to be gained spiritually, as well as physically, from creating a garden. And sometimes it just feels good to get dirty."

Along with the gardening plans, Pam had also begun to work out again, although she still could not go to their sports club. She had tried but had to leave when she couldn't stop the memories from reducing her to tears. Even grocery shopping was still difficult. How many carts half full of food had she simply abandoned so she could escape to the car and cry?

Friends would from time to time invite her to join them for

dinner or for a small party, but Pam, who had always been extremely social, just couldn't cut it. On the first two attempts she had to duck out before the meal was even served. The third time she feigned a headache immediately after forcing down the meal. It was just too early, too soon, for that kind of social interaction. Everyone understood.

The long walks with Maggie and sessions on the exercise bike were helping her get back in shape. As she pedaled next to the floor-to-ceiling window in her bedroom, she watched the brook babble busily along as the landscape changed with the days. When she was feeling really down, those endorphins charging through her body helped lift her spirits.

The boys were on sports teams that changed with the seasons, and she was constantly driving to practices and games, cheering from the stands. She never missed any, and often one of the BC or another friend joined to holler along with her.

Jason and David were her lifelines, her most important reasons for breathing. They kept each day busy, as kids do, and there was always something happening.

They were moving on, as everyone said. However, they were not leaving any memories behind. Those memories, their history, were restoring the foundation of their lives that had felt like it was crumbling so many months before. The saying "life goes on" was truly relevant in their lives.

Pam often reminded her sons how proud their dad would be whether it was for shooting a three-pointer in a basketball game or taking on a household chore without being asked. Being normal kids, there were also moments she would include Peter when discipline was called for and express how she knew he would have reacted. His importance and influence in their lives was a constant, and gradually she knew they were letting go some of the pain of their loss and focusing on the positives that would remain forever.

Along with the energy she could feel slowly returning, she was building a plan. A completed application for admission into York University's education degree program sat on her desk. The timetable would allow her to drive to classes after the school bus collected the boys in the morning. She would organize their after-school schedule with help from other friends on the odd day she couldn't return in time. Certainly she had plenty of evenings to spend studying.

If she were fortunate enough to make the cut the following spring, it would be more than a year before she would begin this new phase of her life. In the meantime a close friend at the local school had persuaded her to apply for the position of her teaching assistant in September to gain even more experience. Her push had been pivotal to Pam's decision to go back to university. Once again, an act of friendship that was helpful beyond compare.

Encouraged by Jane and Lynn, dedicated teachers that they were (even though Lynn set her career aside when she had her sons), she had been reminded of how so much of her past pointed to teaching as the logical path to follow. She had taught business subjects at night school before she was married, had more recently been a ski instructor a few days a week, and enjoyed helping in her sons' classrooms. She knew she connected easily with people, particularly children. Teaching elementary school appealed to her in every way.

She was in charge of her future, she kept reminding herself. What a step forward to feel once again that indeed there was a future.

"The most important lesson I've learned from this experience is that each day is a gift and not to be taken for granted," Pam said to Danielle as they sat in the shade on Pam's back deck, enjoying the peace and quiet of the early summer day.

"You know how deeply we've all been touched by it," Danielle answered softly, "and you're so right: no one is guaranteed a tomorrow. How sad that it takes something like this to make everyone stop and think about the important things in life. It has really made Bryce and me take a good look at our lives. He's seriously planning to work toward an early retirement after our kids are through university."

"That's great news. As the saying goes, plan for the future but live for today. Truer words were never spoken."

Standing up and gazing into the ravine, Pam continued, "Another of the many lessons this experience has taught me is the importance for every young girl to grow up knowing how to live independently. If you choose to stay home with your children, be sure to have education or job training to fall back on. I don't mean we should be pessimistic, but we have to be proactive so there is always a safety net. Life should never be taken for granted, because it can change drastically in a heartbeat. Lesson learned."

Danielle joined her at the railing of the deck, saying she had listened to a program recently on CBC addressing that very subject. She was shocked at the statistics relating to the number of young mothers on their own, through either death or divorce. The panel had discussed the need for better preparation and awareness.

"You just never know..." Pam's voice trailed off.

As the warm days of summer set in, the boys prepared to go off to the summer camp they loved. The familiar setting, the good friends, fun, and adventure would be a welcome change. They seemed to be healing as well as one could hope. Kids are so resilient, she thought to herself.

Tears were never far from the surface when they spoke of their father, but that was healthy, and it pleased her that they would talk about him and share memories. Let them find happiness and joy again—let them laugh and be kids and grab on to life with all of its challenges, inspired by the memory of their dad. This was her deepest hope for them..

The idea of three weeks without her sons presented Pam with conflicting feelings. As happy as she was for them to go and have fun at camp, she was suddenly frightened at the prospect of being totally alone. In spite of all the activity around them for the past ten months, she had been acutely aware of the emptiness she still felt inside her home. Now she would have to deal with it. She hoped the experience would be a turning point for her, so that she could live with the emptiness and not dread it.

She had also made plans to go away for a week. This would be a new step on her own.

Saying good-bye to the boys at the bus pickup had not been easy. As they piled on board with their old familiar friends, she knew it was going to be a helpful diversion for them. Their hugs had been brief but intense—other kids were watching after all—and they gave Maggie strict instructions to take care of Mom.

Bonnie had driven over with them and Pam was firm and convincing during a quick lunch together that she wanted to spend the rest of the day and night on her own. She promised to phone if she was struggling.

Her gardens were a distraction for the rest of the day, and she pushed herself to a satisfying fatigue. The compost heap was rewarding her with rich brown humus that helped turn the thick clay into light loamy soil as she spent hours digging and turning, adding old materials to the pile knowing they would transform into something new. Sitting on a stump she pulled off her gardening gloves and surveyed her work, a look of contentment on her dirt-streaked face. *It's true,* she reminded herself, *the digging, watering, weeding, and fertilizing are like what we hope for in our life ... sowing seeds for the future, nurturing our dreams, watching them grow.*

As she slowly surveyed the property, she was aware of how Peter's presence lived on through everything he had dug and built and nurtured. *The same applies to what he left in each of us*, she thought with gratitude rather than tears. *This is a reminder of how we need to pay attention to how we live and what we will leave behind*, she told herself as she walked up the path to the house.

After a long soak up to her ears in a bubble-filled tub, with a quiet she could almost hear, Pam had the cry she knew would come. Yet these were tears of release, not of despair or heartrending pain. Not that the pain was gone, but she felt more in control of its intensity.

Placing a Miles Davis cassette in the stereo, the first time she managed to listen to "their" music on her own, Pam allowed herself to appreciate the soulful sounds that had filled the house for years. Trailed by Maggie and with the cats rubbing around her ankles, she wandered through each room pausing at the many family photos that covered all the surfaces and walls, tracing her fingers over furniture and small treasures that told the story of their lives together. They would remain a visible presence forever.

She would never need to be reminded of how grateful she was to have experienced the eighteen years of their marriage, ups and downs included. Many people were not so fortunate. Their two sons would embody the best of their union. She was not ready to consider the possibility of anyone changing the shape of this family, even though the subject was discreetly mentioned from time to time.

There was a sense of accomplishment about the strength growing within her. *We will be fine*, she kept telling herself. Peter would be proud.

We're so blessed, she reflected, as she often did now, *to have such a supportive family, but even more so to have the remarkable friendships carrying us through the torrent of grief. We have so much help, with no questions asked and no return expected. We're learning a lesson that we should share whenever we can—to cultivate and nurture friendships through life. The garden of life.*

Pam slept soundly that night.

"It's time to get away," Bonnie said two days later as she loaded Pam's new set of golf clubs into the car. They headed off for a seven-day ladies golf camp in Muskoka where Dee and Jane would meet them.

Tuning the car radio to the Oakville oldies station, they sang along as they passed the century farms with their crops well established at this point in the summer. Herds of cattle and sheep peacefully grazed in the warmth of the day. The leisurely drive through the back-roads to their destination was the perfect way to pass the day.

"Be prepared for the love-hate experience of your life, my friend, the sport of golf," warned Bo as they turned into the club's forest-lined driveway, "and one day you're going to thank me. I guarantee it! We're going to golf all day and play bridge every evening for a whole week without anything else to think about."

They did just that, and for the first time in almost a year, Pam could feel enjoyment from something new in her life. With no memories attached to the game of golf, it felt therapeutic to spend hours at the range and on the course. She relished anticipating the next day, and the next. The road ahead was looking smoother, and she recognized her progress in dealing with the potholes, of which there would still be many.

One breath at a time, she reminded herself. Each day is a gift.

It will all work out.

DEAL #5

WEST	NORTH	EAST	SOUTH
			1NT
Pass	3NT	Pass	Pass
Pass			

North: ♠ 8 4 ♥ 10 5 3 ♦ A K 7 5 ♣ K J 9 6

DEALER:	SOUTH
VUL:	E-W
CONTRACT:	3NT
DECLARER:	SOUTH

West: ♠ K Q J 9 6 ♥ A 6 ♦ J 10 4 ♣ 7 4 2

NORTH
WEST EAST
SOUTH

East: ♠ 5 3 2 ♥ Q 9 8 2 ♦ 8 6 3 2 ♣ 5 3

South: ♠ A 10 7 ♥ K J 7 4 ♦ Q 9 ♣ A Q 10 8

SUGGESTED BIDDING

South opens 1NT with a balanced hand and 16 high-card points. West shouldn't come into the auction with a balanced hand, especially vulnerable. North, with 11 high-card points, has enough to raise to 3NT.

OPENING LEAD

West is on lead against 3NT and leads the ♠K, top of the solid sequence.

BRIDGE QUIZ:

Why is East key to defeating the contract when West's hand is so much stronger?

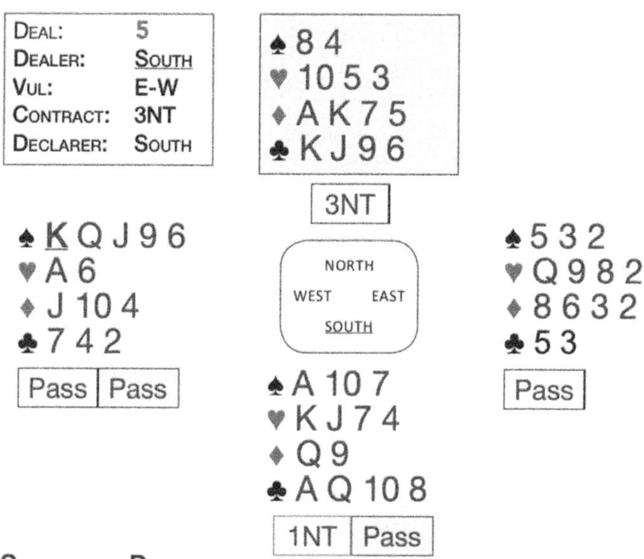

Suggested Defense

West leads the ♠K, top of touching cards from a solid sequence. That's a good lead, however, this deal is all about the diamonds. Declarer has eight tricks and needs only one more. It will come from the diamond suit if East discards a diamond when declarer takes the club winners. East must keep the same diamond length as dummy to prevent dummy's fourth diamond, the ♦7, from becoming a winner.

Suggested Play

Declarer has a spade, three diamonds, and four club tricks. Declarer's basic plan is to hold up the ♠A, until the third round and then hope to get a ninth trick by leading toward the ♥K. However, declarer should first take the club winners, keeping track of diamonds in case dummy's fourth diamond becomes a winner. Then there is no need to get a heart trick.

Conclusion

The defenders try to keep the same length in suits declarer might try to establish. On this deal, East is the only defender who can guard the diamond suit.

7

MARTI'S SOS – 1997

Some of the Bridge Club guessed Marti might say the end of her lengthy affair was her SOS, but she assured them they were mistaken. Their second guess was her marriage and divorce.

"That comes close," said Marti, with a somber tone to her voice. "But ... you'll see."

She was a twenty-year-old stewardess when the affair began in 1965, in the days before the term "flight attendant" became politically correct. She had the hourglass figure and naturally blond hair the airlines prized in those days, combined with a warm, welcoming smile. The Mommas and The Poppas rocked her playlist. Intuitively drawn to helping others and with a strong desire to see the world, there was no job she wanted more.

He was a pilot, or "Sky King," as the BC called him, seventeen years older, married with children.

Their chemistry was immediate and irresistible, and as the years passed the relationship grew as intense emotionally and intellectually as it was sexually. They had never been able to get enough of each other—ever. They imagined that under the right circumstances, theirs might have been a union of the most satisfying lifetime together. Ti-Ming. It simply was not meant to be, and the moment of truth eventually was faced.

When he turned fifty, his children grown, he was ready to divorce and commit himself to Marti. With shocking suddenness, Marti discovered she couldn't live with that reality. As sometimes happens in these situations, she knew his family well, and clearly she would always be the "other woman." She knew she wouldn't be able to handle the guilt. She also appreciated how connected he was to his children, even though his conjugal life was less than perfect. There would be a lot of pain that his family did not deserve. Realizing how much he was prepared to sacrifice for her suddenly made her very uncomfortable and the complexities became overwhelming. As strong as their passion was, ending his marriage simply was not the right option for her. Not that the affair had been the right thing either. But these things happen.

Sorting through these consuming feelings, Marti slowly admitted to herself that the guilt she felt about her lover leaving his family might be a cover. The truth was she was unable to commit to making the relationship legal and permanent now that the choice was offered. There had been an emotional safety zone knowing they could not be together during all those years, and she was shocked as she realized the truth about herself.

The affair had to end.

Shocked, but not really surprised. Marti knew deep inside that her childhood in foster homes had left its residue. She had worked hard to build a strong, confident personality around those insecurities, and she would depend on that now to move her forward. It wouldn't be without a struggle, she noted, as she welcomed her liberation one day and backpedaled with regret the next.

Taking a one-month leave of absence from Air Canada,

Marti began her personal "rehab." To everyone's surprise, she joined a friend who was going to volunteer in the north of India with a church group. That part of the world had suffered horrendous monsoons and help was needed in many ways. To be sure, it was an impulsive decision but one she never regretted. The lessons she learned from the local communities were etched deeply in her soul, and marked the beginning of her ongoing commitment to charity work as well as a fascination with that exotic continent.

She never faltered in her decision to end the affair, even when she cried herself to sleep as she settled into her spartan surroundings in a poverty-stricken village. The first few nights she may have wept for herself, but after that her tears were for the tragedy going on all around her in that devastated area. It was a vivid reminder that she had nothing to complain about.

Upon her return home, lessons learned from that life-altering experience, she made more changes in her life and resigned from the airline. For years a friend had been trying to convince her to become a partner in a small travel agency. Pooling all her savings along with a bank loan, Marti took the plunge. Her love of travel combined with the store of knowledge she had acquired through her years of flying made the work a joy. The effort to get established in that competitive business was a welcome challenge. She had never been one to shy away from risk.

As much as the BC had been aware of the affair, Marti had not drawn them deeply into the details. Throughout the years they had listened when the need was there. On occasion they had expressed their feelings and concerns to her, and she respected the dissenting voices and digested them all. They would talk about it when she felt the need, but Marti knew this was one of those choices for which she alone was accountable. She knew most of them did not want to pass judgment on it, and that was fine with her. Danielle had torn a strip off her more than once, as only she could, but the women were there if she needed them.

Eight years after the affair had ended she surprised everyone again, including herself. After a whirlwind, one-year courtship she was taking the leap into marriage. The BC's consensus was that this was not a union of deep love as much as romantic adventure combined with the thrill of the challenge, which was part of Marti's personality. Marti did not necessarily disagree.

The only challenge she went to great lengths to avoid was driving on winter roads. A frightening accident as a child had left an indelible scar, and the threat of black ice could reduce her to a catatonic state. Otherwise she was ready for anything and having just turned forty she thought perhaps it was time to try marriage.

As daring as she was, she was not reckless or thoughtless. Marti made decisions carefully and stuck to them, a trait borne of hurt and insecurity in her early childhood before she was rescued by a fairy godmother.

Her husband-to-be, Carlos, was a twice-divorced father of two very dear daughters, aged eight and ten at the time of the marriage. A handsome, charming adventurer who definitely had a way with women, he could smooth-talk his way out of any argument without resolving the problem. Or, as was more often the case, he just refused to discuss the problem—full stop.

That was a major red flag as far as the BC was concerned. Marti was convinced she could handle it and in time change it. She was an optimist and figured the wrinkles would smooth out after they were married in spite of the warnings of her more experienced friends.

"We're telling you, Marti—and you can see we're all on the same page here—if you marry this guy with such obvious problems, they're only going to get worse. Good grief! We know you get this. Pay attention to it!" Cass warned, drawing on her own history.

"No kidding," added Jane. "Lots of people have emotional baggage but he's got a full set of Samsonite luggage—including the steamer trunk!"

Bonnie placed her finger and thumb to her temple to mimic a trigger being pulled on a gun. "It's not going to go well, Mar. I can feel it."

"Why not live together for a while and see how that plays out?" asked Pam. "Hopefully you'll prove us all wrong."

Unfortunately that wasn't an option, as Marti had explained to them. "Nope, it's all or nothing. He doesn't want to put up with the flack from his ex. She won't tolerate a live-in situation for the girls. She doesn't want them subjected to a bunch of revolving door relationships. Quite frankly, this is one time when I can see her point."

At the age of forty, Marti had reached a financially comfortable place in her life, the result of hard work and successful investment in the travel business along with a small inheritance. She was proud of her efforts and of this feeling of security in her life after many years of serious budgeting. There was no problem cutting back on her office hours now to devote time to her new relationship.

Spunky from childhood and in spite of her early abandonment issues, she had grown into a smart, funny dynamo. Marti had always wanted to be a mother but gradually accepted it was not in the cards. She hadn't really thought of playing the role of stepmother but quickly developed a close relationship with her stepdaughters and felt fulfilled by it. Suggestions from the BC that she was perhaps marrying the girls rather than the father were deftly deflected.

He was a charmer, the BC unanimously admitted, and they hoped their initial resistance to the marriage was unwarranted.

In spite of his poor marital track record, Carlos offered her a life she felt they would both happily share. In spite of everything, she cared for him deeply and wanted to commit herself in every way to a strong union. She almost saw it as a mission to provide this man with a happy, loving marriage after his two disastrous experiences. Naively perhaps, she thought this was what he wanted and had missed in his life.

Besides, he was her brother-in-law's tennis partner and her sister thought they would make a great match, so she had encouraged the relationship every step of the way.

It wasn't until the second of his daughters left for university, shortly after their ninth wedding anniversary, that she felt the dramatic shift in their relationship. She began to suspect that she had just been needed to provide a solid maternal influence for his girls. Now they were gone most of the time, Carlos seemed to become a different person—and not in a good way.

The last straw came after several months of strange cell phone calls and late evenings with "the guys." In more than one instance the evenings had been proven false by innocent exchanges in conversations. While attempting to have an honest discussion, which for him had never been an easy undertaking, heated words filled the air. Marti had previously been loath to voice her suspicions and she chided herself for this avoidance. The problem was that she had never been in such a position before and she did not know how to deal with feelings of betrayal by someone she had chosen, as an adult, to love and trust.

There was no turning back, though, when the following episode occurred early one evening in their spacious restored Victoria townhouse.

"I hate to hear myself saying these words, but I think you've been cheating."

Slamming his fist on the coffee table, he growled, "I'm not having an affair, if that's what you're saying!" He glared at her in the way that always caused her confused pain. "For Christ's sake, grow up, Marti. No man's going to turn down a quickie, married or not!"

What led to this calamitous moment had been the discovery of a condom in his suit pocket when Marti was preparing to take it to the cleaners. At first he blatantly denied it belonged to him, and then, realizing how totally ridiculous that was, he launched into this even more ludicrous tirade.

Struggling to believe her ears, she had asked, "Are you including yourself in that bizarre statement?"

"I sure am," he responded smugly, "and why should you care as long as I always come home to you? "

Relating it to the group later, she said she had sensed a look of something like pride on his face when he spat out his response. It was like a punch in the stomach, not the first that she'd gotten, but it would be the last. He had spoken to her in an angry, hurtful way a number of times over the years, and each time she had been astounded by the painful physical as well as emotional effect. Any time she had attempted to explain this to him, he would just shrug it off and tell her it was her problem.

Jane spoke through her frown, drumming her fingers on the arm of her chair. "Such a charming guy, and I mean that. It was totally a surprise when you first started telling us about this other side to him. I know we predicted there would be problems, but I don't think any of us thought it would be like this."

Nodding slowly with a veil of sadness slipping across her face, Marti agreed. "Yes, he's charming and has a lot of good qualities. I had such hopes for our marriage. This really has been devastating. The sense of betrayal has been the most overwhelming emotion. It's simply something I would never have looked for or expected. I'm probably reacting like a little kid, but I'm having a bitch of a time with it and my pride is hurt to think he'd want to have sex with someone else. I thought he loved having sex with me. I can't believe how stupid and naive I was."

"But Marti, he said that this other sex didn't mean anything," said Dee, offering her assessment.

Marti sighed. "Well that says to me that sex in general doesn't mean anything to him then. It's candy to him. I can't accept that. It's very obvious to me now that our definitions of love and the commitment one makes in marriage are very different. Living in a marriage by his terms is pointless as far as I'm concerned. He should simply get himself a housekeeper and then screw whoever he wants whenever he wants."

Bonnie spoke up as she walked to the bar to pour another mineral water. "I always was really fond of Carlos—suspicious but fond—which shows what a sweet talker he could be. I'd like to dropkick him for putting you through all this. It just goes to show how adept some people are at presenting themselves as something they are not. He's obviously all charm and no substance, if that's how little he respects you."

"You know, Bo, I don't think it's that he didn't respect me. I think he does love me in his own way. I think he feels that this type of behavior is perfectly acceptable and that it doesn't affect our relationship. Remember what an emotionally dysfunctional history he has. He thinks it's fine to behave this way—lying and deceiving. He doesn't understand how it affects my feelings about him—and about myself, for heaven's sake. I suspect he has always thought this way and we never talked about it until he got ... caught!"

"*Putain*!" muttered Danielle.

"Really! Let me see if I get it," Dee said, always wanting to have the facts straight. "Basically he has told you that he didn't do anything wrong when he was doing stuff you didn't know about. So if he is what other people call unfaithful and you don't know about it then it's okay?"

"You mean, as in what you don't know won't hurt you? This

is getting too bizarre for me," muttered Lynn. "Just give me good old-fashioned values, thank you very much."

"Boring as it sounds, that works for me too," agreed Dee.

At this point, Cass, having returned only weeks before from her eight-year sail-about, spoke up: "You know, the concept of monogamy has been instilled in the West as the only ethical form of marriage. Things are changing—that's for sure—but basically it's how we've been socialized, and it's a value we've embraced as a society. The truth is there are many cultures that have different ideas about it. I'm here to tell you, I heard many opposing opinions and beliefs in many corners of the globe when Dirk and I were traveling. It's a universal issue."

"And yet, here I am," said Marti, pretending to put a noose around her neck and pull it, "exhibit number one—guilty as charged for carrying on an affair with a married man in my past life. Now I'm unable to accept being on the receiving end of infidelity. What goes around, comes around, I guess."

"But Marti," argued Cass, "don't you think that when you committed yourself to marriage you did so based on the values with which you were raised? The values that I recall plagued you during all those years of your affair?"

"In fact, I remember you being very clear when you became engaged that you were elated to build a relationship based on those strong values and not be consumed by guilt as you were in the past," added Pam. "It meant a lot to you and kind of allowed you to make amends for the affair."

Marti absorbed their words and chose hers carefully. "Everything you're saying is right on the mark. I feel like a hypocrite when I compare my past behavior. At the same time, my commitment to this marriage was a hundred percent in every way. I feel like such a dummy for not paying attention to the warning signs before we married, and you all have every right to say 'We told you so'!"

Bonnie stood up. Waving her arms like an orchestra

conductor, she cued the group. "Okay, ladies, on the count of three."

"WE TOLD YOU SO!"

Smiling weakly, Marti shook her head.

Bo was at her side with a hug. "Hey, we're trying to inject a little humor here. You know how badly we all feel about the entire mess."

"And we're well aware," said Danielle, "how happy you were to think you could give Carlos the kind of marriage he claimed he hoped for this time around. To discover he didn't mean that or doesn't appreciate it is a painful betrayal of what he presented to you in the beginning."

As her shoulders collapsed with disappointment, Marti summed it up: "I finally saw that we didn't share the values I thought we did. For the first time I forced myself to acknowledge there was another side to him, one that I had glimpsed but pretended I didn't. I realized he's probably been deceiving me from day one. That's when I found the strength to say I wasn't the woman for him, and he was not the man I thought he was. Way too much water under that bridge. Time to move on."

After that night, Marti moved into a spare room at Bonnie's until she could make some plans for herself and begin to shake off the painful disappointment that engulfed her. Since they both loved all the oldies, they would keep the music going for hours and she would sing her heartbreak along with Roy Orbison or crank up Tina Turner and belt out "What's Love Got to Do With It?" I mean, really, she said to Bo, who needs a heart when a heart can be broken? Bonnie had been asking herself that for years. She could have written those lyrics.

That had been a year earlier.

It's too bad the divorce wasn't her SOS, because it got juicier as more information surfaced. However, she dealt with it and had strong support from her sister, who was horrified, and other close friends, as well as the BC.

It turned out Marti had decided her SOS was a decision she made in the aftermath of her divorce. It was something she felt uncomfortable discussing with anyone except the BC and began one evening as they were gathered at Danielle's house in Moore Park.

The stereo was playing Paul McCartney's newest release and they were all saying how he just didn't sound as good these days, although he was still looking pretty hot. There was nothing to compare to his Beatles days, they commiserated.

"Okay, turn the volume down please. I need the floor. I'm struggling with something here," Marti said as she stood in the middle of the room.

"*Mon tabarnac de ciboire de Saint Sulpice*!" Danielle cursed, "Marti, you haven't changed your mind about Carlos, have you?" Her unusually loud outburst indicated the level of her concern.

"Oh Dani, you know that's my favorite curse of yours! It has such a ring to it." Marti laughed. "Of course not. I haven't looked back once."

"Has Lance the King of Romance," as they had taken to calling him, "made any overtures at reconciliation?" asked Lynn.

"He did suggest we try counseling, which made me laugh out loud."

"Hey, if it looks like a duck, walks like a duck, yadda yadda yadda," was Bo's comment, eliciting laughs and a few quacks around the room.

"He'll never find another woman like you, Martha Elaine," declared Lynn.

Shaking her head with disdain, Marti reached for her drink and lifted it high. "I'm not sure he even wants to, my friends. Good luck to him."

They clinked their glasses to toast the end of something that probably had never even actually existed in the first place.

"I'm not saying it doesn't hurt to acknowledge all this, but when his reaction to my pain was to tell me to get over it, it made my decision somewhat easier. I have no interest in spending my time in that kind of hurtful relationship."

"How are the girls taking it?" asked Pam, who had gotten to know them quite well when Marti brought them out her way to pick apples and berries on occasion.

Marti's deep hazel eyes brightened as she smiled. "They've been really mature about it. In fact, they seem to be very understanding. They've observed some behaviors of their father that, as the young women they are now, they haven't found too appealing. They love him as a dad, of course, but can see where I'm coming from."

"It was obvious to me over the years," Pam interrupted, "that the girls loved and respected you, Marti. So I'm sure your credibility is high with them."

"Thanks Pam," Marti continued. "They've got good values. Dishonesty and deception in any aspect of life are not part of their expectations either. Once they were reassured that my relationship with them wouldn't change in any way, they relaxed about us ending the marriage."

"They must have been sad though," said Lynn.

"Oh for sure," Marti agreed, "but they realize I'm divorcing him, not them. We have a bond and a love that will continue, and for that I am so thankful. After all, they're the family I never had."

Bo signaled a time-out with her hands, obviously wanting to get back to Marti's earlier comment. "Okay, enough of the sad story. It's done and we've moved on, right? Not to be insensitive, but we did deal with this when it happened."

"Absolutely right, enough is enough," Marti agreed, happy to change the subject.

"So what's the powwow about?" Bonnie pressed on.

Leaping to her feet, Marti turned her back to them briefly and then twirled around with her hands pressed to the side of her face. "Get it?" she asked. Everyone looked at her quizzically. Some laughed. Others just shook their heads.

"Mar, to be honest you never have been very good at charades! What are you getting at?" Dee asked with a completely confused look.

Plopping herself back down in her chair and making a face, Marti groaned, "God I wish I still smoked! I would love to light up right now! Oh, but then I might not be able to do what I'm thinking of doing. So..."

"So ... what?" Jane asked.

Cass crumpled up a paper cocktail napkin and threw it at Marti, "Will you tell us what this is all about?"

"You're making us crazy!" shrieked Danielle.

"I'm making *me* crazy too! I cannot believe I feel so self-conscious telling you about this! Honestly, I feel like I'm being so self-absorbed. So narcissistic. So ... so ... anti-feminist! All right, here it is. I'm considering having a facelift."

With an air of exaggerated disappointment, Cass asked, "That's what all the drama was about?"

"No biggie there, Marti," said Pam, palms outstretched and relieved this was all that had been on Marti's mind.

"Go for it—after careful research as to who does the work, of course!" was Dee's typically cautious response.

Marti sat up straighter, nodding as she did. "So you don't think I'm a nut bar or completely into myself? I've been so reluctant to say the words out loud."

"Oh God, Mar, just promise me you won't end up looking like Goldie Hawn in that movie. Remember those lips?" Cass reminded her with a grin.

Laughing and nodding, Marti gestured with her hands as she shook her head. "No overblown lips. I promise!"

"Vanity, thy name is woman," intoned Bonnie. "Even though it was probably some beauty editor and definitely not Shakespeare who said this, it seems to fit."

"Guilty as charged," laughed Marti, "just slap a big V on my forehead!"

"You're not alone," Danielle piped in. "I've got friends who've done Botox, lipo, and these new injectables that help to diminish some facial lines. I'm talking about several different people. None of them had a bad experience, although a couple of friends who tried Botox decided not to do it again because they didn't like the look it gave them."

"But I know a few who love it," countered Marti.

Pam added, "Lots of people are doing stuff like that, and not just women. I've been reading a lot about it, but I'm too chicken to try anything. Apparently a lot of men are going for different procedures too."

Looking around sheepishly, Lynn admitted, "I wasn't supposed to tell a soul about this, but I know it won't leave this room. Jim had his eyes done last year because he was getting huge bags under them. It was driving him crazy! He's always in front of staff giving presentations and was becoming self-conscious about it. I encouraged him to see someone and he finally reached a point where he couldn't stand it anymore and just did it. I'll give you the name of the surgeon he went to if you like. We were both thrilled with the results. I've been thinking about doing the same thing myself, so there you go Marti. I may follow your example!"

"Omigawd Lynn, you're the last one I'd ever imagine doing anything," Pam said. "Talk about feeling comfortable in your own skin. You lost thirty pounds last year on the South Beach diet, let your hair go gray—"

"And of course it didn't go mousey gray but turned out that fab shade of silver. You are gutsy," Danielle agreed. "With that edgy haircut, you're looking great."

"That's what I mean!" exclaimed Marti. "You've got it all working for you, but I don't feel like I do. I just feel old and tired when I look in the mirror and that's what I want to change."

With a big smile and shy acknowledgment, Lynn nodded and admitted she felt really fortunate most of the time, but that didn't mean there weren't things she might someday address. She agreed Jim had felt the same way Marti had just described, and that's why he had his eyes done.

Shaking her finger at Lynn, Jane jokingly chastised her, "I can't believe you didn't say anything to us."

"Well I must admit I almost blabbed a couple of times, but he did it right before we went on vacation for two weeks last year, and when we got back he just looked so natural it kept slipping my mind. Honestly, the whole thing was a piece of cake—just a little bruising and the stitches heal in a few days. We were astounded. When he came back and went into work with his tan, everyone just thought he looked terrific and well rested! Hardly anyone guessed he had any work done!"

"And remember when I got my braces three years ago at the ripe old age of forty-seven?" Danielle reminded her. "That was strictly an ego thing—purely for cosmetic reasons after all those years."

"You agonized over that for thirty years, right, Dani?" teased Bo.

"*Tabarnac*! Talk about procrastinating!" Danielle laughed.

Marti was looking increasingly relieved as she listened to the chatter.

"If you want it and can afford it and have checked out the reputation of the surgeon, then do it," Dee encouraged.

"And what brought this on?" floated out from somewhere in the room.

Marti paused. She truly didn't have to think about her answer, as she had been over it so many times in her head, but this was the first time she had said it out loud, and she hoped it didn't sound shallow and self-serving. "Two things really. This whole marital meltdown seriously tested my self-confidence. So much of my past history has been based on my looks. I keep wondering if getting older was part of the problem in our marriage."

"You've always been your own worst critic, underneath that surface of bravado", Jane broke in, "in spite of the reality."

"True enough, Janey, and I know these feelings can be a natural reaction of women going through divorce, especially when the husband has had a wandering eye."

"Let's not discuss which eye was wandering," Cass muttered, prompting snorts.

Making a face, Marti continued, "The other thing is, like I said before, every time I look in the mirror now I see a face that's old and tired looking back. Yet I've got tons of energy. I feel young and healthy inside."

"I know what you mean," echoed from more than one chair.

"Well, I just don't want to feel that way. I'm not ready. It's not about denying my age. It doesn't bother me at all to tell someone how old I am. It's just a number after all. Although ... fifty? Yikes! That did grate on me a bit."

"You know," said Lynn, fanning herself frantically as she wiped her dripping brow, "turning forty bothered me more than turning fifty. That was before I was cursed with these bloody hot flashes. If I'd realized how horrible they were going to be, I'd have made sure I appreciated my forties more!"

Jane seconded that, since she and Lynn shared the dubious honor of experiencing the worst hot flashes. At least they'd been able to commiserate and exchange whatever remedies they heard about from other women. The only person who had been absolutely no help was Pam, who had sailed right through menopause without one hot flash or any other side effect. She almost felt guilty about it!

"Well, I have to admit I feel lucky that my flashes finally stopped," Marti said, nodding. "I can't complain about that anymore."

"Marti, you're always at the gym and involved in sports. You know your body is in darn good shape."

Flexing her biceps, Marti laughed. "Thanks, Dee. Now I just want to feel as good about my face. I'm tired of the 1950 look."

"The 1950 look? What on earth is that?" asked Pam.

"That, my friends, is when a guy walks by you from the back and thinks you look nineteen but then sees you're actually fifty when he gets to the front ... and his expression shows it. Not a nice feeling!"

After they stopped laughing, Marti continued. "Actually, what started this whole idea was a bitching session during a workout at the gym with my best friend in the whole world—"

"Wanda Woman!" a chorus interrupted, using a nickname they had for Marti's good friend, a high-achieving wonder woman in every aspect of her life.

"Of course!" laughed Marti.

"And?"

Cass interrupted, "Wanda Scott is gorgeous—at least she was the last time I saw her. Come to think about it, it's been a few years, but I'm sure she hasn't changed much. Don't tell me she's thinking about having one as well?""

"Yup, she feels the same way I do about her reflection in the mirror."

"I've always said those huge gym mirrors need to be removed," muttered Dee.

"Besides that," Marti continued, "she has another motivating factor. Her son is getting married next year and she's determined to look as good as her ex-husband's new trophy wife!"

There were all sorts of comments about how Wanda would look better than anyone any time, but Marti went on to explain they were both on the same page with their decision. "You know, it all comes down to how you feel about yourself, right? No matter what anyone else says. The bottom line is that it's a very self-centered decision—but in a good way, I think. It's about feeling happy with yourself outside as well as inside."

"Marti, you're so right. Some of us are going to be happy with the way we age and feel comfortable living with the wrinkles and some of us aren't. Some of us are going to be able to afford to do something if we want to and some of us aren't. That's the way it is. We might feel fine with ourselves now and in a few months or years that could change—or not. Who knows? Whichever way it unfolds, so to speak, is fine," offered Lynn.

"Absolutely," agreed Cass as she lightly played her fingers over her face. "I actually feel a warped sense of affection when I look at some of these lines on my face and remember the sun and wind and experiences that put them there—the laugh lines and worry lines all mixed in together. Kinda the story of my life. But that's just me!"

"God knows this business of aging can be the pits," chimed in Pam. "Marti, check with your surgeon to see if he does eyebrow transplants. Mine are disappearing so fast I can't believe it! You know how we used to comment about older women with those wild, penciled eyebrows?"

"I thought it was just an old-fashioned makeup technique," said Jane. "I can remember watching my grandmother outlining hers when I was a kid. It was quite fascinating then."

"Well," continued Pam, "now I realize their eyebrows had thinned out, turned white and seemed to vanish. Nobody warned me about it though! "

"Mine are disappearing at an alarming rate too," said Bonnie, sending the group into wild laughter as she finished, "but I know what's happening to them. They're growing inward and coming out my chin!"

"Speaking of chins ... on second thought, let's not even go there!" Cass said as she straightened her posture.

"Forget chins, how about our necks? What's going on there?" muttered Dee as she ran her hands over her neck, pulling the skin back and looking hopefully in the mirror behind the sofa. "Turtlenecks and scarves are becoming staples in my wardrobe."

"While we're making comparisons, I'm starting to look like Little Lulu!" said Danielle, as everyone chuckled at the memory of that old comic book character and the absurd suggestion of any likeness. "No eyelashes! I need a magnifying mirror to put on my mascara these days."

"Little Lulu! You have to be our age to remember who she is," Pam nodded.

"One of my all-time favorite comic books!" recalled Bonnie. "And you're right, Dani, come to think about it—she didn't have eyelashes."

"Not when her eyes were open, at least. If I remember correctly," Dee added.

"Jeez, this conversation is really taking a turn for the worse. We're all going to be making appointments with Marti's doctor by the end of the evening!"

This was just the beginning of a long, loud, laughter-filled dinner that covered practically every imaginable topic of women's aging woes. It ended with a pledge that if any one of them were hospitalized for an extended time or in a coma, the BC would make regular visits with tweezers.

Bonnie summed it up: "None of us want to discover we've been lying there looking like a billy goat!"

"Eewww!" echoed around the room.

Marti filled the girls in on the rest of the details. "Wanda and I have a mutual friend who is the cosmetic surgery queen. We've known her for years and she always looks very natural. She's not a raving beauty, just a basic attractive woman who looks like she is aging gracefully without bags and sags. It's a very nice look. So she's our consultant and has given us the names of two doctors to interview. Both have excellent reps, of course, and we'll go with the one with whom we feel most comfortable."

"Sounds like a plan," Danielle confirmed with a clap of her hands.

"How have your daughters reacted to all of this? And your sister?" Pam asked.

Closing her eyes, Marti shook her head. "That's the thing. I can't bring myself to tell anyone else. I'm really quite embarrassed to say anything to anyone except you, and as you can see, this wasn't easy for me."

"You haven't told your sister? You tell her everything!" Cass said.

Marti shook her head vigorously and poured another glass of wine with a slight tremor in her hand.

"She's the last one I'll tell. As open-minded as she normally is, she's so dead against cosmetic surgery she will be furious with me and totally unsupportive. I'm sure she would use all of her arguing skills to talk me out of it. I can't risk telling her until it is a *fait accompli*. Even then I'm sure I'll be in for a tongue lashing!"

With a look of determination in her eyes, she continued, "So I'm relying on you for support through this, and then I'll just tell everyone else I had my eyes done or had a haircut or something. I'll deal with that part later."

Struggling to speak through her laughter, Bonnie stammered, "H-h-had a haircut? Earth to Marti, somehow I don't think anyone will buy that one!"

With that Bo was off, hooting as only she could do. Once she got started, it wouldn't have mattered if the Queen herself were in the room.

Marti acknowledged she might have to come up with a better explanation.

Becoming serious again, Pam asked, "Marti, are you sure about this? I've seen some awful things on the tube about surgeries gone wrong."

Danielle added, "Why risk it? The bottom line is that we can't stop the aging process. It's going to happen no matter what. We all know you don't derive your self-worth from your body image—"

"Yes I do!" Marti interrupted as the others laughed. "Sorry, Dan, I couldn't resist. Please go on."

"Well", Danielle continued, "I was going to blather on about looking on the inside, because that's where our true beauty is ... yadda, yadda, yadda ... looking for an argument to convince you not to do it. But I know that's not the issue. I just think it's kind of scary."

After a thoughtful pause, Marti nodded in agreement, choosing her words carefully. "I know there have been some real disasters, and I've been through all of those conversations with the other women I spoke to who've had work done. Honestly, Wanda and I have done our homework, as you would expect. Procedures have made tremendous advances in the last ten years. I've talked to several women lately who've had all sorts of things worked on and they are all glad they did it. I haven't talked to one person who had anything more serious than nausea from the anesthetic or some lingering numbness in the scalp. Obviously they've chosen their surgeons well."

Jane, who had been quietly listening, suddenly spoke up. "This is like *déjà vu*, no kidding. Sam and I were at a party last weekend and everyone there was our age or older. After dinner we all—men and women—ended up totally involved in a conversation just like this. I couldn't believe it. Everybody's doing it!"

Marti was bouncing with enthusiasm now. "Exactly! The

good thing about that is how much information there is available. You can actually get references to doctors from people you trust, and you can see for yourself the work they've done. Someone else has been the guinea pig, thank you very much!"

"Okay, Mar," Pam said, "just tell us what we need to do and we're in! Right girls? You wouldn't be at this point in the decision making if you hadn't looked into every aspect of it. That we know."

"Not so fast!" Dee was on her feet pacing and looking concerned. "I'm not sure I agree with this, Marti. I'm worried about you. I think it's risky and I don't think you need it. Just stick to age-defying creams or whatever! You look just fine as you are. What if something horrible happens?"

Marti stood, halting her friend in mid-pace, and placed her hands on Dee's shoulders. "You are always the worrier. I did struggle with the same fears, but like I said, polling all those women who without exception have been really pleased helped me turn the corner on this. Having Wanda along on the adventure makes a big difference too, because we keep boosting each other's confidence in this. Needless to say, knowing you guys are behind me is a critical factor too. Why don't you come to the doctor's with me in case you have questions I won't think of?"

"You know," said Jane, "that's a super idea! Dee, do it. It will help you and Marti and make all of us feel better about it."

The doctor appointments were kept, concerns were addressed, and the date was set for the main event. The conversations were numerous in the following weeks as they all did their best to help Marti maintain her positive attitude about her decision. She was so accustomed to putting herself out for others that it was surprisingly difficult for her to feel enthused about making a choice that served only her purposes and her ego.

"Why am I beating myself up about this so much?" she

moaned to the girls at the next Bridge Club evening. "I really, really, really want to do this. I'm sure I'll be happy when it's over. I know lots of women my age do it. It's not such a big deal, but I'm making it one, and I'm driving myself bonkers!"

"Just think how pleased you'll be with the results, how good you'll feel about yourself," Jane tried to reassure her.

"Well, I must admit there's no doubt I'll be thrilled to see a face peering back at me that looks as rested and energetic as I feel," Marti agreed.

The clinic, in an elegant downtown hotel, had been there for decades, establishing a solid reputation. Because Marti and Wanda wanted their procedures done on the same day, they had to wait for openings two months away. That meant two months of everyone doing their best to talk Marti through any anxieties, but they were few and far between.

There were many hilarious cards on the market about women and their looks as they aged, so in true BC fashion it became a game to see who could send her the most outrageous one. In addition to the cards, they also found some excellent articles about cosmetic surgery, both for and against. Marti decided to put them all in a scrapbook, and by the time her surgery date arrived, she had a compilation that they joked about publishing.

The game plan was to check into special rooms booked by the clinic the night before, have surgery early the next morning, and stay over again that night to ensure no post-op issues caused any problems. After five days, the stitches around the eyes would begin to dissolve, and after a week to ten days the other stitches and staples (yikes) would come out. By the end of two to three weeks, the final result would be there for the world to see. Although it would be months before the full benefit of this kind of surgery really was obvious.

Cass had offered to stay at the clinic with her, and everyone agreed her nursing days equipped her to be the least affected by blood, barf, and other such pleasantries.

Marti gratefully accepted her offer and added, "Aren't you glad you stopped sailing around the world so you could come back to this exciting life, Cass? I'm so glad you're home!"

Cass responded with a thumbs-up. "You ladies always make life interesting, and I owe you all big-time for everything you did for me when we were floating about. It's payback time for me. Let me see if I have the details straight. Wanda Woman's husband will be staying with her, and they'll be in the room next to us, right?"

"Right! We can compare notes and see how each of us is handling the post-op. Wanda says she always bruises, so she is expecting to look pretty bad. I hardly ever bruise, so hopefully I'll breeze through," Marti said, her usual confidence returning.

"The nurses were telling us that most often it's a girlfriend or two that comes along to stay with the patient, as a lot of men just can't deal with it. I guess they'll look pretty scary at first," Cass reported to the rest of them. She had replaced Dee at the last appointment to make sure she had the picture of what to expect when taking care of Marti.

"I've just had a great idea!" Marti said excitedly, leaping to her feet. "Why don't all of you come down to the hotel the night before and we'll have a girls' night out. Bring a good movie and we'll order up room service. Well, you will order up room service. I won't be able to eat after 7 p.m. because of the anesthetic. But I can still party on bubbly water with Bo! Say you will—it'll be fun!"

That was all the convincing they needed.

Since it wasn't actually a Bridge Club night, Wanda was invited to hang out with them for a while. Laughingly she acknowledged the honor. Knowing the BC well anyway, she milked the situation for all it was worth, exclaiming how she realized what a privilege it was to be included in their presence. Bowing, they graciously confirmed how right she was!

They had decided to make it a booze-free evening in honor of the two patients, which didn't affect the hilarity one bit.

"This just goes to prove what we always like to say: 'You don't need to drink to have a good time,'" Danielle reminded them, words they often jokingly repeated but which had first been stated at a party in their early years when they were all very much in the bag.

"Haven't we proven that more than once over the years? Especially me now," Bo laughed.

Wanda's husband arrived around nine, and once she bade the group goodnight, the cards came out for an hour or so.

"This is the best way to take my mind off tomorrow, girls. Deal 'em up! I'm so glad you all decided to come down!"

The first surgery was scheduled for 7 a.m., and Marti would be the next one rolled into the operating room at noon. She and Wanda figured they would be comparing notes around six o'clock.

It just goes to show how some things simply can't be predicted. At six in the afternoon, Marti was on her knees embracing the porcelain pony as she threw up non-stop, and Wanda was in the underground shopping arcade browsing with her husband. It was unbelievable. Marti was groaning to Cass she thought she was going to die while, true to form, the Wanda Woman was trying on a new outfit, wearing a pair of sunglasses, with a scarf covering the bandage on her head. They did have a good laugh about it after the fact.

Marti's nausea subsided during the evening. With the help of a sedative she had a decent sleep and felt better the next morning—until she looked in the mirror. If she could have reversed the clock twenty-four hours, she would have cancelled the surgery and never looked back. Her first reaction was horror as she stared at her bruised and swollen face. It was such a bizarre sensation looking into the mirror at this woman she refused to acknowledge as herself. On the reflection before her, she noticed narrow slits above her puffy cheeks where her big bright eyes normally resided. A few brown stitches were visible at the corners, pockets of blood pooled under her now pale skin where bruises were already beginning to form, and her entire head was covered with a bandage that made her look like a ghostly snake charmer.

A snake charmer that had been hit head on by a bus! she thought.

Wanda had enjoyed a peaceful sleep (thanks to some great sex with her husband, in direct contradiction to the doctor's orders) and was astounded to discover the next morning that she had virtually no bruising. Go figure. The bandage, she had to admit, was definitely not making a fashion statement, but she could live with it. She and her husband waited with Cass for Marti to finish her post-op examination with the surgeon.

"So Cass, what do you think? Marti had such a terrible reaction to the anesthetic, didn't she? When I talked to her on the phone this morning she did not sound good."

"Noooo, she definitely was not a happy camper this morning."

Minutes later Marti emerged from the office and tried to squeeze out a smile. "Just keep telling me I'm going to be gorgeous—or at least somewhat normal. I'll be happy with that! That's all I want to hear, over and over and over. Thank you very much. Wanda, you almost look gorgeous now, you bitch. In fact, compared to me you look downright stunning!" They all laughed, hugged, and headed for valet parking.

"I want you to know I feel like shit and wish I had never done this!" moaned Marti. "Just get me home, so I can pull the drapes and sleep for the next five days. Take all the mirrors down, please Cass, and absolutely no visitors! Wanda, you have to call me every day to give me a pep talk."

"Of course, without fail," Wanda promised.

Cass waved good-bye as she helped Marti into the car, with the reminder they would pick up Wanda for the next appointment in five days.

Taking a week of vacation, the plan was for Cass to stay at Marti's until she had the first two appointments. After that she would take Marti to Muskoka, where Cass had been living and working for a couple of months now, for a two-week recovery period. She would be busy with her job but still have time to keep Marti company for a good part of each day. Cass or Lynn, who lived a half-hour away, would drive her back down to the city for the next appointment in two weeks.

Those first five days were a struggle for Marti. She avoided looking at herself in the mirror and kept her eyes down when she was at the sink. Bedrest and a diet of liquids for two days and then a shift to soft solids for another couple of days were part of the regime. The antibiotics caused her stomach to feel a bit off and she was happy to snooze as often as she could. Cass turned the phone off and just checked it regularly to respond to messages so Marti wouldn't be disturbed. Marti stuck to her "No Visitors" rule and passed the time watching TV, reading, or playing cribbage and Scrabble with Cass.

As promised, Wanda called every day and Marti spoke with her when Cass returned the call. However the chat didn't make Marti feel any better as she listened to how her friend was breezing through her recuperation.

"Wanda, I'm happy for you but you are really pissing me off," Marti told her. "I can't tell you how awful I feel—and look."

Cass had confessed to a few of the girls that she was a bit concerned about how things were going. "I guess it takes more time than I thought," she said, "because the swelling and bruising still don't look much better, but I'm probably being paranoid. I hope everything is all right. "

The five-day follow-up appointment went very well, according to the doctor. He kept repeating how pleased he was with the way everything was healing and how happy Marti was going to be with the final result. She still was not convinced, particularly since her face had turned into an abstract canvas of red, blue and purple. The bruising was massive and absolutely shocking to her. The doctor once again reassured her. Right.

Now that the bandage was unwrapped from her head and she was able to wash her hair, she began to feel human again. The swelling around her eyes was slowly subsiding, but she still looked like The Creature From the Black Lagoon as far as she was concerned.

Three days later Marti returned to have the balance of the stitches and staples removed. She was up and about now, although her activities were very limited—doctor's orders. He stressed how important it was to take it easy and give her face time to heal. Nothing more strenuous than going for quiet walks was allowed. Marti hadn't anticipated how extensive the work had been and how much healing had to happen. It wasn't as easy for her as it was for Wanda, she told the doctor, and he reiterated how everyone responds differently and that Marti's experience was not out of the norm. She would try not to worry, she promised herself.

"I have to say," admitted Cass as they loaded the car to drive up to Muskoka, "I definitely was not prepared for you to look this scary!" They attempted to find some humor in the situation and Marti's upbeat nature began to reappear. The more distance they put between themselves and the city, the more relaxed she felt.

Cass chuckled as she applied more pressure to the accelerator. "It's an interesting thing about this drive, isn't it? Even in the middle of summer when the congestion is the pits and everyone is crawling along, just the knowledge that you're headed to cottage country is all it takes to put you in a good mood. But it's so much more a pleasure to sail through at this time of year."

"That and of course a stop at Webers on the way," agreed Marti. "After being on that restricted diet for the past few days, I'm starving!" They fist-pumped and discussed what today's order would include at the popular roadside stop.

"You'll have to go in for me though. I'm not ready to face the world yet."

"No worries about that," Cass quickly agreed. "I wouldn't want you to cause a stampede when the customers see you walk in."

"The Return of Frankenstein's Bride—in living color..." Marti murmured.

After stuffing themselves with Webers' distinctive burgers "with sautéed onions, tomatoes, lettuce, and mayo—hold the fries!" and creamy chocolate milkshakes, they carried on eager to reach their destination.

The last hour of the drive flew by. Soon they were quickly settled with a blazing fire in the woodstove and a book in hand ... and not long before they both were sound asleep where they sat. The tone for the recuperation period was set. The doctor's orders had been strict.

They had a fine time relaxing at the boathouse. Watching spring begin to transform the winter palette around the rocky shores of Lake Muskoka, they waited for Marti's face to be transformed as well. In spite of the cold packs she was applying, it was a slow process and now she was noticing a lack of feeling in some parts of her face. A worried phone call to the doctor's office had again brought reassurances, but Marti was still concerned.

"Maybe this surgery wasn't such a good idea after all," she muttered to Cass. "How long should this be taking? From what I've read, I should be looking much better. Wanda is back at her office, for God's sake, and I'm still not fit for public viewing. I'm getting paranoid that something went wrong."

"Marti, you've got to be patient," Cass reminded her. "Your surgeon has an excellent reputation. Look how his office calls every couple of days to see how you are doing. That's very impressive. If they thought things weren't going well, they'd have you back down there in a flash."

When she wasn't fretting about how her facelift was going to turn out, Marti took advantage of the time she had to herself to quietly take stock of her life. For reasons she was searching to discover, she felt the desire for change. She was also enjoying working her way through the stack of books she had brought with her. At other times she could be found reading bridge books and laying out hands that she and Cass would tackle in the evening. Cass had a new bridge program for her computer and both of them were becoming addicted. Time was passing quickly.

Along with all the activity, there was plenty of time for good conversation. Cass listened as Marti reflected about life. Only half joking, Marti said she wondered if this facelift experience was as much about spiritual change for her as cosmetic. She wanted to do some things differently now.

Gazing daily through the wall of windows overlooking the lake, she began to sense that something inside her was changing. Not like a thunderbolt, but rather a calm wave that was gently washing over her and through her into all the nooks and crannies of her mind and body.

"You know, Cass, when I look back over the last thirty years, I feel like I've been pretty self-centered in many of the choices

I've made, particularly in my relationships with men. I really haven't been too smart in that regard. I've learned some important lessons and I'm going to think differently about where I'm headed in this next phase of my life."

"I hear you, but don't beat yourself up over nothing. Do you think you're feeling that you were a bit self-indulgent in having the facelift? Are you having a wee guilt trip?"

Marti shook her head and explained that she felt motivated to put her energy towards a cause where she was benefiting others, not just raking in a big salary. "My first experience with volunteering in India all those years ago was really humbling and the charity work I've done since then has always given back so much to me. I'm going to look for work with those types of organizations when I start to job hunt. I've had more than enough time to put my thoughts in order lately."

"Oops, I know what it is." Cass smiled. "We've had one too many tokes while we've been up here—purely for medicinal purposes, of course—and that's got you thinking about changing your life. We've been there before."

Marti laughed before she became solemn again. "Nope, it has nothing to do with a guilt trip—or the grass. This whole experience has simply jump-started me into taking another look at my life. I'm so glad I've had this time up here to seriously consider everything."

"Sounds like you've had more lifted than just your face, my friend," said Cass as she opened the patio doors and they strolled down to the dock. "I must admit living in this environment has given me a lot of time to pause and think too. I feel content here, even though it's only been a few months."

The waves lapped rhythmically against the weathered boards, as Cass contemplated the choices she had made through the years that brought her to finally settle in this peaceful place. *Well, close to peaceful*, she thought as she gave a quick, sharp slap to her neck, adding another notch to her black-fly tally. *Nothing's perfect.*

Marti interrupted Cass's thoughts as she picked up the thread of the conversation. "I've really loved the challenge of making my business viable and enjoyed the benefits I've reaped. Not just feeding my wanderlust but also for the flexibility to take time off when I want, like I did for the surgery. I feel ready to commit now to something new for the long term. Considering my humble beginnings—and forgetting my somewhat regrettable choices in men—I've been fortunate to end up financially comfortable and rich in friends. It's time for me to do something in a more meaningful way."

Marti was on a roll and she continued to look back over her past, her relationships, and in particular the disappointing mess her marriage had finally become before it ended. Change was coming in her life, Marti predicted, and she welcomed it.

"In spite of the bad times, we really can't complain. When I take a look around at some of the dreadful situations many people have to deal with, I know I have a lot of blessings to count," Cass said. "Not much money to count, but lots of blessings," she finished with a laugh.

"Better that than lots of money and no blessings, girlfriend."

For a few minutes the quiet was interrupted only by gentle waves slapping against the dock and a motorboat fading away in the darkness.

"It's interesting, Cass, isn't it? You and I were the first ones of the Bridge Club who were in serious romantic relationships, or so we thought, and now here we are, closing in on our sixties and living life on our own."

"Hey! Don't rush us! We still have a few years to go before the big 6-0. But you know, Marti, I feel just fine about that. I've had some great times in all of my relationships, and if that's it for me, then so be it. I'm not saying I wouldn't welcome a good connection with a man again, but I'm happy to say it doesn't top my agenda. Unlike the old days, I don't want sex just for the sake of it."

Marti stared off into space for a second. "What was that Woody quote Jane used to throw out at us? I'm vaguely hearing it in my mind..."

Cass laughed. "Oooh yeah, it was something like, 'Sex without love is a meaningless experience, but as meaningless experiences go it's pretty damn good.'"

"Uh-huh, that's it," Marti laughed. "There was a day."

"No question," Cass agreed, with a nostalgic smile, "but finally I feel as if I really know myself. I'm very happy to enjoy my own company, my crazy friends and of course, Jake."

"I have a feeling you will meet someone, I really do," Marti said as she settled herself at the edge of the dock. Leaning over she pulled her hand through the water, refreshing in spite of its chill.

"You never know," Cass replied. "Look at Pam, happily in a relationship now, when that was the last thing she ever foresaw. She spent eight years on her own and was at peace with herself. That's how I feel now: at peace with myself."

They both sat silently for several minutes, wrapped in thought and the serenity of their surroundings, before Marti continued. " I'd like to get to the same space you're in, but the divorce still causes me a lot of pain and I don't think I'll risk another relationship. For me, it's a trust issue. Of course it goes all the way back to my childhood, and I'm not sure I can get past it after being let down in my marriage. Probably part of it was even my fault. Who knows?"

"Mar, you know from your counseling that's not so, but it's going to take time to put it behind you. The best part of that fiasco is your two beautiful stepdaughters and the great relationship you maintain with them."

"So true," Marti agreed, "they mean the world to me."

Cass continued, her voice filled with enthusiasm, "The good news is you're already full of exciting ideas. I don't have to remind you that part of making the most of life is having plans and dreams—big ones or small. Stuff to think about and work towards. Hope! You already know that."

Marti's face lit up as she considered the future and all it had to offer. "I'm excited about not knowing exactly what I'm going to do next, you're right about that. Hey! Maybe I learned this from you! It's energizing when it's a choice and not forced. I needed to do this nip and tuck thing for me. Wanting to do something for others now is equally selfish, I suppose. I feel this strong urge to give back."

Along with the quiet talks, there were more than a few times when they loaded the CD player and listened to some great rocking sounds, laughing as they revisited old memories and made plans for new ones. Hitting the replay button over and over again, they sang with abandon to Elton John's "I'm Still Standing."

Let's never stop reminding ourselves how fortunate we are, they promised.

"Ya, ya, ya!"

Marti had read, and the surgeon had confirmed, that taking long walks now was a helpful part of the recovery period, as it helped circulate the blood. So, in the second week, along with the relaxing, reading, and talking, the two old friends would set off a couple of times each day on trails through the property. Cass was grateful the flexibility of her work allowed for these breaks.

They marveled at the gentle beauty of the white-tailed deer frequently spotted moving silently through the maze of leafless trees that offered the slightest hint of green from their bud-tipped branches. The day they caught sight of the first red-winged blackbird, confirming winter was definitely over, Marti felt she had turned the corner too and could actually feel good about what she was seeing in the mirror. She was forging into the next season with no regrets about change and new resolutions about the future.

"Onward!"

This, she told Cass, was her new motto.

Back in the city after the two weeks, gasps filled the room when Marti strolled through the door of Dee's place. A silk scarf over her head, partially covered her face.

"Okay, let's have the unveiling!" Bonnie demanded.

With a *ta-daaaa* from Cass, Marti slipped off the scarf and shyly grinned.

True to her promise, she had spent the afternoon having her long blonde hair styled into a trendy bob with subtle highlights added.

"Wow, Marti!"

"Like my haircut?" Marti asked. Bo laughed, knowing exactly why.

"You look amazing!" said Jane.

"Where do I sign up?" asked Pam.

Dee, who had never really ceased worrying about this surgery, had been the recipient of several phone calls during Marti's recuperation reassuring her everything had gone well. Nevertheless she was relieved to see the proof.

Danielle was caught in the middle of making her usual sign of the cross. In a loud voice she offered up a few words of thanks to the Power above. A chorus of "Amen" followed.

Agreement was unanimous that the surgery had been a huge success and that Marti looked herself, only "refreshed," as the magazines like to say.

"Ten years younger at least! Really Marti, you look wonderful, and the best part of it is you don't look like you had a facelift. Nothing looks tight or pulled. It's all so natural. It's fantastic!" Pam gushed.

"And you were right about the haircut idea," admitted Bo. "It does kind of act as a distraction. You look like you've been away on the best vacation ever!"

Marti smiled modestly, bowed, and graciously accepted the compliments. "Thanks! I have to say I'm happy. The doc accomplished just what I hoped he would. I love looking in the mirror now and not seeing a tired face staring back, and Wanda feels the same way, so we are two very satisfied customers."

Lynn, who had been quietly sitting and fanning herself, spoke up. "I can't tell you how relieved I am! My only exposure to facelifts has been when I've noticed someone who obviously has had one, and you know that usually means it doesn't look great. I was terrified you were going to look overdone—you know, kind of stretched and pulled and, well, just not exactly normal. But everyone is right. You look great!"

Marti said, "As happy as I feel with the results, hearing your comments does me the world of good"

They spent the rest of the cocktail hour asking endless questions and checking out her face, commenting on the fine work of the surgeon.

"I can't believe they actually put staples in your head," Danielle said, screwing up her face.

"I know," Marti grimaced, "it sounds so gross, but amazingly you don't feel any pain with them. It's just weird when you touch them."

"It boggles my mind how quickly everything heals," Pam commented, thinking she might be a future candidate after all.

"Truly amazing. But it didn't seem to be going quickly and I did have paranoid moments fearing I was going to look pretty messed up."

"I can attest to that," Cass assured them.

"Cass," Marti said, going over to give her a hug, "You were the best caregiver. Thank you a thousand times over."

Laughing, Cass replied, "Oh you owe me bigtime—as I reminded you several times during these last three weeks."

"So, in all honesty, how bad was it?" Jane asked.

Marti paused in thought before answering. "The worst part —except for my barf-fest the first night—was the damn bruising. It made me look like I'd gone a few rounds with Mohammed Ali, and even the camouflage makeup they give you can't completely hide it. There really was surprisingly little pain—"

"Not true," Cass interrupted. "It was extremely painful to look at her—and I'm not kidding! After watching this, I know for sure I'll never do it!"

"You're right, I looked a mess," Marti agreed, "and I know it appeared like I must be in a lot of pain. But I wasn't. I had a bit of discomfort and some odd numbness that is still there, but it's getting better. I'm not saying I would recommend going through this to anyone else because I sure had a couple of weeks that weren't too pleasant. However, ask me six months from now and see what I say."

"And then, of course, there was Wanda," added Cass.

"Oh, goddam Wanda!" Marti griped before laughing. "Can you believe her? She breezed through without any problems, hardly any bruising. We've had a few good laughs about it and she actually drove up to Cass's with a friend last week to see me. Nice, huh?"

"And how did she look?" asked Dee.

Cass and Marti were in agreement that Wanda looked gorgeous and she was thrilled with the results. Wanda had voiced the same about Marti, but Marti hesitated to believe it. "We're so critical of ourselves for the most part, aren't we? I'm not quite at the point where I can ignore small flaws. But all in all I must admit I'm feeling pretty good about the work."

Marti's smile radiated happiness as she accepted more compliments. "Okay, this is getting to be a one-note song—me, me, me. I'll stop going on about myself and we can talk about something else." She paused briefly for dramatic effect and then said, "So what do *you* think about me?"

She put up her hands to fend off the barrage of cushions and wadded up cocktail napkins tossed at her.

While she had their attention and before they got off on all sorts of unplanned tangents, as was their style, Marti filled them in on the decisions she had been making for her future. The changes she planned were not simply cosmetic, and Marti felt excited about the path she was choosing by selling her share in her company and going to work in community service.

"You're getting rid of wrinkles on the inside as well," Bo observed with a chuckle.

"So true! And be prepared at the card table, I feel so good that I think this whole process has improved my bridge game too!" She explained that up north, when Cass was busy working, she spent a lot of time reading bridge books and playing bridge on the computer. "I'm warning you, beware! You're gonna line up to have me as your partner! Let's get dinner out of the way and bring those cards out!"

DEAL #6

West	North	East	South
1♥	Dbl	Pass	1♠
2♥	3♠	Pass	4♠
Pass	Pass	Pass	

North
♠ A K J 10
♥ Q J
♦ A K Q 8
♣ 6 4 2

Dealer:	West
Vul:	None
Contract:	4♠
Declarer:	South

West
♠ 4
♥ A K 10 9 4 3
♦ 10 6 5
♣ A Q 9

East
♠ 7 6 2
♥ 5
♦ J 9 7 4 3
♣ 10 8 7 3

South
♠ Q 9 8 5 3
♥ 8 7 6 2
♦ 2
♣ K J 5

Suggested Bidding

West opens with 1♥ with 13 high-card points plus 2 length points for the six-card heart suit. North has 20 high-card points and support for the unbid suits. North makes a takeout double. East passes, and South advances to 1♠.

West has enough to compete to 2♥. North shows a very strong hand with a jump raise to 3♠ – South might have nothing. South, with 6 high-card points and a length point for the fifth spade, has enough to go on to 4♠.

Opening Lead

West is on lead against 4♠.

Bridge Quiz:

What would West lead?

What should happen at trick two?

What should happen at trick three?

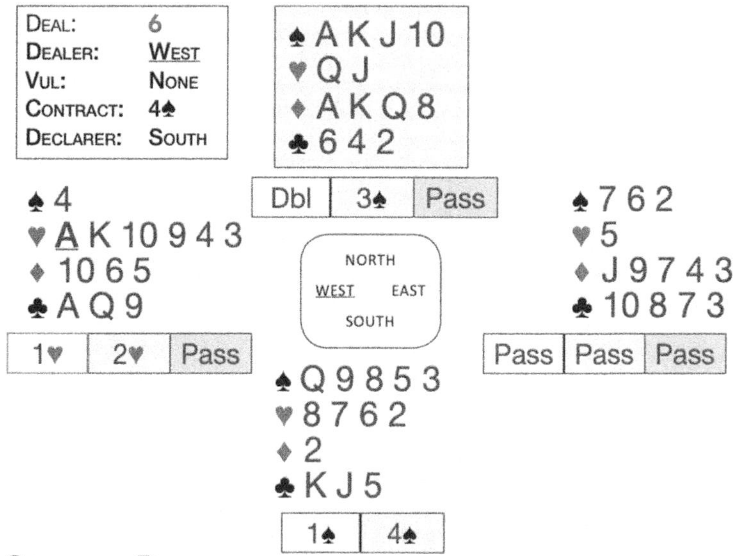

Suggested Defense

West leads the ♥A, top of the touching honors. After winning the first trick, West continues with the ♥K. East can see the defense isn't getting any more heart tricks so the only hope is for the defense to get two club tricks. Unless West holds the ♣A-K, clubs need to be led by East. East has to ruff the second heart and lead a club so the defenders can take a defensive club finesse.

Suggested Play

Declarer plans to ruff two heart losers in dummy and discard two clubs on dummy's diamonds, losing only two hearts and a club.

Conclusion

East has the weakest hand at the table but uses the only opportunity to gain the lead for a defensive club finesse.

When this famous deal was played, it was common to lead the king from ace-king. West, Al Sobel, led the ♥K followed by the ♥A. Although players are warned not to trump partner's ace, Al Sobel's wife, the great Helen Sobel, ruffed the ♥A and led a club. At the end of the deal, Al said, "Thanks for ruffing my ace!"

8

DEE'S SOS – 2001

On the eighteenth tee, Dee assumed the position after lining up her shot. With a mighty swing of the new oversized Ping driver, held in her soft but steady grip and following through with perfect timing, she looked up not a moment too soon to see her ball landing well along the fairway.

"Great shot, partner," she heard as she reached down to retrieve the biodegradable tee (even golf was going green) and put it back in her pocket. Murmurs of praise followed from the other two women, their opponents in this interclub match. Smiling wanly in return, Dee tried to look as if she really cared about winning, which normally she did. She liked to win. Big time.

"Thank God this is the last hole," she thought to herself. "My concentration is shot."

After scores were tallied, cold drinks were the order on this warm September day, as the four women sat at a linen covered wrought iron table on the verdant lawn outside the century-old brick clubhouse. Even after all these years as a member of this oldest golf club in Ontario, Dee never failed to appreciate the beauty of the historical structures and the riotously blooming

English gardens throughout the grounds that encouraged relaxation after a serious game. However, today it just wasn't working for her.

Managing to nurse an icy glass of fresh lemonade and do the post-game socializing thing for a half-hour before she excused herself to the locker room, Dee quickly showered and changed. Finally she folded her tall lanky frame into her compact sports car and sped off.

As if on autopilot, she guided her trusty ten-year-old convertible through the maze of side roads and country lines after leaving the madness of traffic on the 401.

The tires crunched up the gravel drive leading to Pam's rustic log house, where the rest of the Bridge Club was already relaxing. Relieved to be there, Dee laughed in spite of herself as the Rolling Stones' "Satisfaction" blared from around the back of the house with the familiar sound of the Bridge Club backup singers in full voice. Mick and the boys, Sir Elton, Sir Paul, Stevie Nicks, and the Bridge Club—still rockin' as they headed for sixty.

One of the pluses of living in the country, she thought. *You never have to worry about the volume.*

The spacious cedar deck at Pam's had witnessed many great parties over the years, and Dee knew precisely what the scene would be as she took the stone steps two at a time and rounded the corner of the house.

"*I can't get no, I can't get no. Hey, hey, hey-y.*"

The singing stopped mid-chorus as they welcomed the latecomer.

"Yay! Look who's finally arrived!"

"Our first lady of the links!"

"How did the match go?"

Scarcely noticing a glass of white wine slipped into her hand, she made the rounds to get everyone's latest news. Although she appeared subdued to several of the women, nothing was said. It was simply assumed she was tired from her day of golf. Of all the group, Dee was the most low key and conservative. She saved her moments of exuberance for very select occasions.

Cocktails at seven, dinner at eight was the tradition, and sometimes they actually made it happen. Tonight was one of those nights, so Dee had only about twenty minutes of chitchat outside before they sat down at the 150-year-old pine kitchen table for a late summer feast of BBQ ribs, free-range chicken from the farm down the road, accompanied by fresh corn, new potatoes, and field tomatoes all picked that afternoon. It was a traditional meal at this time of year. But Dee, known for the huge portions she could consume without gaining an ounce, wasn't eating much on this particular evening.

"I've got a lump in my breast," she blurted partway through dinner. Practically choking en masse, they demanded details and berated her for not mentioning it earlier. Did she know anything else? Did she discover it? Had she been to the doctor?

"I wasn't going to say anything, but I couldn't keep it inside," she confessed.

"Not mention it? Dee, don't be ridiculous. Tell us everything!" implored Lynn as Danielle mouthed a soundless prayer and crossed herself quickly.

"Well, I just kind of feel like I'm overreacting, being alarmist," said Dee in her usual calm manner, which today held a hint of anxiety. "You know me, Ms. Worst Case Scenario."

It turned out she had discovered this lump, which felt different from past lumps, during a self-examination and was seen by her physician within days. The doctor felt it was nothing serious, having read a clean mammogram report only a month earlier and considering Dee's past experiences of benign cysts.

"We'll keep an eye on it," the doctor had advised her.

"Eye, shmye," said Bonnie indignantly. "You have to march

right back to demand an ultrasound and a biopsy! You should have insisted on that!"

"You know, Dee, with your family history, I'm amazed the doctor didn't immediately schedule all of that in spite of the mammogram result. He must have had a very busy day," Lynn commented angrily, pursing her lips as she finished speaking.

Looking unusually vulnerable, Dee said the fault was probably as much hers as her doctor's. "With my family history, I reacted in the classic head-in-the-sand manner. I don't want to hear bad news. As soon as he said we could just keep an eye on it, that was good enough for me."

"Dee!" Bonnie chided her.

"I know. I know!" said Dee. She promised she would call first thing in the morning.

"And another thing. Take Ken or someone else with you," Pam added softly.

Ken, as the BC called him, but always Kenneth to Dee (or so they thought), was her husband. All the Bridge Club adored him. They clearly recalled the crisis in Dee's family in 1970, when she had run off to Barbados and married him. Mixed marriage was not common in those days. The Bridge Club had a typically riotous belated bridal shower for Dee, one they continued to reminisce over, while the guys in their group organized a golf tournament stag for Ken. The couple had met at an international golf challenge organized by the teams of their respective universities. Sadly there had been a few years of estrangement from her very traditional establishment family before they realized what a fine match the couple was.

"Oh for heaven's sake," Dee replied, "I can go myself. Besides, Kenneth is in China on business."

Bonnie hooted, "I love it! China! It used to be that a business trip abroad might mean London or Paris or Rome. Now everyone is rushing off to India and China!"

"Nope! Not acceptable for you to go alone," insisted Marti,

returning to the matter at hand. "One of us can go too, I'm sure!"

After everyone volunteered, Marti argued she had the most flexible schedule. There was no need for anyone to accompany her, Dee insisted, but Pam was convincing.

"Dee, of course we're all thinking positively here, but I know this from experience and I read it in articles all the time. When you have a doctor's appointment that might involve bad news, you should take someone with you to listen attentively and even take notes or record the conversation so you are clear afterwards on what was said. Trust me, it is excellent advice."

"Even though we've called you 'Steel Trap' all these years with your awesome memory, Pam is absolutely right. You still should have another pair of ears with you, Dee," Jane agreed.

"Besides," added Marti, hoping to lighten the mood, "it's also a good excuse for us to go for lunch."

Dee called the doctor's office the next morning and was squeezed in for the first appointment the following day.

Marti arrived extra early in the midst of a tremendous thunderstorm. The car crawled through rush hour traffic, reaching the medical building just in time. When Dee expressed her anxieties to her doctor, he agreed she was right to pursue the matter with him. He apologized as he admitted he absolutely should have ordered up the tests right away.

"I beg your pardon, Dorothea. It was my oversight. The crazy workload we take on these days is simply no excuse."

Marti shook her head as they left the office, commenting to Dee, "Boy, that sure was a reminder of how we need to advocate for ourselves when it comes to medical issues."

Dee agreed and added that it also was a bonus to have a long-standing relationship with a GP who would go to bat for you and make things happen in a hurry. "Some people have to wait weeks or months to get appointments, so I know how lucky I am to have this moving so quickly."

They went to the diagnostic radiology department where, thanks to the storm, several morning cancellations had left an opening for her ultrasound. The Ti-Ming thing was definitely working for her right now. The radiologist would fax the results right up.

Dr. Herner held the report in his hands when the women returned to his office, after being sent to the coffee bar for an hour. His face projected concern. Marti tried to conceal her alarm.

Dee watched his face intently as he held the paper in front of him. "Since we both behaved like ostriches the other day, please be painfully honest with me now. I can take it."

"Well," Dr. Herner began, "the ultrasound does suggest there may be a problem. I want you to have a fine needle biopsy performed in the lab downstairs, and we'll have the results in a few days. My secretary just checked, and with the heavy rain this morning they also have some openings. You can go there now."

The procedure did not take long, but lunch fell off the agenda as food now seemed particularly unappealing.

"Damn, damn, damn," said Dee, slamming the passenger door of Marti's car as they prepared to drive home, "this is not going to be good news. I just know it. Marti, I am so frightened." With that she lost control and burst into tears.

Pulling herself together after what seemed forever but was only seconds, Dee ran her fingers through her short-cropped hair and straightened up with a shudder as Marti fumbled for words and gripped her hand. The two women sat staring through the front windshield, saying nothing.

Marti put the car in gear but went nowhere. "We have to think positively until we have a reason not to. We always assume the worst at times like this, and most of the time we're wrong. Let's just wait. I can go back with you later this week if we have to. Since it's well into the afternoon and the weather has cleared, let's go play nine holes at my club. I'll drop you off to change and pick you up in an hour. Sound like a plan?"

"I don't know," muttered Dee. "Maybe I should just go home and wallow."

"No point in wallowing over nothing, and that's what we know so far—nothing. We always berate ourselves for worrying in advance, and this is a classic example. Look at this day now that the storm has passed. It's made for golf. Let's go!"

"Oh all right. It'll force me to focus on something else. You know how I don't like to lose."

Marti choked on her laugh. "As if I ever come close to beating you on the golf course!"

"There's always a first time." Dee smiled thinly and then added, "But it's not going to be today!"

Marti was glad to see her friend pull up her socks and, figuratively, slip into a slightly more positive pair of shoes for a while. She hoped a golf game would provide the necessary distraction, although she had to admit her own anxiety.

A half hour later they were on their way to the club, and Dee's passion for the game allowed her to shift her thoughts for a few hours. Marti was right about that.

Three days later, Dee and Marti were once again sitting across from Dr. Herner. If it hadn't been Friday, she would have waited to schedule her appointment after Ken's arrival, but she couldn't deal with the suspense a weekend would hold.

The physician fidgeted with papers as he spoke. "You do have a malignancy. I'm sorry. We will have to do some more tests right away to determine the details so we can establish a treatment plan."

Dee had never felt more frightened or out of control. In spite of attempting to be in charge of her emotions, she felt she was babbling incoherently and afterwards could not recall exactly what anyone had said. Thank goodness she had taken Marti with her. Pam had been right about that.

Back in the car, she asked Marti to call the BC, knowing they would be waiting to hear.

"Please ask them not to call me today. I'll talk to them after Kenneth gets home and we've discussed things." Thankfully it was not a long distance to Dee's. The drive home was filled with gaps of silence as both women searched for something positive to say. It wasn't easy.

Dee sent Marti off saying she wanted some time alone, but now she wasn't certain that had been such a good idea. It would be an excruciating wait for the next eighteen hours until Kenneth arrived home after a long and complicated rescheduled flight.

Later that afternoon the phone rang just as Dee had poured a scotch and sat down to stare blankly out onto the back garden. Bonnie was on the other end.

"Marti called," she began, without needing to say more.

Dee tried to articulate a response but could only manage "I can't talk now." Losing control, she hung up.

An hour later, Bonnie was at the condo door with an order of Dee's favorite Pad Thai. Stepping into Bonnie's open arms without hesitation, Dee burst into tears.

Of all the Bridge Club, Bonnie was one of the two women most able to keep their emotions in check. Now she was crying herself.

"Hey..." she gulped, her voice hoarse as she struggled for control. "Since you couldn't talk on the phone, I decided to come here. Also thought you might get hungry at some point."

Dee nodded, her lips tightly pursed, eyes squeezed shut, as her tears soaked Bonnie's shoulder.

They stood like that for a moment more before Dee stepped back, sniffing loudly. "I need a tissue ... seriously."

Following her into the kitchen, Bonnie explained, "I know you told Marti you wanted to be alone, but I figured you'd probably have had enough alone time by now. It's going to seem like forever before Ken arrives."

Dee murmured through her tears, "You know me better than I know myself sometimes, Bo. I'm glad you're here."

Wiping her eyes, she watched as Bonnie put the Thai takeout bag on the kitchen counter. "Thanks for the Pad."

They sat talking by the bay window with the soft baroque tones of Vivaldi in the background. Daylight faded and the dramatic skyline view, open all the way to the CN Tower, came alive with its evening illuminations.

"Do you remember how often you just showed up at my place through bad times when I was drinking?" Bonnie asked as she poured them both a steaming cup of tea. "I wouldn't have made it through some of those days and nights if you and the rest of the girls had not been so in my face. Often, the times we think we want to be alone are exactly the times we shouldn't be."

As she stroked the cat purring loudly on her lap, Dee wanted to talk about her mom, whom Bonnie had known as a second mother herself. The fact that her mother had died of breast cancer when Dee was twelve had been a part of her psyche ever since. Bonnie had been with her through that. Two young girls on the brink of puberty in 1957, curled up on the frilly coverlet of Dee's four-poster bed, sobbing and trying to make sense of their shattered world.

Those childhood memories of her mother's touch, her voice, the scent of her Evening in Paris perfume, lived in Dee's heart. It was painful, yet comforting, for both of them to reminisce about her now.

Even though Dee felt she had successfully buried the cancer worry as she matured, she considered now that perhaps she had been expecting it to catch up with her all along. There was, she also knew, no logical reason for that, because when genetic testing became available to her as an adult she had immediately participated. The results indicated she was at a very low risk.

Hah! she now thought cynically.

"I mean really, Bo, it's pretty ironic, isn't it? I have hands-down, absolutely no question about it, the smallest boobs in the world."

"Well, in the Bridge Club anyway," Bonnie corrected her.

"Whatever," Dee went on, "I haven't been nicknamed "Teeny Kupchinski" all these years for nothing, and now I'm the one who gets breast cancer. Size sure means nothing in this case."

"You've always won the Tiny Tits prize, no argument there," agreed Bonnie, "not that it matters. Like most women, we've all been looking over our shoulders wondering when we would get hit. The disease seems to be everywhere these days. I would have said you were the least likely candidate though."

It was so unjust, they agreed. But then, wasn't it always?

Dee was the one who, shortly after their group forty-fifth birthday, had organized the Bridge Club to go to the impressive Breast Cancer Department at Toronto Women's Hospital to attend their immersion afternoon, learning everything they should about this insidious disease. She was the one who reminded them each year about booking their mammogram. Always up to date on information about statistics, treatments, or new techniques for self-examination, she unfailingly passed it on to the BC. She did all the right things.

She ate right. She exercised right. She lived right. She still got it.

After a while, Dee admitted some of that Pad Thai would hit the spot. She hadn't eaten since breakfast and even then her nerves were so frayed that half a bagel was all she managed to digest.

"Remember, you don't have the whole picture yet," Bonnie continued as she put the food in a glass container and nuked it.

"I know," said Dee, a traumatized look in her eyes, "but obviously there is more. It's that unknown I'm scared of now. I'm so surprised at how this whole issue of mortality has hit me. It's always somebody else, but now I'm the one. Ever since I heard the word 'cancer' I can't get past my feelings about facing death."

"It's not unusual to get caught up in those thoughts."

"Bo, I'm totally overreacting. I know it, but I can't get a handle on it. I'm embarrassed to tell you I sat down this afternoon after Marti left and wrote out instructions for my funeral. My funeral! Can you believe it? I wrote out ten pages of instructions for Kenneth about business stuff, personal matters, and every detail of my funeral—ten pages! Talk about being anal."

"Well," said Bonnie slowly as she grasped for the right positive words, "remember how we all got our wills and things organized years ago? It's not a bad thing to have all those details written down. We know that."

"Yes, but I'm doing it right now because I think I'm going to die. Why can't I be positive about this? I have to stop thinking this way!"

"I understand, I truly do. You must keep reminding yourself it's not necessarily the worst-case scenario that I know you're imagining. Try and be positive until you know what you're up against—and even more so then. Remember you're in shock at first when you get this kind of news. I'm certain once Ken gets home you'll begin to feel better."

"I sure hope you're right," sighed Dee, taking her half empty plate over to the counter and covering it before she put it in the fridge. "I'll finish this later. I promise."

"Come on. Let's take Corfu for a walk," suggested Bonnie, knowing anything to do with Dee's beloved canine would help lift her spirits.

They ambled along the nearby Yorkville streets, avoiding Cumberland Avenue which was filling quickly with cars and pedestrians heading to the many restaurants and bars. Bonnie was doing her best to distract Dee from her immediate problems.

She commented on the impressive tiny front yards belonging to the rows of narrow Victorian townhouses. Most of the lots had been transformed in recent years into perennial gardens with no grass in sight. "It's so nice to see how boomers have gotten back into gardening, like their grandparents, isn't it?" she said, hoping to get more than a one-word response.

Dee and Ken had vast flower beds which they had developed over the decades at their farm property near Collingwood. That shared interest had turned into part of the couple's regular routine.

"Mm-hmm," said Dee with a modicum of enthusiasm. "Our parents' generation seemed to get so hung up on lawns. It's really fun to see the creativity people are using now, especially since pesticides are banned."

As they passed the façade of 100 Yorkville Avenue, Bonnie recalled it was the original site of Mount Sinai Hospital in the 1920s. "Every Jewish doctor in the city joined when it opened as no other hospitals would hire them in those days."

"Oh gosh, I'd forgotten about that. What a shameful time in our history that was. I just remember it as a seniors' residence, in the 60s, with old folks sitting in the yard in wheelchairs watching the hippie parade. It seemed so bizarre to have that here as we all staggered by when the bars closed."

"I'm looking around and having a major sentimental journey," Bo said with a nostalgic grin, sensing this might be a better distraction. "Yorkville in the 1960s..."

"The heart of the bohemian scene in the early days, that's for sure—beatniks, poets, musicians..." Dee smiled as her thoughts wandered back to those days of revolution in the air or was it marijuana?

"Remember when these streets were lined with hippy head shops, folk singers, coffeehouses, clubs? The Mousehole, the Purple Onion around the corner on Avenue Road, Lenny Breau, The Mynah Bird—"

Dee jumped on the sweetly memory-driven bandwagon. "Omigawd, yes, Gord Lightfoot and Joni Mitchell at the Riverboat as we all jammed into that narrow room, smoking up a storm. Neil Young. Those were the days. This was a real Mecca of music."

Bonnie was on a roll now: "The Paupers, Luke and the Apostles, Robbie Lane and the Disciples—what was it with the Biblical references anyway? You know Robbie Lane is still going strong in Toronto? Unbelievable."

"Ian and Sylvia at the Village Corner. Oh, yeah and Margaret Atwood doing readings at the Bohemian Embassy. Wow, wow, wow—those are good memories," Dee laughed, caught up in the moment. "I loved Buffy Sainte-Marie. She seemed so fearless and exotic."

"It was a different world, that's for sure, and we did have a blast down here," sighed Bo.

"And of course there was the seedy side," Dee reminded her.

"Ah! Let's forget the seedy side for tonight!" Bonnie nudged Dee with a smile. "Deal?"

"Deal!" agreed Dee, as they continued, with one memory leading to another.

"Who'd ever guess now how it was then?" Bonnie said wistfully, looking around at all the high-end shops. "You had to be there."

"Yup, by the 1970s it had all begun to change. Oops, Corfu, not there." Dee guided her dog to the edge of the street so she could stoop and scoop.

Bonnie had to chuckle when she looked into the mutt's bright eyes. "I can't believe you found two dogs over the years that look exactly the same. I swear, I've never seen any like them—first the original Corfu, and after his passing, this replacement Corfu at the pound. Two peas in a pod!"

This was a good topic to get Dee going on as they continued to stroll. There was no question how important her beloved pets were in her life. "Even more amazing is that we found one that looks like this after falling in love with that mongrel in Greece on our honeymoon. Do you remember the story, Bo?"

"I think I'm about to be reminded."

It took Dee most of the remainder of the walk to repeat in great detail her tale of finding a mangy cur in the streets of Corfu on her honeymoon and smuggling him to the hotel. Every evening she and Ken would put out food and water and he showed up without fail. Often they would find him tagging along on their daily hikes, exploring the island, and she was disconsolate to leave him behind the day of their departure.

Weeks later, shopping downtown in Toronto, she passed a scruffy young man at a bus stop with an equally scruffy dog so closely resembling the one in Greece that she uncharacteristically spoke to the stranger. It turned out his dog was pregnant. Ti-Ming! Some weeks later Dee and Ken gingerly navigated the filthy hallways of Rochdale College to the room of this hippy drug dealer to collect their puppy. He had instructed them on the phone to simply bring him a case of beer as payment and when they entered his apartment they could see why. The entire apartment was filled with stacks of empty beer bottles and every piece of "furniture" was made of beer cases, including a maze-like run for the dogs. Totally out of their element, Dee and Ken made a quick exit with the pup of their choice. "Corfu" was the obvious name.

"Serendipitous," said Bo, "and what a great pet Corfu Number One was. The only 'outsider' ever allowed on the

Bridge Club ski weekend—along with Corfu Number Two of course."

Dee brightened at the memory. "That's right. We were so glad to have rescued her from the unfortunate mess that Rochdale had become."

"Ah yes," replied Bonnie, shaking her head as if to loosen more memories. "Rochdale College was a whole other world in those early days," she said, referring to the experimental co-op communal living facility at the University of Toronto. "Remember? It began as a Free School with the residents-slash-students in control of everything. Counter-culture to the extreme. Now it's a seniors' home. I wonder if any of those early residents are wandering its halls in their bathrobes and slippers today."

They both laughed out loud at that thought.

"Hah! It was pretty much 'out there' at the time, but what a disaster..." Dee's voice trailed off at the thought. The Rochdale concept had seemed like a good idea in those heady days, when universities were the centers of political idealism and anti-establishment experimentation. But it didn't take long to deteriorate into an uncontrollable mess—with party animals, drug dealers, and vagrants in the majority.

Bo rolled her eyes in mock disgust as she confessed, "I must admit I put in an appearance at a few wild parties in the early days before the university students were displaced and all hell broke loose. I read somewhere that if you can remember Rochdale, then you weren't really there." She interrupted herself with a hoot of laughter. "'Peace parties,' we called them. Everyone wandered around being groovy and getting stoned. Booze was always my drug of choice, but no need to remind you of that. Fortunately I was never enticed by the so-called transformative powers of dope, acid, and that sort of stuff. We would end up on the roof, drinks or doobs in hand, celebrating the sunrise, music blasting—Janis Joplin, the Doors, Jimi Hendrix, Pink Floyd..."

"Santana—then and now! Imagine that! Even though classical music is my first love, I've always been a Santana fan and here he is, back on the charts, thirty years later. We've lived through some interesting times, Bo," said Dee, reaching down to give Corfu a rub on his back, "and this was one good thing to come out of it for us. Corfu Number One sure gave us years of pleasure, as has this old fellow."

Still spritely after almost fourteen years, he pulled eagerly at the lead as he recognized they had turned the corner heading home.

"Dee, stray dogs were following you home from the time you were eight years old. I remember Buddy and Blackie and..."

Dee chuckled as Bonnie pulled up those distant memories, and they recalled the long list of pets that had taken up residence with Dee and her family over the years. The reminiscing lifted Dee's spirits.

Bonnie was pleased that she had managed to divert Dee's attention to some happier topics during their walk. Once back at the condo, they chatted briefly over a cup of warm milk before heading for bed.

By the way Bo," Dee mentioned as they sat at the kitchen table, "I was very aware you didn't have a single cigarette while we were walking."

Bonnie grimaced. "Ha! It's making me crazy, but I've decided I better try to quit now that we're involved with cancer. Don't know how successful I'll be, but I'm having a bit of a reality check."

"Way to go! I know it won't be easy," Dee congratulated her as they hugged goodnight.

Bonnie could hear the tossing and turning in Dee's bedroom and knew it would be difficult for her to fall asleep, but she also realized it was time to give her some space.

Ken had cut his business trip short to get back to her as

quickly as he could get a flight from Beijing. Bonnie left a few hours before he arrived, with a grateful Dee repeating several times she was very, very thankful her friend had shown up the previous night.

Now it was time for Dee and Ken to face the situation together.

"I'm so scared," she cried. They were standing in the entrance hall with his unpacked bags on the floor, where he dropped them as he came through the door.

"Me too," Ken whispered, his pain raw, as he pulled her closely into his arms.

"The flight back was hell. Every minute just dragged and I couldn't think of anything but you and how you must be feeling. You sounded so together on the phone. I know you did that for me."

Dee tried to answer but could only weep, and Ken found himself doing the same. Finally they were actually holding each other. The emotions of the reality facing them soared straight to the surface more so than words across endless kilometers on the telephone or in e-mails.

Drained, momentarily, they wiped each other's eyes and looked deeply into them, transmitting a clear message of strength. "Okay, DeeDee. The battle is on. Let's slip into our armor and plan the attack. Most women survive breast cancer these days, and you're going to be one of them."

"Cupcake," she replied gently, using her secret nickname for him, "I knew you would come home and be strong and help me, but I can't get there yet. I'm terrified. All I've been doing the past two days is analyzing everything and trying to figure out what I've done wrong. Is it just genetics? Was it inevitable? Is there something I could have done to avoid it and I missed it?

Did I worry too much? Too much stress? I keep thinking I'm going to die and..."

They remained wrapped in an embrace for a long time as he tried his best to assure her. He knew no matter how much courage they could summon in this fight there would be more moments like this.

Sensing Dee was on firmer ground after a while, Ken got up and flipped on the stereo to play a Mozart CD. "Let's have a glass of wine and let Wolfie soothe our souls a bit. That always seems to help when things aren't going right."

Dee closed her eyes and let the music enfold her, longing for some peace. With her husband on one side of her and Corfu on the other, she felt relief seep into her body. Within seconds their cat, Mulligan, was curling himself into a ball on her lap. Pets just seem to know when to bring their own special kind of comfort, she thought to herself.

Days later at the next appointment, Ken took out his pocket recorder and turned it on so they would not worry about forgetting anything he said.

"Excellent idea. I wish more of my patients would do that," the doctor said.

He had scheduled them for the last appointment of the day so he could take his time to explain all the treatment options and answer their questions.

"You have a very common type of breast cancer, Dee. Infiltrating ductal carcinoma. Here's a brochure that will provide you with a lot of information, but let me reassure you by saying the tumor is not large and I believe we have caught the cancer early."

"It sounds awful no matter how small it is. I'm very frightened."

"Of course you are. I understand. It's a shock. However as we progress and you learn more about the situation, you'll begin to feel more optimistic about it. I guarantee that."

Dee turned to look at Kenneth, who was holding her hand and perspiring on his upper lip, ever so slightly, as he always did under stress.

Dr. Herner continued, drawing diagrams as he described the various treatment combinations and options she had to consider. She watched his mouth move and heard the sounds, but comprehension was just not happening. It was all a blur and unlike anything this bright, organized, and extremely competent woman had ever been through. She felt as though she was having an out-of-body experience.

"Since the tumor is less than 2.5 cm and in a relatively accessible location, you are a very good candidate for a lumpectomy. Of course you can have a mastectomy if you feel strongly about it, but I see no need for that. We would follow up with radiation and then a program of medication. You should do very well. Please believe me. Having said all this, I'll now be sending you on to extremely capable specialists who will take care of matters from here on."

Dee nodded silently, unable to get her mouth to work, and Ken responded for both of them. "Thank you, Dr. Herner. You didn't mention chemotherapy. Don't all cancer patients have that?"

"Not at all. It depends upon a number of things, including the size of the tumor and whether the cancer has spread. The first indications here are that only radiation will be needed before the pills. Having said that, a number of tests need to be done to give us more information. After the surgery, your oncologist will confirm the plan of action."

Ken had brought a list of questions with him that Pam had e-mailed to them.

"Here's another good bit of advice, Ken. Don't be afraid to ask questions," wrote Pam, "and be sure to say you don't understand if something isn't clear."

Ken recorded all the conversation. Dr. Herner came around

the desk to sit on the front of it as he reached over and took his long-time patient's hand. "You're going to be in the hands of very knowledgeable physicians, nurses and technicians, and you need to place your complete trust in them."

Nodding again with an immense thickening in her throat, Dee acknowledged she understood completely.

Before they left the office, Dr. Herner gave them a file of printed matter that included a long list of breast cancer Web sites. The surgeon's office would call them with an appointment.

Three long weeks later, they had their initial appointment with the surgeon, who drew more diagrams and confirmed the lumpectomy for three weeks hence.

"You're giving us confidence for the prognosis of Dee's condition. What's our first step?" Ken asked, hoping to project optimism and boost Dee's spirits.

"I would like to schedule a sentinel node biopsy, which we'll do along with your lumpectomy. I'm assuming that's your choice?"

Dee managed to speak, quietly asking questions about one choice over the other. He offered her information, statistics, and his own experience before she and Ken agreed that they felt comfortable choosing to have the lumpectomy over the more drastic mastectomy.

"I believe you've made the right decision. Mastectomies are not nearly as common in this type of diagnosis as in earlier years, but they're still offered as an option."

The couple exchanged a look of relief that they were making good choices. Reassurance from the doctor was something they recognized they needed.

"This additional biopsy is to confirm that the cancer is

confined to the tumor and has not spread. Your case looks promising, and this will simply clarify the situation. You'll have a general anesthetic, and most patients simply go home and rest afterwards. Unless you have a reaction to the general, you should feel fine with just a little tenderness in your chest and underarm."

Dee continued to nod silently as she had been for some time, her voice lost many minutes before in the fog that was enveloping her mind. She shook the surgeon's hand as they left. His secretary would call the next day to let them know the time of the procedure.

As soon as they left the office, with Ken's arm around her shoulder, she burst into tears. "I'm sorry. I just can't help myself. I'm a basket case!"

"Shhh," he said tenderly, pulling her tighter to him, "if you feel you need to cry, then you just do it. It's going to get better. We'll see to that."

This second biopsy brought some unexpected news. The pathology reports indicated there was a very tiny cancer spot in the sentinel node. It was big enough to cause a change in the treatment plan. There would be a lumpectomy, followed by chemotherapy which would precede radiation.

The procedure was quickly scheduled. Unexpectedly afterwards, the surgeon was not happy with the results of the margins around the tumor and wanted to go back in to obtain more clear tissue around it. Dee could feel her fear returning.

"Of course, it's your decision. The risk is remote that the cancer has spread beyond that one node since the spot is so microscopic, but we want to be certain."

There was no need for Dee and Ken to hesitate. They picked up the appointment card on the way out for the next surgery.

The Bridge Club had been collectively pacing since Dee's first diagnosis, and Ken had agreed that the little surprise they were planning might be just what Dee needed. They would have to wait until he felt the time was right though.

Bonnie had remained the primary contact and would speak with Ken and then e-mail the rest of the group. Dee refused to speak on the phone to anyone through the initial weeks of tests, although she did respond to e-mail promptly. This allowed her to feel connected but not have to project false hope into her voice.

"She'll come around, Bo," Ken reported after her weeks of seclusion. "We all know that. She's struggling with processing everything, and naturally she's consumed with memories of her mom. We're working through it, but I think the time has come for some very active involvement from her friends. It's so good to know you're there. Keep those e-mails and cards coming. I know she sent all of you a message when she received that phenomenal flower basket, and the book will make her laugh when she is up to reading it. Right now all she can do is cry, and I'm getting concerned. I've never seen her like this."

The second surgery appeared successful, with the rest of the nodes indicating they were clear as well as the tumor site. The basic pathology was in the surgeon's hands by morning and he confirmed the procedure was a success, discharging her after a night's stay.

"We feel we caught this early," he said, looking up from her chart with a smile, "and your prognosis with your follow-up treatment is excellent." That was the first good news.

The next bright spot was waiting for Dee as she walked out into the lobby with Ken to discover the Bridge Club sitting there. Her surprise and broad smile were all they needed to see.

"We couldn't wait any longer to see you. Ken gave us the go ahead," Pam squeaked out through her tears.

"Besides that, we figured it was time you had a few hands of bridge!" Bonnie announced, her voice cracking with emotion.

Looking at her husband's anxious face, Dee grabbed his

cheeks in her hands and said, "Kenneth! You are the best person at keeping secrets! Thanks for doing this."

"Hey, I did nothing," he replied, smiling with relief at her response. "It was all their idea. They've already dropped lunch off at our condo and set up the bridge tables."

"We even brought you a card holder in case your arm was sore," Jane told her. Danielle pulled it out of her purse and waved it around.

"What do you think, Dee? Good idea?" Marti asked, hoping with all her heart to see a happy smile from their friend.

"Great idea!" Dee sniffled, wiping her cheeks as she broke into another huge grin. "Let's go!"

Cass had been standing back a bit before she handed Dee a huge bouquet of her favorite lilies.

Ken waved and left for the office, breathing a large sigh at Dee's reaction. It had been worth the risk.

The afternoon, with the BC wearing pink ribbon pins, stretched into the evening as they played bridge and traded breast cancer stories they knew from other friends. From their myriad experiences they could all vouch how helpful it was to learn from others' lessons. Along with a large box of chocolates, the ladies had brought Dee a copy of *Dr. Susan Love's Breast Book,* which everyone said was the bible of breast cancer. The attack was on and they wanted to provide the best backup fire they could.

"Now when we click on the Breast Cancer Site each morning, it's a personal click for you, Dee," said Jane. Dee had encouraged them for years to bookmark this site and go to it when they went online. Most of them would automatically click on the linked sites for hunger, child literacy, and other worthwhile global charities while they were at it. It took about ten seconds of a person's time, and all were accredited links, no scams.

"Right on," agreed Lynn. "I know we've all spent a lot of

time on various breast cancer Web sites over the past few weeks, Dee. It's overwhelming to see the amount of information and support on the Internet. What a difference it makes in our lives, eh?"

"To be honest," Dee told them, "I was nervous about looking up stuff about my condition online. Surprisingly, it turned out to be one of the most effective sources of comfort and encouragement. I've lost myself for hours getting caught up in it all."

That day was a coming out party of sorts, Dee thought later. For the first time she talked openly with her friends about her condition, her hopes and her fears. They had reminded her of her approach and attitude towards her golf game and the character-building lessons learned over the years of working down to her 12 handicap. Some of that grit and determination would be useful in this new challenge she was facing. She did have the right stuff, they assured her.

"Jeez, Dee, how many times have you chided one of us on the golf course with your famous anonymous quote: *Golf is life. If you can't take golf, you can't take life,*" Marti reminded her in a teasing tone.

"Right," laughed Bo, "we never knew exactly whether that made any sense, but you make it sound like it does. One thing for certain is that you, my friend, most certainly can take golf. The rest goes without saying."

Dee got their point.

Lying in bed early one morning after another restless night, Dee took Ken's hand in hers and kissed it before she spoke. "Cupcake, you've taken so much time away from work to be with me I'm starting to feel guilty. I've done nothing in our business since this whole mess began."

"DeeDee, trust you to worry about work. Everything is fine. We're lucky we can set our own schedules so stop stressing about it. It's simply not an issue for now, and I know that very soon you're going to be back at it again—as you like to be. I've been thinking, though, that from here on in, we both need to ease up and smell the roses a bit more. We've forgotten about that for too long."

Dee and Ken had been a team in every way since their marriage and after many years of doing management consulting for a large firm they had established their own business. They loved the challenge and thrived on the long hours. Early on they had realized that they were work junkies and golf-a-holics and really had no interest in hearing the pitter-patter of little feet in their lives. At least not two-footed creatures. They received tremendous enjoyment from the children of their friends and family but much preferred dedicating themselves to their professions, their golf game, and the constant presence of a variety of dogs and cats.

Ken was confident that Dee's love of life would begin to resurface as the initial shock of her diagnosis faded and she began to get through her treatment. He hoped he was right. His dedication to that end was all consuming.

At the next appointment, the oncologist informed her that her cancer was "stage 2" and "grade 3," along with a lengthy list of other numbers and terms with which she would become very familiar, like all cancer patients.

"Although there is no evidence of any further metastases," he explained, "your test results indicate that your type of tumor was aggressive, so we want to attack it as effectively as possible. The good news is, the tumors that score the higher grades, as yours did, tend to respond better to chemo."

Somehow Dee had trouble feeling enthused at the news.

However as they were leaving the room, the oncologist added one more remark and this one did make a difference. "I want to assure you that your disease is highly treatable. Trust me."

After days of talking to herself, with Ken working to reinforce her confidence and positive attitude, Dee announced he did not need to accompany her on the first chemotherapy session.

"I've always stood solidly on my own two feet in the past. Why the hell am I stopping now? I've got to get a grip."

Ken wasn't certain this first session was the time to be on her own, but he wanted to support Dee as she rebuilt her resolve. She seemed so determined, like her old self. He kicked himself for it after Dee had left in a taxi, torn by a desire to be there with her.

Walking briskly through the halls of Princess Margaret Hospital, Toronto's top cancer treatment facility, Dee felt her calm slipping as she observed many other chemo patients taking their treatment, in various stages of the disease. In the reception area she was promptly greeted by a volunteer, who asked if this was her first visit. Dee opened her mouth to respond. All that came out was a muffled sob. The fear of the unknown viciously gripped her and wiped out all her resolve in a flash.

This was clearly a common experience for the volunteer, who offered Dee a tissue and led her to a quiet corner for privacy. In a reassuring voice, she explained what would happen over the next hour or so, walking Dee through the process and encouraging questions.

"We know how intimidating the first visit is, and your reaction is perfectly normal. Don't think for a minute that it isn't. Is there someone with you?"

Dee explained she had wanted to be there on her own, had insisted on it. The volunteer nodded and said it was interesting how many women made just that choice.

Grateful for the understanding, Dee gradually composed

herself and tried to dispel her embarrassment at losing her cool in public. It just wasn't her style. Then she recalled the number of people who had told her that when you first discover you have cancer, nothing feels normal. It doesn't seem to matter how much in control you usually are; your whole world is scattered, full stop. It takes time to pull it back together.

Another friendly volunteer ushered Dee into a treatment room, where the nurse told her she had healthy veins and proceeded to insert her IV with ease. The nurses and technicians were warm and encouraging, creating a calm, quiet environment. Time passed quickly as she alternated reading her book and snoozing. Before her session was over, Dee was approached by a woman, who introduced herself as a volunteer for Wellspring Cancer Centre. A cancer survivor herself, she gave Dee a booklet filled with answers to questions and lists of workshops and other available services.

As they spoke, Dee appreciated the information she was offered, but even more so the intelligent and soothing attitude this woman conveyed.

Walking out of the hospital, she felt almost upbeat for the first time. If only she could convince herself to believe in the future.

"You know, that was fine," she described to Ken later. "I didn't realize I was so frightened until I tried to answer the first person who helped me. She was incredibly kind and understanding. As it turned out I could have driven instead of taking a taxi. I guess that might change, but if this is how it's going to be, you don't have to worry about me going on my own. The support there is amazing."

"That's such good news. But you know, I still think you should have someone with you all the time—just to chat with, to get you a drink of water or juice while you're hooked up, whatever."

"Maybe you're right. I won't have any trouble finding company."

The chemotherapy sessions were scheduled approximately four weeks apart. In between she would have her blood checked regularly and have to be very careful about hygiene, avoiding anyone with even a hint of the sniffles.

The chemo would attack the cancer but not do anything good to her immune system in the process. Each chemo "cocktail" was based on that day's blood results, so there was always a waiting process, and she realized she would be spending a lot more time sitting around the hospital. Having Ken or a friend along turned out to be a very good idea.

Discovering after the first session that she was pretty wiped out for a day or two, she took advantage of the down time to read for her own enjoyment instead of burying her head in business files.

Not one for popping pills, she decided to see if she could do without the anti-nausea medication. Returning the medication to the surprised nurse at her second session, Dee suggested she give them to someone who really needed them and did not have a drug plan to pay for them, since OHIP didn't cover them. She felt good about that and got along just fine without them. More good luck, she told herself.

Dee was amazed at the world into which this experience had transported her. All the caregivers—medical and support staff—were unfailingly positive, informative, and helpful. They offered endless tips and advice on how to cope with the myriad side effects that patients experienced in different ways. She had read articles about this aspect of the breast cancer story, and now she was living it. What an effect it had. She simply felt you could not help but begin to buy into the positive atmosphere.

But it did take time. After the initial weeks of feeling sorry for herself and fearing for her life, planning her funeral, and imagining how her Cupcake would carry on without her, she had given herself a shake and attempted to step onto a new path of optimism and hope.

The Christmas season passed quietly, without the standard frenzy of parties as the couple focused on keeping Dee out of crowds and healthy. Knowing Dee and Ken would miss their usual Christmas golf trip, the BC presented her with a high-tech putting mat when she mentioned she was hoping to focus on improving that part of her game.

"How much better is this attitude?" she asked herself as she began the new year with daily self-talk about how she would meet this challenge head on. Purpose and direction were two buzzwords she applied to everything—now more so than ever. She would do it not simply on her own but also by accepting the remarkable support being offered to her. It was time to wage war, to fight the good fight like never before.

It had to happen. Her hair had begun to fall out, and she hated finding it all over the place. It would soon be time to simply get rid of it instead of constantly cleaning up the mess everywhere she looked.

Jane and Bonnie accompanied Dee to a recommended wig store. She had read it was a good idea to look for one before your hair loss became severe and while you still had reasonable energy. So she did.

The woman working in the shop seconded that idea: "Alternate the wig with your own hair for a week or so while you become used to it. Then just do the deed and have a friend or your hairdresser shave your head while you sip your favorite libation. Make it an event and remember, it will grow back and it will be beautiful. This part of the cancer treatment is often harder for some women than anything else, no matter how much we are warned."

Dee acknowledged she was struggling and was not looking forward to it. "I guess it's a good thing that my hair is relatively short."

"Honestly Dee, the one you have on now looks completely natural and it's almost a perfect match to your color, maybe even a little better!" Jane said, amazed at the quality of the hairpieces.

The woman explained how she encouraged her customers to go a shade lighter as skin color sometimes changes as a result of chemo and the lighter hair would not make it as noticeable. She also gave Dee a brochure about a program called Look Good, Feel Better, which ran workshops at many of the hospitals in the city for cancer patients. The volunteer from Wellspring had also mentioned the program.

Jane and Bonnie tried a few wigs on themselves.

"You know, I'm learning there are a lot of good things about wearing a wig. I'm tempted to get one myself," Bonnie said, thinking how great it would be not to have to bother fixing her hair every day."

"And I could throw away my curling iron forever!" Jane exclaimed, looking very excited at the prospect.

"You girls are always focused on the bright side—and I truly appreciate it—but let's be real here. It's going to be itchy, and that'll drive me crazy, but I'll just have to deal with it. My ego will overcome it," Dee muttered.

Lynn went to a Look Good, Feel Better workshop with Dee and they passed around tips to the BC the following month. Both women were blown away by the positive energy of the workshop and the transformations that took place there. You could feel the changes in the air, hear confidence returning to voices, see pleasure appear on tired faces as the two hours progressed and everyone began to live the words of the workshop. You did feel better when you felt you looked good. No question about it.

"Dee, this is great. It's no consolation for what you're going through, but we never would have known some of these tips were it not for your workshop," Pam thanked her.

Those Bridge Club Tuesdays each month were Dee's only social life, with everyone wearing masks and gloves since her immunity was weakened and a simple cold germ could cause problems. She refused to give that evening up. The format was shortened, with everyone agreeing to skip the dining component. They simply spent an hour or two together with a few hands of bridge in the early evening until Dee's strength returned.

Pam came into the city early for the February Bridge Club night, which was to be held at Jane's. She wanted to sit down at Dee's and talk for a while.

"It's been a long few months, let me tell you. Thanks for giving me the space to work through everything."

"Remember, you're talking to me," Pam reminded her gently. "I know precisely what you're up against. Everyone has to come to terms with something like this in his or her own way. It's such a shock."

"I realize that more than ever now, Pam. I thought of you and Peter a lot during those first weeks. I kept trying to appreciate all of the successful treatments and results there are for breast cancer. I know you didn't have that option with his pancreatic cancer, but in spite of that you never gave up hope. I'm beating myself up for not valuing my good fortune. I can't seem to convince myself to be grateful!"

Pam squeezed Dee's hand. "Hope fuels the drive to survive. You have to keep fighting through this dark period and force yourself to see the light at the end of the tunnel. You'll overcome this and be healthy again. I just know it! You're so fortunate to know that's an option. Remember, Dee, one breath at a time."

Dee nodded as she quietly expressed to Pam how she and

Kenneth had learned such lessons from Peter's death about appreciating each day. "And now, twelve years later, we realize how we've slipped back into our old frenetic lifestyle. We haven't taken a relaxing vacation in years," she admitted. "We really lost sight of the importance of every single day; there's so much more to life than business and golf. Now we're being reminded again."

Pam wiped her eyes and nodded. It was simply human nature, she said, to need an occasional tap on the shoulder to slow down and remember each day is a gift. "God knows I still need that tap every once in a while."

The two women gave each other a strong look and an even stronger embrace that made any further words pointless. Then they walked and window-shopped along Bloor Street. Bundled up just enough to enjoy the unusually mild winter weather, they rang Jane's buzzer just in time for the seven o'clock cocktail hour.

Cass and Lynn rushed through the door behind them, and they all grinned madly in the elevator as they recognized that the old Dee was on her way back. It was great to be there and feel sort of normal again, whatever normal is, Dee thought.

They packed up the cards a bit earlier than usual when Dee mentioned she was beginning to fade. Cass drove her home along with Pam, who had left her car at Dee's earlier. Tired as she was, Dee admitted she felt good after this girls' night out.

The weeks began to pass quickly, and on a Sunday morning, Ken suggested they go for a drive and do brunch downtown. As they approached the city hall, Dee noticed people milling about but didn't pay particular attention to it as they entered the parking garage. Spring was in the air, and there was often something going on in the center of the vibrant downtown area.

Upon exiting the garage, there was no mistaking what all the commotion was about. They were in the midst of the crowds supporting the annual Spring Run to Find the Cure. This event had been growing for the last ten years into a hugely popular fundraiser for innovative and relevant breast cancer research, education, and awareness programs across Canada.

"Wow, look at this turnout! It's kind of a coincidence we parked here given what's going on in our life these days," she said to Ken as they wove their way through the throng.

"You've got to love the energy and mood of it all. It's inspiring, isn't it?" she asked, not needing an answer as Ken led her by the hand to what appeared to be the finish line.

"Let's stand here for a few minutes and just take it all in," he suggested.

It was impossible to avoid being caught up in the happy atmosphere. Individual walkers crossing the line mixed with groups organized into teams with matching outfits, crazy hats, and assorted accessories. Pink was definitely the color of the day.

Ken and Dee stood smiling, arm in arm, basking in the positive vibes and excitement in the air. Dee suddenly let out a yell as she focused on a large group, crossing the finish line and heading straight toward her, including the Bridge Club and assorted friends from all aspects of her life. There were men, women, kids and dogs, dear friends, and some she had never seen before, all wearing pink tee-shirts that said "Doin' it for Dee!"

"Oh my, my, my," was all she could repeat as her shrieks caught in her throat and she laughed and cried at the same time. There were hugs all around and high fives as everyone cheered and talked at once. Pam made certain she snapped photos of the entire event.

"You got me again! I'm completely overwhelmed!" said Dee, shaking her head in utter surprise. "How did you all get organized?"

The story gradually unfolded over lunch and lemonade served in Nathan Phillips Square in front of city hall, with no one person taking credit, as they had previously arranged. They were unanimous in expressing what an uplifting experience it had been and how Dee would be right in there with them next year doing her part. She couldn't wait!

As she spoke on the phone several days later making thank-you calls to everyone, Dee couldn't stop repeating what a gift Sunday had been. She felt it was the catalyst that finally got her head straightened out.

"You know me, Mar, it's about time I took my own advice and put my mantra into action."

"Purpose and direction. You've sure drilled those words at us often enough," said Marti, her smile making itself felt over the phone.

Dee nodded and pumped her fist soundlessly in the air. She thanked Marti for keeping her company during her chemo earlier that week and explained the changes she and Kenneth were making to their routines and their lives.

"You know how the early rounds of chemo made me feel exhausted. I've slept and read and taken it easy—a big change for me. It dawned on me this is the first time in years I've taken so much time away from my work other than on the golf course? Been quite a treat, actually, to read whatever and watch movies I've missed. Kenneth has cut his hours back too."

"This part is all sounding good, Dee ... very good," Marti agreed.

"It's been another epiphany," Dee said. "We'd become so insular and work focused without even realizing it. We're determined to change that."

After six months Dee's chemo sessions were completed, and everyone hoped the treatment had done its part.

Golf continued to be one of her ultimate goals. She was not swinging a club or going to the indoor range, as her surgery had left her with a lump in her armpit that made movement uncomfortable. Always serious about her sports, Dee religiously exercised her arm so as not to lose any range of motion as the lump began getting smaller. She would be ready for the next golf season come hell or high water.

The next BC evening was a celebration as the masks and gloves were ceremoniously dumped in the trash. During dinner and in between bridge hands, Marti cajoled Dee to spend an afternoon helping her at the shelter for abused women where she was the director.

The work had become Marti's focus even though it was frequently emotionally draining. The satisfaction was worth it, she always said. Now she sensed it might provide a good distraction for Dee, since it was still too early in the spring for golf.

"Besides, the shelter is right on the edge of Little India, so we can go for some great curry."

"Oh *mon Dieu*," exclaimed Danielle, clapping her hands. "Bryce and I went to that area for dinner with friends a couple of weekends ago and it was fun! It's so colorful, the smell of spices everywhere—lots of restaurants, cafes, and shops. You'll love it, Dee!"

Dee appreciated the suggestion and the enthusiasm. "I'm embarrassed to admit I'm in a bit of a funk—as if I ever should be again! I thought I'd be able start hitting golf balls right away, but the doc has given me the word that it won't be for a few months yet. Can you believe, after all I've been through, that actually upset me? I've been moping about it."

"Give yourself a shake!" said Cass. "You'll be swinging those clubs soon enough."

"I know I'm being a twit about the whole thing," Dee acknowledged, "Maybe a delicious 'blow-the-top-of-my-head-off' curry is just what I need."

The following Wednesday Marti picked Dee up at noon after a morning full of meetings. To Dee's surprise, the afternoon flew by at the shelter, organizing supplies, answering the phone, and helping residents, which sometimes was as simple as taking time to listen while Marti dealt with one crisis after another. When they finally left, they walked a couple of blocks along Gerrard Street and, as Danielle had described, found themselves in a very different world of sights, smells, and sounds.

"We live in a good city, don't we?' Dee remarked. "Too bad we often don't get out to these places unless we're tourists somewhere else."

"So true," agreed Marti as she absorbed the pleasing assault on her senses, "The cultural mosaic of Canada is alive and well in this neck of the woods!"

"Marti, I liked helping at the shelter. What if I come next week for a full day if I'm feeling fine?"

Marti was delighted for several reasons. Not only could she use an extra pair of highly efficient hands, but more importantly, she felt that Dee was looking at life a little differently. She sensed an even more positive tone in her voice.

Next on the agenda were Dee's radiation "tattoos" and her first session. The whole process seemed a breeze after the chemo. There was no waiting, and the treatment time was short. After three weeks she had the usual sunburn effect, which was painful but helped by a soothing cream. Five weeks later that chapter was over, and a whole new outlook had been the major side effect. Always the worrier, Dee knew she had learned from this entire experience that anxiety really got you nowhere. Stuff happens whether you worry or not.

Then it was on to the final phase of medications. Since she was postmenopausal, tamoxifen was the drug of choice and the side effects should be minimal, she was told. She chose to believe them.

She related at Bonnie's place the BC Tuesday after her final treatment, "I know I've been hearing for years that I should relax and enjoy life more but it took this kind of a scare to finally get through to me. I spent the first weeks after I received my diagnosis, totally wrapped up in my misfortune and giving no consideration to the life-altering experience it would be. I owe so much to the support from all of you, my family, and the incredible people I have connected with during my cancer treatment."

"We've watched you grow, Dee, in a different way," Jane noted in her straightforward, positive manner.

Dee looked a little self-conscious at the praise, saying, "I have to thank the women at Marti's shelter as well. I've learned so much from being involved in their stories. I never would have taken the time to be a part of that had I not gotten sick."

"There we go again," smiled Cass, "Ti-Ming."

Dee and Marti were often joined for a lunch or dinner by one or more of the BC as they enjoyed their forays into Little India, Greektown, Cabbagetown, or over to Chinatown. As months passed they moved farther afield to explore the Corsa Italia and Little Italy as well as the old but newly marketed Portuguese area. They became enthused once again about taking the time to appreciate their multicultural city and all it had to offer.

Pam had come across a quote of Albert Einstein's when she was coping with her grief so many years before, and she hoped Dee would find the same inspiration: *"Learn from yesterday, live for today, and hope for tomorrow."* She had Cass print it in calligraphy for Dee, who photocopied it, framed it, and placed several around the condo.

"Words of wisdom," was Kenneth's response when she showed it to him the first time. "Let's make it our motto and focus on positive changes in our approach to this incredible life we share."

It wasn't that the changes Dee and Ken made were immense. It wasn't that life had not been good before. The shifts made that good life even better. Dee became a more empathetic listener as each week passed at the shelter, and she felt satisfied about the time she was spending there and the contributions she was making to others. The more she listened to the women in the shelter, the more she realized how few her problems were.

Weekends at their farm near Collingwood had been their only down times, but now she and Ken made time for relaxation during the week and together they rediscovered their city, including the districts to which Marti and the gang had taken her. They both recognized that as much as they were benefiting from spending more time enjoying life and each other, their business was not suffering noticeably. Dee was happy to return to work but dramatically cut back her hours. She felt she was still accomplishing what she wanted with far less stress.

What had they been thinking before? They questioned what they had been thinking before and wondered how they got into such a rut. Now they made a pact to remind each other there was so much more to life than work and golf.

One of their first actions was to book a trip overseas. They would leave right after her three-month checkup, Dee reported, as the BC was digging into dessert around Danielle's dining table. The trip would mark the successful end to her treatments and the beginning of appreciating the rest of their lives in a way they otherwise might have missed. No one knew what the future might hold.

Eyes shone, glasses were raised, and voices were filled with gratitude and hope.

"To life!"

"Hurry up and finish eating," urged Dee. "Get the cards out, Dani."

DEAL #7

West	North	East	South
	1♦	Pass	1♥
Dbl	2♥	Pass	4♥
Pass	Pass	Pass	

Dealer:	North
Vul:	Both
Contract:	4♥
Declarer:	South

North
♠ 9 5
♥ Q J 8 2
♦ A K Q J
♣ 10 9 4

West
♠ K 10 4 2
♥ K 7
♦ 8 5 3
♣ A Q 8 5

East
♠ Q J 7 3
♥ 5 3
♦ 9 6 4
♣ 7 6 3 2

South
♠ A 8 6
♥ A 10 9 6 4
♦ 10 7 2
♣ K J

Suggested Bidding

North opens 1♦ with 13 high-card points, East passes, and South responds 1♥ with 12 high-card points plus 1 length point for the five-card heart suit.

West has support for both unbid suits and 12 high-card points plus 1 dummy point for the doubleton heart. That's enough to make a takeout double.

North, with four-card heart support and a minimum opening, raises to 2♥. East doesn't have enough to compete and passes. With 13 points and having found a heart fit, South takes the partnership to game in hearts.

Opening Lead

West doesn't want to lead either of the opponents' suits and doesn't want to lead away from the ♣A. West chooses to lead the ♠2.

Bridge Quiz:

How will the play go to the first trick?

How will that help the defense take all the tricks to which it is entitled?

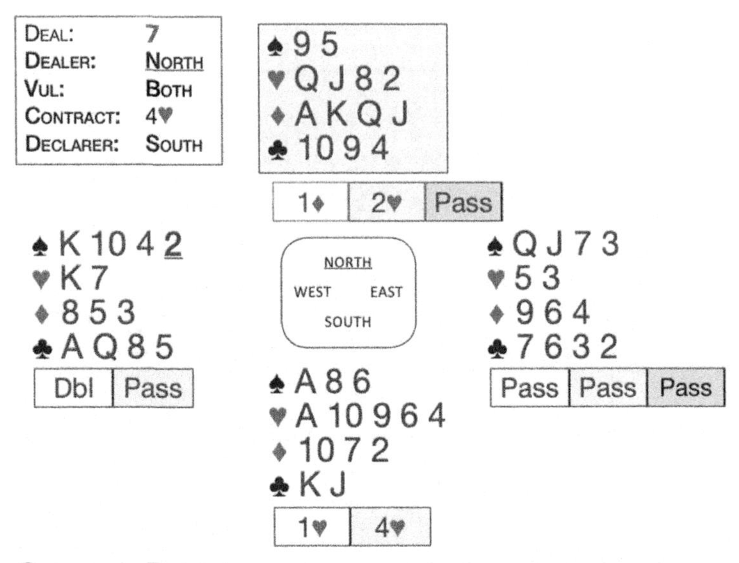

Suggested Defense

When the ♠2 is led and a low spade is played from dummy, East plays third hand high, trying to win the trick for the defense. With touching honors, however, East plays the ♠J, only as high as necessary. When declarer wins the ♠A, West knows East must hold the ♠Q.

Declarer crosses to dummy with a diamond to try the heart finesse, which loses to West's ♥K. Now West plays the ♠4 to East's promoted ♠Q. East can lead a club, following the maxim to lead through strength and up to weakness in the dummy. This traps declarer's ♣K and allows the defense to get two club tricks, in addition to the ♥K and ♠Q, to defeat the contract.

Suggested Play

After winning the ♥K, if West takes the ♠K, declarer, on regaining the lead, can finish drawing trumps and discard a club loser on dummy's extra diamond winner.

Conclusion

Playing third hand only as high as necessary helps the defenders set up a defensive club finesse.

9

DANIELLE'S SOS – 2004

Danielle, whose formative years had been strictly manipulated by the stern-faced but kindly sisters of the Holy Order of Mary, Joseph, and Jesus, experienced her SOS only a year before the group sixtieth. It was still pretty raw, but at least it hadn't lasted long. Quick and dirty, she said with a touch of irony.

Her reputation as the Bridge Club's "queen of clean" had never been disputed. Who would have thought that one of her monthly, high-intensity housecleaning binges would uncover the dirt it did?

Dani and Bryce had been married for thirty-six very normal, happy years during which their two very normal, happy children had been raised in a very normal, happy home environment. Sounds too simple, but it happens.

They had been besotted with each other since day one. Driving down Highway 400 from cottage country in their new 1968 MGB, Bryce and his brother blew by the TR3 in the middle lane when they noticed the two attractive occupants. The girls had already spotted them—the car first, truth be told. Small British sports cars were hot items in those days.

The guys crossed over to the slow lane and eased up on the accelerator until the girls pulled alongside, also decelerating. There was some serious eye contact, but when the guys signaled to the girls to pull over, their response was vigorous headshaking. Even in those days you never knew what sort of weirdos were out there. The girls did slow down to keep pace though. With the tops down on both cars, Bryce leaned halfway out of the convertible, waving a piece of paper in his hand. Danielle, the passenger, reached out and somehow, as Jane avoided contact with very little distance between the two moving vehicles, grabbed the paper. On it was a name, phone number, and the message: "Call me please! I need to know you!"

Danielle and Jane, friends in their last year of university, were driving back from a Georgian Bay weekend. Jane's lifelong friend Lynn and some other keen bridge players had rented a rambling old cottage for a girls' getaway. It had been a blast, and one of the first times all of the women who ultimately would become the Bridge Club had been together.

Danielle did make the phone call, and she and Bryce never looked back.

That first impression had not been wrong. They were married within the year and never ceased to find each other interesting, challenging, and attractive in all the ways that mattered. Bryce had been raised in a strongly Roman Catholic family, and their shared faith was a vital part of their relationship. If anything, he was even more committed to his religion than she was. This was the main reason he had been able to break through some of the barriers set up by the teachings of the blessed sisters.

The nuns would no doubt have felt stirrings of pride to know that Danielle was a virgin on her wedding night. However, their satisfaction might have faded quickly as the blushing bride realized what the joys of sexual freedom meant to her and the commitment she made to discover all she had been missing. Bryce was a most willing and capable partner.

Not that there hadn't been blips along the way, periods when they were "out of sync" as they called it. Of course they argued and had disagreements like everyone else, but it never became personal, and if hurtful words were said there were apologies and forgiveness. They both understood fully how unnecessary and destructive a negative attitude was.

Communication was a natural strength they shared. Accountability was paramount in the way they raised their children and the way they approached life. It certainly seemed to have paid off, as they sailed through the teenage years with little more than the standard missed curfews, some underage drinking, and messy rooms.

Their values were strong and clearly demonstrated and the core of the family was solid. Honesty was a given, the foundation on which everything was built.

There were times when others commented to Dani and Bryce how the bond between them was abnormally strong, but there was never a moment they wanted to change things. As boring as it might seem to others, they were perfectly happy and comfortable with their lives. Danielle never thought about something going wrong with their marriage, and that's why when the shit hit the fan, she really wasn't certain she could find the strength to handle the mess.

In 2000, Dani had retired from her position as an art historian at the Art Gallery of Ontario. She had enjoyed the challenges and rewards of her career and remained a committed volunteer at the AGO. As much as she missed the conviviality of her coworkers and the lunchtime strolls along Queen Street West, she quickly immersed herself in planning trips she and Bryce had dreamt of through the years.

Bryce was able to re-organize his financial management career and move into semi-retirement handling the accounts of his clients, from wherever in the world he happened to be, thanks to his laptop and cell phone.

The messages in those "Freedom Fifty-five" ads had come in loud and clear, and they wasted no time living the dream of early retirement.

Basking in the warmth of their sun-filled two-bedroom condo, Danielle stood at the floor-to-ceiling windows. *It feels like I could simply leap out onto the deck of one of those sailboats,* she thought, watching them bobbing at their moorings directly below. The view over Lake Ontario to the city skyline never disappointed and could be enjoyed from every room.

"Who knew?" She and Bryce had asked each other when they downsized their home, moved to the Etobicoke lakeshore, and discovered it was perfect for them.

"What a fine job the city did on this waterfront development," Bryce commented to Danielle during a walk as they stopped for a drink at a small bistro.

"I love it," she enthused. "The butterfly habitats, all the wildflowers and grasses, such good ideas."

They would often bike to the Saint Lawrence Market and have one of the traditional back bacon sandwiches before loading their packs with treats for dinner. Other times they would pedal to the end of the Martin Goodman Trail at the Beaches (or Beach depending on what name you voted for), which felt like suddenly arriving in some small ocean-side town in California.

Living by the lake, they discovered a whole new dimension to this city they already loved and knew this was the neighborhood they would call home.

Compacting their lives into one quarter the size of their spacious home had been a challenge, resulting in the repetition of a new mantra: "A place for everything and everything in its place." This was essential to avoid instant clutter and was a natural coping strategy given Dani's history as a neat freak.

There simply was no room for stuff to just lie around and collect.

Shortly after moving, they were scheduled to leave for their annual two-week September vacation in the Eastern Townships of Quebec. Before departing, they had knocked themselves out unpacking crates and boxes and were pleased with how organized they had been. Nevertheless there were some items that had not found their "place" in the new space. As a result, one closet had been designated for storage, to be dealt with in the future. Danielle shoved all the left over stuff into the small space. Later.

Loading their gear in the car, they headed off on the easy seven-hour drive. Most of it would be along the boring but speedy Highway 401 before they stopped for lunch at an invitingly dumpy diner in the outskirts of Montreal. Madame Tremblay had been serving up her French-Canadian cuisine here for decades.

Since the very first time, over thirty years before, there was never any question what their order would be. It was the one meal where all rules of good nutrition went out the window for these two travelers.

"*Deux poutines comme toujours, mes chers amis?*" Madame Tremblay's strong, throaty voice sang out their regular order of two poutines. Next they recovered from the customary bearhug after they walked through the door. After all these years she considered them regulars and noticed if they were late for a seasonal visit.

Freshly cut potatoes filled the plate, fried in two different oils, topped with her homemade gravy that was light but still rich and full of flavor. Finely grated Quebec cheddar and local curds topped the masterpiece. Artery clogging, perhaps, but so delicious they could never resist.

"Mmmm ... yummm," murmured Danielle. Bryce nodded in return with a satisfied grin.

In between bites they caught up on family news with their old friend before a strong espresso sent them out the door for the last two hours, cruising along scenic Highway 10 to their destination.

Danielle's roots in les Cantons de l'Est were long and deep. Her extended family shared their typically French homestead on the shores of Petit Lac Magog with assorted cousins for a couple of generations ever since the great-grandparents had passed on. They had all negotiated a schedule that seemed to work so that each family enjoyed time there during all four seasons. The leaves would be presenting their blazing autumn exhibition during their stay, and hiking the gently rolling hills would offer a visual feast.

It hadn't been a hard sell to entice Bryce to accompany her to this part of her world when they were first together, and he had soon felt as connected to the Townships as she did.

Back in Toronto after the vacation, Danielle rolled up her sleeves one morning after first cranking up Beatles music on her iPod. For over thirty years that was her music of choice to clean by. Today she was going to give the place a good once over. She moved all the furniture, cleaned every nook and cranny, and decided to tackle the storage closet. Bryce was off on his annual four-day fishing weekend at an isolated island lodge in Georgian Bay with the guys, so it was the perfect opportunity to turn things upside down.

Standing tiptoe on the top rung of the small stepladder, she momentarily lost her balance and knocked one of Bryce's old briefcases to the floor. Working from home now and with files all stored on a laptop, he really didn't use them anymore. This particular case had always been her favorite, with a soft, rich leather the color of roasted chestnuts and classic brass fittings. It had such a fine quality look to it that suited Bryce. As silly as it sounded, she had loved to see him carrying it.

The briefcase hit the floor with a sharp thud, and the locks popped open. Her heart stopped as her brain tried to make sense of what her eyes were seeing. Strewn across the carpet at her feet was a jumble of sex toys, condoms, pills, and porn DVDs more graphic than any she had ever seen. Danielle stared in disbelief, her face burning. She shut off her iPod.

Jumping to conclusions was not an option, because none of them made any sense. Dani sat stunned. Then, slowly, she examined each item with her eyes, too repulsed to touch them.

She tried to imagine that perhaps he simply wanted to use them by himself to satisfy some longing he did not feel comfortable sharing with her. As crazy as it seemed, was he seeking moments of private satisfaction, living out some sexual fantasy into which he chose not to invite her?

It simply did not compute. Their sex life had always been a big part of their relationship, she thought, with experimentation that pleased and excited them both. Bryce had never indicated he was dissatisfied in any way. Besides, she was ignoring the reality of what she was seeing. She forced herself to accept the evidence in front of her. These items definitely were meant for the participation of more than one person. You don't have a strap-on dildo to screw yourself. No one needs condoms to have sex alone. And Viagra? What was that all about? Bryce had always told her he would never even think of trying it because of the risk with his high blood pressure. Surely he would not consider sex with someone else worth that risk. That thought was almost too much to bear.

The sense of betrayal was overwhelming, even physical. All color drained from her face and she looked as sick as she felt. Suddenly she clutched her stomach and dashed to the powder room just in time to violently retch. Disbelief, anger, and sorrow swirled through her mind as she clung to the sink, her legs weak. Soaking a hand towel in cold water, she held it to her face until she felt some relief and slowly returned to the scene. Stunned once more by what lay strewn before her, she sank onto the floor and leaned against the sofa. Dazed and nauseated she sat there for a long while before she stood up, furiously kicked everything into the case, and shoved it back on the shelf.

Danielle knew she had to digest this. She had to find a way to be calm and rational before she could begin to make sense of it all. Certainly she could not speak of it in the shape she found herself at that moment. Never had she imagined a problem like this could exist between them—whatever the problem was. Her confusion was overwhelming, her thoughts erratic as she tried to convince herself she might be jumping to conclusions.

Bryce, like most guys, always had an appreciative eye for a beautiful woman and Dani would frequently be his point guard, issuing a "babe alert." She didn't feel it was being sexist, just enjoying nature's bounties. He would return the favor with "hunk alerts" for her. At times they would just look at each other and roar with laughter at the frivolity of it all. Their fidelity, though, their commitment to their union, was unequivocal. So she thought.

So what the hell had happened?

Dani sat by the window trying to rid herself of the horrible smothering sensation. She had to get a grip. Perhaps there really was an easy explanation that she just could not see. Thinking back over the past few months, she wondered if she had missed something.

Certainly for the past year or so, Bryce had alternately complained and joked about *Monsieur Magique* losing his touch. There had been times when he had been frustrated by what he considered a less than stellar sexual performance. But it had never been a real issue—or so she thought. They always found other ways to satisfy each other and agreed that some change was to be expected as the years went by. Was that it?

She had to admit there were some odd moments while they were in the Eastern Townships, just weeks ago. She hadn't dwelt upon those incidents for more than a moment. Now they came flooding back and she sensed a bit of a jolt recalling some weird feelings.

The trip had begun so well.

"As soon as we get organized here," Bryce had announced upon their arrival at the cottage, "I'm calling to make our traditional dinner reservation. Oooo-la-la, I can taste that mouthwatering Brome Lake duckling already."

"Okay, *mon cher*," Dani had replied. "After that I'll call the yoga studio to confirm our three-day retreat next week, *comme d'habitude*."

Then the first disappointment occurred.

"Uh, Dani… " Bryce had stammered uncharacteristically, "I know you won't be happy about this, but I have to beg off this year. I've too much work to do. I thought I would spend that time on business stuff so I won't have to take time away from our other plans."

"*Merde!* But we've gone to that retreat for the last eighteen years! Are you sure? I'm so sad … but if you can't, you can't."

Typically their stay consisted of healthy outdoor activity combined with scrumptious meals, visits with friends and relatives, meandering drives down country roads with stops for tastings of wine, cheese, ciders or buying fresh fall produce and home-baked goods at the many farm stalls. No visit was complete without at least one stop at L'Abbaye St. Benôit du Lac on Lac Memphremagog to experience the deep spirituality of Gregorian chanting ringing through the golden chambers of this Benedictine cloister. The ciders and cheeses produced by the monks were on sale to take care of more earthly desires.

It should have been another perfect holiday in the townships, but it wasn't.

There was something amiss between them, and the most unsettling part was that Danielle could not put her finger on it. She felt it, but when she mentioned it to Bryce he assured her she was imagining things.

Pulling her into his arms, he hugged her warmly as he always did and brushed his lips across her forehead. "Don't be silly, *mon amour*. Aren't we having a fabulous time as always?"

Dani returned the hug and brought her lips up to meet his. *Something is wrong*, she thought. Her words told him he was right, but she knew deep down he wasn't. She wished she could figure out why.

The fact he had cancelled out of the yoga workshop had been most upsetting, because he actually did not seem to have such a great workload with him. She could judge from the time he spent on the telephone just how busy he was and he had not been on it much. But he sure had been glued to his computer.

At times he appeared to be trying too hard to be his usual relaxed self. Although his words would indicate he was having fun and was not distracted by anything, his body language and tight smile indicated otherwise.

Bryce had been his usual exuberant self when they were hiking and biking although she noticed they spent less time at it. At the cottage he had been withdrawn at times and blamed some big accounts for making extra demands on the computer for him, often staying up later and slipping into bed after she had fallen asleep.

They definitely had not made love as much as usual, and he was the one who always referred to himself as "horny in Hatley" when they were down there. Danielle had been keenly aware of this but said nothing. She simply reminded herself that he would tell her what was on his mind in due course. He always did. At least that was what she thought.

Now, as she stared unseeing out the living room window, she wondered if her vague anxieties perhaps were well founded. She made a few attempts to find solace in some meditation. It wasn't working. She tried to look for an answer through prayer. That didn't work either.

Sinking into the softly cushioned wingback chair, Danielle lost herself in the lake view. The afternoons were quickly becoming shorter, and as she watched the sun dip lower in the sky, her heart sank with it. Abruptly she rose with a shake and walked into the bedroom.

Standing before the full-length mirror, she slowly dropped her clothes to the floor and studied her naked form. People were always surprised when she mentioned in passing how old she was. She had been told so often that she didn't look her age, she had almost allowed herself to believe it.

Her shoulder length blunt-cut black hair was shiny, full of life. The straight-cut bangs gave her a schoolgirl look and her regular hairdresser would tease her, suggesting she let him give her a trendier style. But her old style was easy to maintain and Bryce always said he loved her hair, so she kept it that way.

Bryce made her feel desired and attractive, which gave her the confidence to feel that perhaps she still was. Sure, her average-sized breasts were no longer perky, but they were still firm and round with a slight sag that was not unappealing. Her waist remained distinctly there, although it didn't create the curvaceous effect it once did. There was no denying the noticeable bulge where her flat stomach had once resided, but her abs were strong and she could still suck it in and feel good about tucking tops into her skirts or wearing the spandex sports gear so popular now. Her regimen of yoga and walking combined with biking and golf kept the weight off, and even though her thighs were fuller than before, they weren't in the "thunder" category.

She was no spring chicken she had to admit as she examined her reflection more critically than ever. Bryce had consistently told her over the years she had great legs, even though she thought her ankles were bony. Her eyes rested now at the top of her legs and then quickly filled with tears as she felt her anger take over. Between her legs was the sexy little secret she shared with her husband.

Years ago on a steamy night of lovemaking, she had gone into the shower and shaved her pubic hair on a whim. She had read in some article how this was a turn-on for men and thought she would surprise her lover. The nuns would not have approved! Bryce reacted just as she had hoped and she had continued the practice, discreetly concealing her body in the gym change rooms, saving the secret just for her lover, her husband, her trusted partner. She had felt pleased with herself that even approaching sixty, she could act and feel as erotic as when she was in her prime. Now she felt humiliated and stupid and foolish for not acting her age—whatever that was.

The trust she always had in her husband was the key to the intimacy they shared and the confidence she had in herself physically. She was shattered at the thought that this trust had somehow been broken. She threw herself on the bed and stayed there for a long while, attempting to clear her head before she crawled under the covers.

On Sunday she was a wreck after a sleepless night. Since she was up anyway, she went to the 8 a.m. early mass, which she knew would bring her some comfort and peace. Not this time. Her head simply would not allow her religious beliefs to get involved in this situation. She couldn't figure it out, but God was not getting through to her right now.

After splashing cold water on her face, she forced herself to sit and drink a cup of tea before throwing on a jacket and taking a long walk by the lake. Inhaling the cool autumn air, she followed one of the many paths through the Butterfly Garden to the rocks that lined the shore of Humber Bay. The sight of the afternoon sun washing over the downtown skyline across the harbor was always a pleasing view. Today it wasn't doing anything for her. Her mind was blank at this point. After an hour she slowly made her way home.

Bryce flew in the door late in the afternoon with his predictable high energy, and Dani had the makings of their favorite martini waiting. She had decided to keep up a façade for the moment in the hope there would be some sign that she was totally off the mark. Curious, she thought, how we are able to fool ourselves into not accepting the obvious.

She expected that he would entertain her with the weekend's report, which she could always count on to give them several good laughs. Oddly, this time he was short on conversation.

"Bryce, is everything all right?" she asked, hoping her voice sounded normal.

"Yeah, sure ... why not?" he replied a bit curtly as he drained his glass and smiled at her in not quite his usual way before he turned his gaze out the window.

This was her chance to tell him what happened, but she blew it. Her fear of hearing something she so desperately did not want to hear overrode her hope of hearing she had been totally mistaken. She quickly stood, taking the empty glasses to the kitchen, saying over her shoulder, "Oh nothing ... I guess, nothing..."

Normally this kind of a conversation would not have been left hanging, but today it was. Bryce muttered he had to get to his computer, saying he had reports to read.

Nothing felt right, but Danielle hoped it was her now out of control imagination. She simply could not bring herself to raise the issue and that was disturbing in its own way. This was not the way they handled problems, she reminded herself. Her inability to express herself was so out of character it was frightening her as much as her awareness that Bryce was hiding something.

Time. She needed some time. She also needed to run this whole scenario by someone she trusted who could listen without being judgmental. Thankfully, Bridge Club Tuesday was just three days away.

Somehow she would carry on until then and say nothing. Definitely this was not something she could address with anyone in the family. She would work on a plan and run it by the BC. She had to believe the reality surely wasn't the ongoing X-rated video that wouldn't stop playing in her mind.

The next two days dragged by with Dani's explanation of a flu bug covering her subdued behavior. It offered an excuse for her physical distance from Bryce in bed, but now she was even more aware that he wasn't really interested anyway. In many ways he was his considerate self and yet there was definitely something off kilter. Deception simply was not his style. Each time she thought he was keeping secrets or blatantly lying to her, she felt desperately out of control. At times she just had to sit down and try to catch her breath as she struggled to banish her harsh, scrambled thoughts.

There were moments she was certain she was going to completely lose it, but first thing in the morning both days she slipped out to her yoga class anticipating the strength it would give her. The focus on mantras and positions, the total letting go of everything else around her, brought her to a meditative space now and helped hold her together.

Yoga had been a part of her life since her artistic mother introduced her to it as a child in Quebec. It was through her teaching that Danielle had come to understand how yoga and religion complement and support each other in many ways.

She gave both an equal place in her psyche, although yoga was a subject most definitely not approved of by the nuns of her youth. It wasn't until she was a young mother and yoga studios became more of a trendy thing that she immersed herself in the study.

She was thankful now more than ever for the peaceful place she could reach through the practice. As much as she was committed to her religion, she knew it was to yoga she would turn for help with this problem. She just didn't think God would get it.

Danielle had discovered an amazing teacher in Toronto many years before. At ninety-one years of age, Constance had been practicing yoga since she was five years old and, although she preferred not to mention it, had achieved the highly respected and rarely achieved ultimate level of swami. She also drove a convertible, had the best sense of humor, could do a headstand forever, and had a totally up-to-date hairstyle: definitely role model material.

Yogis believe that we all have the power to find the goodness in ourselves—that place deep within us that is eternally at peace and shelters our true identity.

"That place from which we can at least find an understanding of what the hell is going on," Dani would tell her non-yoga friends.

Constance had been instrumental in guiding Danielle to explore her own path, and this was an important part of how she lived her life, despite the eye-rolls of some of her friends. She would need to find her center now, she told herself, and spent extra time in a private meditation area attempting to do just that.

Tuesday evening finally arrived with Pam collecting Dani to drive to Dee's place.

"Hey girl, you look absolutely awful. What's wrong?"

"I've got the flu," answered Danielle as she flopped into the front seat and closed the car door with a bit of a slam.

Pam shot her a second look and said, "Yeah, right!"

Running her hands through her hair, Danielle pulled it back into a tense knot at the nape of her neck and grimly looked straight ahead. "That's my story and I'm sticking to it."

Pam continued to peer intently at her friend with questioning concern before she slipped the car into gear. Recognizing distress in Danielle's voice, she studied her face and instantly knew there was a problem.

"Sure ... *not*! What's going on?"

Danielle's dark eyes began to fill but she managed to maintain her composure.

"I have to wait until we're all together so I don't have to go through the story twice. I'm not sure I can repeat it."

"Fine, now that you've really got me worried, at least tell me it's not cancer or a serious problem with the kids or anything like that before you make me totally crazy!"

"Fortunately it's not, and maybe I'm wrong about the whole thing. We'll see."

Pam reached across the seat and squeezed Dani's hand. They forced themselves into an almost normal conversation, catching up on family news before they switched to the close mayoral race that was energizing the city.

The late rush hour traffic was dragging on. Spotting a chance to make a quick right turn, Pam slipped into a Starbucks drive-through lane. "I think a couple of skinny lattes would go down well as we crawl along."

Dani nodded and managed a weak smile, grateful for a shot of caffeine. "Trust you to make the thoughtful gesture."

"Well, not to belabor the point, my friend, but you know my perspective on things since Peter died. I've been to the bottom of the well so nothing else can be that bad for me. I know we can deal with whatever challenges us. I want to help."

"I want that too. And I know you will once I get it out."

Respecting the need for quiet now, Pam pulled back into the traffic while Danielle turned her head to the window and sipped her latte.

The gardens in the spacious University Avenue boulevards were overflowing with colorful and exotic plantings this year, a pleasant distraction Danielle appreciated. With Toronto being such a green city and the downtown area full of parks and planters, the hot, humid summer had created magnificent floral showcases on street after street. With autumn approaching, every bloom appeared to be at its peak before it succumbed to nature's call to seed and quietly wither away. Today Danielle found herself staring vacantly at the passing scenery and wished she didn't feel like she, too, was withering away.

She was relieved to see they were the last to arrive at Dee's. Soothing classical music underscored the welcome as the mouthwatering aroma of roast pork wafted from the kitchen. Danielle gladly accepted a glass of wine and immediately had everyone's attention. The pain on her face gave her away.

All eyes were riveted on her as she told her story more calmly than she had anticipated. She neglected to identify the strap-on item from the briefcase to the BC, too embarrassed for her sake and Bryce's, no matter how upset with him she was. As always, the color of her cheeks quickly changing from pink to raging crimson proclaimed the intensity of her feelings. As the last sentence spilled out, her floodgates opened and tears covered her cheeks.

Putting her arm around Danielle's shoulders, Jane said, "What a shock coming upon that stuff out of the blue."

"Totally bizarre!" Lynn sputtered, with a shake of her head.

"But maybe it's nothing," suggested Cass.

"Yes," agreed Pam, "maybe there's some simple explanation ... although I'm not coming up with one."

"And," Danielle sobbed, "I've spent the last couple of days

wondering if my marriage is over. I know I'm overreacting but I'm so scared ... so confused. I never would have imagined us ever having any problems—certainly not involving something like this! Have I been completely out of touch with reality or so unaware I didn't see...?"

Jane drew Danielle into her arms until her shoulders stopped heaving and she pulled herself together a bit.

"I can't believe how this is making me crazy. Why couldn't I just ask him about it, like I normally would? It's like I'm in a really bad dream..." her voice trailed off.

"This is so weird," muttered Cass. "I mean, Bryce of all people. Mr. Cool, Upfront, No Bullshit, Love of Your Life, Good Catholic Boy, Regular Guy Bryce."

"Unreal," agreed Lynn.

Danielle abruptly rose, moving quickly down the hall and into the powder room. Pressing a cold washcloth on her face, she held her hands firmly over her eyes for a minute working to force the tears to stop. Returning to the living room, she rubbed her fingertips on her temples as she sat back down.

"I'm sorry I'm being such a drama queen, but I just feel so, well..." She inhaled and shuddered as if to give herself a shake, searching for the right word. "Shattered—that's it, shattered. What the hell do I do next? How do I figure out what's going on?"

After batting around all sorts of possibilities, there seemed to be a consensus. The first thought was an affair. But nothing really added up to that, since he was always around.

"But what explains his bag of tricks then?" wondered Bonnie. "Dani had a point when she said you don't need Viagra and condoms unless someone else is involved. Something doesn't add up."

Nodding her head, Danielle sadly agreed. "Why would Bryce be unfaithful to me, unless I've been unbelievably stupid? We've always told each other how lucky we are to have such a great relationship. You guys have teased me incessantly over the years about how we still act like newlyweds!"

They all agreed it had been a standing joke through the almost forty years.

"Up until just a while ago he would still catch me at times, back me up against the wall, and kiss me like he meant it. Sometimes we'd just get it on right there and then!"

"Whoa, TMI!" hollered Bo, holding up her open palms, "More information than we need, thanks."

Dani nodded, smiling weakly. "Just wanted you to see the passion was still there and not so long ago."

"Think carefully, Dan," Pam asked sympathetically. "Do you think you can pinpoint when something changed?"

Danielle held her head in her hands for a few seconds and brushed back the hair that had fallen across her face. "There is something else, now that I'm forced to think about it." She paused as she lost herself in thought once again. Speaking slowly, she went on, "You know, he's been acting a bit differently lately, but I put it down to all the changes in our life, with selling our home and the move and, well, just some normal aging issues…" She trailed off again.

Taking a long, deep breath, she asked no one in particular, "Remember when I went to visit my sister for two weeks in May?"

"Yes, she was home from rehab after her knee replacement and you went to see her and help with the family because her husband had to leave on a business trip," Dee reminded the rest of the women.

"How could we forget? It was one of the very few times you and Bryce have been apart for more than a day or two after all these years of marriage," Pam teased, hoping to get a smile from Dani. "We called you our Paul and Linda McCartney."

"We kidded you about behaving like an anxious young wife

leaving her mate to fend for himself!" Bonnie now tried to win a smile from her.

They chuckled, all except Danielle.

"Well, I didn't mention this before, because I wanted to think it was nothing. A few days after my return, I went to play a yoga DVD and there was already a disk in the machine. As I replaced it I saw it was a porn DVD. I put it back in and didn't say a word about it."

"Were you upset?" Cass asked.

"Dumbfounded, at first, is more the word. Then, astonished. It occurred to me that maybe I hadn't tuned in to how deeply Bryce is affected by the recent problems he's having with his—uh, shall we say—sexual performance at times, or at least the problems he thinks he's having. I mean, I realize it's a major psychological issue, although he hasn't talked much about it to me, which is so unlike him. What surprises me is that I'm walking on egg shells. I can't bring myself to start the conversation."

"It's not an easy one to casually launch into, that's for sure," Jane agreed with a serious air, absent-mindedly tapping her long nails on the lamp table next to her.

"But it's not an issue for me," Danielle exclaimed firmly, "and I know we can work around it. I guess it's really a crisis for him."

"The dreaded ED—one of those nasty problems many men have to deal with as they age. It's good to see it's getting a lot of attention... " said Lynn.

"The ads are everywhere," Dee interrupted.

"That's for sure. Everyone is more aware it's not uncommon," Lynn continued.

"I've got friends whose husbands are struggling with the problem. It seems to go with the territory around our age," said Pam.

"Do you think Bryce has been taking any medication for it? Maybe that's why he had the Viagra," Marti said.

With a shrug of her shoulders, Danielle replied she'd never seen any sign of them. "If he is, he's hiding them, which would be really weird."

"Maybe not weird to him. He might be really embarrassed, no matter how open you are with each other," said Pam. "From what I've read, problems like that are tough for men to accept."

The talk deviated momentarily to the many ads on television, with couples of a certain age either exchanging come-hither glances or awash in post-coital glow.

"Some of those pill ads are hilarious!" Bonnie hooted, raising four fingers.

"Particularly the warnings about four-hour erections," Cass added with a wicked grin, "Call me ... please!"

Even Danielle had to laugh at that outburst.

Pam returned to the serious side of the conversation. "Oh brother, here we go again. Laughing when we're trying to be serious. There are options to treat erectile dysfunction, you know, Dani. Bryce doesn't need to feel like it's the end of the world."

"And obviously his problems aren't that bad. We still have sex, just not as often and not like it used to be," Danielle said as she shook her head slowly. "I just deal with it but I guess he can't."

"So get back to when you found the porn DVD. What did you do afterwards?" Analytical Dee was gathering all the data. "Why didn't you say something to Bryce then?"

"Well," explained Danielle, "after I decided his problem has been driving him crazy, I thought he probably was watching something erotic to see if it might help. It didn't really bother me once I got over the surprise. I figured he would tell me about it in good time, so I didn't even mention it."

Everyone was immersed in her own thoughts for a moment

before Danielle continued, “When we were first married, Bryce had a few old stag movies, as they were called then, that we watched from time to time. He seemed to get off on them, but I couldn’t stop laughing because they were soooo amateurishly shot.”

“Oh God, I remember those,” Jane said with a laugh, “and the ‘stars’ all looked like such losers. They were hilarious, really!”

Cass leapt up, performing a shimmy a la Dita Von Teese that could have been a showstopper on any stage. “Debbie Does Dallas has nothing on me!”

Flopped on the couch, Bo announced, “I’d join you, Cass but I was at a business meeting this afternoon and I’m still wearing my industrial strength Spanx. I can hardly move!”

She crossed her eyes, making a face that got the point across all too clearly. Laughter filled the room.

Marti was next to perform, flashing her lacey bra, “And don’t you think I could be in the next version of *Bodacious Tatas*? The seniors’ version, of course.”

Dani couldn’t help laughing again. “Both of you could be stars, no question!”

“Sorry to interrupt. I just don’t get too many opportunities to behave like that these days,” said Cass. Marti seconded that.

“When didn’t we make each other laugh? I appreciate the humor, trust me,” Danielle assured them before continuing, “As I was saying, it was hard to get turned on with those old blue movies—you’d end up on the floor laughing rather than screwing. I guess we all had a peek at some of them back in the day.”

Dee held up her hand, “If I remember correctly through the haze of that evening, I do believe we had some of those black and white cinematic gems at my bridal stagette. Did we not?”

“For comedic value only!” Jane said.

The room was filled with snorts of laughter and a number of funny flashbacks to that event before they returned to

Danielle's dilemma. They were all relieved to see that their attempts at humor had brought smiles to Danielle's face, if only briefly.

"Did watching that stuff seem to be a big deal to Bryce then?" asked Marti, getting back on topic.

Danielle continued, "Not at all. I always told him I'd rather do it than watch it. He seemed to like that!"

"Back in the 70s lots of us tuned into CityTV's *Baby Blue Movie* before the novelty wore off, remember those?" asked Pam. "They caused a big uproar at the time, but today no one would give them a second thought."

"That's for sure!"

Danielle grimaced, wishing she could simply stop talking. She could not recall a time in her life when she had felt such anxiety. "Well, before finding the one I just told you about, I've not been aware of anything like that in the house. The one I found is still there in a cupboard, and I don't think I'd care if he said he wanted to watch it, but then again ... maybe I would... " She paused and took in a deep inhalation, blowing it out noisily and shaking her head as if to clear it. "What I do care about is all this secrecy. As I said before, we just don't have secrets from each other. At least, I thought we don't. I mean, what's the use of that behavior?"

A look of frustration filled her face. "I don't know what to think anymore."

"In my opinion, couples who keep secrets from each other have much deeper issues," said Lynn.

"Well, I don't necessarily think you have to tell each other everything," offered Dee. "Why not keep some things to yourself?"

"I'm telling you, Dee," Pam said in a strong voice, "you can see this confirmed in article after article: secrets in a marriage, once exposed, cause feelings of deceit and betrayal—just like Dani. I know I would feel the same!"

"Don't get me wrong ladies," said Cass. "I'm completely on board with the honesty issue. However I'm positive that tons of people look at porn from time to time and don't say anything about it. That's not being dishonest."

"You're right, Cass. But it doesn't sound like what's happening with Bryce is as simple as that," countered Danielle.

"Of course you don't have to report every little detail of your day, but most couples in a good relationship do share the mundane stuff. You know what I mean—who you talked to that day, what they said, where you went, what you did. It's just natural. You might forget something and never mention it. That's perfectly normal. But to feel you have to hide anything even if it's a little off the norm, like the fact that you watch porn or stop in at a strip club with the guys—that's not the way it works in a good relationship. That speaks to a deeper problem," said Lynn with a look of clear conviction.

"I completely agree," Pam said with a nod.

"So do I," said Danielle, "that's my point."

Marti felt herself being thrown back into that very dark time of her life when she had been faced with her own husband's lies and the pain it caused. She interrupted quietly, "Don't forget I'm the poster child in this group for having a marriage ruined by deceit. There's nothing better than honesty in a relationship—in every way."

It was fair to say that put an end to that debate.

As out of character as it seemed, they wondered if Bryce might be inclined to make a quick pickup at a bar, use an escort service, or something like that, while going through a "late" midlife crisis.

Dani found that possibility unacceptable. "I feel strongly that this is not what's going on, but then again, why did he have all that stuff?" She shook her head slowly, frown lines deepening.

Closing her eyes for a moment, she sat surrounded by

silence again, everyone's mind working overtime. Then she continued.

"Years ago, he enjoyed hitting a strip club or two on a boys' night out."

She recalled that he always expressed a certain disdain for the married guys who were so hard up they got their pleasure paying for lap dances (and whatever else might follow in these liberated times). He always said it was much more fun to "get horny and go home." A night like that never failed to end in a fast drive home and a trail of clothes leading to the bedroom.

She reminded them how in the early days, before kids, they sometimes went with other couples in a noisy group to the old Victory Burlesque House at Dundas and Spadina and then stopped in at one of the great delis down the street after the show. Innocent fun at the time. Amateur night was the best laugh. "So there's no logical reason for him not to mention stuff like that."

"I just can't get a handle on the situation. I have to ask myself if I've been insensitive about his ED and haven't responded properly. I've always been supportive and loving and tried to make him feel good, even if Steve and the twins were AWOL—if you get my drift." They all chuckled at her use of the familiar slang expression from their younger days and then nodded sympathetically.

"Maybe it's my fault," she wondered sadly. "Maybe I just don't turn him on anymore. Maybe he wakes up in the morning and just sees me as an old lady instead of the girl he fell in love with."

"Dani, stop beating yourself up. There has to be another answer. When two people are as close as you've always seemed, they see past the aging. They feel the love that was always there," Pam reassured her.

"Right," said Bonnie, "and they just keep the lights off."

"Oh, ha ha ha," Cass responded with a cynical laugh. "Too true to be funny."

Danielle sat quietly looking off into space, turning something over in her mind, and then she spoke again. "The only obvious competition I've felt recently is Bryce's laptop. He is joined at the hip to that thing and seems to prefer having his nightcap with it instead of me these days."

"Hmmm—that comment gives me a thought," muttered Cass. As much as she hated to even suggest it, it had to be considered. Unthinkable as it might seem, this suggestion did offer a certain logic and, at the very least, a path to pursue.

Taking a large swig from her rum and Coke, Cass spoke softly. "Dani, you're not going to like what I'm going to say, but I seriously think it's a possibility. I wonder if Bryce is caught up in Internet pornography."

Dani's reaction was immediate. "Absolutely not! He's not the type!"

"Just what is 'the type'?" questioned Pam.

Bonnie was quick to respond. "From what I read these days, Internet smut has been a magnet for all sorts of 'types.' It's unreal how out there it is. Oprah has even done a couple of shows about it, so that tells you something! I assure you from my experience with addiction that no one can claim immunity if they choose to get involved."

"Internet porn, cybersex—if you're involved in one it often leads to the other for those that are so inclined. It's a problem all right," agreed Jane, tapping on her glass. "You've heard some of my stories of the situations we're having with high school students and these issues. It's pervasive—especially now that everyone has the Internet and cameras on their cell phones."

"No kidding," said Lynn, "what a challenge for teachers these days."

"Obviously something very out of character for Bryce has

been going on and you need to consider all options if you want to get to the truth of it," Dee said.

Cass gently urged Danielle to simply consider the facts and see if anything struck a nerve with her.

"Well, speaking of the *type*," Pam said, rolling her eyes as she shook her head, "I can't believe we're having this conversation. I just had lunch with a friend at work the other day who confided in me that, after discovering some large charges on her phone bill, her husband admitted he was calling phone sex numbers. Sweet Mother of God, as you might say Dani, what's going on out there? Here's another guy you would never point the finger at for that sort of thing."

"Ahem," Marti interjected, "and let us not forget my ghost of husbands past, dear Carlos, who valued random sex more than an honest relationship."

"*Fils de salope*!" muttered Danielle, making a face.

Lynn had been quietly listening. The only sign of her reaction to the conversation was the increasingly rapid jiggling of her right foot. With her right leg crossed over her left knee, at this moment she could probably power a generator with the energy she was creating.

Now she spoke up, "Porn, porn, porn! I'm so sick of porn. It's everywhere these days and quite frankly I think it's been more damaging to society than helpful."

"I'm with you there. It's way out of control," said Pam. There were murmurs of agreement from the rest.

Lynn continued, "I wouldn't watch it if you paid me—and not because I'm a prude, as you all well know! I love a good roll in the hay with Jim. It doesn't happen as often as it used to, mind you..."

"Oh boohoo, have a little cheese and crackers with your whine." Bonnie smiled with mock sympathy as she passed a plate with just that to Lynn.

Lynn grinned at the comment and helped herself to some

cheddar before she continued. With dinner on hold everyone was getting a little hungry. "But, I mean ... more often we simply feel warm and fuzzy because of all the things we share in our lives and a snuggle is as good as it gets."

There wasn't anyone in the room who didn't agree there was a lot to be said for a good snuggle at any age. The love and comfort exchanged in a couple's warm embrace was irreplaceable. Depending on the moment, bliss or relief or security or all three were transferred.

"I have to say that's what I miss the most being on my own," Marti said quietly. Bonnie nodded. She knew the feeling.

"I couldn't agree more," said Danielle, "We've always been huggers and cuddlers. It's a big part of what we do. We just never had a problem keeping the old fires going too."

"Some do and some don't," said Lynn. "I know couples who haven't had sex as part of their marriage for years. I wondered how they could really be as happy as they appeared, but as more years go by, I have to say I get it. Intimacy is experienced in many ways in a good relationship as we age. Priorities shift."

"That's just the way life goes. It doesn't take long for the honeymoon to end—jobs, kids, and all the whatevers in life start taking over. It's more common than not, I would say," added Pam."

"Making good memories keeps the foundation strong in a marriage and that's what's most important, in my humble opinion," said Dee, standing and stretching before she headed to the kitchen. It was time for a break.

"Humble, my friend," countered Bonnie, "is not a word I would use to describe any of your opinions!" She flashed a teasing smile. "Just kidding Dee, just kidding."

"I know," Dee laughed back. "Just partially kidding."

"Family, memories, mutual respect and understanding, plans for the future, shared and separate interests, even enjoying doing nothing at times. That's my description of a happy marriage at our age," offered Lynn, "and if it's important to people, a good sex life is a bonus."

"Well you know my feelings on the subject of sex," laughed Cass with a wicked grin, as eyes rolled around the room accompanied by a few sniggers and chuckles.

"That would be a perfect example of how some things in life just never change!" Jane responded to great acknowledgement.

"And then there are those who just kind of fall into a rut and stay there, some content and some not," Marti observed.

"And sometimes what one sees as a rut is a perfectly happy situation for another," Pam countered philosophically. "Honestly, I can see how sex gets put into the 'been there, done that' category at our age."

"Whatever turns you on—or not—as long as both are in agreement. That's the bottom line," said Cass.

Marti was waving her hand with greater intensity. "Not to hog the stage in this conversation, but look at me again. I haven't closed the door on another physical relationship, but if it never happens I'm cool with that too. It's a good thing to know you can be happy on your own and no one else needs to complicate things—especially at our age. Honestly, I am so over having sex as a priority in my life!"

"Hear, hear," Bonnie cheered. "There are a lot of us perfectly happy single ladies to be found."

Danielle had been listening quietly to the conversation, one in which she would normally have been actively participating. Shaking her head and pursing her lips in a look of total exasperation, she asked no one in particular, "So where did we go wrong then? I thought we had good communication, but obviously Bryce was not talking to me about something."

"You're going to think I'm joking, but I'm not," said Bo. "I think you should send an e-mail to Sue Johanson. I still catch her show from time to time."

"If you can't laugh at sex, you shouldn't be doing it," Dee intoned, quoting a well-known line of the popular sex therapist.

"Omigawd," sputtered Lynn, "the *Sunday Night Sex Show* on Q107! Remember how I flipped out when I discovered my boys listening to it when they weren't even teenagers back in the 80s? Transistor radios under the covers!"

"Oh yeah, and then we all ended up tuning in. She was great—I guess she still is," said Jane."

"We tune in to her cable call-in show from time to time," said Pam. "She's so smart and funny—and I have to say I'm still learning from her even though her main audience is much younger. Her advice guided me through a few tricky times with my boys when they were teenagers."

"That's not a bad idea at all, Bo." said Cass.

"Hey, anything will help," agreed Danielle. "Let's check her Web site."

"Okay, let's see what we can find," Dee said after she had gone to turn the oven down. Good thing roast pork was delicious served cold or hot, she thought. It was going to be a late dinner tonight; that was obvious.

Bringing her laptop into the living room, Dee flipped it open and began to key in some words. "Well, we all know the saying '*Men see body parts, women see relationships*.' Most of this information talks about the male addiction to porn. Of course some women get involved too but it's not a demand by women that's created this inundation, I guarantee you that!"

"Why can't we just go back to the good old days when guys bought *Playboy* and looked at the pictures? That seemed to do the trick then," wondered Lynn.

For a few minutes they ranted on the state of the pornography industry today with the worst aspect of it being the accessibility to children. Now, jaws dropping, they listened as Dee read facts she was pulling up on the Internet. They had to admit they just hadn't given the subject much attention lately.

"You said it, Bo. Anybody is 'the type' and the problem is growing."

Most of the BC had been recipients of unwanted porn to their e-mail addresses and had shared solutions offered by anti-spam software. Sometimes they had received hilarious jokes from friends that were soft porn but which then caused them to be bombarded by all sorts of other unwanted spam that definitely stretched the boundaries of acceptability. They heard the same story from everyone they talked to about it.

"You know," said Danielle, "the Catholic church considers any association with pornography a grave sin. That's another reason why I would be amazed at Bryce dabbling in anything except the stupid soft porn we've been talking about. You know how he is about the Church."

Some were more open minded about the topic than others. There was no disagreement however that the Internet, unlike any medium before, unleashes sexuality in ways that traditionally were controlled through censorship in the past. They all agreed it was not a bad thing to have some rules. Otherwise things just got completely out of control.

"Say no more," said Lynn with a shrug.

The discussion grew loud at times. There was complete consensus on their abhorrence of the flood of hardcore pornography and the ease of access. You had to be living under a rock not to know it was a multi-billion dollar industry.

The parents in the Bridge Club had often expressed frustrations when their teenagers became aware of what was out there after 1994. Porn sites appearing on the family computer had happened more than once, and they heard their kids argue it was an accepted part of computer activities for their generation. There had been discipline and discussions or arguments about values, morals, rights, expectations. Parenting was no easy road, and the Internet certainly added complications in spite of all the positives.

Now they sputtered agreement that this problem of curiosity turning into addiction to porn was shocking and eye opening.

"The crack cocaine of the porn industry," was a term on several Web articles Dee pulled up. Site after site stressed how Internet porn is insidious and can be addictive because it is accessible, anonymous, and affordable until you are hooked, which can then cause huge debts.

"Oh hell," muttered Dee, scanning the information that appeared to be endless, "forget the wine and pour me a double scotch please. Listen to this. I'll skip the really gross stuff. "*People who get hooked on Internet porn run the risk of developing a serious, potentially dangerous addiction to fantasies of virtual sex that can ruin lives, threatening jobs and families.*"

The more she read, the darker the mood became in the room.

Jane sensed the need to lighten up, explaining, "This is the perfect time to use a line from *Annie Hall*: 'Don't knock masturbation. It's sex with someone I love!' She was rewarded with groans from everyone.

"Instead of suffering from erectile dysfunction, now some of these guys need to have connectile dysfunction. Get it? No access to Internet." Cass added her effort at humor.

Bonnie reminded them of the *Seinfeld* episode about masturbation that had an entire viewing audience in stitches. "Omigawd, every time I see that episode I nearly pee my pants. Dani, I remember you talking about it with tears of laughter running down your cheeks."

"Ladies, ladies! Enough with the jokes. We're supposed to be helping Danielle figure out what's going on in her marriage," Pam reminded them.

"It's okay, Pam. We always manage to laugh our way

through most situations, don't we? That *Seinfeld* was one of the funniest I've ever seen." Danielle reassured her.

Dee kept pulling up Web sites and reading bits to them. The information continued to substantiate that a certain percentage who habitually watch porn require increasingly graphic images as they need more stimulation to get aroused. Dee read out loud how a user with a problem is capable of going into debt on Internet porn and could get drawn into sites where simple viewing leads to having personal e-mails arrive addressing the user by name. This casual intimacy builds a feeling of developing a personal relationship with one or several participants.

"This is getting seriously scary," Dee said, as she continued to read. "An attached response to acting out fantasies might be received that same day with the user's name moaned and sighed erotically to draw them in even more. Web cameras add more avenues to instant gratification. The user gets to design his or her own customized sexual rush and participate in the kind of bold fantasies that might never be a part of real life."

As informed and worldly as the BC considered themselves, they were shocked.

Some sites went so far as to allow users to connect with a real person in their town or city.

"Just keep in mind that this is focusing on the smaller percentage of people who develop a problem. Obviously this doesn't apply to most people," Dee reminded them, "but it also points out that the problem is growing and anyone is vulnerable. Age does not factor in."

"Speaking of age," said Lynn, "the subject of Internet pornography has come up in conversation when my sons have been home. I have to tell you that even though that generation is more relaxed about it, my daughters-in-law have said that they and the majority of their girlfriends feel the same way we do. So we're not just being fuddy-duddies about this."

The flow of facts was endless. Informative articles, research papers, chat rooms, and blogs all offered way more information than any of these women wanted to know.

And it was getting a bit overwhelming. "Oh man, I need a break," Bo muttered, heading for the balcony with her cigarettes, her efforts to quit still unsuccessful.

Pam stood and stretched telling Bo she would keep her company. Besides, she had an idea she wanted to run by her.

Dee's uber-affectionate cat, Mulligan, had taken advantage of the abundance of laps in the room and was quietly making the rounds. His calming presence didn't go unnoticed.

Danielle sat quietly stroking the cat's silky coat, attempting to digest everything she was hearing so she could connect it to images filling her mind. Like the strange e-mail addresses she found from time to time during the past year on the screen of the desktop computer they occasionally shared. Bryce had quickly moved to delete them, expressing ignorance and questioning their source himself.

She recalled sensing at the time that he was acting rather oddly, commenting vigorously that he had no idea what they were or how they got there. But she naively banished those thoughts as ridiculous, just as she had when she thought she noticed him quickly changing the screen when she entered the room.

Rethinking it, she had to admit that the occasional instance had grown into regular occurrences. She said nothing but had felt he was strangely nonchalant a few times, giving her the distinct impression he was hiding something, even though that was totally out of character. It had crossed her mind once or twice that perhaps he had been looking at a porn site, but she accepted he wasn't doing anything some other guy might do. She just wondered why he didn't say anything about it.

It would have been more like him to say, "Hey Dan, take a look at this." Since secrecy or deceit was something she would never expect of him, she really didn't give the behavior too much thought at the time. Thinking about everything now, though, it seemed to add up to a different picture; one that upset her very, very much.

Cass introduced another aspect to the topic. "You know, ladies, I think we have to stop for a moment and look at another side of this. We've been totally focused on the smutty, sleazy, denigrating kind of porn that's out there. There are also films that fall under the category of erotica that are very sensual, sexual, and would be considered in good taste by a lot of men and women."

"You're right, Cass. Maybe that's what Bryce was looking at," Pam agreed, hoping for perhaps some sort of acceptable compromise.

"Exactly," Cass continued, "there are some good erotic films out there that are artistic, tastefully shot, and not demeaning to women in any way."

"Hah! I read somewhere that the difference between porn and erotica is the lighting!" said Lynn.

"Very funny," Cass replied, "but I beg to differ. I've watched some films categorized as erotic that were good stories, well-acted, and beautifully shot. Most of them were foreign films with subtitles, I must admit. And some of them were a turn-on, no question.

"I'd feel better if that were the case," Danielle admitted, feeling her temperature start to rise, "but somehow the evidence doesn't point to it. That goddamn fucking—pardon my French—DVD I found was definitely nothing but classic smut, judging by the label."

"Dani, we all like Bryce so much. He's the last person we would ever imagine to get caught up in this, but ... what are you thinking?" Marti asked.

No one wanted to jump to any conclusions, but there did appear to be a pattern evolving from her words.

"Hmmm, when you start putting all the pieces together, the possibility of the problem being Internet related starts to make sense, doesn't it?" Cass was becoming more convinced she was right in her suspicion.

Pacing the room as her anger and frustration kicked into high gear, Danielle thought out loud, "What is really making me feel so sick and crazy is the fact that he bought all that stash I found for a reason. It's bad enough to think he has an addiction to porn on the Internet, but now I have to wonder how much farther he has been sucked in—if you'll pardon the expression. God, how can I joke at a time like this? I just feel like screaming and kicking something. I'm beyond upset."

"You have every right to feel this way. There are few worse feelings than that of betrayal," Marti said, sitting beside her, a sympathetic hand on her back.

Standing up after a few minutes, with a look of resolve, Danielle paced as she spoke. "I *am* feeling relieved that I've gotten this out in the open. God knows I couldn't tell anyone else."

"Of course you're upset, angry, and disappointed in Bryce at this point. It could be worse, though. Put it into perspective. It's not like he's a mass murderer," said Bonnie.

"Right. Something is obviously off track, but surely fixable. Your feelings will mend once everything is aired out. I can't believe Bryce is deliberately trying to hurt you or is being unfaithful," Lynn suggested, shaking her head in frustration.

"There *is* a solution to whatever this is. It will all work out," Pam said softly.

Staring into the blackness out the window, Danielle straightened her back, as if the action of physically pulling herself together would bring her emotions into line as well.

"Let's assume you're right. What's the next step? The man I love has a problem, and I've got to get to the bottom of it before it really messes him up—and us. In all honesty, now that I've finished feeling sorry for myself, I'm really angry with him at this particular moment—problem or no problem—and what I feel like doing right now is grabbing him by the balls and giving them a good twist!“

“But you might scramble his brains if you did that!” Bonnie said, drawing snickers.

“The perennial question pondered by women. Why do so many men think with their dicks?” Marti asked rhetorically.

“Who would have ever thought that of Bryce?” muttered Dee.

“If the President of the U.S. of A. can't control himself in the Oval Office, for heaven's sake, why should we be surprised about anyone else?“ asked Jane to cynical smirks around the room.

“I can't believe you didn't say something to Bryce right away. I would've left that stuff on the floor so he could trip over it as he walked in! I wouldn't have had the control you showed,” said Cass.

Bo was quick to add her creativity to the situation. “I'd have crushed one or two of those Viagra pills and slipped it in his coffee before he left for his morning bike ride. That might have gotten his attention.” Everyone burst out laughing at that visual, including Danielle.

The room was soon filled with other equally wild suggestions, until a shrill whistle from Jane interrupted them. She was the only one among them who could do that great fingers-in-your-mouth, ear-splitting whistle, and they all envied it.

Dee signaled time out.

“Dani, I really hope that somehow we're helping here, in spite of the last couple of minutes of craziness,” said Jane, who was now standing behind the counter in the open kitchen tossing the salad while Dee reheated the roasted veggies.

"Maybe we're getting somewhere. As upsetting as this is, I hope you're beginning to feel it could be a lot worse."

"So true," offered Cass, attempting to choose the right words to encourage a look at another point of view. "Remember what I said—it's not all ugly and immoral. We have to keep things in perspective."

Danielle ran her fingers slowly through her hair, collecting her thoughts. "I'm so drained after holding this inside. I felt like I had fallen into another world—Alice down the rabbit hole, you know? It seems a lot longer than a few days but maybe we're on the right track."

"You know we'll keep working on it until you want to stop," Marti reassured her.

"I know that and I don't want to stop. It's all helping me somewhat get past my confusion, anger, and sense of betrayal. I never expected to have those emotions connected to my marriage! Spoiled, huh?"

Pam spoke up. "Spoiled nothing. You have strong values and you've always known what was important to you in your marriage. You've both worked hard to build a solid union."

Dee carried the roast on a platter to the table and waved the carving knife in her hand now as she spoke. "There are lots of people who don't have that kind of honest, trust-filled relationship—and there are some who say they wouldn't want it. Too confining."

"I always think that's such bullshit when people say they need more freedom in their marriage! Why bother getting married then? Deep down I'll bet most couples would treasure what you have," Lynn interrupted.

"Not so," argued Bonnie. "Not everybody looks for the conventional, and we all know that, but this isn't the issue here anyway. Let's stay on track."

Jane, salad-tossing duties completed, wiped her hands on the dishtowel slung over her shoulder and hugged Danielle.

"You and Bryce have had a great marriage and this bump in the road isn't going to destroy it."

"Right," agreed Bonnie, "I mean, you guys even wallpaper together!"

"Ha! The litmus test of a good relationship as far as I'm concerned," laughed Dee, to which the others agreed heartily. "Okay! Everyone to the table!"

"I'm starving," announced Cass, heading for the dining room.

"Me too!" said Danielle. "I've hardly eaten for days and dinner smells divine. Let's eat. I still feel terrible, but a lot better than when I first came through the door."

Walking to the table, Bo expressed a thought that made a lot of sense to the others. "I'll talk to some people at the Addiction Centre and see what they suggest. There's no better place to find help for this kind of problem."

"Good idea!" Jane seconded, nodding vigorously, "why didn't we think of that earlier?"

"Actually Pam planted the seed when I went out to have my smoke and it makes a lot of sense," Bonnie told them. "They'll be able to give you sound advice. They might even assure you that this isn't an addiction issue based on what you can tell them. Certainly their advice can only help."

"Are you still counseling there, Bonnie?" Danielle asked, with a growing sense of relief that support might actually be out there.

"I stopped counseling last year but still sit on a few committees so I'm there on a regular basis. I'll find out everything I can tomorrow with a few phone calls. In the meantime you've got to try and live as normally as possible. Give Bryce the benefit of the doubt for now, even though it won't be easy. We're all just a phone call away if things get tough."

Danielle breathed in deeply, trying to slowly release some of the tension. "I'll have to do double duty with yoga this week.

If we're right about Bryce's problem, I'm going to need all the good karma I can muster. As much as I've tried turning to prayer with this, it's not working for me right now. Call me as soon as you know something Bo."

"Of course I will," Bonnie reassured her.

"In the meantime, Dani, why don't you and I go for lunch after our yoga tomorrow and then take a walk by the lake," Pam suggested.

Dinner finished, the cards were dealt. Danielle felt they had talked the problem to the limit for that night, and she had the beginning of a plan. Playing a few hours of bridge would be a welcome diversion now.

True to her word, Bonnie called later the next afternoon. Danielle's yoga and the talk with the BC had helped to put her in a better place emotionally. She was ready to try and fix what was wrong.

Beginning with an apology, Bo explained that she had to wait several hours for her call to the director of counseling to be returned. He steered her to a counselor who specialized exclusively in the relatively new and demanding issue of sexual addictions, including Internet porn and cybersex, and coincidentally Bonnie knew the fellow quite well.

"I was able to give him as much detail as he initially needs," said Bo "and he was prepared to get involved without seeing you first. He wants you to phone him first thing tomorrow. If he feels confident about the situation after talking to you, then he'll advise you how to proceed. If not, he'll have you down to his office before starting anything. Believe me, you'll feel better after you speak with him because he has a very empathetic manner and a wealth of experience."

After her conversation with him the next morning, Danielle

had to agree with Bonnie. Mike, the counselor, did convey a sense of trust and knowledge. Danielle quickly lost her initial feelings of embarrassment but knew she was blushing over the phone in spite of herself. Nevertheless she was able to describe the incidents and articulate her concerns and suspicions.

"Don't get hung up on the word *addiction,* " he cautioned. "There are other possibilities that may not be as daunting. The first thing we need is more documented information about his behavior as this will be instrumental in our first meeting with your husband."

He asked about her reactions and feelings, pressing her to make certain she felt prepared to deal with whatever lay ahead. It could be very unsettling. She had to know she was strong enough.

They talked about the state of her marriage as he probed to ensure there were no other infringing issues. Mike mentioned to her that Bonnie had told him about the strong support network in her group of friends. Dani expressed how much that meant to her as she in no way wanted to say anything to her family about the problem.

For two weeks Danielle was to keep a daily journal of her observations of Bryce's behavior and her feelings as she reacted to her perceptions. The amount of time he spent on the computer, unexplained absences, and any hostile, indifferent, or otherwise unnatural attitudes needed to be noted. Mike asked if there had been any abnormal charges on any of their credit cards. Danielle indicated she hadn't noticed any, but she would take another look. At the same time it was vital for her own mental health that Dani did not feel as if she was spying, but rather taking a positive step to discovering the truth of the problem. Then a program to resolve it could begin. After giving her his cell number, Mike's parting words were supportive and encouraging.

"Let me reassure you, Danielle, you are not alone. This type of problem is growing at an alarming rate. I know it seems very big to you right now. Painful and personal. From what I've learned talking with you and Bonnie, I truly feel you will get this sorted out and move past it. I daresay your relationship with your husband will be even stronger as a result. It may not be nearly as bad as you think it is. Try to believe it."

She would try. With all of her heart she would try.

It was an interesting challenge to suddenly pay attention to all of the normally insignificant moments in the day. It didn't take more than a few days to confirm that Bryce was more than preoccupied with his computer. Now that she was focused on it, he also seemed to be working at being relaxed. Or was it Danielle that was working at that?

She almost hated to leave the condo to go to yoga, out for groceries, or any other reason, because she couldn't stop her mind from imagining what Bryce was doing. She wished she could follow him when he went out. It was a horrible way to feel. She detested the fact that she had set the infamous briefcase in a certain way so she could tell if it had been moved. Horrible. She did not want to think what she was thinking.

Usually they met at yoga a couple of mornings a week, but now Pam picked her up for it. Bonnie called each afternoon just to make contact and offer encouragement. The others kept in touch by e-mail or texting so she would not have to keep repeating herself. She told Pam and Bonnie she was using them as her crutches during this time. Their help was her lifeline.

After five days, Danielle called Bonnie at her wits' end.

"I can't keep doing this Bo. I am 99.9% sure it's an Internet problem. It's obvious. I just need to confront him with it. I have a feeling that he won't be able to lie if I put the cards on the table. Even if he objects to talking about this I have my strength back and won't accept that."

They talked over the pros and cons and finally Bonnie

suggested Danielle contact Mike and see what he would say. She did.

"Danielle, you are one strong woman. I trust your instincts."

"You know, Mike, I feel I have nothing to lose at this point. I can't keep being Sherlock Holmes. I hate it and I can't pretend any more. When he is home, he is married to his computer, and when I come into his space he becomes ingratiating in the most unnatural way. Truly abnormal behavior. I looked on Bryce's computer when he wasn't home and even though he keeps his history clear most of the time—which by the way he never used to do months ago—I've found a few porn sites. I've even gone as far as looking when he has gone into the bathroom, but he makes sure he leaves things in a way that makes it difficult. It's bizarre. He never would do things like that before. I just know we're right about what he's doing. I mean, we don't know exactly, but it's not good. If he wants to deny it, then we have a different issue. He's never deceived me until this situation cropped up. I really believe that. I know this is something new, and this is not his true nature. I've got to try this now."

"Good luck," said Mike. "Call me back when you can."

Danielle hung up the phone, closed her eyes, and said a silent prayer asking for strength, compassion, and understanding. She would need all that. Forgiveness would come later. She hoped. It was interesting, she noted, that now she was more involved in helping fix the problem rather than purely feeling hurt and betrayed, she could once again find some strength from her faith.

She called Bo again and told her what her plan was. She listened to Bonnie's words of advice and promised to call or e-mail her later that night. "No matter how late," said Bo, "I need to know you are okay. Be calm. Good luck."

An hour later Danielle poured two scotches and sat down beside Bryce, who was watching the BBC news.

"Ah, cocktail hour. Thanks babe."

Dani leaned down and kissed Bryce lightly as she handed him his drink.

"Cocktail hour and time for a serious talk, B."

Their eyes met and held until Bryce dropped his for a second. Turning off the TV, he looked back at Danielle. "What's up?"

Taking a deep breath, Danielle maintained her strong gaze and took a deep swig of her scotch before she answered. Once she began, the words spilled out with her barely pausing.

"Bryce, one of the best parts of everything between us has always been the honesty we share. Something's going on. I know it. You know it. The difference is I don't know what the hell it is and you do. I'm hoping now that I'm being honest, you will be the same. I suspect it's going to be painful for both of us. I don't want to insult you by telling you what my suspicions are. I would rather you took the high road, as I believe you always have until recently, and tell me truthfully what you've been doing. Take a few minutes to think about it. I love you. I want us to fix whatever is wrong."

Getting up, she went to the closet, picked up the incriminating briefcase, and set it on the floor in front of him. Her eyes welling with tears, Danielle turned away and composed herself. Then she looked back at him. She could handle this now she had begun, she told herself.

Bryce had been staring into his drink. Looking up, his jaw set and he blinked at the sight of the briefcase. Standing abruptly, he placed his drink on the fireplace mantle, and without turning back to her said, "I've got to take a walk. Give me an hour."

Danielle sat rooted to the spot, as she heard him open and close the hall closet before the front door clicked shut. This wasn't what she had expected.

With her mood shifting from irritated impatience to suffocating anxiety, she worked at pulling herself together. After a few moments she wandered out to the hall and felt encouraged to see his car keys and cell phone sitting on the table. This was a good thing, she said to herself.

Turning the lights out so the room was bathed only in the pastels of the fading sunset, she flipped on the sound system to her meditation CD. The mystical words of the gayatri mantra floated through the air, accompanied by the rich mellow tones of a single flute. Soothing and calming, the ancient sacred Sanskrit chanted so melodically at the same time emanated such power. Seated cross-legged on the carpet with her palms up, resting on her knees, Danielle closed her eyes and allowed herself to be carried to a place of harmony deep inside her.

"I am power. I am light. I am peace," she repeated, silently reaffirming her strength and her belief in herself, in her marriage, in their ability to fix what was wrong.

It is written, she reminded herself, that yoga is the end of sorrow. She felt she had gained the strength from yoga to move past her hurt and focus on the future.

When she was ready, Danielle lit some candles before she stood at the window to appreciate the barely visible panorama of the lake with the western tip of the Toronto Islands caught in the horizon. In the dusky light, the never-ending parade of dog-walkers, roller bladers, joggers, and strollers provided a distraction. What a great place to live, she reminded herself, then started slightly as she recognized her own husband in the midst of the activity below. He appeared to be headed back to their building, and she was ready to get on with things.

The apartment door opened quietly. Bryce quickly came up to Dani without removing his jacket and took her in his arms. Holding her very close, she could feel his throat tightening as he struggled to speak.

"I've been such an idiot," he whispered hoarsely. "I can't believe the way I've been behaving and what I've done. I owe you such an apology."

They stayed as they were for several minutes. Two bodies welded together in love and pain.

"Where did I put my drink?" mumbled Bryce. "I'm going to need it. Let me get you another one too."

"No thanks, B. Really, just a glass of water is all I want right now."

They talked long into the night. Bryce began by reassuring Danielle how the choices he had been making had nothing to do with her and everything to do with his deep-seated, self-centered conflict over what he perceived to be his loss of sexual prowess.

"Honestly Dani, you can't imagine how painful an issue this is for a man. I felt all my self-confidence, my self-worth, just slipping away. I felt like such a loser. I know this sounds crazy and way out of proportion, but that's how it hit me. I was filled with an almost uncontrollable sense of desperation."

She listened in amazement as he spoke of his frustration, using words like "humiliation" and "despair." Attempting to digest his words and put his feelings ahead of hers, she realized how unaware she had been at the importance of this change in his body.

Danielle responded sympathetically, "I'm so sorry Bryce. I had no idea it affected you like that. Why didn't you talk to me about it like always?"

Shaking his head and knocking back some scotch, Bryce tried to explain the overwhelming feelings that consumed him about his fear of becoming impotent. "Talking about it now and saying all of these things out loud, I feel like an idiot, but as the whole issue of ED took over it was like I was a different person. I started going to the porn sites, even though it didn't help my problem much. I kept trying to find something there that would. When you were away for those two weeks at your sister's, I just went over the edge since I had no constrictions. I mean, I really lost it and just became obsessed with sex on the

Internet. I don't know if I'll ever be able to admit how bad it became."

Horrified at that revelation, Dani knew she had to find compassion at this point until she had the whole story.

"I even spent a couple of evenings getting very drunk at the House of Lancaster, if you can imagine that!" he said, referring to a seedy 'gentlemen's club' that had been around for decades, not more than ten minutes from the condo.

"And that's when I bought all the stuff you found and..." His speech faltered and he took a long sip of scotch before continuing, "and this is the part I'm truly ashamed of ... I actually made arrangements to rent one of the private 'studios with hostess,' but at the last minute I chickened out—or came to my senses, or whatever—because all I could see was your face in my mind, and even in my drunken haze I knew I was making a very wrong choice. I staggered out and grabbed a cab home."

As Bryce told her everything, she stared at him numbly. It was distressing, bizarre to say the least, yet at the same time almost a relief. He had not been unfaithful. He loved her as he always had. He had a problem that grabbed hold of him and took him on a ride that quickly got out of control.

As they talked their way through the evening, he agreed some professional help was needed and implored her to remain by his side. He repeatedly emphasized how his behavior was driving him crazy and how he wanted to put a stop to it. He felt disgusted with the choices he had been making.

They were also able to talk about seeing their family doctor about the ED. "I've been reading about it and there are lots of possibilities available to improve things," Danielle told him. "We're not the only couple our age facing this kind of issue."

Bryce agreed he was ready to talk about the problem now that it was out in the open and expressed how he felt a huge weight had been lifted from his shoulders. He had not wanted to hurt her but had become consumed with his feelings of embarrassment, shame, and anger as he feared losing what had always been so much a part of him.

"My God," he agonized, "you know this is not like me. For the first time in all our years together I just could not open up and talk about the problem with you. I really lost my ability to think straight. I feel the worst about breaking the trust you have in me. I know my credibility has taken a serious hit and rightly so. I'm begging your forgiveness."

Danielle reassured him she would do whatever was necessary to get them through this crisis. She also let him know at the same time how deeply hurt she had felt and how frightened she had been at the thought their marriage was in trouble. As much as he wanted her help, he also needed to know some of the consequences of his actions. They would get through this, they agreed.

When they climbed into bed that night, Danielle was acutely aware that her defenses were up. It takes a while to recover from a breach of trust. They kissed each other lightly, saying "I love you," and lay sleepless and wide-eyed on their own sides of the bed for hours, just holding hands.

The following week she felt optimistic as she told the Bridge Club how she and Bryce were progressing. "It's almost as if he was hoping to be caught. Facing up to the situation and talking openly about his problems—which essentially were his loss of self-esteem due to the ED and his desperation to find some solution—has made all the difference to him. He was as much in shock at his loss of control with the Internet as I was."

"Was Mike able to help at the Addiction Centre?" asked Bo.

"He has been great, Bo. Thanks so much for putting us on to him. I called him the day after I confronted Bryce and he saw us last Friday. He guided us both through a lot of painful moments and gave us good advice to help work through things. I couldn't believe he could get to the bottom of it so quickly. He feels Bryce is going to be able to control his impulses, as this type of behavior was not his nature but rather an extreme reaction. Don't get me wrong, though, we're still going to need some help."

"But is it as easy as that?" Lynn asked.

Danielle told them how Mike had compared the boundary between healthy viewing of Internet sex Web sites and secretive, compulsive use to the boundary between moderate social use of alcohol and excessive drinking. He explained the similarities in the addiction: the inability to discontinue the use despite adverse consequences. The first step to recovery he told them was admitting the problem and asking for help.

"I thought of you, Bo, and all we learned from you."

Bonnie nodded, her eyes confirming Danielle was right to think of that.

Danielle related how Bryce had, without hesitation, admitted to Mike and her that he had violated his own moral code. He recognized how he had been deceitful in his actions. He had told Mike how remorseful he was for causing such a breach in his marriage. It all came out.

Her voice broke slightly as she said, "Bryce even overcame his own mortification and confessed to Mike in no uncertain terms the reason he got caught up in cybersex. He told him about his issues with ED and that this was all about him. I felt embarrassed for him and proud of him at the same time."

Bonnie's voice was strong, her experience from her own rehab and as a counselor giving credence. "The fact that Bryce can focus on how his behavior has affected your relationship is the key to resolution, no question. His capacity to speak the truth right off the bat shows he can overcome this with help. I really feel encouraged."

"What about speaking with your priest," asked Lynn, "since you both are so connected to your church? Would that help as well?"

"You know..." Danielle hesitated, composing her thoughts, "I'm looking to my faith to help me find compassion and forgiveness. Yoga brought me the strength to get to that place. Bryce is looking for guidance and strength through prayer. To be honest, though, we're not so narrow minded to think our religion is going to solve this problem. Goodness knows when it comes to sins of the flesh, so to speak, the Catholic Church doesn't exactly inspire confidence."

"I'll second that!" Pam immediately responded.

Danielle continued, "So to answer your question, it's probably not going to be as easy as it sounds. I have to get rid of my suspicious feelings. We put blocks on Bryce's computer to help me feel comfortable as much as to help him. "

"How does Bryce feel about that?" asked Dee.

"He is completely cool with everything he needs to do to get past this, As Mike put it," said Danielle, "it's not that easy to resist the unlimited smorgasbord of sexual feasts from the biggest porn shop in the world."

"That kind of sums it up," muttered Marti.

"Oh yeah, we will be looking to Mike for support for a while," Danielle said, but with an air of optimism.

"Time, Dani, time... " said Dee hopefully.

Danielle continued to explain, "Mike feels that Bryce's history of being so grounded ... his level of communication in all other aspects of his life ... is the critical factor here. He says someone who has always been a deceitful person would not have as good a chance to get past this as quickly. This whole situation has been such an aberration."

"Kind of a slightly delayed mid-life crisis," said Bonnie.

"Could have been a lot worse though," Jane said. "I know this was horrible for you, but the good news is it looks like everything is going to work out. You know Bryce didn't mean to hurt you or damage your marriage. He got caught up in something he couldn't control."

"Yes, all that is true, but we know it's going to take counseling to help us heal the hurt. No matter how much you love someone, it's amazing how difficult it is to rebuild damaged credibility."

"Don't I know it," muttered Marti. "You are so right. It takes two to tango. I didn't have the right dance partner, but the good news is you do. You both have the skills and the desire."

"Yes," sighed Danielle, "we do have that going for us. I know a lot of marriages face worse challenges. We'll be back on track with some outside help. I truly do believe that."

"Who'da thunk it?" murmured Cass.

"There you go. Even the best of relationships sometimes need support. There's no shame in that," said Bonnie.

Looking around the room Danielle continued, "No question help is essential to get this sorted out, but before I could reach that point I sure needed you guys. Thanks for steering me through this mess. Not just in figuring out what might be going on but for keeping me on an even keel."

She pulled her hands to her heart center, as they say in yoga-speak, and bowed low, "Namaste. You are the best. Now let's play bridge."

Bonnie looked at Danielle and asked, "Uh, aren't you forgetting something, Dani?"

Without missing a beat, Danielle quickly crossed herself.

"And please, God, while you're at it, give me some good cards tonight."

DEAL #8

WEST	NORTH	EAST	SOUTH
	1♦	Pass	1♥
Pass	2♦	Pass	3NT
Pass	Pass	Pass	

DEALER:	NORTH
VUL:	NONE
CONTRACT:	3NT
DECLARER:	SOUTH

North
♠ J 6 5
♥ K 5
♦ A Q J 10 7 3
♣ 8 3

West
♠ 7 4 3
♥ 10 9 8 3
♦ 4
♣ K 10 7 5 4

East
♠ K Q 8 2
♥ 7 4 2
♦ K 6 5
♣ A 9 2

South
♠ A 10 9
♥ A Q J 6
♦ 9 8 2
♣ Q J 6

SUGGESTED BIDDING

North has enough to open 1♦ with 11 high-card points plus 2 length points for the six-card diamond suit. South, with 14 high-card points, responds 1♥, planning to get to game on the rebid. North rebids the six-card suit, and now South settles for game in 3NT.

OPENING LEAD

West is on lead against 3NT.

BRIDGE QUIZ:

What is the challenge if West leads the fourth best club against 3NT, hoping to get enough tricks through length to defeat the contract?

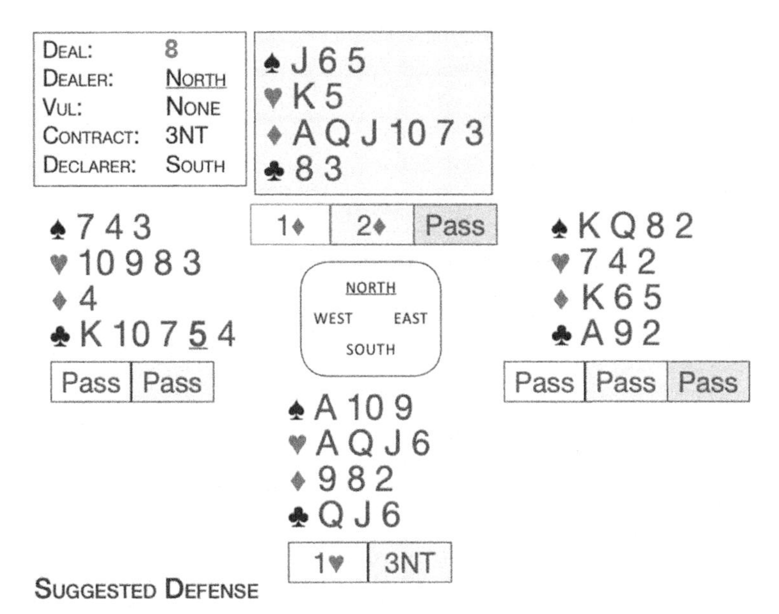

Suggested Defense

West leads the ♣5, fourth best from the long suit. East wins the ♣A and returns the ♣9, higher of the two remaining clubs. South plays the ♣Q. West knows South also has the ♣J. East would return the ♣Q or ♣J if holding the ♣Q-9 or ♣J-9.

To establish and take the club winners, West needs an entry to the winners once they are established. Since West has no entry other than the ♣K, West has to hold up on the second club trick, playing the ♣4. West has to hope East has another club and will gain the lead before declarer has nine tricks. When East gains the lead with the ♦K, East still has the ♣2 to return. The defense gets the ♦K, ♣A, ♣K, and two more club tricks through length.

Suggested Play

Declarer should play the ♣Q at trick two to tempt West into winning the ♣K.

Conclusion

To get tricks through length, the defenders often need to keep an entry within the long suit in case partner can gain the lead, and has a link card to reach the winners.

10

THE HAND DEALT – 2007

Back to where this story began.

The Bridge Club's laughter and chatter had been interrupted more than once by weather conditions as they drove north through the rapidly worsening snowstorm. With mixed emotions they arrived at their destination.

Dee's Victorian farmhouse awaited offering comfort and warmth. The drift-filled driveway unfolded in the headlights. Snow-laden limbs of ancient oaks lined the way, forming arches like a crumbling cathedral's and momentarily creating a darkened, somber effect. The Suburban ploughed up the lane and crunched to a stop at the side porch.

Their agenda had been set decades before. When it came to this particular weekend they were, to a great extent, creatures of habit. The tasks of unloading ski equipment, groceries, and weekend bags were accomplished quickly in the bitterly cold evening air. Tumbling up the porch steps and through the mudroom, each one set about doing what had years before become routine. In no time the delectable aromas of a beef stew warming in the oven drew them to the table.

Even so, the lack of appetite in these normally hearty eaters did not go unnoticed.

A vigorous fire blazed and crackled. The house filled with sweet smells of burning apple wood that had been added to the aged oak and beech logs. Through the frosted windows, the rural landscape was disappearing as the storm intensified.

"Let's have our pie in comfort by the fire before we get out the cards," Dee suggested.

Settling into the down-filled sofas and chairs, perched on the hearth or cross-legged by the fireplace, none refused the warm bumbleberry pie with a sliver of vanilla ice cream. Dessert was part of their tradition, the eat-a-thon as they called it, and they were determined the weekend would progress step by step as they worked their way through it. They had made a pact. They intended to keep it.

The conversation occasionally lagged, involving just one or two at a time as opposed to the normally raucous banter, while each woman silently contemplated what had brought her to this point. This weekend. This promise. This bond.

Just a few months earlier it had begun.

For years the Bridge Club had been sharing stories about "senior moments." They commiserated with each other's experiences, tried to find the humor in it, and declared membership in the CRAFT Club. As in Can't Remember A F*cking Thing.

Consequently, she didn't pay much attention to her incidents of forgetfulness. It seemed to be happening to everyone her age.

The previous winter she had mentioned it in passing to her family doctor, trying not to sound paranoid. Dr. Chang had run some tests, patted her hand, and suggested she simply try to relax a bit more. It was nothing more than stress, she was assured, even though they both knew she was not one to get stressed. The tests had shown nothing untoward, and she put it out of her mind.

On a perfect October afternoon the bright sun blazed, creating a vivid autumn palette of crimson and gold in the densely treed neighborhood. Accelerating slowly when a traffic light turned green, she steered her car through a busy intersection. It gradually occurred to her she had absolutely no idea where she was going. Pulling over to the side of the road, she tried to calm the anxious feeling overtaking her.

Obviously she must have been on her way somewhere to do something or she would not be in the car. She looked in her purse, checked the passenger seat as well as the back for something that might give her a clue—a shopping list, an appointment card, library books. No sports gear. Goddamit, there must be something here! She checked what she was wearing. Maybe she was on her way to some identifiable activity, but her attire told her nothing.

After long moments of fruitless searching, physically and mentally, she turned the car towards home. Hopefully she could remember where that was, she muttered to herself, wiping her tears and driving slowly to maintain concentration. Flooded with relief as she turned into her street, she knew precisely what the next step would be.

The nurse/receptionist put her on hold briefly as she recognized the concerned voice on the phone. Her family doctor would see her the next day, squeezing her in before the afternoon appointments. She had been going to this physician for twenty years, a woman ten years younger, with whom she felt a comfortable connection and the staff knew her well enough to notice something serious was troubling her.

Aware it was probably not good thinking, she nevertheless began checking the Internet to research the options going through her head. She knew deep inside she'd inevitably end up with a self-diagnosis, which was also a bad idea. Earlier in the year when she first spoke with Dr. Chang about being forgetful she'd surfed the net looking for answers but then told herself she was being alarmist and stopped. Within a short time now her anxiety had returned and after bookmarking some pages she left her desk in a state of complete agitation.

She ignored the phone the few times it rang and decided to pick up her messages later. The only one that mattered was from a friend asking why she had missed the monthly book club meeting that afternoon. After an unsuccessful attempt to convince herself she was hungry, she sat in front of the television for a while, absorbing nothing, and then went to bed early. The night was spent tossing and turning with sleep managing to edge in for brief intervals as her mind incessantly replayed the day's events.

The next afternoon, looking wan, she was quickly ushered into the office of her GP. Having kept her concerns to herself, she had no one with her.

"Well," Dr. Chang began after listening to her story, which included several other incidents she had not previously considered meaningful, "let's do a basic physical since you're almost due for yours anyway. When you talked to me about this some months ago we didn't do one."

Dr. Chang was exceptionally thorough as she conducted the physical examination, asking pertinent questions about her patient's sleep patterns, changes in her life, and possible family or external issues, exploring the feasibility of being overtired or depressed.

"The only thing that's depressing me is worrying about what happened yesterday and those other times I mentioned!"

With a gentle voice the doctor told her they would talk once she had dressed and quickly left the examining room.

Minutes later, she was seated across from Dr. Chang, who

was making more notes. They spoke until it seemed there was nothing they had left unexplored.

"I'm going to give you a requisition for tests and we'll see what we can find. You've always been in fine health and kept up your annual visits. We'll do all we can to diagnose this as quickly as possible and get you back on track. Your earlier tests showed nothing untoward, but to be safe I'm going to run them again along with some new ones. In the meantime try not to worry, although I know that's easier said than done."

"Dr. Chang, you know I've never been one to suffer from stress. I've always enjoyed every aspect of my life and I retired last spring so life is one big holiday now! Trust me on that. What else do you think this might be?"

The doctor shuffled the file in front of her, avoiding eye contact. "If it's okay with you I'd rather not speculate. Let's see what the tests show. Perhaps it's a minor problem with a simple solution. No point fretting over something we don't know. Are you comfortable with that?"

"I guess I'll have to be," she replied. "Let's just get on with it, and thank you for seeing me so quickly. I know how tight doctors' schedules are these days."

"You're welcome. Have my secretary book you for a follow-up in two weeks. And bring someone with you. That's important."

This was the catalyst, the beginning of talking about the end. She never thought it would happen to her, but it was quite possible the unimagined was now her reality.

It was after this appointment that she had first voiced her feelings to the Bridge Club.

She was relieved to be hosting this month and served up a chicken potpie and salad before saying a word about what was really on her mind. She actually had wanted to wait until her doctor got back to her, but partway through dinner they knew something was wrong.

"You're awfully quiet tonight," was the first comment directed to her.

"My God, what's happened? You should see your face," was the next.

She thought she could be calm, logical, strong. After all, nothing was definite.

As she finished relating the conversation with her doctor and admitting her earlier visit, she cut through to the heart of the matter. "I have to be blunt about this. Beating around the bush isn't our style."

"Well, it also isn't our style to have a problem and not say anything to us for seven months," came the first response, supported by general agreement and mild chastising.

"You know me, I never have health issues and I've always felt lucky about that! I just decided to take the doctor's word it was nothing and that was that. It was what I wanted to hear."

She got up from the table, where everyone had suddenly lost their appetite, and busied herself clearing dishes as the rest of them leapt to help.

Oddly she realized she was speaking as though the subject was an everyday topic. She heard herself stating very matter-of-factly, "If I have the worst diagnosis—and I mean the "A" word —if my life will change forever in every way, with no hope for recovery ... I'm outa here." She finished by drawing her finger across her throat.

A heavy silence met her words, followed by a torrent of responses.

"Don't be crazy."

"You can't mean it."

"No way! Talk about taking a worst case scenario to the extreme!"

"This is not like you! There have to be alternatives."

"You can't just give up. Besides lots of people live for ages with Alzheimer's."

"Fuck!"

It wasn't as if they hadn't mulled over the possibilities before, but the conversation had always been about other people's situations and the talk had been general. Now it was personal, which changed the tone of everything. The opinions were strong, diverse, and resulted in difficult debates. The saving grace was the fact nothing had been diagnosed, so they all, deep inside and desperately, could hold on to the hope that this was just talk.

Looking exasperated, she interrupted, "Let's put this whole issue on the back burner for now. We're not throwing out our views in general this time...I mean, we're talking about a life here. My life. I'm pushing the rest of you into thinking about this and I know it's not fair. With any luck it's not necessary."

"I cannot believe we're even having this conversation."

"Fuck, fuck, fuck..."

"It's frightening the life out of me."

"It's frightening me too—don't get me wrong—in fact, I'm terrified. I can't believe what may be happening." With that she turned her back on them and stared through a window into the night, seeing nothing.

They looked at each other with stunned expressions, too shocked to comment.

She turned around to face them, pulling them back into the moment with an almost calm, logical suggestion. "Maybe we should step back and think about this on our own until I hear from the doc. You're right—I'm probably reading too much into this."

"Good idea. My God, this was getting very difficult. The tests you're having will clear up the unknown, the problem will be solvable, and then we won't even have to have this discussion again."

Not everyone agreed. Maybe, they argued, it was good to talk about it.

"You know, it's something that's an issue with our generation, and it's going to keep rearing its ugly head," said another, searching faces for confirmation .

"It's tough to get down to the bare bones on this, but it's an important issue. I can't believe you didn't say anything about this when I called you yesterday," said another with a frown.

Shaking her head in a voiceless response, she listened as they went on, unable to drop the issue now that she had started it.

"I don't want to talk about this ever again, but I can see how serious you are, so of course I will. It's just so hard for me to even think about it," another exclaimed.

"I really do not want to go there."

"But we have to," a weak voice persisted, "like it or not."

Her clenched fists resting in her lap combined with her tightly drawn jaw betrayed the tension she was attempting to control. "Who could've imagined we might face this together?"

Tears welled in her eyes as she slowly stood, all attention fixed on her. Pacing the room, she gathered herself and continued, "I need to tell you that I haven't said anything to anyone else, but I have bad vibes about this."

"Hey! I get bad vibes about all sorts of things. It doesn't mean I'm right and you probably aren't either."

"Mmm, no, seriously, this is different," she said, pausing to search for the right words to describe the fuzzy thinking, the disorientation. "I've been feeling strange for a while now. It's not even so much about forgetting stuff as just not being able to figure out answers. You know, like suddenly having no idea what I'm holding in my hand."

"Like what?"

"Yeah, what exactly do you mean? Are you saying that you don't recognize stuff you should?"

"Precisely. The recognition comes and goes," she explained. "I had a flashlight in my hand the other day and suddenly had no idea what it was, let alone what I needed to do with it. Later on in the day I saw it on my desk and knew what it was but had no idea why it was there. I had a vague memory of holding it earlier and being confused—it was totally bizarre—and then I just started to cry."

"Scary!"

"Yes and that's just the one time I remember! It's intensely confusing and probably stuff is happening that I don't notice. That's the worst part. It's different from what we joke about."

This was the beginning of what would become an ongoing education on the subject of Alzheimer's disease for all of them.

"And it's other things too. My friend Cathy, in my Bruce Trail hiking group, has told me a few times lately that I'm lurching as we're going along. It's not very obvious, nobody else mentioned it, and I'm not aware of it."

"Well, none of us noticed anything like that. Right?"

Everyone agreed they hadn't, desperate to find something positive to say.

"When I told Dr. Chang she indicated this was significant, and I have to say I didn't like the look on her face."

Looking for direction, they asked what the next step was.

"If the diagnosis is what I suspect I'll talk this over here at home first obviously."

"You mean you haven't said a word to ..."

She cut them off with the wave of her hand.

"Not yet. I know what I want will absolutely not be accepted ... no question. I don't know how I'm going to handle that. But I will tell my doctor immediately. Then I'll tell you my plan."

"You already have a plan?"

Silence settled in the room with each one trapped in jumbled thoughts. Disbelief was visible on every face. The whole situation was surreal.

"You know," she said abruptly, "I think we've hashed this over enough. Let's drop it for the rest of the night and leave our talking until I hear the test results. I never thought I would hear myself say this, but to those of you who are still believers in one way or another, perhaps some prayer would help. That tells you how desperate I am."

There was no response, not a word. It was simply too overwhelming.

She was first to break the stillness and try to pull them back to a better place, "More wine please. And get out the cards. We need to focus on something else for a while. It's not exactly going to be easy to concentrate."

Everyone gaped at her.

"No way."

"Not tonight."

"This is bigger than all of us. We need to keep talking."

Her brow wrinkled and eyes filled momentarily again, as the strength she had summoned threatened to fade. "Of course ... you're right. I want to face this situation with clarity as much as I can ... but it's going to be a lot harder for you to grasp. I feel like I'm on one side of the fence and you're all on the other. I want you to want to come over to my side."

"Remember we're still talking about a hypothetical situation here."

Nodding again, she agreed but with a worried caveat. "You know me. I've never been one to get caught up in worst-case scenarios. But now I'm feeling if ... if we don't talk about this soon ... I'm terrified there won't be enough time later."

Needing to somehow put a positive spin on things, they struggled to point their thoughts and words in another direction. There were other possible diagnoses, for example.

She was ready for encouragement, to hope for some good to prevail, and they were just the friends to try and convince her to let go of her mindset, at least for now.

Which is exactly what they worked on until it was finally agreed they had to go home and sleep on it. There was no question they were emotionally exhausted. They slowly stood, a collectively subconscious movement, and held each other. The enormity of the discussion was overwhelming and frightening. It simply could not be happening.

At the follow-up appointment her cousin Steven, a recently retired physician, accompanied her with a promise to tell no one else. He of all her family would handle things best. So far nothing conclusive had turned up and Dr. Chang had already sent a referral to a neurologist. Attempting to gain a better idea of her situation, she decided to be bold and ask directly about the chances of her having Alzheimer's. *Let's not beat around the bush*, she thought to herself.

"We need more information before making any diagnosis," the doctor responded. "So far nothing concrete is indicated but we are eliminating possibilities."

Steven tried to be reassuring on the way home and used all of his expertise to convince her there was no foregone conclusion. She didn't believe either one of them.

Phone calls and e-mails flew back and forth for the next few weeks as the Bridge Club shared their thoughts, reactions, fears, and suggestions. Google was worked overtime. Each woman read all the information she could find, searching for something that offered hope. Each made time to drop by her place, go walking, catch a movie, and a lot of other things they didn't normally do. Twice she had failed to show up as planned and they knew they needed to phone her to remind her on the day and then pick her up.

The following month, she updated them on another batch of tests, whose final results had not yet arrived. She mentioned she thought her doctor was stalling. Dr. Chang had sent her to a neurologist, and there had been endless blood tests, an EEG, an MRI, and a humiliating neuropsychological test. She had breezed through the first part recalling familiar information such as her address and birthdate and identifying line drawings. But she had totally blown most that pertained to short-term memory and drawing the time on clock faces. Now she was scheduled for something new in nuclear medicine called SPECT.

"What does that do?"

"Single photo emission computed tomography," she read. "I'm becoming an expert. It's amazing I can remember this stuff when I can't remember where I put my toothbrush. Here, my cousin wrote this all down in the notebook we use at appointments. *This procedure can pick up the rare isotopes in the brain that indicate Alzheimer's.* The neurologist says it will be the determining test for me after everything else they have done. Really what they do is figure out what I don't have before Alzheimer's is considered as a diagnosis."

Arguments were offered. Other possibilities with happier endings were once more discussed in hopeful tones.

"We're grasping here, girls, grasping," she said with a dismissive wave of her hand.

"Yup, we'll keep grasping until we know that we can't grasp anymore."

"Sounds to me like it's time for the old Dylan Thomas battle cry."

And they recited together, with an intensity not felt before, "*Do not go gently into that good night. Rage, rage, against the dying of the light.*"

"Rage! It's been our weapon against aging. How can we forget that?"

She nodded as a cloud of regret scudded across her face. "I know this goes against everything we've planned for ourselves, but this disease won't allow me to rage for very long and then I won't know what I'm raging against. Trust me, if I could I would. You know that."

"We do know that—for certain."

"Okay, I have a suggestion and I think we should unanimously agree to commit to it." She paused, gazing apologetically around the room. "Sorry," she continued, "I didn't mean to sound so pushy about this."

Another emotion-charged silence filled the room.

She held a slim paperback in her hand.

"I've read this book and it helped me to understand my feelings. I know I'm not alone in them. It's given me the confidence to feel informed and calm—well, somewhat calm, I guess—about the choice I'm making. You need to read it too so I took the liberty of getting a copy for each of you. It was on the *New York Times'* bestseller list for eighteen weeks in 1991, which tells you there are more than a few people who want to know about this option in life."

She gave them a rundown on the contents of the book, *Final Exit*, and it turned out some were already familiar with it although none had read it.

"You have to keep on letting us help, keep on talking, keep on leaning on us as much as possible until we find out where this is taking you."

She nodded, admitting to relief they had decided to call it an early night.

Her struggle was becoming more obvious. She and Steven confided in her immediate family, including the one who loved her the most. As she knew it would be, that was the hardest.

They all tried to absorb the shock as they waited for answers. They were making phone calls, asking questions, and searching for answers and information wherever possible.

Two weeks later the Bridge Club hastily responded to her phone summons and gathered at her place after dinner. She told them she would be alone. There had been complications as to what time some could be there but by 8 p.m. all were present. She had a diagnosis. This was most definitely not a regular BC evening.

The test results, including additional ones and repeats, were in hand. The neurologist had sent his findings and report to the GP, giving her the task of bearing the bad tidings. The previous day, Steven had held her hand in Dr. Chang's office and asked the important questions. Notes had been taken and the details discussed in disbelief. She and Steven had cried in the parking lot after their shell-shocked exit from the building. She had prescriptions for medication that probably would not help and another appointment in a week to talk. Dr. Chang recognized they would need some time to formulate questions.

Essentially, though, the facts were clear and she shared them now.

"I just needed to be with you for a while tonight," she said softly.

All they could do was sit helplessly, tears filling their eyes, looking from one to the other. Finally, each held only her in their gaze. Fear, sorrow, anger, and confusion contorted their faces.

Before anyone could make a move to deliver a comforting embrace, surely the predictable and natural response, she cleared her throat and attempted to steer everyone into the next moment.

"It sounds crazy to say I was kind of hoping for a brain tumor, but I was. This diagnosis is the last thing I wanted to hear: early Alzheimer's with a clearly rapidly advancing pattern." Her voice was trembling now. "You can read it in the report yourself."

She gulped back a sob and opened her mouth to continue

speaking but no sound was heard. Her head dropped into her open hands. With that she began to weep, her face buried in her palms, her shoulders heaving. Anguish filled the room.

The ache flowed from her into each of them: a power surge of hot, searing pain. Silent rage. Denial. They held each other and let the tears flow, knowing that nothing could be said or done until they somehow managed to get on top of their emotions.

Outraged cursing and blasphemous oaths followed. It all had to come out. Incredulous questioning as to why these things happen required no responses. There were none. Shit happens, and this was one of the worst kinds.

Pulling herself together as best she could and taking a deep breath, she began again, "Okay, now you need to listen to me. I must say this out loud in order to truly get a handle on it myself. Pour the wine."

The scotch was also set on the table and more than one stiff double ordered up.

She told them there was nothing new to say. "Everything I said two weeks ago still stands. Then it was all speculation. Now it's reality. I feel more committed than ever to following through on my plan for self-deliverance and I need you to know this. I'm feeling guilt-ridden for dragging you along on this ride and I want you to seriously consider how you feel about it. Don't even try to express your opinion now. Think about it."

The evening was short but emotional. They would have their regular Tuesday BC evening as scheduled in another two weeks and they would breathe not a word of her thoughts to anyone else.

The days flew by and before they knew it, they were picking up where they had left off. Everyone had thought of nothing else since the evening they learned her truth.

As they waited for her to arrive, none of them could speak of anything else.

"What would you do?"

The issue consumed them and soon they were back into the thick of the storm.

She continued her pitch with urgency in her voice that compelled them to listen without argument. It was a torrent of words, fast-moving and forceful. "I know I'm asking you for something that stretches the boundaries of friendship to the limit. It may be completely unfair of me to even put you in this position, and I ... I'm sorry ... for that. I feel I have two options. One is to keep this totally to myself, not involve anyone. The other option is this, and it's really what I want ... to share my decision with everyone important to me and then..." Hesitating, her voice dropped to almost a whisper, "to ask you, and you alone, to be with me when... "

Her look told them what her voice at this moment could not.

"Keep talking," they urged, in wide-eyed disbelief. "We're here ... "

"We just aren't sure how..."

"Or if ... we really can do it."

Wringing her hands slowly, she closed her eyes and inhaled as deeply as she could, searching for the power to go on. There was no question in her mind what she wanted to say, but speaking it out loud required a strength for which she had to dig deeper than she imagined.

"It's critical to me that you understand how I reached this mindset and how clear of thought I truly am about it. If I'd been diagnosed with cancer or anything like that, I'd take up the sword. I'd engage in hand-to-hand combat, call up the cavalry, do whatever was humanly possible with whatever treatments, strategies, medications, and surgeries available to me. You know how I am—voodoo might even be an option. I believe with all my heart that it's important in those situations to hold onto whatever hope you can: to fight with all of your might."

She let this sink in before continuing, "We all know there are some incredible stories of remission, cure, and happily-ever-after, or at least valuable and worthwhile extra time. Look at my good friend Sue, who has battled MS for fifteen years and is the best role model in the world for keeping a strong spirit and making the most of every day in spite of the challenges. And Leah Patterson, who received a terminal cancer diagnosis last year and is running a half-marathon months after she was supposed to be gone. I just don't have that option."

"But you do have some options—look how we stood up to breast cancer not that many years ago."

Holding up her hand to stop the onslaught of comments, she pressed on. "I've searched everywhere. I have no options that are acceptable to me. They might be options that help others deal with my illness but they do not help me in any way. When we faced breast cancer together there was one key ingredient, which is glaringly missing here."

"And that was?"

"Hope. You must have hope. There's not a shred of hope here. Not with my particular condition. I've checked."

Again voices were raised in pleading dissent.

"Surely there must be some possibilities to consider. There's so much research being done. New medications."

"Trust me. We've spoken with other specialists in the past two weeks. Steven used all his connections too. Bless him. Since the diagnosis, my family has researched every conceivable option to get information on new treatments, care, and future prospects. You've all told me that you've been checking things out since we first had a hint of this. Honestly we have to admit we're pretty darn knowledgeable right now about what's ahead of me." She was putting on her game face at the moment, and they recognized it.

Jaws tightened and worry lines appeared on other faces; others simply looked dejected. "Yes, you're right, we've been researching, talking, and desperately hunting for positives. That doesn't mean that we're ready to give up on you. We don't want to ... to lose you..."

Her eyes filled as she struggled to respond. "I-I-I don't want to lose me either. I don't want to leave my family, my friends ... you ... my wonderful life ... I'm so thankful for all of..." Overcome, words failed her temporarily as she closed her eyes and swallowed hard, unaware they all had done the same, "but ... I only have a brief window of time where I'll be able to think rationally about it..."

Tears covered her face now. Everyone had given up all attempts to stifle what needed to be let out and they wept together.

Through her tears she spoke softly but fiercely. "Remember these words: *I'll regret dying but I have no regrets about my life.* We all know where we heard that before, and I for one have never forgotten. I've had an amazing life, with all of its ups and downs. That sustains me. It gives me strength in the decisions I'm making now."

Wiping her eyes with the back of her hands and taking her time, her resolve returned as she looked squarely at each of her friends. "You know, this has been on my mind from time to time even when it wasn't about me. Remember the shock about Judith last year?"

They began talking all at once about a woman known to most of them who had received a diagnosis just the year before. Everyone who knew Judith thought she was developing a serious drinking problem, until she finally was forced by her daughter to see a doctor. She was sent to Sunnybrook Hospital for tests and immediately diagnosed with frontal lobe dementia. Everyone was in shock—except her.

The reason Judith didn't react was because the disease already had a stranglehold on her brain, stealthily taking over in the preceding months. She remained in a secured psychiatric ward with no understanding of her situation, her short-term memory rapidly vanishing, while on the surface she appeared quite normal. Her ability to make rational decisions was seriously diminished. Her conversation typically consisted of repetitive stories tied to a box of photographs kept in her room.

The bottom line was that, at the age of fifty-three, Judith would be confined to a supervised, locked residence for the rest of her life and deteriorate intellectually although her physical health might remain intact for many years. Bizarre behavior would gradually affect her ability to interact socially, and contact outside the institution would all but cease. The Bridge Club had agonized over that situation, vented, ranted, and argued about how they would want such a scenario dealt with if they were so stricken.

"Oh my gosh yes, poor Judith. That was such a tragedy."

"A terrible shock."

"Unbelievable."

"Well," she said, "I want you to remember what you had to say then as we talk about my situation now. Think of it as a dress rehearsal. I mean, how many times has one or the other of us said, 'If that happens, just shoot me."

"Yes, but—"

Raising her hand again, "No 'yes buts' about it. We all said it. That's what this boils down to. I'm just making a less messy choice."

There was no response to that.

"After I had time to absorb my diagnosis, I called Judith's best friend, Liz, who visits her religiously every week. I mean, talk about a true and compassionate friend. Judith's family doesn't see her that often! I went along with Liz on her next visit and came home thoroughly convinced of my decision. I saw Judith's condition as a fate worse than death. Without question, to me, death would be the better choice. That experience truly freed me."

"Yes, but Judith doesn't know what's going on, so what does it matter to her?"

"You know," she said, "I'm so sick of hearing that argument. It's what people have been saying for years since Alzheimer's and dementia really became issues people talk about. Why the hell should being unaware make it okay? Personally I find that offensive."

It was obvious everyone was laboring to develop a valid argument by the concentrated looks on their faces.

"Here's another way to look at it—and trust me, I believe I've thought of them all. If I were in the hospital on life support and they were going to pull the plug, as requested in my living will, you would all be gathered around to say good-bye. Right? It's what the loved ones do, it seems to me."

There was a general muttered agreement.

"And even though everyone would be sad, they would feel they were honoring my wishes that no artificial means of support be used to keep me alive."

"But that's completely different!"

"I disagree," she countered, eyes flashing with emotion. "This is really the same thing except I'm pulling my own plug. Keeping my physical being alive while I'm out to lunch in a nursing home is, to me, just like life support. That's not everyone's opinion, but it's mine, and I'm asking my wishes to be honored. I do not want life support under any circumstances! Does that help make it clearer?"

After a moment of thunderous silence a tortured voice

quietly responded, "I see your point, but it's just so hard to come to terms with it."

Stifling sobs, two of the women hurriedly left the room. The rest sat deep in thought, saying nothing, and waited until they were all prepared to continue.

Thankful for the pause, she slowly brought her neglected glass of merlot to her lips. A comforting hand gently rubbed her back. She struggled to maintain focus and control.

Once everyone had regrouped, a calmer voice reminded her, "It's not like we haven't talked about stuff like this concerning our parents."

"Yeah, but they're facing issues about mortality and quality of life in their eighties and nineties."

She thought about her mom. At ninety-two, widowed for ten years, her impressive memory and intellect were still sharp even as her body failed her. A former nurse, she was all too aware of her conditions but soldiered on without complaining. Her mom could hold her own conversing on any topic: sports, politics, investments. She loved a good laugh and commented regularly on the positives in life. At the same time in recent years she frequently expressed her wish to go to sleep and not wake up. She wasn't depressed, just tired of the constant struggle. Her feelings were understandable and she would have liked to have a choice.

"How will your mother react to your decision? Have you considered her feelings?"

Nodding, she spoke in a solemn voice. "Mom continues to amaze me. Before I could get to the truth of my situation, she leaned over, took my hand in hers, and said that she would support any decision I made. I mean ... she knew before I told her. I cried. She didn't at first. She said losing me this way would not be as bad as losing me for the rest of her life to an institution. It would break her heart to think of me with Alzheimer's, but she would always have happy memories remembering me as I am now. She held me and I cried and then we both cried."

There were tears all around again and it was moments before she continued, "And I know that I'm responsible for her welfare, but whether I leave the way I'm planning or whether Alzheimer's removed me from her, someone else will have to take over. My family will continue to care for my mother in the best way. That's a given."

The other women expressed praise and admiration for the way her mother managed life in spite of her challenges.

Then there was Cuppie, they recalled, who still went to Florida for the winter at age ninety-seven and enjoyed the casino, the races, and a good game of bridge. And Constance, the esteemed yoga teacher and swami, still doing perfect headstands in her nineties and driving a convertible. And Joan, eighty-eight, playing nine holes of golf every nice day in the summer and always walking the course. Or Lillian, legally blind and in a wheel chair, getting around by WheelTrans and the help of friends and never without a smile and cheery words.

Great role models all. There were many.

"For sure," she agreed. "It's so admirable to see people make the most of life in spite of the challenges of aging and illness. It's how I imagined my future. We should all be so lucky!"

Her voice grew strong and confident again. "In the book I gave you, the author describes the empathy he hears from much of the public about an individual's right to make decisions. He suggests how much kinder it would be to offer people choices ... wait a sec..."

Reaching for her bag, she pulled out her well-worn copy of the book, turned to a page with a fluorescent yellow Post-It tag, and asked one of them to read the highlighted words, *An alternative that would enable them to live right up to the extent of their life's potential, and then choose to die with certainty and dignity when the time is right for them.*

"That page is tagged to show how much of an impression those words made upon me," she said, looking at each face to establish her point, "and they resonate within me every day. *Certainty and dignity.*"

Some repeated the words, acknowledging their importance.

She continued, obviously in control now and aware of precisely what she wanted to express. "We're all just over sixty with so much life left to live—which is absolutely right, except now the quality of that life is being taken from me. I have at best—*at best*—another year or so of deterioration before I will need to be institutionalized or have a permanent caregiver. There are some new drugs that help slow the process, but most often in cases far less severe than mine. My greatest fear is that I won't act in time and I'll lose my ability to make the decision myself. I'll become Judith. I cannot—I will not—let that happen."

She hesitated briefly to let this sink in. She knew she had to keep striking. "This will be hard enough on everyone as it is, but I'm determined to make it a conscious and intelligent decision on my part and to handle it to the end with integrity. Integrity, that's my key word. Apart from losing life itself, that's the most important issue to me now." Taking a deep breath with barely a pause, she pressed on forcefully, "I will not accept the possibility of recognizing no one and needing care in the most personal of matters. I refuse to draw my family into that situation, even though they all insist they would do it with love and the strongest desire to provide me with the best quality of life. Of course they would. Of course you all would. I know this."

She again gestured to stop the avalanche of assurances and arguments.

"I'm almost finished with my tirade, but let's be honest.

We've been talking about this for years now. We all have friends who've had Alzheimer's touch their family in different ways. We know how much love and effort families put into taking care of the one afflicted. It's to be admired. It's wonderful. We also know how much of a drain this kind of care can be, emotionally and financially, and for what benefit to me? Excuse me for being selfish here, but this is precisely my point. I'm in a position to say what I want. Whose life are we considering here. Mine or everyone else's?"

She looked beseechingly at each of her dear friends, wanting desperately for them to understand. "What will it matter to me how good the care is? I won't be aware of any of it, and you will be dealing with someone who might as well be a stranger."

"But—"

"*No* buts," she reminded them, "my personality is going to die but my body may live on for years. I won't be me. I won't be living my life. I'll be some other presence living in this body. I'm not going to list all of the unpleasant aspects of the conditions that await me. We are all too aware of how this disease progresses. It's all documented. I've been reading everything I can get my hands on. I'm not suggesting this is the choice anyone else should make. I'm simply saying it's mine, and I should have the right to decide whether this is how I choose to continue in this life or not. I can't stand the thought of not being in control of myself. I won't end life in this state ... I won't!"

She leaned back into her chair and pressed her head against the firm upholstery. Folding her arms across her chest, she swept her eyes deliberately around the room. They all recognized that look. She knew exactly what she was doing.

"I have a plan, and I'll tell you what it is after we talk this through. Now it's your turn. Thanks for listening so patiently."

This was an emotional earthquake, and the aftershocks

rippled through each one of them. They sat rooted to their spots trying to organize thoughts before words slowly began to flow.

After listening carefully to one another, without judging or sermonizing, they reached a consensus. Whatever she wanted them to do, they would. Whatever she asked of them in terms of support and help, they would give. Some of them were really pushing themselves to make this commitment, but more importantly they did not want to let her down when she was so certain of her intent. Stronger together than alone, as they had so often said.

But what did the rest of her family say?

"When I first had the tests, I just said I'd been feeling a little unwell and was having some investigations. I had been vague to this point with everyone except, of course, Steven. We've had some huge arguments but he has respected my desire for privacy so far. He understands how this would affect my marriage. Every day from this point on at home would be torture. So I have to keep my plan a secret."

"But now everyone knows your diagnosis?"

"Yes and everyone is being proactive and getting information about Alzheimer's. It's a natural reaction these days. I've really tried to appear only mildly worried. Those old days in little theatre are paying off. Oh, I just had this flashback! Remember in *Fiddler on the Roof* when I had the wardrobe malfunction during the big dance number?"

"I can't believe you're trying to make us laugh in the middle of this conversation."

"We have to keep laughing or we'll do nothing but cry," she insisted, "and I don't want this to become a weepfest. Personally, I'm pretty much cried out. I don't want to feel sorry for myself anymore. I want to feel at peace with my decision. Once we've all managed to accept this—if we do, that is—you have no idea how much it will mean to me and how you will enable me to proceed with my plan."

"Which is?"

"How do you know anything about doing something like this ... how do any of us know?"

She closed her eyes and took a deep breath before continuing with strength and clarity.

"Well you should ask," she agreed, "it's all in this book I just showed you. I want you all to read it. Please, it's short. There's a cocktail of pills—"

"How are you going to get those pills?"

"They're commonly prescribed, nothing exotic. You just have to have enough. I have a feeling that my doctor is going to be supportive in her own way."

"You've got to be kidding. How?"

"The day she talked to me about the diagnosis, she was amazing. She couldn't have been more sensitive and empathetic. She listened. She put her arms around me when I broke down. We talked at length about my feelings now and how I would be able to accept and deal with the future. I didn't come right out with it, but we did speak in general terms about choices in life. I then steered the conversation into choices about death."

"I can't believe she didn't cut you off right there and then. Most doctors would."

"I know," she agreed, "but it was a natural progression in a philosophical discussion. I watched her responses very, very carefully and measured her words. I definitely got the impression that she understood where I was going, even though she stressed living and moving forward, as you would expect from a principled physician. I think I can take a chance and be more forthright at our next appointment ... which is ... uh, soon."

"So how do you see this playing out? Have you really thought the whole thing through?"

"Crazy as it sounds, coming to terms with this idea and figuring out how to make it work has brought me more solace than anything. I feel like I'm taking the worst possible situation and making something positive out of it. I feel like I'm keeping my integrity intact and going out with dignity. It's empowering."

"Choice—it's the foundation of everything in life, isn't it? It determines how we live our life, whether or not we bring another life into this world. So why shouldn't we have the choice of how to end our life as well? Most people would not abuse this. It's human nature to value life over death."

"Interestingly," came an interruption, "many articles predict that the laws around self-deliverance, as you call it, and euthanasia will change in the next few decades as government struggles to deal with the healthcare costs of aging baby boomers."

A voice of support came from across the room. Several of the women spoke of reading articles about legislation passed in Oregon that supports euthanasia in certain situations. Of the number of people who qualify to apply for it due to terminal illnesses, only a small majority actually end up following through. But the government has recognized their right to choose."

The aroma of freshly brewed coffee was filling the room—decaf for some and a good strong espresso for those who desired a jolt. They needed to focus. The talk continued.

"Here's what I'm hoping will happen. This is going to be difficult for you to hear, so stop me when you feel the need. Tell me honestly what you think. I have to know that I'm not causing any of you more pain than you can handle. I need to assure you that you aren't going to be charged with assisting suicide. I know that has probably crossed everyone's mind."

"For sure. Remember the Sue Rodriguez case in British Columbia several years ago, all the press?"

"Exactly," she agreed. "It's only natural to be concerned. I've spoken with a couple of lawyers about the situation—in general. Obviously I didn't refer to myself."

"But that's what we are doing: assisting your su-su..." The word was caught in a choke.

"No, you're not. No one needs to know that you were aware of my timing. It's as simple as that. I wouldn't consider this for one second if I thought any of you would be held responsible. Just because you're on the premises when the act occurs doesn't make you culpable in any way, and I'll leave a letter explaining my actions."

One voice broke in, supported by the nods and murmurs of agreement from the other six. "As the saying goes: one for all and all for one. That's us, right? That's always been us—for more than forty years. As we listen to you and understand how you feel about this, we may come to terms with it. But if not, the dissenting voices must be heard. We all have to be on board here."

She met the painfully sympathetic gaze of each one. "Absolutely! You know that I wouldn't ask any one of you to do anything to which you can't commit. Opting out of this is the right of each of you, and I'd understand."

The silence in the room was lighter now. Each of them was closer to knowing what she would do and why.

She continued to explain, "I think my doctor will prescribe the sleeping pills I need over the next two months. I'll save them. In fact, I'll need to have one of you collect them from me so I don't forget what I'm doing with them or where I put them. I'm already using Post-It notes all over the house and writing everything down in this notebook. It's the only way I can function now. I feel the changes already."

"We'll take turns going to your next appointments with you."

"Well," she replied quietly, "obviously there are others to be considered ... one in particular, who will not even discuss this.

We have to work around them too." Her voice drifted off for a few seconds.

She straightened her posture once again as her gaze flashed like a laser around the room. "The Bridge Club ski weekend is my target date—two months from now. I just hope I can make it."

Eyes widened and they collectively inhaled.

"I know this will be too difficult for anyone in my family to handle ... including ..." her voice caught and she stopped herself from saying the name. "I don't want any of them with me. I'm afraid one of them might try to stop me at the last minute. But with you, I know that if we agree, we can make it work. This would sound crazy to some people, but my last two days will be fun and full of love and laughter. Even though I know you'll be struggling, I can't allow myself that liberty any more. I know if we agree, we'll succeed. We always do."

"But are you going to tell your family exactly what you plan to do?"

"Almost. It's imperative to me that they understand or at least try. I wouldn't want any of them to feel I had deceived them in any way. I'll be completely truthful and will explain why I'm choosing to do this with you and not them. I just won't tell them my precise timeframe. They all know the BC history, and I'm trusting they'll respect my wishes. Having said that, I'm also certain some will be angry with me."

"Well, I'm sure they will be angry with us too when it's all over. Don't you think they will try to stop you from coming to the ski weekend?"

A thin smile flickered faintly across her lips as she explained that she hoped to convince everyone things were going well up to that weekend. She hoped they would be happy that she was having a few days away with the friends they all knew meant so much to her. "It will take a performance, but I plan to leave on an upbeat note. I want everyone to understand that."

A strangled voice broke from the group, "This is bigger than any of us. I hear you. I get what you're saying. I think I might even feel the same as you do if I had this diagnosis. But I'm really scared."

There was no disagreement with that. Others expressed strongly how they could never take this step, even though they could see where she was coming from.

She explained to them how she'd worked her way through her initial fear, anger, and tears and how every step of learning and planning had strengthened and calmed her. She hoped her experience would convince them that this was right for her. "I've always said to you I want to face this disease squarely, head on, no pretensions. In one of the books I read, Alzheimer's is described as a disease that slowly devours you from the inside out. It's happening to me. I can feel it, and I have to get away from it before it takes over. I simply cannot end up like Judith. That's what this is all about."

The rest of the Bridge Club would all agree later that her argument and decision had taken on a whole new perspective for each of them after she described her reaction to Judith's situation.

"After all the countless hours of rip-roaring arguments we've had about religion, I know some of you are going to struggle with that. Just remember what I've always said about rolling up to the pearly gates, if indeed the opportunity presents itself. If there is a God, as some of us believe and some of us don't, He or She will be forgiving and let me in based on my track record. The values and principles that govern how we live our life will be weighed more heavily than the number of times we attend church or say our prayers or how our life ended. I have no doubts about that."

There was no question in any of their minds about her beliefs. They had been strong and consistent through the years.

She assured them unequivocally. "Think about it. You're not making any choices that go against your religious beliefs or basic values. I'm the one making the choice and you'll be offering me comfort and support. Surely your beliefs encourage that kind of help to someone who is suffering. Mine do."

"Have you made a living will?'

"I have," she replied, standing up and pacing, ticking points off on her fingers as she spoke. "That was the first thing I did to begin preparing myself, even though I won't need it now. I've already started to put all of my ducks in a row and get my stuff organized. I'm telling you, this is an empowering experience."

They were beginning to believe her.

"I'm past the sentiment for the most part and just feel an intense desire to make this work. I feel the pressure of time to do these things while I can still make good decisions. Everything is in the top drawer of my desk. I've left very clear instructions to the last detail thanks to help from all of you—my estate, my possessions, the wake—even down to the music I want played and where to order the food. I'm going to make a video to be played at the wake, with your help. I want the day to be a celebration of the good things in life and an opportunity for me to say thank you. Of course there will be tears, but hopefully in a good way—no moping allowed! I've also stipulated I want my body left to science, with organ donation and Alzheimer's disease research the priorities. It's the least I can do. Taking care of the details has made me realize how we all should deal with these matters while we're healthy."

With that, she fell back into her chair and blew out a long breath.

"Jeez Louise, no stone left unturned."

"You're absolutely right, and I have to tell you it's given me immense satisfaction, crazy as it sounds. Remember that Erma Bombeck e-mail that circulated after she died?"

"Everyone I know got it—and more than once!"

"Well, go back and look at it again, because she said a lot of the things I want to. Grab life and live it and don't worry about grass stains. Don't sweat the small stuff. Use the good china. Make sure the people you love know it."

There were murmurs of agreement, acknowledging their awareness of how important all this was and how most of us lose sight of it from day to day.

"Don't get me wrong, I still have bad moments." Her face tightened briefly before she continued, her voice a tone softer. "But I know what I'm doing and why. My initial feelings of despair have mostly changed to relief as I've worked through this."

Dinner was hardly touched. Most of the wine bottles were still corked. The cards stayed in the deck. The women were drained.

Still they forced themselves to talk, question. The one underlying fact they all agreed on was that she needed them to help her with this most important decision of her life.

The amount of reading and research she had done was impressive. Her arguments were logical and supported by intelligent thought, even as she sometimes struggled to find the right words. They were beginning to see the signs she had been describing.

"I want you to listen to this excerpt from a book that was written by a younger woman with my diagnosis. It's a good example of how I'm not alone in my opinion about my situation."

In a clear voice in spite of the odd stumble and need for gentle assistance, she read the words that echoed her own thoughts. This writer had ultimately decided not to take her life. At the same time, this woman had agreed that it should be a matter of personal choice rather than a legal or religious matter. The writer expressed succinctly how our society has associations to assist suffering animals to a peaceful end but does not extend the same charity to humans.

Raising her head slowly from the page, she met every set of eyes with a look of fierce intensity. "I need to know that you see others share my point of view. I need to feel that somehow you understand where I'm coming from and that you're not feeling forced into this."

The evening was not a late one. They had much to consider.

During the following weeks she spent time with each of them, one on one. Each was given an item that was meant for her to treasure. Each had left knowing without a doubt that this was a decision reached by a woman of sound mind and full heart. She lent them books and gave them a list of many more she had borrowed from the library.

Might any of the others have made the same decision? Not one of them could say for certain, and some most emphatically knew that it wasn't. But it wasn't their decision they reminded each other. After all their history together, how could they not respect that and set aside personal bias?

One of them had a book her book club was reading and bought seven more copies. "This is an important story, so well written, and everyone should read it no matter what age you are," they were told, as each received a copy of *Still Alice*.

It was the fictional story of a fifty-year-old university professor's descent into Alzheimer's and how she and her family were affected and reacted to it. "It's a difficult story from which we can all learn so much, and it's very current."

After they had read it she felt she had an even stronger case for not wanting this experience for herself or her family. She admired that family's love and commitment but that was their story and this was hers.

It was obvious to everyone close to her how this insidious

disease was all too quickly robbing her of independence. One of the most difficult moments had been when she was asked to hand over her car keys. Driving was simply too dangerous for her and for innocent people around her. For the last few weeks, the BC had taken turns giving relief to her family members so that she was never alone. They knew they needed that close contact as much as she needed them.

At the last Bridge Club night before the ski weekend, they talked about how they'd try to work through their grief in the aftermath of all this. No one was pretending it would be easy. She cried when they told her they had all committed themselves to working with the Toronto Alzheimer's Association in whatever capacity was needed in the future. They felt it was one way to honor her and begin to do their own healing.

"And promise, one more time," she urged, "that going through this with me will only strengthen your resolve to living life to the fullest, to being appreciative and grateful and involved like always—only more so. Swear to me you will help each other not to be totally bummed out by this. I need to hear it one more time."

And so they swore to her and meant it. The end result of all this had to impact their lives in a positive way. They would need each other's help. No question about that.

"Let me try to put how I'm feeling now in perspective." she said with an unexpected cynical grin, "We all know that saying ... you know, we've seen it on t-shirts and in e-mails ... about kicking the bucket with wine ... and chocolate. I wrote it down here somewhere."

"Aha! You mean "*I plan to leave this life with a glass of chardonnay in one hand, chocolate in the other, skidding sideways and yelling 'wooohooo, what a ride!*'"

"Yeah! Well, that's kinda my plan! Get it?"

They did get it. They just never thought it would come to this. Not in their wildest dreams.

There had been long talks, without her knowledge, among themselves about each one's struggles to come to grips with the whole unbelievable scenario. It wasn't about them, they kept reminding each other.

They tried to keep the conversation light through the cocktail hour but inevitably it would return to her and how she was coping. "I feel myself slipping. Confusion is becoming a familiar part of my life but it comes and goes. It's frustrating, frightening..." She stopped as her voice trailed off.

Her favorite meal was served and at her insistence they played bridge—as best they could—spending more time talking and laughing to cover the obvious difficulties she was encountering. Before long an excuse to end the cards arose from the chatter as an idea began to take shape.

"Okay! We'll each draw one of our names from this hat. We've learned so much from each other, let's put it all together at the ski weekend. Write in as few words as possible—"

"A challenge in itself," one of them interrupted with a laugh.

"True! But as I was saying, write down what that person has brought to the BC as we've ridden the waves of our lives together."

Names were written on paper slips and drawn. They would have a month to put together their response.

Someone else had brought along a book she had been reading in her efforts to come to grips with the situation they faced. She shared the thoughts that had stayed with her from the book, explaining how they had put her perspective in focus.

"What we need to do is set aside everything else and show up for you, to say we are with you. It's as simple as that."

They looked at each other and, without a word, stood up and high-fived.

That was then. Now here they were. The Bridge Club ski weekend was in full gear, with everyone determined to make this, as she had requested, "the last best time."

"Okay, dessert's over, unless someone wants seconds."

"We're all going to have to help each other in every way over the next two days."

"And that includes eating dessert, so I'll have a refill, thanks," said Jane. Bo quickly passed her own plate, stressing she was never one to shirk responsibility.

Responding with forced chuckles and weak smiles, they were attempting to maintain a certain level of their traditional weekend relaxed atmosphere and somehow avoid the only focus there could possibly be.

She got up after dessert to help clear the dishes but then stood rooted to the spot, placing her hand on the mantle to steady herself. Her every movement and expression transmitted to the radar each of the other women felt implanted in them this weekend. She did have their attention.

"Listen up," she began, with a noticeable catch in her voice. "I'm determined to keep this from becoming gloomy or weepy. We promised, together and separately, we would not go there. Just let me say this one more time. I love you and am deeply, deeply grateful for all that we've shared through these years. You are the best. Remember our vow: no more tears. I know they will come again later when I can't berate you. Now we need to relive memories of all that we've shared and celebrate how lucky we are! I wrote the name of this author in my notebook that you know has been my lifeline. Listen: '*What better way to die than celebrating life.*"

Eyes glistened around the room but incredibly, they agreed weeks later, no one lost control. Their resolve was strong.

"I remember that quote," one replied, anxious to move the conversation forward. "When you gave me the book written by Thomas DeBaggio, my whole perspective about what you face seemed to fall into place. I hope somehow he knows how much good his searing, honest writing has accomplished."

"None of us could be here this weekend without reading the books you steered us to and the stories, articles, and videos we all discovered or had recommended by others."

"Talk about an education. I just wish there had been another reason for it."

"That's the reality of it all. Most of us don't learn about stuff like this until it affects someone we love."

"Well, a lot of people will never realize how helpful they were. It wouldn't have been possible to truly grasp your challenge or to reach a decision about our role without learning as much as we did. We were pushed to reach within ourselves."

"What amazed me was discovering how many people have very productive lives as they cope with Alzheimer's disease. I wish you felt you had the same possibility."

Her eyes welled as she responded, unable to give them what they really wanted to hear. "I wish I did too. No turning back now."

A moment of intense quiet followed this exchange, a moment when their connection was almost palpable, with no doubt or hesitation. Their strength flowed from one to the other and bound them together as never before.

And then the familiar words were heard.

"Okay. Let's get these dishes cleared and play bridge. Deal 'em up!"

While a few cleaned up the kitchen, others set up the card tables and chairs by the fireplace. The cards were shuffled as they all randomly took seats. They would switch partners after every four hands just for the fun of it so it didn't matter where anyone sat. This was kitchen bridge at its best, with plenty of laughter mixed in.

They had all brought along photos from the past forty years and dropped them in some of Dee's old wicker baskets to be sifted through from time to time. Often when one of the group was dummy, that woman would wander over, pull out a handful to look at, and then pass them to the others at the end of that hand. The stories and laughter that accompanied the photos made for lengthy breaks.

Truth be told, her ability to play bridge was fading and it was easier to keep the chatter going so they didn't have to work at faking the game.

"Pam, there's no question you win the award for the most changes in coiffures! Your seventies afro takes the cake though. Look at this shot. Talk about big hair!" There followed a determined effort to see how many photos they could pull out showing Pam with a totally different look and then put them in chronological order: a forty-year history of hairstyles.

"Omigawd, here we are in our aprons, serving spoons at the ready, dishing up breakfast at the homeless soup kitchen. We've had a long history there, but I think this is the only photo we have of it."

"Must have been our first day or close to it, judging from those fresh young smiling faces."

"Here's one of my favorites, twenty years later, I might add —us standing in front of the Duomo in Florence on our Tuscany trip."

"What a gorgeous shot! Mamma mia, did we have a great time there or what?"

"Well, what's more gorgeous here? The beauty and history of that magnificent structure or us loaded down with our shopping bags from the Mercato San Lorenzo down the street? I don't know which was making us smile more!"

"Bella Daniella! Remember the next door neighbor who couldn't take his eyes off you?" Danielle's cheeks typically blushed crimson red in seconds at that memory and she quickly attempted to change the topic.

"Thank you, thank you, thank you, Cass. What a stroke of

luck it was for all of us when you met those Italians and bartered to have the use of their villa."

Cass assured them that the best part for her had been having the chance to spend those two weeks with the BC. "I tell you, those memories helped me through a few down times when we were sailing. There weren't a ton of bad days on the boat, but there were some and I pulled up a lot of good memories to get me through."

"Well Cass, here's one that certainly doesn't look like a bad time. You sent it to us from Greece. Someone took a photo of you sitting on the bow of your boat taking a photo of Dirk the Jerk behind the captain's wheel. It's simply spectacular with the turquoise water and a sunbaked village tumbling down to the sea in the background."

"Truly breathtaking!"

"Jake took that on one of his holidays with us. You're right, what an adventure we had," agreed Cass looking wistfully at the images that brought with them a flood of memories that were more than purely visual. Words, textures, sounds, smells, not to mention emotions, could return with a glance at one of those shots.

A few more hands of bridge would be played before there was another interruption, and so it went. The evening progressed uproariously, in spite of themselves, with familiar stories repeated for the umpteenth time.

To be sure there were moments during the breaks when an exchange of looks or a squeeze on the arm would cause two or three to slip unnoticed from the living room. Quietly, down the hall or upstairs, fears and anxieties that surfaced were quelled. This weekend would not be easy but they would see it through, each helping the other. They had promised.

"Trite as it sounds, whoever first said a picture is worth a thousand words is one of my heroes. It's so true."

"Here we are at a ski weekend doing a chorus line to show off the socks Jane knit us in those wild, psychedelic colors."

"I've got mine with me this weekend. Never ski without them!"

"Me too!"

"Jane, look at these! Some super action shots of you skiing including doing a three-sixty!"

"Oh sure," said Jane, grinning as she reached for a photo, "and is it an action shot in the air or in the midst of one of my spectacular face plants?"

Bo sifted through the basket with Lynn, who waved a photo at her. "Now here's what I call an action shot! It's you at the BBQ with the biggest pile of ribs I've ever seen."

"Mmmm, we've had a lifetime of great meals from our Bo and her BBQ. No argument there!"

"Lucky us. Now that you mention eating, pass Lynn's cookies over here, please."

"Oh Dani, remember this?"

"Yup, that was at our group fifty-fifth in Muskoka," said Dani, a wide smile lighting her face. They chuckled at the picture of her holding her sides, collapsed in uncontrollable laughter on a sofa. "Bo had just finished telling us that now we were getting on in years we needed to be aware of the 'three N's of aging,' which I have not forgotten."

She shook her hands wildly at the memory and chortled as she began to lose it again while other voices in the room came to her assistance, "Never pass a restroom. Never ignore an erection. Never trust a fart!"

"Words of deep wisdom," affirmed Bo, grinning as she hoisted her ice water and toasted Danielle, who was still doubled over with laughter. "Even at our mature age, anything to do with flatulence causes our Sainte Danielle to totally lose it. And of course she gets us all going."

"I still think it all goes back to the nuns."

"Well, Danielle, I'm warning you right now," Cass said with mock gravity, "don't stay too close to me or you will be cracking up constantly. It seems every time I bend over these days I inadvertently fart. Another joy of aging!"

There were empathetic nods mixed with the laughter.

"Let's face it, in some ways we'll never grow up."

Reminiscing continued before they got back to the business of dealing a few more hands. However, the photo baskets were like magnets, and finally they realized they needed to put away the cards and lose themselves in the plethora of memories that lay waiting.

Draped over the arms of the softly-plumped chairs, sinking into down-filled sofas or lazily stretched out on the carpet, they passed the basket from one to another with the fire roaring inside and storm raging outside.

Another whoop of laughter filled the room as Dee fanned the air wildly with the photo in her hand, barely managing to get her words out. "Without question the award-winning group shot from the ski weekend at the Alton Spa, when my farmhouse was being renovated."

"What a weekend that was!"

"We know without looking exactly which one it is! In the restaurant Marti had been rather over-served, as our kids like to say, and when we went back to our cottage on the grounds we partied on."

"To put it mildly. Remember Lynn sitting in the veggie dip?"

"She insisted it was okay for her to do that because she had brought it."

"Trust me. You both have portraits in the Hangover Hall of Fame after that night!"

Tears were rolling down cheeks as they relived so many good times and recalled frequent silly behavior that does everyone a lot of good every once in a while no matter what age. Particularly when you're with people you trust who won't judge you.

Lynn rolled her eyes and nodded. "How can I forget those youthful hangovers? It's amazing how having kids gets you right out of that habit!"

"Or having to be on call for clients 24/7. Running the shelter certainly put an end to those days for me—although in a perverted way I kind of miss that bad behavior," Marti finished with a sigh and a giggle.

"Marti, you still manage to encourage us all into bad behavior from time to time. We've simply become adept at not needing booze to fuel it."

"Wait, wait, wait." Danielle was rummaging through the basket. "There's one more shot from that weekend that I must find."

Waving the photo triumphantly, she passed it around to more peals of laughter at the image of them unloading all the gear for skating on the pond and cross-country skiing from the car. "I love this. We had such plans for that Saturday. Unpacked all of our equipment only to pack it all up again unused. Nobody could move after our party that first night except to go out to the hot tub."

"And I brought all those outfits for nothing," moaned Cass, who always managed to have some wild costume in her bag to make any event special.

"Yup! No question though, your day at the races with the polka dot skirt and matching tulle hat with the brim no one could see around still is the prize-winning couture moment."

"Yuh think?"

They laughed until their sides ached recounting other stories. If one of them did not get the details exactly right, someone else did. Their forty years had been too full for one person to remember everything although Dee was the acknowledged master retainer of detail. They had not called her "Steel Trap" for nothing. However these days it definitely took a group effort, which was one of the reasons it was so much fun reminiscing.

"*La recherche du temps perdu,*" sighed Danielle, rubbing her eyes and yawning. "Such great times."

Agreeing it was time to call it a night, Pam set the camera timer as they organized themselves in a disorganized fashion in front of the fireplace. Complaining, joking, and mugging were part of the process and she always insisted on more than one shot. Everyone knew, but no one said out loud, these would be the last group photos with eight of them.

They were not ignoring the outcome of this weekend but rather immersing themselves in the memories that would be needed to carry them all through the difficult moments ahead. The tough part was not just in helping with this decision of hers but also in coming to terms with the finality of it. They all knew exactly how much they would miss that eighth part of their whole being that was the Bridge Club.

On the other hand, they had all reached a place where they felt they had found the strength that was needed. After struggling together to achieve that goal over the preceding weeks, now there was something that felt almost like pride at how they were helping make this final wish attainable. Fear, guilt, anxiety, indecision ... all this and more had stalked each of them in one way or another as they had worked to come to terms with it all. They were united now in their commitment.

Sleep did not come easily to anyone that night, but morning came, as it always does, and was met with determination to face the day as they knew they must.

The drive to Blue Mountain on Saturday morning was tricky, but the Suburban was up to the challenge. It was well worth the effort as only the hardcore skiers bothered to tackle the slippery, drift-filled roads, and the hills were not busy. The wind had subsided and the day would remain relatively calm before the blustering returned later in the afternoon. The snowfall continued, light but steady.

"It's still a buzz cruising the runs after all these years. Even if it is a stretch to call them mountains."

"And to have conditions like this in Ontario, instead of our usual boilerplate, is unbelievable. Wooohooooo!"

Someone was always by her on the hills, in front and behind, so she didn't forget where she was or where she was going. They were aware of how she had gotten lost several times finding her way back from washrooms, and she became very anxious if she felt she was on her own. There was always company waiting for her in the clubhouse when she wanted a break. But on her boards she still rocked and her pleasure showed in the elated grin upon her frost-flecked face as she skied with her usual intensity.

Upon their return to the farmhouse, she was the first to flop in the unspoiled blanket of snow by the side entrance. "Snow-angel time! I want a beautiful band of angels outside my window tonight. Tonight of all nights."

And soon there were eight.

Around the dining table that evening, the photo baskets circulated along with the traditional prime rib roast, which was barely touched.

"Has anyone noticed how many pictures there are with us eating? Food has been a big part of what we do together."

"Bo, check out this shot of you at the barbecue whipping up your famous beef on a bun. This one goes back a few years, eh."

"Oh yeah, like about forty years. Look at that barbecue—no propane tank to be seen. I was on the skinny side then too! Hard to believe!"

"Speaking of food, da-daaaaaa," Bo sang. "Here's a close-up shot of the famous Bundt cake! Remember that, Dee?"

Everyone was laughing and talking at once as Dee blushed.

"How could I forget? Apart from the fact that none of you would let me!"

"It was our first ski weekend after Bo finished her rehab and we had no alcohol, of course."

"Until you placed your Bundt cake on the table and the whole kitchen reeked of rum!"

By this time Dee had her hands over her face, her cheeks burning. "I felt like such an idiot! Bo, how many times have I apologized for that?"

"Dee, you'd been making that recipe for years and just didn't think about it. We all knew that."

"I tell you," said Bo, making a face, "the worst part was seeing that whole cake go into the trash in spite of my protests that you should eat it. I knew what we were missing!"

"Yikes!" hollered Jane, staring at another photo. "How can we forget those days when Pam and Danielle were both extremely pregnant just a few weeks apart?"

"*Mon Dieu*, we were a sight!"

"Well the wardrobe for 'ladies in waiting' back in the seventies didn't help much. We look like we're wearing circus tents!"

Lynn rose to stir the smoldering embers, speaking softly, "It's incredible, isn't it? Going from being kids to having kids to seeing our kids having kids ... and yet it hardly feels as if time has passed at all."

She added a few logs to the dying fire as the heartwarming smell of the well-seasoned wood beginning to blaze again filled the room.

"Okay, let's get serious for a minute." They sifted through the baskets and pulled up photos from Habitat for Humanity weekends, breast cancer walks, and other things like potluck dinners to raise money for Women for Women in Afghanistan, a favorite of theirs since Lynn had read about it in *Homemakers* magazine many years ago.

"There's no denying we've all learned that giving is contagious. The more you do, the more you want to. It's not always about the party as we well know."

"It isn't?" Bo said, feigning surprise. "I've been duped!"

Everyone grinned at a photo taken at the fiftieth birthday weekend, when Cass was still sailing the world. They had made certain she was in the group pictures in absentia.

That weekend they had rented an old, slightly rickety cottage perched on the rocks of a small island in Lake Muskoka.

A headshot of Cass had been enlarged to an eight by ten, taped to a wooden ruler, and they had taken turns being responsible for making certain her face appeared in the photos. All the shots were very funny, but the consensus was that the best one was the hat photo.

"Right, thanks to Jane! You had us all complaining about the hat decorating activity you were forcing upon us and then our competitive juices kicked in and we were out of control."

"Those hats were works of art!"

"Good or bad art, is the question."

"I remember when you sent me this photograph. I cried for days at first whenever I looked at it and after that I taped it to my mirror and smiled at the thought of it from then on," said Cass, holding it up for all to see. It was her headshot with a wide-brimmed, lavishly over-decorated hat perched on top of her photo.

Laughter rolled around the table as they remembered how they each took a hand in creating Cass's hat when theirs were finished. They were only allowed to choose one decorating item, but there was no control on the quantity and things got a little out of hand with the sequins, ribbons, sparkles, feathers, and glue gun.

"But there's an even more important shot that I taped to my mirror as well," Cass said as she dug around the basket and pulled up the group shot from that weekend which showed all of them wearing their fine chapeaux. Bo held the headshot of Cass sporting her creation in the midst of them.

"That's the most significant Bridge Club photo to me," said Cass, "even when one of us is not here, we still are."

"And always will be."

"Amen to that."

This was a moment when they might all have totally lost control, given the circumstances, but instead they leapt into action. The table was cleared, the rugs were rolled back, the music cranked up, and the party was on. The activity of the day had simply been the warm-up for the evening's main event. Saturday night was party night with the oldies but goodies (music as well as the Bridge Club, they said in more recent years), shaking the golden-hued pine floorboards that had well over a century of Saturday nights worn into them. Sixty might have been a reality, but the girls could boogie with the best of them.

It seemed like yesterday they used to stack the LPs on the turntable, and they recalled the excitement of the advent of cassettes and then CDs. Now, thanks mainly to encouragement by younger generations in their families, they had their music on iPods and could pick and choose whatever they wanted to listen to with the greatest of ease.

The energy was electric as they jived to Elvis, to the Beatles, to Van Morrison, to the Red Hot Chili Peppers. They would jive to anything! They had always professed jiving should be compulsory in the high school curriculum. There was no other type of dancing that was more fun.

They twisted to Chubby Checker, strolled to Fats Domino, did the Mashed Potato and the Pony with shrieks of laughter, and swayed to Sinatra and Streisand and Bublé with off-key voices blending and arms draped around each other. Cass provided her usual moments of interpretive whatever. She hadn't lost her touch.

All of their old standbys were blasting, the louder the better. They belted it out word for word—the Stones, the Beatles, all the Motowners, Roy Orbison, Rod Stewart, the Guess Who, The Four Seasons, The BeeGees, and any other Golden Oldies you might name. They sang their hearts out. Cass performed her outrageous Tina Turner routine. Any tune by Diana Ross and the Supremes prompted a karaoke-style performance featuring Jane, Pam, and Marti—a tradition through the decades that never failed to crack everyone up.

It was her party. Her last best time.

A much-needed rest to catch their breath presented a good time to bring out their responses to the names drawn from the hat at the previous month's BC evening.

"Dorky as it sounds, along with the craziness we've shared, we've brought some substance to each other's lives as well. And before we start arguing about getting top billing, let's do it in alphabetical order of first names. Toss your slip of paper back in this hat and we'll dump them on the coffee table. That will solve that!"

Each had been instructed to type her response as they would guess afterwards who had written what. They did enjoy their games. Even now. Especially now.

Bonnie—Take responsibility for your life and cushion it all with laughter. Loud laughter!

Cass—Dare to dream. Dance on to the next adventure knowing your family and friends are in the chorus line!

Danielle—Be strong in your beliefs. Find the goodness within yourself and experience life one breath at a time. Expletive deleted – ooops - Namaste.

Dee—Purpose and direction. Keep your head down, keep your eye on the ball, and follow through!

Jane—Accept people as they are/ find forgiveness in your heart/ live life to the extreme.

Lynn—Family is what you make it so make it your priority. Respect each other AND the environment, and teach your kids to play bridge.

Marti—It's never too late for change, inside or out. Choose a life that matters and pay it forward.

Pam—Plan for the future but live for the present and appreciate that each day is a gift. Cultivate your garden.

As the list unfolded, they became more serious, smiling acknowledgement at these lessons in life that had been brought to the table.

Guessing who had picked which name brought the laughter and teasing back, particularly when it was noted that all of them had been able to accomplish the task in less than twenty-five words. An amazing feat for a few of them! They concluded that, considering the amount of time they spent learning rules for playing bridge through the decades, this list might be the Bridge Club's rules for living life.

"Every game needs rules, right?"

"Ha! Nothing bigger than this game of life!"

"As trite as it sounds, I have to say it. Even after all these years, there's no better way for everyone to live than by the Golden Rule. That should be the header for our list."

Hands on hearts and drinks held high, they recited the axiom they had all learned in the first grade: "*Do unto others as you would have them do unto you!*"

Talk about keeping things simple.

"And let us not forget our steadfast belief in the so-called ancient Chinese art of Ti-Ming," she added with mock solemnity, flipping through her notebook. "Here's a perfect example —I mean, how karmic is the timing of me finding this? *A friend is someone who knows the song in your heart and can sing it back to you when you have forgotten the words.* Thank you for the singing you have done for me these past few months."

There were no words now, no laughs.

She was the one who said it was time.

She told them she could do this part alone.

She knew how deeply they had dug to get this far.

"You know you don't have to stay in the bedroom with me. I'll be fine," she reassured them in her typical manner. There's no question this was an option some had considered, but in the end all had rejected. Every detail had been talked through until there was no need to talk any more. They knew what they would do. With love and an indescribable amount of pain.

The climb up the stairs felt endless, their footsteps heavy. A decision had been made in the planning stages that they would not change from their clothes. They did not want to risk interrupting the momentum of their actions.

Extra mattresses had been hauled up to the big attic with its king-sized bed and two sets of bunks. For years, this had been the room Dee's many nieces and nephews took over on their visits to the farm. With so many snorers in the BC, they normally chose bedrooms that guaranteed them a bit of soundproofing. This night they would all lie together.

The keeper of the pills had slipped out with her earlier and together they precisely followed the instructions carefully copied. The potion was mixed before dinner while the others were having a cocktail in front of the fire. She had taken her anti-nausea pills then too. Hot chocolate was added to counteract the bitterness of the pills and the mugs they now held looked no different from hers.

The time for talk was over. One last embrace from each of them. One last I love you. One last you'll be in our hearts forever.

"Remember, it's the journey, not the destination, and we've had one hell of a trip together. You owe it to me to make certain it continues," she said in a strong voice. "This is my decision—my choice. You've made it possible for me to move on to ... whatever ... feeling at peace and loved. I ... I could never thank you enough. It's been a wonderful weekend ... a wonderful life."

A wave of immense gratitude washed through her as she looked at the faces of these women with whom she had shared so much for so long. She was grateful beyond words for their friendship, for this sisterhood that had been such an integral part of her world, and for their ability to move beyond their own barriers to support her at this moment in this ultimate act of love. She was grateful for her wonderful family and other friends and the experiences that had filled her life. She was grateful she had been able to express these feelings to everyone who mattered over the past two months. She was grateful she had remained focused on her ability to make this choice at this moment in spite of the clouds of confusion that were closing in on her mind. No regrets now—the time for them was long past. It was time to go.

She felt her resolve slip for a moment. Her voice suddenly became soft and fragile before she willed it to be how she knew it must. "I'll be in touch from the other side," she said into the stillness that enclosed them. If anyone could, she would.

Raising their mugs, they choked back tears to stay strong for her. They had promises to keep. Their own internal struggles would have to get in line.

She could do it, needed to do it. No turning back. One thought held her focus: swallow.

The warm liquid slid easily down her throat. The chocolate was almost pleasing, not quite masking the bitterness.

Within minutes, so surprisingly quickly, she was fading, her breath slow and shallow as the empty mug was gently taken from her hand. Life was leaving her as she wished. One massaged her feet. One held her hand. Another stroked her hair. She was loved.

Some clasped hands and others buried their face in their pillows as they lay quietly in the darkness until they knew that the deepest sleep of all had claimed her.

It was done.

Done for her. Not for them.

Slowly, when it was confirmed she was truly gone from them, they gradually slipped out of the room in their own time. One, then another, sometimes two, realizing this was not so easy to accept. With one exception. They had made certain one would lie with her until dawn. As much for herself as anything, that one had said. Hot tears slipped down the sides of her face and soaked the pillow as hours passed. There would be no sleep for anyone else this night, this longest of nights.

Downstairs the reactions were as different as the women themselves. Sorrow, anger, relief, regret, loss, and confusion swirled around them like the storm outside. There was nothing to be said yet.

Deep sighs filled empty spaces. Mournful gazes pierced frosted windows. Tears fell: some silently, some with wailing sobs. Long embraces were scattered through this place of mourning.

Outside the wind gusted causing windows to rattle. Snow

continued to fall creating a curtain around their sorrowful space. The night seemed unending, as if a darkness had fallen that might never lift.

She had asked them to promise the next day would be as close as possible to the way it traditionally had been. They had vowed they would try their best. They had talked together about how it could be their private time of grieving as they prepared to face her family and everyone else in the following days and carry her messages and fulfill her requests as she wished. They knew how important it was to her that they not fail. They swore they would not.

Picking at fruit and cereal and tanking up on caffeine, they continued to find comfort from silence even as they wept in each other's arms. There were no words that would bring solace. Not yet.

One of them noticed a bag at the end of the kitchen counter and inside found seven small gift-wrapped packages. A note from her sat on top.

A last goodbye from me. I hope you hear me saying these words. I love you and will always be with you.

Each had received a simple silver frame containing an elegantly calligraphed quotation.

Death is nothing at all.
I have only slipped away into the next room.
I am I and you are you;
Whatever we were to each other, that we still are.
Call me by my old familiar name.
Speak to me in the easy way which you always used,
Put no difference in your tone,
Wear no forced air of solemnity or sorrow.

Laugh as we always laughed at the little jokes we shared together.
Let my name ever be the household word that it always was.
Let it be spoken without effect, without the trace of a shadow on it.
Life means all that it ever meant.
It is the same as it ever was, there is unbroken continuity.
Why should I be out of mind because I am out of sight?
I am waiting for you, for an interval, somewhere very near, just around the corner.
All is well.
Henry Scott Holland, Canon of St. Paul's Cathedral, London (1847 – 1918).

A heavy silence filled the house. Leaving this gift was so typical of her.

Some sat together, still feeling no need to speak. Others moved to a quiet spot on their own.

The storm continued to rage but as noon approached they knew they could not put off the next step. The phone call.

"Do not, under any circumstances, call 911," she had told them. "If you do, then the police have to do an investigation. Read that part in the book again if you have any doubts. If you simply call the doctor whose name and number I am giving you, he will come and can issue a death certificate and that will be the end of it. My doctor spoke to him weeks ago. She could not tell him our plans but said she is certain he will understand the situation when you give him my note. Call him at least twelve hours after we go to bed, not before."

They were not convinced the police would not be involved. But if the doctor insisted the authorities be called and they did investigate, the women were unconcerned. They knew no wrong had been done and whatever heat there was, they could take it.

Since no one had much appetite for dinner the night before, they encouraged each other, without great success, to eat now in order to meet the demands of the day. Sorrow was filling them faster than any food. Grief would wrap its tentacles around each of them in its own time.

The sleepless night began to take its toll as fatigue dropped some into naps where they sat.

With the roads still closed, the doctor had called back to confirm he had arranged transport to the farmhouse as soon as it was possible to get through. There was no saying when that would be.

Strapping on cross-country skis later that afternoon, they fought their way across the open meadow. Heads down, they punched their arms and pushed their legs against the snow and wind, the combined forces of which attempted to blow them back to the house.

Reaching the protection of the centuries old forest, they glided silently amongst the aromatic pines and cedars. The deep new snow had obliterated the trail but the cut through the trees made it easy to find the way they knew by heart after all these years. The calm in the forest was a welcome relief from the frenzy out in the open. It was as if they had entered a comforting chamber that offered whatever was needed at that particular moment—understanding, forgiveness, acceptance, peace.

Time passed with no words spoken. Tears froze on cheeks dusted with snow. Each remained immersed in her private well of quiet.

The pain of loss would linger, weaving its threads into the fabric of their being. This they knew. It was impossible to be their age and not have learned that sad lesson in life.

The silence was broken when one voice gently off-key began to sing "Amazing Grace." Sporadically others softly joined in or hummed along with her.

It was just what they needed to open the floodgates. They began to speak in bursts about their thoughts and feelings now that her wish was granted. As their voices rose, their skis glided quietly on. In spite of the overwhelming sorrow, they felt proud of her and of themselves for standing by her.

It had been a brave decision, rooted in her heart as well as her mind. Brave for her. Brave for them. She had known it would not be understood by everyone and words of moral outrage would be heard after the fact. Judgment would be passed. She had trusted she would be supported in her final quest by this sisterhood that had been such an important part of her life. They had given so much to each other through all the years. She had reached for the life raft one last time, and in true Bridge Club fashion they had not let her down.

Sleep in heavenly peace.

Sleep in heavenly peace.

EPILOGUE – 2020

If you asked any one of the Bridge Club whether the last thirteen years had gone by in a flash, you would get unanimous agreement. Definitely.

The women steadfastly kept to their routine of getting together monthly. They had skipped a big celebration when they reached 65. It had been too soon after losing her.

They were witness to the ongoing changes in one another, most of them typical for those years bringing them to seventy-five: white hair, health issues, family disruptions, retirements and for some, best of all, grandchildren.

And, worst of all, loss.

After the fateful ski weekend in 2007 when Jane had chosen her final exit, mourning had permeated their lives. It had settled into their psyches in ways unique to each of them.

Their admiration for Jane's choice to die with dignity was a given. The BC's support had not wavered once they were all on board in the months before that weekend, after listening to her reasoning.

They had agreed it was all about her, not about them. They had been there for her in every way and had felt how vital that was to Jane. In the aftermath of the intense grief of the final weekend, as their hearts began to empty of pain, the space left was quickly filled with memories of Jane. She would be forever present in their lives.

Danielle struggled the most because of her strong religious beliefs. The priest at her church had helped her work through anxieties and begin to reach an acceptance of Jane's decision. She still sought his counsel long after Jane's exit and, even so, Dani knew she would always feel a sliver of torment about it. As the years went by and the Canadian government passed laws to allow medically assisted dying, Danielle felt compelled to become an active supporter of the right to die with dignity.

As Marti worked through her grief, she found peace after she set aside thoughts of finding a new man. "Honestly, Mar, why bother?" Jane had asked more than once. "Find contentment within yourself. You've done so much for others. Now focus on you." So, instead of internet dating, Marti embraced her emotional and social independence. Her step-daughters were married and brought grandchildren to her life, which gave her new love affairs. Completely smitten, Marti gladly settled into her role of Nana.

Lynn found peace too in dedicating more time to her parents and volunteering in the community. After her father died, she persuaded her mother to move to a senior's residence on the lake, minutes from her own home. When her mother began to shows signs of senility, Lynn was thankful her years of volunteering in the hospital's Alzheimer's wing after Jane's passing gave her the tools to offer the most effective support. She often thanked Jane in her heart for helping her to fill those last years with her mother with understanding and love. The arrival of grandchildren into Lynn and Jim's lives was also a bonus.

Many years after she had been widowed, Pam was introduced by friends to Steven Ashworth who was ten years older than she, an accountant and a widower with adult children. He and Pam enjoyed spending time together but were also content to be apart.

They often spent weekends at his cottage on Lake Simcoe and occasionally travelled together. Their mutual respect and enjoyment of each other's company and interests brought them many happy years.

On one of their final walks together, Jane had said to Pam, "I'm not suggesting Steven is replacing Peter in your heart. But he is a good man and obviously cares deeply for you. I can see you care for him too in your own way. Spend more time with him. Travel the world. He has told me he would love you to do that, but would never put pressure on you." So Pam retired the following spring, and invested more time and emotion in the relationship. She never stopped being grateful to Jane for the nudge.

Bonnie went back to counselling others for drug and alcohol addiction at Havenwood once a week. She felt that having been intimately involved through Jane's passing gave her an added dimension of empathy on which to draw. In time she also offered grief counselling. Cuppie, her mother was alert and interested in everything to the end of her ninety-six years. She remained Bo's primary concern until she passed away a few years after Jane. Bonnie stayed involved in her mother's retirement home by being on the Board and also helping out in the Alzheimer's wing. She already knew many at the home from her daily visits to her mom. Her vibrant personality had a positive effect on staff as well as patients and she was happy to bring some small cheer to their lives.

In their early seventies, Cass and Nick stopped working on the Kelly property, which had now been taken over by a younger generation of the family. They lived sparingly in a small apartment in town on the lake and continued to be avid sailors. They doted on three grandchildren Jake and his wife had given them and one from one of Nick's daughters. After setting up her loom at the community craft center and co-op, Cass had partially eased her grief by spending more time weaving. She promised herself to make a greater commitment to her own creativity and to seriously invest herself in each piece. To everyone's delight, a nature-inspired wall hanging she crafted that incorporated leaves, twigs, and milkweed silk won first prize in a Muskoka arts competition. Cass called it "An Autumn Walk with Jane".

During Jane's final months, Pam often brought her up to Dee's farm in Grey County, sometimes along with Jane's mom, Estelle, who was still adept in her nineties. Together they had planned a new flowerbed to be dug in the spring. Jane chose each plant species to specifically represent a member of the Bridge Club. They had bent the rule of "no outsiders", which made Jane laugh as she added a plant for Sam.

In her typical take-charge way Jane had instructed, "Promise me you will not call it a memorial garden. No way! It's a garden of hope and continuance, and each of you has to commit to weeding it." She had finished that comment with her catchy laugh.

The following spring, Kenneth had tilled the soil, under specific instructions, and the BC had driven up to plant it as Jane wanted. Return trips occurred to weed and reminisce. The flowerbed flourished through the years and each spring, summer, and autumn overflowed with abundance.

Each summer Sam visited the farm and took back a large bouquet for herself and Estelle until Jane's mom passed. Dee's neighbors were welcome to take cuttings whenever they wished. The BC knew Jane would have approved.

Life, as it does, slowly established a rhythm as the years slipped by. And Jane's absence was part of that new normal.

Many years later, a dark shadow once again fell across the Bridge Club, in a way none of them could have imagined.

On the Friday of Thanksgiving weekend in October, 2018, Dee had come down from the farm for an overnight at Bonnie's because a mutual friend was visiting from out of town. They enjoyed one of Bo's classic meals on the grill, and after an evening of laughter and reminiscing, including a political diatribe to be sure, the friend had left. Not long afterward, Bonnie fell asleep in her usual position on the couch. Dee left her snoring lightly, and went to the guestroom knowing Bonnie would make her way to bed at some point in the night.

The next morning Dee awoke early and slipped out for a brisk walk on the well-worn path that hugged the shore of Lake Ontario. Autumn colors wrapped around her and leaves in shades of red, gold and orange carpeted the trail she chose, crunching underfoot. She planned to have the traditional Saturday morning bacon, eggs and hash browns breakfast with Bo and then drive back to the farm to prepare for her family, who would arrive on Sunday for a Thanksgiving feast. The night before, Bonnie had spoken of her eager anticipation to spend Thanksgiving with her brother and nephews. From the years they were best friends as kids, the two women always agreed it was their favorite holiday.

Dee was surprised that Bo was not up when she returned. She went to the bedroom to waken her and discovered, to her horror, Bonnie's lifeless body.

"Peacefully died in her sleep." The coroner said there was no need for an autopsy.

The shock was indescribable as phone calls were made.

Stunned disbelief hung in the air the following week as funeral plans were arranged by Bo's beloved niece and nephews. After her mother passed away four years earlier, Bonnie had made it known that when her turn came she wanted exactly the same service.

The century-old stone church was overflowing for the funeral. The Bridge Club sat together, and the organ boomed uplifting, traditional hymns, beginning with *How Great Thou Art*. As the first notes rang out, tears flooded Pam's face and did not stop for the next hour. Later, the solo vocal of Leonard Cohen's *Hallelujah*, caused audible sobs throughout the congregation. Bonnie had chosen well, and afterward the BC swore they could hear her rousing voice singing along.

Winter came and went with little happening to ease the shock of her loss.

Still the Bridge Club survivors continued on each month. Even though they were now just six, there was never any suggestion of inviting others. The "no outsiders" rule was still in force. They took turns rotating through hands of bridge and always made it work. But the absentees were sorely missed and spoken of often.

Earlier in 2018, Bonnie had led the Bridge Club in planning a memorable trip for their seventy-fifth joint birthday celebration in 2020.

"We have to start planning now to make sure we have all details covered and can get reservations where we want," she'd declared. "We all know how long it takes us to make decisions!"

"Oh mon Dieu," Danielle moaned, "Remember how many trips we began planning that never happened because we did not get our acts together?"

"And remember how many times we laughed talking about those trips that never happened?" Lynn reminded them. "Let's not blow this one."

So the discussions had begun early and in earnest.

Since they all still laughed at the stories of their adventures in Europe in the 1960's, and they had already taken an unforgettable group trip to Italy, they chose France as their destination with surprisingly little debate .

"We'll hit Paris first," Bonnie suggested. "I've always wanted to follow in Hemingway's footsteps there!"

"And then the French Riviera, please ... rosé, the Med, the markets, Provence ..." the others had chimed in with their ideas.

It was agreed. Pam and Lynn volunteered to help Bonnie gather the preliminary information.

After Bonnie died, the plan for the birthday trip hung in the air. In truth, enthusiasm had dampened. Bonnie had always been the catalyst. Then Cass and Danielle admitted they were concerned they could not really afford it. Marti wondered if it was a good decision for her.

"I don't feel right travelling without Nick," Cass said. "Especially since our savings are not enormous and he would like to take a break somewhere too. Since the Kelly's are not well enough to go south anymore, we don't have the luxury of them taking us along."

Danielle had been widowed for three years. Things had never been the same for them after Bryce's discovered sex addiction. They had stayed together in a mostly unhappy environment that she could not find the courage to leave. Bryce became increasingly foul-tempered, often berating Dani with unwarranted expletive-ridden criticism. After his death from a massive heart attack, the family was shocked to discover Bryce had lost a good portion of their savings through unwise investments. Danielle had admitted to the BC, after months of being a widow, that she was relishing her freedom.

"If I could offer advice to other women when a long marriage goes sour, it would be to take a deep breath and leave," she often said. "Give yourself permission to have the life you deserve. Don't feel tied down to old habits that are no longer satisfying or appreciated. Above all, there is never a good reason to accept disrespect and abuse of any kind. And pay attention to finances, which I foolishly never did. Bryce kept telling me to trust him and so I did. Big mistake! Being on my own now makes me realize how much time I wasted and how my financial security has been jeopardized. I was not smart."

Dani and Bryce had visited their daughter and her family in Australia three times and now she was planning to rent an apartment near their Melbourne home for six months.

"You know I'm on a strict saving plan to visit the kids next year. They offered to help me go to France on our trip, but with them both starting new jobs, I don't feel right about that. I want my own place so I can keep enjoying my freedom, tightly budgeted as it is, but close enough to see them whenever we want."

Danielle's son was a freelance writer who lived in Vancouver and planned to join her in Australia for part of that time.

Marti was on the fence about the trip too. "Living on a fixed income now really does cut into this kind of travel for me. Good thing we did so much when we were young. It will be a push, but I will make this trip happen if everyone else wants to."

After more soul searching, they all agreed that their seventy-fifth celebration could be less extravagant. The important thing was to be together.

"A weekend at Dee's farm is always our best time. Let's just do that again in the summer of 2020," Lynn said. It was unanimous.

Even so, Pam, Dee and Lynn were adamant about carrying out Bonnie's wishes. The others kicked in what they could manage to help, insisting they needed to feel a part of it. The August after Bonnie's death, the trio flew to Paris with some of Bo's ashes in an intricately carved wooden box small enough to fit in the palm of a hand.

They spent a week in Paris visiting some of Hemingway's haunts, as Bonnie had been so eager to do. They took turns leaving sprinkles of her ashes as they strolled along the quays of the Seine and sipped espressos at Les Deux Magots brasserie. They toasted her memory with Champagne at the bar in the Ritz, discreetly depositing a sprinkle in brass planters that had once been ashtrays. They knew she would applaud that decision and imagined her loud laugh as they did it.

Then they took the TGV, a high speed train, to Nice. An entertaining taxi driver by the name of Bernadette collected them and took them to the Villa des Violettes bed and breakfast in Antibes. Bonnie had chosen this small inn when she first began planning the trip for the group. She'd loved the description which said there were dogs, cats, chickens and a splendid view.

The women were surprised to discover that their hostess, Katherine, was from Toronto. She had married a Frenchman, Philippe, who was the *fromager* at the daily local market. The couple were relaxed and welcoming and, since there were no other guests, they joined the Bridge Club trio for drinks together on the terrace each late afternoon.

It was a coincidence to discover that Katherine knew how to play bridge and so they had a fourth for the duration of their stay.

At the BC's first gathering after their return home, the women agreed that the final act of gently scattering Bonnie's ashes on the calm waves of the Mediterranean during a brilliant sunset, had been a fitting end to the trip. It was a goodbye that would have won Bo's approval.

And then the pandemic hit in March 2020.

Not even the shocking and terrible Covid-19 virus could

break the Bridge Club, although it turned everyone's world upside down.

It meant from that time on, the women met for Zoom chats and played bridge together in online cardrooms. But they still did so every month and carried on in the new ways the fast-changing world demanded. And somehow, they all stayed healthy.

Still, it was not an easy time.

Pam's longtime partner, Steven, succumbed to the virus as it mercilessly plowed through the nursing home where he was slowly recovering from a debilitating stroke. Left with a weakened immune system, he simply did not have the strength to fight the virus. His passing occurred early in April and was made all the more difficult because no one he loved was allowed to be with him. COVID-19 had caused lockdowns around the world and new, strict rules were quickly enforced. Perhaps the harshest of all was the rule that no visitors were allowed in nursing homes and senior residences, where, shockingly, the virus was rampant.

Pam and her sons were saddened by his loss and the boys worried about their mother being on her own now. They checked in with her every day and both had invited her to move into their homes.

Now, with summer well under way, southern Ontario entered into Stage Three of reopening from the lockdown. Since indoor gatherings of up to ten people were now allowed, the Bridge Club birthday party at Dee's farm was going to happen after hours of planning in Zoom calls.

Pam and Danielle were driving there together in the warm August weather with the windows down and tunes playing.

Pam's eight-year-old wheaten terrier, Murphy, her third one since Maggie, was snoozing in the back.

"I still prefer having the windows open instead of the a/c on," Dani said, as she ran her fingers through her hair.

"I couldn't agree more," said Pam. "And, by the way, congratulations on letting your hair go white! I love it! Obviously I'm still coloring mine and can't quite give in."

"Well, you all watched on Zoom as my roots turned white and got longer and longer. It just made sense to let it go and, honestly, there's something freeing about it! No kidding!"

"You may convince me yet. Lynn has always said that too," Pam replied. "I guess I kind of blew it."

"Never mind," Danielle said. "The important thing is that we all came through the lockdown in good health. We are so lucky we can get together now."

Individually, the women had taken COVID tests that week after isolating in preparation for their visit to Dee's. They were determined to create a safe bubble.

"After more than fifty years of traveling these roads, you'd think we would take the scenery for granted, but I still love the views," Pam said as she navigated the winding secondary road that took them up hills and down into verdant valleys. Panoramas of undulating farmland and thick forests unfolded before them in swaths of every shade of green, often stretching to the horizon. Colorful displays of wildflowers ~ white daisies, yellow buttercups and blue chicory ~ lined both sides of the road and often drifted into the fields and woodlands.

Danielle nodded. "I feel the same. Although the presence of those massive wind turbines sprouting in field after field really doesn't sit well with me. I hope they truly are helping the environment ..." Her voice trailed off before she finished with a mutter. "Forgive me but I just try to ignore them."

"Honestly, I don't mind them. I want to be a believer. I look past them and still love how far these views extend. Oh-h-h ...

and those flocks of sheep and herds of cows grazing here and there. Of course, cows still remind me of Bo."

Dani chuckled. "Always."

Irrigation had kept fields of potatoes and soybeans lush. The corn was high and roadside stands indicated it was ready early. With the bright blue sky and warm sunshine, one could almost forget they were in the midst of a public health crisis.

"It's truly bizarre this is all still thriving in the middle of the pandemic," Pam said and Dani agreed. Their conversation segued into the confusion and concerns about what dangers they really were facing.

"It's so hard to get a handle on all of this ... wearing masks, hand washing, social distancing, staying home." Dani sighed.

"But we can see that all helps," Pam said. "I'm glad to hear most people are doing their part."

They were silent again for a few minutes, turning their attention to the countryside.

"Fresh corn and field tomatoes! My favorite foods this time of year!" Dani exclaimed, changing the subject.

"And peaches!" Pam added. "Even though this is apple country, it's a little early for them."

"Let's stop at that market near Dee's and stock up."

"Okay, but I'm sure Dee has a good supply. She told me a while ago she had a bumper crop of field tomatoes," Pam said. "Let's call and check first. Cass and Lynn will arrive with blueberries, no question about that."

"Muffins and pies, for sure. Lynn was busy baking when I spoke to her this week."

"After seeing the menu list that Dee sent us, I know we are all arriving with stuffed coolers like the ones we have in the trunk. There will be no shortage of delicious meals."

"That's something that has not changed through all of our decades of eating together – good food!" Danielle laughed, then added, "Lynn called this morning to say the tests she and Cass had this week were negative like ours, as were Marti's and Dee's. So we are all good to go!"

"This truly is a crazy world," Pam said. "Who could ever have imagined having to do these things?"

Danielle nodded, then pinched her lips together and swallowed hard before she continued. "*Putain. Incroyable*! I wake up each morning hoping it has been a bad dream."

"That makes two of us, and probably most of the world's population," Pam replied, followed by a long sigh.

"Anyway," Danielle went on, "Kenneth drove down to the city two weeks ago. So no one has been around to burst our bubble, so to speak."

Their talk turned to discussing how Marti, Dee and Ken seemed to have easily settled into living together at the farm since the confinement period began in the middle of March.

"That worked out well," Pam agreed. "What a coincidence that the pandemic happened when Marti was visiting with them in Florida and they had to drive back to Toronto together when the flights were cancelled. They just made it back before the border was closed."

Danielle frowned. "I still can't process how this whole virus thing has turned the world upside down. Who knows when I will ever get to see the kids in Melbourne now. Things there are shocking and no visitors are allowed into the country."

Pam nodded. "I hear you. It's sad how many lives have been impacted forever ... loved ones passing, jobs disappearing, homes lost, businesses closing. Changes big and small. When it was decided on the drive home that Marti should come and stay here at the farm during the lockdown, no one imagined it was going to last so long."

Marti had gone to her townhouse in downtown Toronto just long enough to pack warmer clothes. She had called a co-worker at the women's shelter where she worked, knowing that family was struggling already because the husband, a cook, had lost his job. Now the woman would lose her income too, so Marti offered them her place. It was an ideal arrangement for all of them.

Then she had driven to Dee and Ken's farm in Grey County and settled in to the apartment they had built over the drive shed.

"I'm quite sure Marti will say this to all of us when we are together," Pam said, as she swerved to avoid turkey vultures feasting on roadkill on the shoulder of the road. "She told me recently that it was a great decision and in spite of the forced isolation she was loving living there. In fact, she said Dee and Kenneth have told her she can stay forever. That reminds me, please text Dee and tell her we are 20 minutes away."

Danielle sent the text as she reacted to Pam's comment about Marti. "Wow! Do you think she might?"

"Marti said she would consider it if they will allow her to pay rent and be a proper tenant. At the very least, she said she is going to stay up in The Blue Mountains area and never live in the city again. How is that for a complete change?"

"I have a feeling a lot of people are going to be making decisions like that. What good is it to be stuck in the city when you can't go to the theatre, shops or restaurants like usual and the parks are jammed with everyone desperate to get out in the fresh air?"

They rode in silence for a few minutes.

At length Danielle reached over, putting her hand on Pam's shoulder. "And how are you doing?"

Pam's half-hearted smile told her story, as her eyes suddenly filled.

"Sorry" she apologized, wiping away a tear. "As you can see, I'm still feeling a little fragile. But honestly, I am okay."

Danielle passed her a tissue. "You and Steven had a lovely relationship. He was such a good man."

"Yes he was. Our hearts were broken that he had to die

alone and could only hear our voices and see us on the nurses' iPads and phones. But at least there was that and everyone who loved him had a chance to say a final goodbye to him."

"You have been loved by two fine men in your life, Pam."

Pam touched her palm to her heart. "For that I am grateful."

The dirt road changed to loose gravel as Pam turned the car up the driveway to the farmhouse. Both women burst into laughter at the same time as they saw what was waiting for them.

The entire parking area was ringed by colorful balloons. A large banner printed with "Happy 75th!" and strung with streamers, hung over the side entrance to the farmhouse. As Pam and Danielle got out of the car, Dee, Marti, Cass and Lynn emerged from the house, wearing multicolored feather boas around their necks and sequin-covered party hats that sparkled in the sun. Dee was carrying a tray of full Champagne glasses and the sound of Queen's *We Are The Champions* filled the air.

The celebration was on.

They greeted each other with air kisses and high fives, which they had already agreed would be more COVID appropriate in spite of all their precautions.

Wooden Muskoka chairs were set out under the pergola by the side of the house. The picnic table had Champagne and sparkling water in ice buckets. Platters of assorted appetizers were brought out from the kitchen.

"Even the weather has decided to make this party a success!" Cass cried, twirling gracefully in the sunshine and floating her boa in the air.

"Those knee replacements haven't cramped your style, Cass," Lynn said, grinning. "It's not so easy with this cane of mine."

Dee's most recent rescue dog, a long-haired dachshund, made the rounds greeting everyone before he scampered off to find Murphy, who was already chasing squirrels.

After settling in, the women shared toasts and expressed their wonder at the reality of what they were celebrating - and their gratitude for the lifetime of love, loyalty and laughter that had carried them through all of the down times.

"Friendship at its best!"

"Seventy-frickin'-five years!" was repeated in this manner, and others, as the afternoon light faded.

There were toasts to many of the milestones they had met together and to the card game that had been such an important part of all those decades.

"And let's raise a glass to women everywhere who have shared friendships like ours!" Lynn said.

"Um, or kinda like ours ..." Cass murmured. "I mean, look at all we've gone through. Imagine how many other stories there are."

"But here's the thing," Marti said. "Listen to us ... seventy-five years of age and we still don't feel old ... just experienced!"

"And as we all know," Dee added, "so much of life is about Ti-Ming."

Pam stood and picked up a tray. "Exactly. I can hear Bo's voice reminding us timing is everything and that it's time to pass the appetizers again."

Laughter rippled through the air. Glasses were refilled. Appetizers were passed.

Pam set up her camera on a tripod for the obligatory group shots. The late afternoon was spent reminiscing as well as talking about how life was changing due to the lockdown and virus. They agreed it was a challenge to come to terms with how the entire world was being upturned, especially on top of facing the challenges of ageing.

Gratitude wrapped around them for having these next few

days together. Of course there was an agenda of hiking, biking, reading, relaxing, looking through photos, wining and dining and, it went without saying ... bridge.

As the sun began to set, mouthwatering aromas wafted from the open wood oven in the barbecue area. A leg of locally-raised lamb had been slow-cooking over embers, while intermittent trips had been made to the kitchen to prepare the salad and vegetables. And definitely dessert!

Tidying up, the women moved inside.

The dining table, draped in a white linen tablecloth and matching napkins, was set with Dee's good china and the family silver that had graced their formal dinners together for over fifty years. A glass vase held eight roses from the garden.

There were eight places laid. They had agreed that all of them would be present, at least in spirit. They had been eight from the beginning and always would be.

The End

ACKNOWLEDGMENTS

I wish to express my deepest respect for everyone whose life is touched in any way by Alzheimer's disease. We live with hope every day that a cure will be found.

This story is fiction (based on some fact) and, apart from the Bridge Club members, any resemblance of characters to real persons is a coincidence and unintentional. The opinions expressed are purely those of the author and are in no way meant to suggest they should be embraced by others. No disrespect is intended.

In the original edition, I purposely obscured the identity of the woman in the final chapter to emphasize that it could have been any one of those women, just as this could happen to any one of us. I did not wish this to be a story about how extended family was affected, but rather how a bond of friendship can overcome every obstacle and remain strong and true in the face of such a crisis. In adding content to this new addition, my feelings were the same as to how that chapter was written.

However, after ten years of readers politely inquiring, I felt it was appropriate to divulge the identity now.

In order to reach that exciting point where a manuscript is finally ready to publish, a tremendous amount of support and assistance is essential. I'm grateful to everyone who contributed in his or her own personal way to bringing the original and now *The Bridge Club Tenth Anniversary Edition* to readers.

My first expression of thanks must be to the multitude of authors of the reports, articles, Internet sites, and books that were available to me for research as my story unfolded. My personal education during the writing of this book was a satisfying and ongoing part of the process. In particular I want to mention Diana Friel McGowan (*Living In The Labyrinth*), Ellen Goodman and Patricia O'Brien (*I Know Just What You Mean*), the late Thomas DeBaggio (*Losing My Mind: An Intimate Look At Living with Alzheimer's*) and Derek Humphry (*Final Exit*).

Thank you to my family for their unfailing support, in particular my dear husband, Dr. Maher Anis, whose patience and encouragement never waned. Thank you to my brother Terry Murphy, a writer himself, who persuaded me to take the leap of faith and allow him to be the first to read my manuscript. Your stamp of approval kept me going.

For Peter, David and Jason there are no words strong enough.

For the original version of *The Bridge Club* ~ Ron Jacques, a freelance editor who paddles his canoe in Muskoka, was an early motivator. I owe more gratitude than I can ever express to Gail Johnston, Gloria Epstein, Lisa Sands, Carol Howitt, Barbara Herner, Liz Bialkowski, Ofra Landman, May Cunerty, Yasmin McNeilly and Susan Henderson, even though they probably don't realize it. My thanks to Maria Price and Kim Lake for permitting me to share part of their history. To those trusted readers who patiently slogged through chapters that were works in progress and offered valuable feedback, *merci mille fois*. I include in that group the anonymous Book Club members from Halton, who gave my novel its first "test read" and offered me their invaluable opinions and critiques. Thanks again, Barb!

Thank you to Patsy McCartney for your unbroken friendship from halfway around the world and for allowing me to tap into your experience as a respected bridge professional. Thank you for the bridge hands you created for the first edition of *The Bridge Club*. The technical assistance of Alison McCartney was most appreciated.

In publishing the original novel in 2010, I am grateful for everything (and it was plenty) I learned through the efforts and guidance of Editors Elizabeth Day and David Bernardi.

For this tenth anniversary edition, I'm honored to include bridge hands contributed by Canada's Audrey Grant, an internationally respected professional educator and contract bridge teacher. As well as a wealth of bridge books, Audrey Grant also publishes the bi-monthly Better Bridge magazine and a daily online bridge column. In 2015 she was inducted into the ACBL Hall of Fame. (It was a delightful surprise to discover Audrey was a fan of *The Bridge Club* when it was published in 2010. I cherish our friendship that resulted.)

Please go to Betterbridge.com to connect with the wealth of bridge information and opportunities Audrey offers on her extensive website.

This new edition of *The Bridge Club* would not have been possible without the able assistance of Carolyn Ring, editor Dinah Forbes and beta readers extraordinaire, Gail Johnston and Martha Paley Francescato. Many other advance readers helped bring this final version to publication and my thanks goes out to them as well.

Special thanks for the knowledge and assistance of Kate Rock, Tonni Callan, Annie Horsky McDonnell.

And to all the members of the Blue Sky Book Chat group , especially my talented co-hosts, my Lake Union Authors family, and to my friends in Patricia's Readers' Rendezvous, *mille mercis* ... a thousand thanks!

I'm so grateful to the writing community of which I'm proud to be a part. The collegiality, friendship and support found there is truly remarkable. Thank you to the many reviewers and bloggers who take the time to read our novels, review and write about them. I include in my thanks talented designers who create meaningful and beautiful graphics. You all are the lifeline to sharing news about our writing and helping expand our readership. The tremendous effort you put into your work is most appreciated. I began to write out a list and it became so long, I had to stop. The number of excellent online reader groups, bloggers, reviewers, and bookstagrammers could fill its own chapter and I did not want to inadvertently omit anyone. Some of these sites have thousands of followers and some are small and personal. All of them provide invaluable assistance to authors. I send a sincere thank you and hope I share my gratitude often with you personally. You all are an integral part of the village it takes to reach readers.

Which leads to more gratitude to all the readers who buy our books. I love hearing from you and appreciate the time you take to share your thoughts with me and with others. If you write reviews and spread the word, even better. And if you do none of that, that's okay too. As long as you find pleasure in the books we write, that is our greatest reward.

I'm grateful to Sharon Clare for her patience and her artistic talent in designing the beautiful cover.

Most of all, thanks to my treasured Bridge Club—for the story, the support, the feedback, and more than anything the non-stop laughter and friendship through the past fifty years. This tenth anniversary edition is dedicated to our beloved Bonnie.

And to women of all ages everywhere I encourage you to treasure your friendships, to nurture them, and to believe in them. To have a good friend, you must be a good friend.

AUTHOR'S NOTE

Bringing The Bridge Club to new readers has been a labour of love. Even though the original story is the same as in 2010, the new content at the end brings readers old and new up to date with this group of women who touched the hearts of so many. That is something that has been requested through the last ten years and the timing felt right in this tenth anniversary year.

With COVID-19 putting the brakes on travel for all of us, spending time in Canada on the pages of the story also seemed like the right place to be. Hopefully I will be back in France next year with new stories and experiences.

Thank you to everyone who has written to me through the years or messaged me on social media. I love hearing from readers! I value your thoughts and opinions, so please continue to share them with me at patriciasandsauthor@gmail.com.

Have you signed up for my newsletter? It goes out once a month with all sorts of giveaways from my author friends and information about what's coming next. Just click on "subscribe" at my website patriciasandsauthor.com. If you enjoy the photos I share online, please follow me on Instagram. I'll be happy to follow you back.

If you would like to find yourself in some of the beautiful settings in my photos, you might want to consider coming on a tour I co-lead each summer with my BFF, Deborah Bine (aka Barefoot Blogger). We take 16 women on a 12-day magical journey through the parts of the south of France we love the most. Many women come on their own while others come with a friend or friends (your book club?) or a sister, mother, daughter. It's all good. What we love the most are the wonderful friendships that develop on this journey every single time. Simply email me at patriciasandsauthor@gmail.com or go to this website – Absolutely Southern France Travel – to see the details of our tour.

There are photos of past tours on my website. The 2021 details will be online in the new year. In the meantime you can look at past years' tours as the itinerary is always basically the same kind of awesomeness.

I love to visit with book clubs, so please don't hesitate to ask! We usually do this through FaceTime or Zoom and it works perfectly. I would love to meet your group to chat about books, life and whatever you like. Details are all on my website.

Any time you take a moment to write a review, please know your efforts are appreciated. Comments from readers are helpful and inspiring to me. You are the reason I write and your words encourage others to read my books. *Merci mille fois!* Thanks a million!

And now . . . on to the next book. See you there!

GUIDE FOR BOOK CLUB DISCUSSION

1. What elements of this book would make you recommend it to others?
2. To which particular chapter/character did you relate more? What similar life experiences have you encountered?
3. What moral/ethical choices did the characters make in their individual chapters and in The Hand Dealt - 2007? How did you feel about their decisions?
4. How did you feel about the original ending (2010) and do you support the author not naming the character, although she dropped clues? Do you agree with the author naming the character in the 2020 Epilogue?
5. Which character did you think died before you found out in the Epilogue? Or was it not important for you to know?
6. If you were Jane and confronted with a similar diagnosis, what choice would make for yourself? How would you feel if a close friend of yours asked you to support such a decision.
7. Do you share a similar longstanding friendship with a person or particular group of people? How do you feel this has impacted your life?
8. Was the author's vision optimistic? In what ways does the story inspire hope?
9. What is the most important message that you'll take away from this story?
10. Are you a bridge player? Did you play the bridge hands in the book?

Made in the USA
Monee, IL
17 June 2021

71573720R00260